ALYSSA GOODNIGHT

Unladylike Pursuits

Impress Ink

This is a work of fiction. Names, characters, places, and incidents are products of the author's imagination or are used fictitiously and are not to be construed as real. Any resemblance to actual events, locales, organizations, or persons, living or dead, is entirely coincidental.

For
Jason,

who is, as ever, a constant source of amazement
and wildly successful at making dreams come true.

Acknowledgments

My most profound thanks to

Kelly Martin,
*Without whom, I would never have started this book
and with whom, I would never have finished it.*

Judith Braun,
*Who has endured a lifetime of supplying the tedious
affirmation I require, most recently in the form of revision
critiques.*

And
Whitney Martin,
Whose esteemed opinion of her mother is a lesson to us all.

1

"You may consider yourself engaged, dear nephew, and I know I may trust you with the secret. Bridal jitters are giving us a bit of trouble, and I fear good sense has run amok. Still, you mustn't worry..."

LETTER FROM LADY BEATRICE SINCLAIR TO MR. DESMOND RICHLY
25 OCTOBER 1818

"Ahhh, here you are, Emily dear."

Emily's father had looked up at precisely the moment she'd entered the room, but his lips hadn't moved, and the voice wasn't his. Her instinctive cringing should have been a sufficient clue—her stepmother was here. Somewhere.

Hearing a murmured question from his estate manager standing at his elbow, her father glanced down again at the papers spread out before him on his massive mahogany desk. Reminding herself that she could be at ease with the woman now, Emily glanced cautiously about the room for her stepmother. A week had passed since her birthday, and having reached the safe haven of five and twenty years, Emily considered herself quite securely 'on the shelf'. And, as such, out-of-reach of both heiress-seeking gentlemen and her stepmother's well-meant, but nevertheless tedious, matchmaking schemes. She could ignore all of them, and eventually, they would all go away. She hoped.

As her eyes lit on the generous figure of her stepmother, tucked carefully into a chair that appeared to be gasping for breath, Emily dutifully lifted the corners of her mouth, thereby preventing their impending downturn. Beatrice would not be making her departure anytime soon, and when she did, it was possible that they would first need a very large shoehorn to extract her. The image cheered her quite a little bit.

"As summoned," Emily answered with a nod of her head and a dramatic flourish of her arm.

"Surely you were not thinking of going riding?" Beatrice was eyeing Emily's deep green velvet riding dress with disbelief. "Tis quite out of the question. And as you shall shortly discover, you've absolutely no time to waste on such frivolity."

No doubt recognizing the signs of an impending argument from her stepdaughter, she quickly hurried on, "Never fear, my dear, I assure you, you've something much more diverting in store."

"Indeed?" Emily queried with feigned interest—she and Beatrice had very different ideas with regard to amusements, "Well then you mustn't keep me in suspense."

Her stepmother opened her mouth to reply but shut it again quickly with a little shake of her head, "Oh, I do wish to tell you, my dear, but your father insists it should be him." She then stole a petulant glance at her husband while Emily shifted her eyes to study him as well. If her father had devised a diversion, likely it was a worthy one. Perhaps it was to be his way of welcoming her into newfound independence.

"However…"

Emily dragged her eyes back to her stepmother.

"I'd be remiss in my duty if I allowed you to carry on in such a manner without the wisdom of my…words."

Beatrice clearly hadn't appreciated the implication inherent in the use of the word 'years'.

In fact, judging by her expression, she was quite proud of herself for the improvised substitution. "Tis much too chilly on a day like today for you to even consider being outdoors—even the sun does not wish to come out. You must remember, my dear, a reddened nose isn't at all flattering on any lady, and someone of your unfortunate coloring must be especially careful."

Faced with Emily's impassive countenance, Beatrice dutifully reminded, "Your hair, dear, is quite red enough on its own."

"You've a very keen eye, Beatrice" Emily offered, determined not to be drawn into an all-too-familiar conversation.

"No matter what you may think, my dear, cheekiness is never attractive."

"Particularly pink cheekiness, I should imagine," Emily countered, simply unable to help herself.

Beatrice's lips promptly disappeared, so compressed were they in disapproval. Faced with such an incongruous picture, Emily couldn't help but conjure a fairy tale ending of her own. It involved a meddlesome stepmother who'd had a curse put upon her, sealing her lips until such a time as she decided to say something nice. As Emily fondly imagined years passing in pleasant silence, she thought it best to turn away. It wouldn't do at all for Beatrice to see the mischievous smile now in bloom on her face.

She wanted to giggle when she heard Beatrice playing along. Displeasure was being huffed out in audible sighs— words were obviously not necessary. Perhaps Beatrice would learn from this experience. Not likely, Emily knew, but they would manage. Beatrice would gradually become more tolerable as the reality of Emily's spinster status finally took hold. Then, with any luck, her stepmother would pronounce her a lost cause and leave her blissfully alone. Until then, Emily would obligingly cast herself in the role of much put-upon stepdaughter.

As difficult as it was to believe, she and Beatrice had still not managed to call a truce with regard to her hapless hair color. Emily had no idea what exactly it was that Beatrice expected her to do about it other than acknowledge her bad luck in being saddled with it, but even that was too much. She rather liked being different. Just slightly more so than she enjoyed provoking her stepmother.

Suddenly the skirts of her stepmother's gown began to rustle and billow outward, seemingly of their own accord. So Lady Priscilla was to be joining them as well.

Wonderful. Lady Sinclair's immaculately groomed Roseneath terrier would certainly have plenty to add to the discussion, being even more vocal in her disapproval of Emily than her ladyship, and taking every opportunity to yip in agreement with any reprimands or admonishments that her mama chose to bestow.

Emily had nicknamed the annoying little creature Prissy almost as soon as they had been introduced, a choice which had proven itself very fitting indeed. Even now the little beast was eyeing Emily with haughty reproof.

"The rest can wait, Jamieson," her father announced, promptly pulling her attention back to him.

With a nod the man gathered up the sheaf of papers and hurried from the room, gently closing the door behind him. Had she not now been eagerly anticipating the surprise her father had in store, she would have been envious of the man. Typically a summons meant a lecture, most often on propriety, paired with a summary of her disappointing lack of adherence.

As was her custom, she would insert a "Yes, Father," whenever he seemed to expect it, and when it appeared that he was finished, she would offer a final demure nod, indicating that she would make every effort to do better, when, in fact, she had no intention of doing any such thing.

No promises made, no promises broken. A fine line but a clear delineation.

But today was to be different; henceforward all of her days would likely be different. She was a spinster now and needn't have such a care for her reputation. She could be deemed eccentric, and no one would so much as blink in her direction. How glorious it would to be! She grinned at her father and even tossed a relieved smile in the Ladies' direction.

"Emily, my dear, please sit down," her father invited. "I've a matter of some importance to discuss with you."

"Yes, I know," came the giddy reply.

Her father looked puzzled and slanted a glance at his wife, "You know?"

"Well, not everything, certainly. But I *do* have my

suspicions, and there's been a bit of a hint of something else as well." Emily slanted her own glance at her stepmother. "Come. No more secrets, Father. I'm ready, no matter what it is you've planned for me."

"Really?" Her father met her stepmother's eyes and then brought them back to rest on his daughter. "I wouldn't have expected this, but you always were a fearless little thing."

"Patient, too, Father," she reminded him, smiling, "We mustn't forget that."

"No, I suppose not." So saying, he kept silent for an excruciating moment, gazing at her rather quizzically, before appearing to collect himself and his thoughts. "Yes, well, you likely realize that circumstances will change significantly. You cannot carry on in the manner in which you have been."

"And that, I assure you, is a great relief."

Her father was frowning at her now, quite obviously unaffected by the wide smile she was bestowing upon him. "What precisely is it that you believe to be at issue here, Emily?"

"Everything!" she answered buoyantly.

"Perhaps you could be a bit more specific," he lured.

"My birthday has come and gone—I'm five and twenty, and a week besides. 'Tis finally official, and in truth, I'm relieved. I sit before you now an ape leader, long-in-the-tooth and on-the-shelf. A spinster without the shame. My reputation is no longer so fragile—I can do precisely as I wish with no one to care overly much. I've the freedom to explore a bit and have adventures. I can assist you with estate matters and linger in the stables whenever I wish. It even *sounds* glorious just to say it out loud!"

Beatrice gasped out a, "Good heavens!" and followed her words with a hiccup. Her father was nodding slowly, as if everything now made perfect sense. His tone was lighter but remained serious as he answered.

"I don't imagine your husband would agree with you, my dear."

"Likely not, so it's a mighty good thing that I've settled

into life as an old maid." Emily felt like chuckling a bit herself. Finally, she was at ease with the subject matter—finally, she could afford to be. Relaxing back into her chair, she smoothed her hands over the kitten-soft nap of her skirt.

"Perhaps you should unsettle yourself a bit."

Emily grinned at her father, willing him to shed his seriousness in exchange for a light-hearted smile, "I do believe you are funning, Father. Did you intend a pun?"

"I don't believe I've ever intended a pun, Emily." The heaviness had returned to his voice, and suddenly she felt her nerves start to thrum. "You need to understand that your life as a spinster is coming to a quick end, my dear." He threaded his fingers, looking gravely down upon them. He then glanced from wife to daughter, keeping his countenance sober.

"But it's just beginning! I've not yet even had a chance to take advantage of my newfound status."

"And that, my dear, is a great relief to us all. But I'm afraid this is the way it is to be."

"But why? This makes no sense."

"The idea that a gently bred young lady should settle down, marry, build a home for herself, mother a family? Preposterous notions, all of them." Her father waved them off with his hand. "And yet here I sit, condemning you to just such a fate."

"Well, I wouldn't say I agree with all of that precisely..." Emily's words faded away, just as she supposed her smile had, both steadily chipped away with each chink of her father's words. Numb with nerves and shock, she didn't want to move for fear that something awful might happen.

"I've no doubt that marriage is the furthest thing from your mind," her father continued, now putting her in mind of a honeybee droning persistently in her ear. She desperately wished she could swat his words away from her. Glancing at Beatrice and Prissy, seeing their smugly superior expressions, she wished she could swat them too.

"...but I very much believe that you are in need of a husband."

Emily spared a glance for her stepmother. Both she and little Prissy were nodding with the air of worldly wise matrons. Swinging her no-doubt hunted eyes back to her father, Emily was determined to lead the conversation back onto familiar ground.

"Father, please," she entreated, striving to keep the hint of panic from her voice, "I do *not* need a husband. A husband would ruin everything!"

She didn't consider this pessimism but rather probability. Having reached the advanced age of five and twenty without ever having a man form the subject of her daydreams or enkindle any degree of longing, she felt was telling indeed. Many gentlemen had inspired her to strong emotion, but she didn't suppose a fierce desire to be rid of their presence should be counted.

The wondrous enthusiasm and blind naïveté of youth had long since worn off, and romance was not something she aspired to any longer. She'd come to understand that marriage wasn't to be the next chapter in her life, and she was content with that reality. She planned instead on adding page after page of delightful adventures. It was better, she thought, to stay true to herself and not be disappointed than to continue searching in vain for a man who simply did not exist. One who would desire her for what she was, not for whom she should become.

Emily saw her stepmother stop nodding to look expectantly toward her husband. Her father's eyes looked troubled but unwavering. He sighed heavily and looked down at his desk. When he once again lifted his head, Emily realized she had been holding her breath.

"Well it seems we disagree." Never a good thing.

Emily's eyes darted frantically about the room, the ticking of her father's handled ormolu desk clock setting the tempo for the progression. First skimming over her father's determined but seemingly regretful expression, then her stepmother's unmistakably triumphant one, and on to Prissy's malicious sneer.

She felt herself deflating slightly as the glowing triumph of spinsterhood started to slip away from her. Couldn't anyone besides her see that a husband was a preposterous suggestion, especially at her age?

"And as I suspect you haven't yet begun to take me seriously, it is unlikely that you will shortly be of a disposition to choose for yourself. Luckily, your stepmother and I have selected someone suitable."

Emily didn't view this news as the slightest bit fortuitous.

"I think you remember Mr. Desmond Richly from our dinner party a few weeks ago?"

She narrowed her eyes and nodded that she did, not yet certain where her father might be leading her, other than to distasteful memories.

"He spoke to me that evening regarding a union, and I put him off, but in light of today's discussion, I've decided to send word that his suit has been accepted." His tone gentled a bit, "I'm afraid you've given me no other options, my dear," but promptly resumed its detachment, "We'll plan an engagement ball for one month hence."

"Only one month," Lady Sinclair twittered, clapping her hands together in delighted approval. "We'd best get started with all the arrangements, my dear." Her fisted hands were now quivering in excitement. "I fully expect us to be inseparable in the weeks ahead," she enthused.

Her stepmother's prediction, on the heels of her father's announcement, had Emily fighting down a wave of nausea. Almost inconceivably, it appeared matters had just gotten worse.

"Mr. Richly?! Is this the surprise? Is *he* the surprise?" Emily tossed a horrified stare at her stepmother who was positively beaming. Emily decided it best to ignore her and turned her attention back to her father, "You can't possibly be serious. He's not the slightest bit suitable—far, far from it." She crossed her arms in defiance, "I can't marry him—I won't. The very idea is horrendous."

Silence pervaded every corner, a resounding warning of misjudgment.

Lady Priscilla, as ever, was the first to condemn her, growling low in her throat. Her mama was quite unexpectedly at a loss for words and so only managed to gasp in outrage before fanning herself vigorously with her unattended needlework.

"Your remarks, Emily, are unbecoming and intolerable. If you'll recall, you are speaking of a relation of your stepmother's," her father reminded with uncharacteristic harshness. "Be aware that you have just undermined any hope you might have had in convincing me to postpone the engagement. You are quite obviously in need of a husband's guiding hand. Once wed, I am certain you shall quickly find yourself sufficiently occupied so as to forget any objections you may at this moment dream up."

Emily felt a leaden weight on her heart pulling her further and further down and away. Out of reach of anything familiar. Instinctively she struggled against it.

"But—"

"Often it's best not to say anything at all," her father informed her with a hint of steel in his voice.

Emily caught his eye and breathed out a quivering, steadying breath. Very well, she would change tactics. If she took her father at his word—a seemingly wise choice—she was to be married off. That was one thing. Being married to Richly was something entirely different. It was an eventuality to be avoided at all costs, and it called for drastic measures. Swallowing a lump in her throat, Emily prepared herself for drastic action.

"I...I do beg your pardon, Father, Beatrice." Emily stuttered to a start, humbling herself by nodding her head solemnly at each of them in turn. "In future, I will endeavour to keep my opinions to myself whenever I deem they might be offensive."

Beatrice appeared uncertain as to whether an actual apology had been issued, and Emily fervently hoped the prickly detail would distract the woman for a bit more time yet. She hadn't time to spare for Beatrice's sensibilities, for she was plotting, wondering how soon it would be appropriate to broach an alternative to her father's suggestion.

"It is quite obvious that you are unaware of Desmond's

many wonderful qualities," her stepmother announced, in a tone that was far from conciliatory. "I do believe it would be to your benefit if we discussed them. At length and in detail."

Emily promptly decided time was of the essence.

"Father, what if I could manage to win another gentleman's proposal before the month is through? A *suitable* gentleman," she felt obliged to add, opening her eyes wide in a manner that usually pleaded her case better than words. "We could still go along with the engagement ball…" she cajoled.

"Do you have a gentleman in mind?" He wasn't troubling to conceal his suspicion and curiosity.

"Er…no. But I will," she assured him.

"Em—" her father said.

Emily held both hands out in front of her, willing him to wait. "I know what you are thinking, Father—that there is no one I wish to marry. And a truer statement there could not possibly be. But, as *you've* seen fit to ignore that one crucial detail, isn't it fair to allow me to do so as well? I was looking for a perfect match. Now I can be content with someone…"

Pressing her hands to her stomach, she darted a look at her stepmother whose lips had thinned as she waited for Emily to finish. Emily rapidly considered how not to be offensive.

"Someone…who wouldn't feel as if they'd settled by marrying me. Someone content with the simplicity of country life, without the diverse interests a man of Mr. Richly's stature must claim."

Good grief but the back of her throat was itching. A torrent of uncomplimentary words was tempting her, but she held fast. Her stepmother appeared slightly mollified, but her father's lifted eyebrow conveyed that he wasn't a bit fooled. He looked down at his hands and seemed to be considering. Emily sat tensely, pleating her skirts between nervous fingers while she awaited his response. She wanted to add something, anything, to her argument but couldn't decide what it should be. Then suddenly, time ran out.

His decision made, her father spoke, and so forestalled his wife, who had simultaneously opened her mouth, no doubt with the intent to begin cataloguing Mr. Richly's many desirable qualities.

"Fair enough, Em. If you can find a suitable gentleman and garner his proposal within one month, then you need not marry Mr. Richly. I'll refrain from speaking with him until then. Preparations for the ball will proceed; its outcome is now up to you. You may go."

Emily jumped up to leave before her father could change his mind.

"Edward!" came his wife's shocked admonishment. "What *can* you mean? What of Desmond?"

Emily slipped through the door and pulled it nearly closed as she clung to the knob with her arm curved up behind her. Weak with relief, she lingered for a moment's recovery and so heard her father's response.

"Calm yourself, Beatrice. It will all work out for the best."

Emily believed the sentiment extremely questionable. While it was true she had managed a narrow escape, her efforts had led her to dubious success. Still, at least now she had a choice instead of none at all. She could find an alternative to Richly or fall victim to failure. Failure being as unattractive a prospect as Mr. Richly himself.

At her back, the door nudged open a bit, but before she could release the handle and move away, it was shoved further open, very nearly putting her off balance. Nose in the air, Lady Priscilla appeared and sauntered past her, tossing a sniff in her direction.

One look at the little beast was just the incentive Emily needed. Suddenly, desperately needing to be alone, she spun on her heel and set off in the opposite direction. It seemed she'd walk the long way around in her effort to escape. No matter—she needed the time to think. She would just postpone her reaction to her father's "surprise" a few moments longer. For she needed to be well away before she could let loose the seething fit of aggravation she intended. She planned on it being very loud indeed.

Her long-awaited birthday had finally come and gone. She'd expected a triumph, a victory, a celebration of spinsterhood; what she faced instead was extremely lowering. Rather than indulging in the freedom she'd expected, she had but a month to choose a husband who would surely snatch it straight away from her. The irony was absolutely pitiful. She didn't wish to think of her father's duplicity just now. Why was it that he'd not once seen fit to mention his little birthday surprise? It *had* been a week late in coming, but that was little comfort.

Emily stepped outside, her spirits lifting with her skirts in the gusty wind. She stole a moment, eyes closed, face buffeted by the smell of rain and a tinge of moisture, before purposefully striding around the house towards the gardens.

An image of the detestable Richly rose up to mock her, and she swung out her leg, wanting nothing more than to dispel it. Before the month was over, she knew she very well might wish her boot to connect with the man himself.

"Richly?!" It came out on a distasteful hiss. Emily couldn't fathom what her father had been thinking. His approval of the man had her wondering if he'd been judging against any standards at all. Apparently all that mattered to her father was that she marry a gentleman. Although it was a stretch to even grant Richly that courtesy.

Bending down to take up a leafless holly branch, she swatted it against her palm.

Gossip held that the man was set upon acquiring an heiress in order to cover his gambling debts. Debts, it was rumored, he had accrued in less-than-respectable establishments. Hardly a glowing recommendation no matter what Beatrice cared to add. He even looked the part of a dissolute gambler, a reality of apparently little concern to anyone but her.

Tipping the branch down beside her, she let it scrape along the stepping stones, and found its grating sound perversely comforting.

Almost immediately she realized that her father's less than fastidious attitude could work to her advantage. After all, she was an heiress. She didn't need to marry for money, and she disliked the idea of being married strictly for her own. She wasn't angling for a title, and apparently neither was her father. Society's guidelines for a proper marriage having been smoothly dispatched, Emily realized that her father had left her free to judge against her own criteria.

She moved past the now-dormant rose bushes her mother had once lovingly tended to sit on a carved stone bench recessed in a curve of yew shrubbery. Idly tapping the tips of her fingers on the chilly stone, she supposed it was to be a disadvantage that she'd long known precisely the sort of man she wished to marry. If she hadn't found him in a spinster's lifetime, what were the odds she'd find him in the next month?

Truly, there wasn't much time to spare in daydreams, but she needed a bit of cheering up and so determinedly pushed back reality for a pleasant moment.

Her husband should be a swashbuckling adventurer—delighted to have a bit of fun, but not at the risk of life and limb. He should proudly encourage her dramatic and determined step outside the bounds of propriety. *And*...he should be possessed of a wicked sense of humor, a dangerous amount of charm, and a face that quickened her heart.

She was smiling when she came abruptly back to the present, but not for long. It hardly mattered that she knew precisely the sort of gentleman she was searching for—it wasn't as if her life was being played out in a novel. While any number of penned heroes would smoothly suffice, it was something of a muddle that there wasn't a three-dimensional man of her acquaintance that fit the description. None even made a respectable showing, including Richly. But then, it was wise to remember, he never did.

So truly, she hadn't made a wit of progress. Heaving a pained sigh, she closed her eyes and took a deep, cleansing breath, willing herself to think of anything else. She longed for an escape but was practical enough to realize she wouldn't find one. There *was* no escape, and it looked as though there never would be again. Even the clouds that had spent the morning jockeying for position seemed to sympathize, but oddly she found their grumbling angered her even further, so much so that the twig she'd grasped tightly at both ends snapped neatly in two. Staring down at the remnants, a calm swept over her, and she opened her hands to let them fall away from her.

It seemed she had little choice but to set up the hue and cry—the hunt was on. She felt like a little red fox, hampered by heavy green skirts and her own standards, desperate for any hiding place at all. The hounds would soon catch her scent, and she had no choice but to let one of them catch *her*. In fact her task was considerably more precarious—she needed to go out looking for the beasts. *Where* could she hope to find one that wouldn't send her scurrying even closer to the ogre Richly?

Looking around her at the sheltering greenery, she realized the privacy of the gardens wasn't enough today. Today she very much needed to get away, to escape for a time fated to be temporary. Right now it didn't matter. She needed advice, guidance. Tea.

Sophie would know precisely what should be done. Just thinking about her best friend's practical approach to even the smallest of problems soothed Emily's nerves and saved her from her own disappointed imagination.

Gusts of chilly wind had loosened her hairpins and now sent several wisps dancing across her face. They whipped over her eyes, caught in the corner of her mouth, and went unnoticed as she grimaced over the irony of her latest predicament. She had been waiting impatiently for a bit of adventure for as long as she could remember. Now that she faced the life-altering, and very likely humbling, task of finding a husband, she couldn't imagine why her simple life had ever seemed so disagreeable.

Certain she could manage to arrive at the vicarage before the storm, she raised her skirts and hurried to the stables.

* * *

Emily was settled comfortably in a gallop when the rain started. The perfect complement, she thought resignedly, to the way her day was going thus far. Already cheated out of a pleasant morning, her hopes and dreams trampled, she was now to be soaked to the skin as the afternoon's thunderstorm set about the task of dissolving any shred of optimism left to her. Perhaps she'd be struck by lightning in the next few minutes and escape into oblivion. Not likely. Matters were certain to get worse before they got better, and she suddenly realized how.

Week-old memories sluiced over her as vividly as the rain. She could almost hear her stepmother's voice shrieking on the wind.

"Edward! You *have* warned Emily about the highwayman, haven't you? She really shouldn't be riding about until he's apprehended. It was but three days ago that Lord and Lady Chesterwood were attacked!"

"A highwayman!" Emily had gasped, shocking herself with a feeling of perverse delight. She was so absorbed in an inexplicable sense of excitement that she promptly lost the train of the conversation. Luckily she had resumed attention at exactly the right moment.

"...you simply mustn't ride until they're apprehended," her stepmother had announced emphatically.

Uncertain she had heard correctly, Emily turned to her father.

"Surely she—you—cannot be serious?" she had wondered. "Tis an outrageous demand, preposterous even to suggest—"

"Calm yourself, Emily," her father had said. "You may continue to ride—"

"Thank you, Father. As always, the voice of reason." The last she had paired with a smug smirk aimed in her stepmother's direction.

"—as long as you are accompanied by an armed groom," Lord Sinclair had finished, his voice raised in ill-disguised irritation over the interruption.

"But Father, you cannot seriously expect me to tolerate the tedious presence of an unimaginative groom each time I choose to go out," she had protested.

"I can, and I do. I do not want you out riding alone under any circumstances. You're to take a groom with you, or keep to the house until the villain is apprehended. Have I made myself clear?"

Emily had debated further argument, but her father had appeared convincingly adamant, so she had decided to give in gracefully. More in words than deed.

"Yes, Father."

"Now would you care to elaborate on why you require an 'imaginative' groom, or should we leave that discussion for another time?"

Emily wasn't at all looking forward to that particular discussion, but now definitely wasn't the time to worry over it. Glancing nervously about, she conceded that it might have been wise to heed her father's words of caution. After all, the villain had not yet been apprehended, and having met with such success a fortnight ago, he was bound to try again.

What's more, in the lonely darkness of the sheltering trees, it was difficult to envision him as a daring adventurer with an unknown but noble purpose. It was simple indeed to view him as a dangerous scoundrel intent on thievery and worse.

She glanced anxiously over her shoulder but doubted the rain would allow her much warning. He'd have to be nearly alongside her before she could manage to discern him from her surroundings. She wouldn't think about him, wouldn't look back again.

A reverberating clap of thunder startled Emily to attention, offering audible proof that the spike of lightning she had decided to ignore had definitely been too close for comfort. Rain was coming down in sheets now, soaking her to the skin; she needed to hurry. Perhaps even a prayer or two would be in order.

"Bloody hell," she yelped as her hair caught briefly on the low hanging branch of an oak tree as she flew past it. A few more hairpins lost forever, she mused ruefully. It really was a wonder she had any left. Tangled tendrils of hair now smacked wetly against her face and neck, and her beautiful new riding dress was plastered uncomfortably against her skin.

Beatrice would appreciate the fact that her riding hat was even now sitting high and dry in Gypsy's stable. The mare had simply looked too silly to wear it out, and as Emily had assumed that she'd have looked equally ridiculous, she'd left it.

What she'd hoped would be a shortcut was turning out to be anything but. Strong winds and pelting rain had transformed the less-traveled path into treacherous terrain, making navigation both difficult and dangerous.

She couldn't deny it had been a mistake in judgment. Although, in her own defense, she doubted the decision to shortcut the journey had been a conscious one. Gypsy knew the path to the vicarage as well as she did, perhaps better. With her thoughts in such an uproar, she had probably neglected to give the horse any direction. So here she was.

Well, it simply couldn't be helped. Compared to the storm that had been ravaging her thoughts since her father's surprise announcement, Emily viewed the afternoon's weather as merely a minor inconvenience.

The highwayman, she had already refused to think about.

She was occupied with reminding herself of that very fact when she arrived, rather unexpectedly, at the point where her messy shortcut intercepted the road. As Gypsy plunged out of the trees, a violent movement to their left had Emily hauling back on the reins in shock and uncertainty. Gypsy reacted in outrage over the assumed intrusion and reared back with teeth bared. Already leaning back heavily on the reins, Emily felt as if the bottom had fallen out beneath her. She dug in her heels, tightened her knees, even grabbed at her horse's mane in an effort to keep her seat, but not surprisingly, the beast was slippery all over.

She landed on her backside in a newly formed puddle, her skirts rucked up enough to reveal a good deal more of her leg than she cared to. A slippery coating of mud covered nearly every square inch of her.

Emily groaned, already foreseeing that the bruises that

would result from the fall would be nothing compared to the shrill reprimand she was likely to receive upon returning home. Her riding habit was in pitiful condition, soaked and now filthy as well.

Lovely. Now she looked just as she felt. Hopefully Sophie could set her to rights. That is if she managed to arrive at the vicarage before she perished from cold and self-pity. She scarcely wished to acknowledge that there'd been another rider—it would be easier simply to pretend she'd fallen of her own accord. She could then have merely re-seated herself and ridden away. But there *was* another rider, and manners forbade such an easy escape.

Content to ignore a disapproving stare and even a mild level of censure in the interest of quelling gossip and easing her escape, she pushed back her sodden hair and started to rise, only to find herself caught in the watchful, arrogant gaze of quite the most magnificent stallion she had ever seen. He was midnight black and beautifully formed. She could have stared at him for several oblivious moments, but she wasn't given the chance. Regally the horse side-stepped, and its rider came into view.

Raising her eyes slowly from a glossy-wet, black Wellington boot, Emily took in the tall rain-soaked body, the hard planes of the rider's face, and finally a pair of stormy grey eyes. It seemed the highwayman had found her after all.

2

"...She does have an unfortunate habit of riding about the countryside unescorted, and in the most unladylike fashion..."

LETTER FROM LADY BEATRICE SINCLAIR TO MR. DESMOND RICHLY
22 OCTOBER 1818

Not certain what she should expect of this mysterious stranger, Emily drew her breath in sharply and waited. When he did nothing but continue to stare down at her in apparent disapproval, she decided he must be a calculating villain intent on first flustering his victims with nervous uncertainty. Or...with luck he was merely a harmless gentleman thoroughly unfamiliar with the dictates of chivalry.

"What is your intention, sir?" she inquired warily.

"An apology," he informed her in apparent surprise.

"Very well," she allowed expansively. Obviously he wished to choose his words carefully. She would be particularly gracious in her acceptance.

Neither spoke; neither moved, except to simultaneously raise a single eyebrow in question.

"I'm waiting!" Emily exclaimed finally, more irritated with this awkward delay than with her painful, messy fall.

"Yes, I've noticed. I confess I've no idea as to why you might choose to do that. We are, after all, out in the elements, and I don't suppose you're at all comfortable."

Judging from the laughter twitching his lips and shining in his eyes, he thought the entire situation amusing. She wished she could enjoy such a luxury. But today was likely to hold very little pleasantness at all.

"If you are possessed of any manners whatsoever," she informed him slowly, "you'll apologize for knocking me off my horse, and help me up."

"I am not in the habit of issuing apologies—"

"I'd puzzled that out for myself," came the muttered interruption.

"—for matters in which I am clearly not at fault," he finished, his smile still firmly in place.

"Say no more. It has become unattractively clear that your arrogance forbids such a courtesy."

"Not arrogance, love, competence. Not to mention sitting clearly in the right of matters. If I'm not mistaken, it was *I* riding along the path, and *you* plunging recklessly through the trees with nary a thought for the more…ah…civilized travelers."

Emily's eyes skewered him, willing him to adopt a more somber, less irksome attitude, wishing him, and his wicked smile, far, far away. "Indeed. Then I must offer *my* apologies."

"Ah…at long last."

She would not smile. It would be horrendously misinterpreted.

"Or, perhaps my condolences would be more appropriate. I fear you've either been struck by lightning or smacked by an errant tree branch." Her feigned sympathy transitioned smoothly to conviction, "Because it is clear that your judgment is lacking—you are most definitely at fault. The road, when wet, is a bog, whereas the path through the trees is sufficiently layered with leaves as to make it easily passable." She was only slightly fibbing after all. If it wasn't actually storming, the shortcut through the trees was a preferable choice. Still, he didn't need to know the particulars.

She'd been willing to concede partial blame for the accident—*full* blame if the rider was an acquaintance of her father's, strictly in the interest of self-preservation, but this stranger was a different matter. His presumption had grated, and now she hadn't the slightest intention of giving him the satisfaction. Neither did she wish to further encourage his affably superior demeanor.

"Your concern is heartwarming but misplaced. Only one of us was unseated, a single reputation muddied, so to speak."

Emily sucked in her breath with an exasperated hiss and seriously considered muddying a good bit of his despicable person.

Despite his mocking tone, he obediently dismounted and held out his gloved hand, a much-delayed picture of chivalry.

"I am indeed a gentleman. When it suits me. And as such, it is my duty to assist even ill-mannered ladies. He raised his eyebrows with a challenge of his own. "I am at your service, Miss…?"

Emily pointedly ignored both hand and query and slowly stood, tense with anger and stiff with soreness.

"I could quite easily have been injured you know." Faced with his obvious, and rather insulting, lack of concern, she couldn't help but point out this possibility.

"A cursory inspection provided sufficient assurance that the only injury of any consequence was to your pride. Never fear—judging by the look of you, it will recover quite nicely."

With no ready quip on her tongue, Emily clenched her teeth and wished it were possible to actually 'stare daggers' at someone.

He nodded his head, quite obviously under the assumption that the matter had been tidily dispatched, and then turned slightly away. But not quite enough to hide his grin.

Using her sleeve to wipe the mud from her face, she surreptitiously studied him from beneath her lashes, reluctantly conceding the existence of a single redeeming quality. He was inescapably, inarguably, a magnificent specimen. But quite obviously for display only, not to be touched or tampered with. And never to be spoken to.

Odd that she hadn't noticed until now.

He was quite tall, she imagined at least six feet, and

despite the obvious bulk of hard-earned muscle, he wore his sodden clothes with an ease she envied in her own sorry state. His dark hair had gotten so wet that it was impossible to determine its true color, but it was plainly longer than fashion dictated. His movements had been smooth and efficient, and he clearly had an enviable rapport with his stallion. She was fairly certain that under different circumstances she would have admired him very much. At least until he opened his mouth.

Now that she considered it, his mouth was quite nice, and she could have stared at it for some time. She had even noticed a slight dimple as he'd turned away, and she supposed he knew precisely how to put it to good use where the fairer sex was concerned. Such thoughts had her pulse quickening, which was surely ridiculous.

He had a strong nose and slashing brows over heavy-lidded eyes that appeared dark grey, lit with flecks of gold. Emily was busy pondering that strange combination when she realized that those very eyes now stared mockingly back. Startled, she looked quickly away, hoping he wouldn't notice the color that had likely settled on her cheeks.

"Hasn't anyone ever warned you about staring at a man in such a fashion?" he inquired.

Turning back to him, she noticed the tense line of his shoulders.

"I hardly think you are in any position to instruct me on the subject of manners."

"Nor do I desire the task. Tempt me further though, and it will be my pleasure to enlighten you on other, considerably more diverting, matters."

Emily was certain her blush deepened well past flattering, but she hadn't expected the odd fluttering around her heart. It had the exuberance of dancers and, all at once, her breath came short. She wanted to reach her hand up to press against the rhythmic beat, to stifle it if she could, but then changed her mind against it. It wasn't particularly unpleasant, and beyond that, she didn't need this stranger thinking any more of himself than he already did. Needing, however, a moment to regain her composure, she tossed her leg over Gypsy and settled herself back in the saddle before responding.

"And it will be mine to acquaint you with my boot," she parried prettily.

She watched as he assessed her, apparently deciding how best to deal with the messy picture she presented. She smiled a chilly bit of encouragement.

"Very well, I'll offer only a bit of advice. In future, you may wish to either adopt a slower pace or consider a less spirited mount," he suggested blandly.

Emily stiffened. She took inordinate pride in her abilities as a horsewoman and immediately took his suggestion as a challenge. Raising her chin a few inches, she gave him a look of disdain.

"I'd wager I could manage your stallion."

"I rather doubt it. But as I don't plan to offer you the opportunity, your ability will remain uncontested."

"Perhaps you'd care to race then? A true test of horseflesh versus skill? You may boast the former, I the latter." While absently patting Gypsy, she stared down the stranger, willing him to agree. Faced with his narrowed eyes and lack of response, she bit her lip to hold back a grin and tossed out, "Not arrogance, but competence, remember?"

The stranger's lips twitched, and Emily could well imagine the train of his thoughts. *She's but a slip of a girl. What can she be thinking in boldly challenging a strange gentleman to a race? She needs to be taught a lesson. And it would be my pleasure to oblige…*

"Are you certain your pride could manage the end result?" came his answer, all but confirming her suspicions.

"I daresay considerably better than yours as I plan to win," she quipped.

"In that case, I accept," he announced with a confident smile. "Will one week from today suit you?"

"Do you need the time to practice?" she inquired prettily.

"Sheath your claws," he said around a chuckle, "I have

business in Cornwall and can't be certain when I'll return."

"Very well then, one week," she conceded, a smile pulling at her lips.

"At the north edge of this blasted forest," he declared, running his fingers through his hair and sending rivulets of rainwater slipping down the sides of his neck to disappear into the *V* of his shirt.

"Come at dawn," she ordered imperiously, determined not to ponder over those daring rivulets any further.

Nodding his head in deference to her curt demand, he quietly answered, "Until then."

Smug with satisfaction, Emily could easily imagine herself victorious, could even imagine her boot positioned on his chest pressing him into the mud. "Victory will be sweet," she murmured to herself.

"Indeed." Apparently he'd heard her. His smile was wicked and mocking both, and Emily could think of no appropriate response. She paused in the act of swinging her mare away from him when she heard his voice once again, smooth and almost seductive, "But not as sweet as its prize."

Feeling strangely unsteady and oddly confused, she nudged Gypsy around and attempted to make a dignified exit. She wished she had not felt compelled to glance back over her shoulder. For there he stood, an enigmatic smile on his lips, waiting for her to succumb to that very weakness.

Devil take the man!

His grin set her heart aflutter a second time, and worse, this time she was almost certain he knew it.

Such a reaction would have been disturbing enough in its unexpectedness, but it was considerably more so when paired with the awareness that this…stranger…had been responsible for the only times it had ever happened.

She would make certain it was his last victory over her.

* * *

The faeries had bewitched him.

He was almost certain of it, and that was curious indeed

as he was equally certain that he didn't believe in such creatures.

Yet what other explanation could there be?

He'd wanted, quite simply, to tuck her into his pocket and keep her for his own. And had felt ridiculous because of it.

Apparently the faeries didn't understand the rules of British society. Either that or they had merely been intent on making mischief. A lady, whom she had most assuredly been, was not meant for dalliance but for marriage.

As such, he had no business thinking of her in the way that he had been.

But he was only a man, and whether she realized it or not, she had tempted him, very nearly lured him, away from gentlemanly behavior.

By God, she'd challenged him to a race!

He wanted to regret his acceptance, but couldn't. Instead he anticipated their dawn appointment knowing it would be bittersweet. He'd relish the minx's company, no matter how fleeting, and then regret the necessity of parting.

He wouldn't trouble to deny the fact that they would indeed part. For he had absolutely no intention of getting married, and the curious effects of today's faerie storm weren't about to change his mind.

It had been an extremely sensible decision, made long ago and reaffirmed every day since.

Certainly he had nothing against the fairer sex. He'd been charmed, besotted, and enchanted more times than he cared to count—today included. But it had never lasted, never taken hold. And it never would. While he might occasionally engage in a bit of harmless flirtation with a woman of his class, any further indulgence would be taken on society's fringe.

If he'd had use for a wife he might have been willing to reconsider, but for now there simply was no rationalization for such a life-altering commitment. Martyred innocence didn't appeal to him on any level. A virgin bride was utterly unnecessary. So, too, was an heiress; he had funds of his own. Contrary to his father's belief, and apparently everyone else's as well, he would manage very nicely without an heir. What difference did it make if a distant relation inherited the title and all that came with it? Let them inherit now, instead of him. It would be as a weight lifted off his soul.

He'd been warned of the possibility of loneliness but remained unconcerned. Loneliness had been his shadow companion for a very long time, and a wife hadn't a chance of displacing it.

The sudden hollowness in his chest felt like a whisper of grief moving through him, an unpleasant, inescapable reminder of the impact tragedy had had on his life. Quite simply, it had changed everything.

He'd lost his brother—his father's heir—and as next in line for the title, it seemed he'd been poised to lose himself as well. So he'd gone. Left everything behind for the chance to make something of his life beyond what his father intended and the title demanded.

Disappointing second son to the Earl of Chase, Brandon Davenport had made a comfortable fortune in the West Indies and returned to England the heir to a viscountcy. Now, with title, estate, and money of his own, Lord Brandon Davenport, Viscount Ashwood was much sought after. And rather disturbingly, by everyone he didn't care to know. As a result, life in London had left him feeling oddly anonymous.

Polite society imagined itself fascinated with him, and yet the *ton* was utterly content that he remain an enigma. Swirling innuendoes and whispered speculation were capable of entertaining indefinitely. The truth would bore them into silence, and then what would they do?

Pertinent details were, of course, the exception—those had been clarified immediately.

On the morning of his return he'd rented a modest bachelor residence. By the afternoon, all of society had known that he'd made his fortune, acquired a title, and stood in line to improve his status on both counts as heir to the Earl of Chase. They also knew of a certainty that he was looking for a bride.

Denial, he knew, would be a waste of time.

When it became apparent that he was intentionally dancing only a single dance with any given young lady, and in fact, rarely stayed long enough at any function to partner more than a very few, they were ready with an explanation.

Quite surprisingly, it was the correct one.

It was put about that he was tenaciously 'clinging to bachelorhood', but rather than deter anyone, the news had the opposite effect.

Now not only a catch, he was labeled a challenge as well. The latter, he had quickly found, was most definitely worse than the former, garnering him the devoted attention of the most complacent and overbearing of young ladies. And their mothers.

Since his arrival in London little more than a fortnight ago, he'd been inundated with invitations. With the season and the summer months past, the *ton* was apparently plagued with ennui. It appeared the town's hostesses were eager to pull off a *coup*, and with him in attendance at their routs, balls, and parties, they imagined they had a better chance of success.

He had to admit to being initially amused over the flirting, fluttering, and gushing that had accompanied every introduction, but before long it had smothered him, as oppressive as the crush of bodies.

The widows had been more forward than he remembered, the debutantes more determined. And why not? No matter how inadvertently, he had given them more reason to be.

Desperation had fairly hung in the air.

Conversation was banal and underscored with intent, dancing was remarked upon and not worth the effort, and flirtations were far from harmless. Everyone, it seemed, was focused on chances and choices, if not their own then someone else's.

Before long, they had all blurred together, utterly indistinguishable, and he very much doubted he could remember a single one of their names or faces.

He'd begun spending every evening at his club, but he'd

quickly found that in London, one was always within reach. Avoiding the social whirl didn't preclude the gossip, the rumors, the betting books, or the aggravation.

Everything he did or said was dissected, interpreted and discussed.   In gentlemen's clubs over whiskey and in drawing rooms over afternoon tea, for God's sake! He perversely hoped he'd managed to have the ladies lingering over their biscuits in avid curiosity over a careless comment.

Tired of it all after but a few days, he had wished only to escape. A stroke of good luck had come in the form of an invitation from his old friend, Lord Colin Willoughsby.

He and Colin had been commissioned into the army together, but they'd served side by side for only a matter of weeks.   While Colin had been content to stay on the Continent, well suited to intelligence work, he himself had sold out almost immediately.   Contrary to his father's opinions, he believed himself quite sufficiently disciplined already. So he'd boarded a ship bound for the West Indies and hadn't looked back.

Against a great many odds, Colin's first inquisitive letter had found its way into his hands. Apparently he had felt a proper greeting unwarranted. The brief note had begun, "If you are alive, old man, send a note in a bottle. Otherwise, disregard what follows." Ever since, Brand had valiantly tried to keep up his end of their steady, sporadic correspondence. Colin, it would seem, had the patience of a saint.

Coincidentally, he and his friend had both returned to England within weeks of each other. Colin to assume the title and responsibilities left behind by his father's death, and Brand to enjoy a bit of life before he was forced to do the same.

When Colin had sent word that he had returned to his estates and was eager for a houseguest, it seemed the perfect opportunity. Having put matters in order with his solicitor, Brand was eager to escape the feeling of being under glass. He had promptly sent off his reply of acceptance and followed the letter into a particularly untamed and quiet corner of Devon no more than an hour behind it.

The journey had indeed been invigorating, becoming more and more so the further he traveled from London, but he'd been grateful to sink into a sumptuous leather armchair in Colin's library. Colin had been quite eager to join him.

After their initial greetings and catchings-up, Brand had naïvely imagined they'd share a brandy and a bit of companionable silence. Not so.

His friend had apparently needed to unburden himself, and had promptly revealed half excitedly, half shamefacedly that he planned to marry. He had in fact already chosen a bride, a Miss Emily Sinclair, daughter of Lord Edward Sinclair.

Brand couldn't have been more surprised by the news, and he suspected he might even have been a bit tactless in his initial response.

"Why on earth would you do that?" he'd puzzled.

Colin had laughed boisterously in response, and Brand had known instantly. This was no jest, no mistake. At the very least Colin didn't consider it one, and Brand couldn't imagine it would be a good idea to inquire.

"You needn't worry, old boy. It's relatively common."

"I notice you didn't say 'harmless'," Brand accused with a smirk.

"So I have your blessing?" Colin asked in jest.

"Is it necessary?" Brand asked, interest perked. Perhaps there was a chance to redirect this odd turn of Colin's mind.

"Most definitely not," Colin chuckled. "But I'd like to know why you're so set against it—you don't even know her."

"Do *you*?" Brand probed. He knew he was being rude but couldn't seem to help himself.

"As a matter of fact, I do," Colin said, watching his finger as it traced the rim of his glass.

"Did you arrange all this in short-pants?" Brand asked, pointedly suspicious.

Colin's eyes glanced up and over at his friend, amusement lurking in their depths. "Why in God's name would you ask that?"

"You've been on the Continent for the better part of ten

years and back for less than a month! I wouldn't have expected that was enough time for you to get settled, put your affairs in order, and succumb to the lure of marriage."

Uncrossing his legs and leaning forward in his chair, Brand queried, "When did you meet her? Where?" Remembering London's breed of chameleon ladies, he added, "Do you think she could distinguish you from a group of other wealthy, titled gentlemen?"

Not at all offended by such blatant cynicism, Colin answered good-naturedly. "I certainly hope so. I knew her as a child. She once thought me her hero."

He spoke somewhat abashedly, smiling at the memory, his blue eyes crinkling at the edges. "It was very flattering," he added.

"No doubt."

Sitting forward, Colin wistfully asked, "Do you think it's too much to hope that—"

"Yes," Brand interrupted flatly.

"You must have charmed your way around London," Colin said leaning back. "Or perhaps you simply brooded, a romantic, tragic figure."

"It wouldn't have made the slightest bit of difference. I could have been a vampire, and I would have been eagerly beset by falsely optimistic young ladies."

"Sad but true."

"Ah-ha! So you are not unaware of the single-minded purpose simmering in the minds of every young lady of marriageable age!"

"Of course not. What else would you have them do?" Not wishing an answer, he promptly added, "Beyond that, I do not think it wise to generalize."

"How can you not? What do you know of this Miss Sinclair? She was a chit in the schoolroom when you left."

"My mother informs me that she has remained unmarried."

"No doubt for good reason," Brand muttered.

"Beyond that, I'm optimistic."

"I see. I suppose it was this infallible logic that insured your success as an intelligence officer," Brand offered dryly.

The Willoughsby butler had interrupted the conversation at that point with a sealed letter lying ominously on a silver salver, a dangerous looking opener beside it.

His father's summons, it would appear, had finally served a useful purpose. It would spare him further discussion of his friend's seemingly untenable decision. Colin was behaving like a lovesick youth, yet oddly, it seemed Brand was suffering all of the unpleasant effects. So despite having had only a quarter hour's rest, Brand grasped at the only escape he was offered.

He'd exuberantly tipped back the contents of his brandy, offered his apologies to Colin, and promised to return within a couple of days. He'd been striding towards the door when his friend, still sitting calmly by the fire, had forestalled him.

"I'd be on my guard if I were you, Ashwood. Fate will likely deal you a love match, and the lady will no doubt turn you into a bumbling idiot. I just hope I'm there to see it."

"I assure you, there will be absolutely nothing to see," Brand had said emphatically, "But do try to avoid that embarrassing eventuality yourself," he added, fearing it may already be too late.

"I'd propose a wager, but it's really not necessary. I predict I'll soon have the opportunity to witness your discomfiture, and it will more than sufficiently make up for today's condescending behavior." Tucking his tongue in his cheek, Colin had looked casually away.

"I'll bid you good luck with your endeavors, no matter how ill-conceived," Brand had said shortly, turning away from Colin, his absurd prediction, and the comfort of the fire.

* * *

Having resolved at the rebellious age of three and twenty not to allow his father to control his life through the threat of disinheritance, Brand had earned his freedom but with difficulty. Or so he'd thought. By rights he was free to

ignore his father's feckless bidding, but training himself to
do so was proving to be more difficult than he'd expected.

So it would seem that, newly arrived in Devon, he was
being summoned away to Cornwall, to his father's estate.
He now found himself in a merciless downpour, cursing
himself for his blind obedience, his father for the weather,
which was surely ridiculous, and Colin for the blasted
shortcut he'd suggested. He'd thought briefly about finding
a spot to wait out the storm but quickly discarded the idea
and urged his horse to even greater speed.

Remembering Colin's prediction of love, he'd snorted
with derision.

Had his friend actually believed it possible that he would
fall victim to the wiles of a young lady of quality? Even if
he did, his poor judgment could never be attributable to
something so illusory as love.

How could he possibly love someone who was content
to be in love with a reputation that by its very nature was a
coincidence of birth? In his case, tragedy need also be
accorded a role. The very idea was rather insulting.

Needing to occupy his mind with more practical matters,
namely how to get out of the blasted trees all in one piece,
he had thought no more on the subject and quickly found
himself distracted anew.

The faeries it would seem had been as unappreciative of
Colin's suggested shortcut as he. Either that or his thoughts
had put mischief in their minds. He didn't claim to know
whether the creatures could read a person's thoughts, but
either explanation of their misdeeds seemed just as likely.

Their punishment had been clever indeed—they had
intercepted his path with a fiery temptress that had
bewitched his mind. They had no doubt gotten perverse
pleasure from the fact that she was as unlikely as any he was
wont to choose.

Her horse had seemed to plunge straight out of the trees,
and there she'd sat, gloriously astride. It was due to years of
practice and some steady maneuvering that he'd managed to
avoid a collision that would surely have injured them both.
As it was, he'd watched helplessly as she'd slipped to the

ground and landed in an immense mud puddle at his stallion's fidgety feet, uttering a decidedly unladylike oath.

Annoyance had warred with concern as he'd looked down at her. Just a slip of a girl—the top of her head would barely brush his chin. It was astonishing, really, that she appeared unharmed and in need of nothing more than a good scrubbing and a stern lecture.

He wondered fleetingly who would be responsible for such a lecture—husband or father. Either would certainly be furious if he knew she was cavorting about the countryside looking as she did. Only a fraction of her dishabille could be attributed to her fall.

His body tightened as he remembered: her cheeks had been flushed, her hair curling down around her shoulders, and her riding dress drenched with rain and clinging to every curve. His thorough perusal had assured him that she was definitely more woman than girl, and while not classically pretty, she was sufficiently arresting as to make one stare with appreciation, nonetheless. Considering now, he suspected her appeal may very well have lain in her utter disregard for her appearance.

That one would never belong to the glittering masses of the *ton*. In fact, she probably scoffed at society and all its trappings. Rather than applaud her good sense, he was surprised to discover that he would not object to delivering her a lecture himself. It was one thing to be deemed an Original, quite another to be caught cavorting in the rain, riding astride, with charms boldly on display for any who might care to look…or sample.

Ill-mannered, obstinate, boastful wench. She had thought entirely too much of herself. But then, perhaps, so did he. His smile came easily as he realized, at the very least, she had managed to set herself apart. He would have no trouble remembering her long past their intended race.

3

"...I hesitate to even mention it as it will surely come to naught, but Emily has adopted the strange notion that she must needs choose a husband for herself, and Edward is of a mind to indulge her—for a time. It is merely a girlish whim and of little consequence..."

LETTER FROM LADY BEATRICE SINCLAIR TO MR. DESMOND RICHLY
26 OCTOBER 1818

She couldn't understand it; it made absolutely no sense, but in truth she no longer cared who had caused the mishap. Distance had given her a modicum of clarity. What did it matter really? What harm had been done except to a new riding habit she would have eventually, leisurely muddied on her own? It didn't even bear considering.

Still, the stranger's assessment had been only half-correct. While she *had* managed to come away uninjured, her pride had neither sustained bruise nor scratch. Instead it had remained firmly intact, no doubt assisted by the fact that she didn't trouble to worry over appearances. While the wet, cold, and mud were getting deuced uncomfortable, they would be easily remedied once she arrived at the vicarage. All in all, she felt she had handled herself quite nicely under the circumstances.

The entire encounter might well have sprung from the pages of one of her novels. A threatening thunderstorm hovering over a shadowy forest, a spirited, well-intentioned beauty—it was her imagination after all—and a boorish, sinfully handsome stranger—boorish being the definitive descriptor.

The silence had hummed with tension as it had settled fleetingly around bold taunts, eloquent parries, and regal confidence. It had been deliciously exciting once she'd allowed herself to be drawn in. She'd been immersed in her own actions. And captivated by his.

Shivers, gooseflesh, and a parched tongue wouldn't have been amiss, for all were typical reactions to an enthralling experience. A captivating novel would inspire all three, yet strangely, they'd all been markedly absent today. Instead she'd had flutterings.

Flutterings.

The word was meant to describe little winged creatures, not a heart. But that had been precisely the word that had come to mind. Perhaps a difference was to be expected as she was actually, literally involved in this incident.

Each time he had grinned at her, her heart rate had speeded to a rapid, rhythmic beat, and she had fought to subdue the inexplicable reaction. He had been determined to fluster her, and she had been equally determined not to allow it.

It was a depressing admission to be sure, but the few heated, ill-mannered moments she had shared with a stranger had been the highlight of her entire week. Just a few moments of obnoxious repartee had been the perfect respite from her thoroughly disagreeable predicament. She hadn't wanted to think about husbands, and his very presence had made certain she hadn't.

Having finally tumbled—quite literally and onto her bottom—into an adventure outside one of her novels, she was determined it would be enjoyed and prolonged as thoroughly as she could manage it. Her devilish stranger had gifted her with distraction and offered himself up for a further diversion. In truth he'd eluded to an offer of more, but that was neither here nor there. Beyond the race, she had absolutely no plans to accept whatever it was that he'd been offering, and she rather thought she'd made that clear.

He'd gone his way, and she, hers. For one week.

Shaking her thoughts blessedly free of him, she realized

the rain had finally stopped. As such, she was determined to shrug off her impossible burden a few moments longer to snatch a bit of the day for the sheer pleasure of the crisp, invigorating weather. The chill in the air and the changing leaves brought with them such an exciting feeling of anticipation. Soon the wind would swirl with color as it whipped through the trees, and then, perhaps, icy sheeting rain might give way for a time to a sprinkling or two of snowflakes. The subtle invasion of winter was something she had always looked forward to.

This year left her with somewhat of a paradox. Her favorite time of year was now wrapped around her father's ultimatum. As winter approached, so did an unwanted engagement, and soon after that, a dreaded marriage. Henceforth every year would be a painful reminder of all she'd been forced to sacrifice.

As she looked out over the saturated hills, upholstered in varying shades of green, she felt suddenly very alone. Her whole life was wrapped up in this little corner of Devon, and as mundane as it was, it was still home. She didn't want to leave, not for a life she didn't want. It was lovely here; everything was familiar, and the countryside shimmered and glistened, almost like a dream.

Realization came quickly, followed by the grudging admission that it was perfectly reasonable that she should cry. With only a few moments till her journey's end, a few moments to spare before an explanation would be required, she welcomed the escape of a few weighty tears. Any more would signify she was content to be a victim of circumstances, which she most certainly was not. She would find a way to triumph.

Once again, her fond imagining of the stranger on his back in the mud invaded her consciousness, bringing with it an unavoidable smirk and, this time, a giggle.

With relief Emily realized that her moment of pity had passed. It was time to put Sophie to work.

The rambling heap of grey stone that served as the vicarage came as a decidedly welcome, if blurry, sight. Emily gulped in the frigid air, hoping the chill would temper the heated flush in her face. Believing she'd achieved at least a semblance of calm, she quickly dismounted, tethered her horse, and walked slowly up the brick path Sophie had lined with lovingly tended flowers. Flowers that would soon need to guard themselves against impending winter.

Taking a deep breath, she rapped sharply on the heavy oak door, not wishing to barge in looking so frightfully shabby. It was opened almost immediately by Sophie, who simply stared at her in silent wonder.

After several seconds of mute scrutiny, her friend finally spoke. "However did you manage to get yourself into such a state, Em? It seems beyond even you."

Shaking her head in exasperation, and oblivious to her muddied skirts, Emily started through the doorway, prompting Sophie to whisk her own skirts out of the way.

"I warn you, you will not believe it. Not a single bit of it. It is inconceivable what I've had to deal with today. Really, you reach a point at which anything else is simply beyond endurance—"

"I've reached it," Sophie interrupted dryly.

Emily was silent for a beat. "Very well…" she allowed archly, "If you wish to strip me of the opportunity to—"

"Your opportunity will keep. First I'd very much like to strip you of that filthy gown—there is now a trail of mud on my clean floor. Upstairs," she ordered grimly. "I will hold up your skirts."

"Oh very well," Emily surrendered, moving obediently towards the stairs with Sophie trailing along behind her.

She stubbornly remained silent on the comfortably creaking stairs, in the upstairs hall that smelled pleasantly of beeswax, and even upon reaching the privacy of Sophie's corner bedchamber while she stood shivering as her friend helped her off with the clinging, heavy mass of velveteen.

"Tidy yourself, dry your hair, use the blanket on the chair to get warm, and take your pick of the gowns in the wardrobe—in that order," Sophie instructed with a meaningful glare. "When you come down, you'll sit, have some tea, and visit with Father and me. He's busy writing tomorrow's sermon." She turned away from her friend but then glanced back over her shoulder with a raised eyebrow and added mischievously, "It should be a good one."

Emily had long been privy to the knowledge that Vicar Penrose never actually finished a sermon.   He took extensive and often unintelligible notes, which his only daughter then composed into concise and interesting prose. In his endearing absentmindedness, the vicar never seemed to grasp the fact that the notes from which he read every Sunday were quite different from the ones he had left for Sophie to transcribe.   Rather, he was quite proud of his sermons, finding opportunities to quote them days after their delivery. Emily was not sure anyone acquainted with both father and daughter was fooled, but even so, she enjoyed pretending it was a close-held secret.

With the quiet tap of the door softly hitting the jam, Emily was alone, a smile playing about her lips as she stepped to Sophie's chair and lifted the deep blue woolen blanket, wrapping it cozily around her bare shoulders.

"Yes, ma'am," she dutifully assented, already having forgotten the correct order of things.

Already her troubles had seemingly melted away. Certainly they were there, an unattractive, unpleasant puddle she wished she could step over and around indefinitely, but she could avoid them for a bit and pretend her only concern was tea. Right now, it most certainly was. And taking it with Sophie and her father was a decidedly welcome prospect.

She and Sophie had been best friends for as long as Emily could remember, and she had always been as welcome at the vicarage as in her own home. As of this morning's discussion with her father and stepmother, the scales had apparently tipped in this direction. It seemed here at least both father and daughter accepted her as she was and were happy to have her company as such. While it was true that Sophie nudged and prodded her over many things, both friends were fully aware that such efforts, while habitual, were futile.

Emily selected a simple moss green gown from the carved rosewood wardrobe in the corner of the room and eyed it critically. Deciding it shouldn't be the slightest bit garish paired with her persimmon hair, she pulled it out. Certainly she would have to contend with the considerable difference in height between her and Sophie, but at least she would be warm and dry.

Laying it on the bed, she moved to the washstand, and caught her reflection in the free-standing mirror sitting on Sophie's dressing table.

Egad, but she looked horrid! Wisps of hair had escaped their braids and were now sticking to the spattered mud on her face. She was chafed with cold, pale from shock and recent illness, and sick of heart. She looked hunted.

Good heavens! What must Sophie be thinking?

Apparently that tidiness took precedence over curiosity.

Rolling her eyes in easy acceptance of her friend's little quirks of cleanliness and order, Emily decided to deal with her hair first and so sat down in her chemise and blanket, took up a towel, and went to work. It took only a moment to realize that her thick curly hair was not going to be tamed with an ivory-handled brush and her own tired arms anytime soon. Conceding defeat with a shrug, she secured the still slightly damp mass with a scrap of blue ribbon, content to be merely moderately presentable.

Giving her reflection a final satisfied nod, she made to rise, and then noticed a torn and wrinkled scrap of paper nearly hidden beneath a hand mirror. There it sat, smoothed but wrinkled amid Sophie's few concessions to vanity. Emily wouldn't have given it a second thought were it not for her immediate certainty that the handwriting didn't belong to Sophie.

Conscience warred with curiosity for several moments until, unable to bear it any longer, Emily snatched up the paper and read it quickly.

25 October 1818
> *Choices are no longer mine;*
> *they're now all left to you.*
> *I pray you'll make the right ones*
> *before your time is through.*

Even after rereading it twice, she still didn't understand the cryptic message, other than the date, which was today. And yet the words seemed oddly familiar. Where could she have seen them before? If she'd come across them in a book, she couldn't think which one it might have been, but faced with the alternatives, it seemed likely. If someone had spoken those peculiar words to her, she most certainly would have remembered. And promptly thought he or she a ninny.

Right now the origin of the rhyme was insignificant; it was the origin of the note she needed to be concerned with. Where had it come from? Who had written it? And perhaps more importantly, why had she had to stoop to snooping in order to read it? Why hadn't Sophie confided in her? For clearly, if Sophie had gone to the trouble of placing it amongst her most personal possessions, it must possess a certain measure of importance.

It was a pity Sophie was so adept at avoiding confrontations—on occasion Emily had found that they made everything so much simpler. Emily would have loved to sashay into the parlour holding the slip of paper between finger and thumb, rippling it through the air, waiting for an explanation. But as Sophie never parted with a secret she didn't intend to, such a plan was destined for failure.

Devil take it!

She could still put the note back where she'd found it and forget she'd ever stumbled upon it. Her conscience was already pricking her for reading her friend's private correspondence but not enough to convince her that good manners was the best option. Her insatiable curiosity aside, she was worried about her friend. This was not the sort of message an unmarried young lady, and a vicar's daughter, should be receiving. In fact, its presence in Sophie's bedchamber was quite astonishing indeed.

Gripping the paper with both hands, a shiver ran over her, and she willed herself to calm.

Perhaps she was reading it incorrectly. After all, the handwriting bordered on a scrawl. Still, sparing several moments on an alternate decipher didn't make a whit of difference. Everything else she came up with was even more ambiguous or nonsensical than her initial guess at its meaning.

Considering further, she decided that very little inspired a need for such obscurity. But mischief most certainly did. She knew well from experience that if you danced around a subject, you were not, strictly speaking, guilty of a lie. Merely a little deception.

Could Sophie have somehow gotten involved with unsavory individuals intent on nefarious purposes? Rereading the note a third time, she was convinced that it presented an ultimatum or warning of some kind. The more she considered those last few words, 'before your time is through', the more convinced she was of the possibility that Sophie was being blackmailed.

But for what? Her recipe for ginger-orange scones and a smuggler's crate of embroidered tea cosies? It seemed unlikely.

Utterly confounded, and convinced she must be missing something, Emily rubbed both temples in soothing circles and tried to think.

Considerably more relaxed, she conceded that perhaps the intent of the cryptic message, rather than mischief, was simply caution. It took little more than a careless word or misstep to start a rumor, and once started, it spread as quickly and riotously as a runner weed in an unkept garden. Any unpredictable involvement between two individuals was inevitably discussed at length, particularly if one of the two was a gentleman, and the other, a lady. A hesitant or uncertain pair would wisely wish to avoid the whispered speculation until such a time as it was unavoidable.

Such as an engagement, Emily allowed slowly, sitting down heavily on her friend's tidy bed. Could it possibly be that Sophie was even now considering marriage? Was this curiously ominous rhyme intended as a heartfelt declaration? The notion seemed almost laughable but no more so than her prim and proper friend choosing to court disaster. In fact, comparatively, it seemed downright probable. After all, ladies and gentlemen both were guilty of odd behavior when they believed their hearts engaged.

She simply couldn't decide.

It appeared there was nothing for it. She was going to have to do a bit of sleuthing. And while she didn't mind the necessity, she was irritated on principle. Whether immersed in danger or befuddled by love, Sophie should have confided such a thrilling secret. Best friends were supposed to tell each other everything. Hadn't she just braved perilous weather and a hugely annoying stranger to confide her own problems, only to be forestalled, first, by a layer of mud, and now, a vexing puzzle?

With her luck, an investigation would unearth the disappointing reality that Beatrice had written the mysterious note, and that the ominous warning referred to no greater threat than the seeming perpetuity of Sophie's status as an unmarried young lady. At the moment she couldn't think of a more fitting, and frankly disappointing, end to the day.

It seemed she was now embroiled in a second quandary, and neither of the two was of her doing. The first was the interfering work of her father and stepmother and this one attributable to Sophie's irritatingly close-mouthed way of dealing with secrets.

If Sophie hadn't planned on revealing anything, she shouldn't have been so indiscreet as to leave the note in plain sight beneath a mirror on the vanity table in her room. Really! Talk about a temptation.

Thoroughly exasperated and tense with anxiety, Emily breathed in deeply to calm herself, hoping Sophie wasn't yet wondering what was keeping her. At least not wondering enough to come looking.

She'd have to postpone any further curiosity. Right now she needed to focus on her own dilemma—the sooner it was solved, the sooner she'd be free to explore the devious workings of her friend's mind.

Emily promptly realized it would be best to get rid of the incriminating evidence. She was, after all, still holding the note.

Shoving it beneath the hand mirror that had done such a

poor job of hiding it in the first place, she leaned back a bit and tilted her head to examine its placing. Tugging slightly on the edge revealed a few more scribbled letters, and contented Emily that Sophie wouldn't notice anything amiss.

Now, quickly, she needed to finish getting cleaned up. Tipping a chipped white porcelain pitcher over the hand towel positioned neatly next to the basin, Emily cringed a bit as she wiped the chilly water over her face. The process of scrubbing herself clean took longer than expected as some patches of mud seemed intent on staying put. She felt slightly chagrined to leave Sophie with a brown towel in place of her once-immaculate white one.

Deciding Sophie might be more forgiving if it was neatly replaced, she gave the task her best effort, arranging and rearranging as she realized that something was nagging at the edge of her mind. Everything about Sophie's secret message was suspicious. If it was from a suitor, where were the flowery words of love, the boldly declared devotion, the impatient yearning for another meeting? Where, for heaven's sake, was the courtesy of a clean sheet of paper?

Then again, unsavory individuals likely wouldn't trouble over the date so much as a clarify a demand, would they? Yet there'd been no demand specified. In fact, there'd been no reference to anything other than the possibility of consequences. Had Sophie already been given the details, and this messy little scrap was solely intended to encourage her to consider them wisely? If so, why had she kept it? Nothing made sense, if only because everything Sophie ever did made absolutely perfect sense.

In theory Emily knew she shouldn't worry. But already today one of her theories had been proved utterly untenable. Her expectation of an unhindered slide into spinsterhood had been irrefutably hindered. Her world was currently in a tumult, and she couldn't afford to make assumptions. However, if she were to give Sophie the benefit of the doubt, nothing had happened yet. Plans could still be foiled and reputations saved. She could, at the very least, be optimistic.

Unbidden, comparisons of her friend's situation and her own filled her mind. She herself was desperate to find a suitable gentleman who would enable her to shrug off the abhorrent threat of Mr. Richly. In contrast, it now appeared entirely possible that Sophie may have purposely involved herself with a man who could very well be completely inappropriate. She could but pray that his misdeeds paled in comparison to Richly's.

She very nearly giggled as she imagined Sophie wasting stolen moments lecturing her mysterious gentleman on the consequences of wicked behavior, but she quickly sobered as an extremely disturbing thought rose in her mind like a cake of soap in bathwater.

Straightening quickly from her hunch over the wash basin, she shivered as the icy cold water dripped off her chin and down in tormenting rivulets between her breasts. As she leaned over again to halt their progress, she couldn't help but wonder if Sophie's mysterious gentleman and her enigmatic stranger could be one and the same.

The idea was preposterous, surely, but it wouldn't disappear. Try as she might to submerge it, it kept bobbing up, taunting her with the possibility.

Patting herself dry, she quickly dressed, and reminded herself that all she could do was hope and pray that there would be no more coincidences today. For Sophie's sake of course.

Snapping her skirts in irritation, she quickly made her way downstairs. She could hear Sophie and her father talking quietly, no doubt holding tea for her. Emily stopped a moment in the open parlour doorway and studied her friend unnoticed, determined to be objective. Sophie was a classic beauty with pale blonde hair and intelligent green eyes. She was kind, gracious, dutiful…and unwaveringly loyal.

At least Emily had thought so until she had found a potentially life-altering rhyme on a little scrap of paper, its contents having been kept secret from a purported best friend.

Sophie glanced up at that very moment and motioned

her to join them as she bit her lip in exasperated amusement. Relaxing her own lips into a mild smile, Emily graciously conceded that Sophie's spinster status was indeed astounding. It seemed inconceivable that no one had yet managed to win her friend's hand—Sophie did not share her own opinions of marriage and was, in fact, forever encouraging her to reconsider them.

It seemed likely that their lives might very well be poised to change simultaneously. Yet precisely how either of them would change was to remain a mystery—at least for a short time.

Emily had moved to seat herself on the worn and comfortable burgundy-flowered sofa when Vicar Penrose finally noted her presence. An affectionate smile lit his cherubic face.

"Emily, my dear, delightful as always to see you," he said jovially. Then with a puzzled expression, "Are you shrinking, my dear?"

Emily smiled with affection. "My gown had gotten wet in the rain, and Sophie was gracious enough to lend me one of hers. If only I were as tall as she," she finished wistfully.

"Oh, quite so, quite so," the vicar replied good-naturedly. "You really shouldn't be out in the rain, my dear. You'll catch a nasty cold."

Emily had absolutely nothing to say to that pearl of wisdom and so kept silent and smiled fondly on the man who had offered it. A round little elf with bright pink cheeks and thinning white hair.

Emily had always considered it a miracle that such a diminutive and dreamy man as the vicar had sired the statuesque and imminently efficient Sophie. As far as Emily could tell, the only things father and daughter had in common were their green eyes and their unerring devotion to each other.

"Do sit down, my dear," the vicar was saying to the teapot, "and tell me how you go on. I haven't seen you for, what is it, a month now?"

"Emily visited last Tuesday, Father," Sophie corrected indulgently, offering her friend a challenging stare, all but daring her to reveal what had kept her away so long. Emily didn't suppose it was necessary that she admit to a recent insight into the link between rainstorms and nasty colds. So she smiled at her friend, appreciative of the irony, but content to keep it their little secret.

"She came for tea, and you enlightened us on some of the recent archaeological discoveries on the Continent."

"Tuesday, you say. Oh yes, quite so. I remember the conversation now." His eyes took on a faraway expression as he continued speaking, mostly to himself, "Wonderful to be involved in such thrilling work—ah, to be young again," he finished wistfully.

"Your colleagues correspond with you quite regularly," Sophie reminded, "I daresay there is very little of which you are unaware. Besides, we could not manage here without you, could we, Emily?" Sophie asked with an encouraging nod at her friend.

"It would surely be impossible," Emily answered soberly and without hesitation. She bestowed her most convincing smile on father and daughter and then helped herself to a lemon tart from the tea tray.

Vicar Penrose nodded a bit sheepishly. "You're right, of course. My work is here," he told the fireplace, and then continued earnestly, "But when I think of all the important discoveries now and there still being so much to learn… Why only yesterday I received a most interesting letter from—"

"That sounds fascinating, Father," Sophie interjected quickly, "but we're more than willing to save the details for another afternoon. We quite understand that you need some time alone to finish this week's sermon."

Sophie nodded encouragingly to her father like a mother to her young child.

"Yes, you're right, my dear. I'd forgotten." Patting his pockets, he added, "I seem to have misplaced my spectacles again—it's as if they've a mind of their own. Now where can they have gotten to?" he said, frowning in puzzlement, "I had them not five minutes ago."

"They're on your head, father," Sophie informed him

seriously, smiling indulgently.

"Indeed. Bit of an oversight, eh?" the vicar said vaguely, reaching up to pull them down.

"How very witty, Father," Sophie said with a twinkle.

"Eh, what's that?"

"Your pun, of course," Sophie explained. "Using the word 'oversight' to mean something overlooked as well as where you found your glasses—over your 'sight'."

"Oh, er, yes. That *was* clever of me," the vicar said bemusedly. "Sometimes I surprise myself. Perhaps I'll use it in this week's sermon," he continued with growing enthusiasm. "What do you think, my dear?"

Sophie hid a small shudder. "Hmmm," was all she could manage.

"Well, I'd best get busy on that sermon. They don't write themselves, you know. You'll excuse me, my dears?" he asked of the vase of pink and yellow roses on the table. Without waiting for their dutiful assent, he set his teacup down and shuffled down the hall, mumbling to himself.

Emily was well used to the vicar's habit of addressing inanimate objects rather than people and never felt slighted. She suspected the tendency came from years of addressing a congregation without focusing on any one person in particular. The only other explanation she could think of was that his attention was rarely truly focused on anyone living in the modern world.

The study of ancient civilizations was the vicar's overwhelming passion. One on which he focused to the exclusion of most everything else, even occasionally his sermons.

Sophie's focus was, and had long been, her father, and Emily fervently hoped the note she'd uncovered meant her friend had finally decided to live her own life instead of vicariously living someone else's. She spared a moment to wonder just what level of vicariousness a vicar's life could possibly attain and then mentally applauded Sophie's good sense, no matter how delayed it happened to be.

She watched Sophie stare after her father as he quit the room and disappeared down the hall, and she wondered at the secrets lurking behind that calm, innocent visage. She truly hoped they were inspiring.

Swiveling her eyes away from Sophie, she instead focused her attention on the tea tray. Judging from the spotty arrangement, Sophie and her father had decided not to wait for her. Their impatience had gained her a lucky reprieve. Sophie had no idea she had seen the note, and as such, this may very well be the perfect opportunity for a bit of cautious questioning.

Carefully placing a pair of modest sized scones on her plate, she indulged in a comforting bite. Then arranging her features in a show of innocence, she addressed her friend.

"Delicious as always. I wouldn't want your recipe to ever fall into the wrong hands." She'd intended her words as a bit of delicate probing to see if Sophie reacted to the possibility of a threat.

"Whose hands would those be?" Sophie's only reaction appeared to be utter confusion.

"Uhhh…unsavory ones?" Emily suggested lamely, now wishing she had never said a word.

"Unsavory? Are you meaning unclean? Because my guess would be that yours are the closest the recipe would likely come to such a fate."

All right, perhaps she deserved that. Next time she'd think matters through a bit better before speaking right up. In fact, perhaps she should just postpone her inquiries. Clearly she was too preoccupied for subtlety or even for sensible thinking. She'd indulge in a soothing cup of tea, and temper the sour in her stomach with sweets. Then she'd appeal to Sophie's nurturing, compassionate nature to liberate her from a dreary future with Mr. Richly. She'd deal with the matter of the note later.

Sophie was hardly surprised when her friend fell silent after such a curious comment. She'd been surprised to have as much conversation as they'd had, no matter how bizarre. Emily was typically sufficiently distracted by the tea tray so to remain silent.

As teatime at Sinclair House was now presided over by her stepmother, Emily usually chose to remain absent from that favored afternoon respite. Unfortunately that meant that she did not often get to indulge her fondness for sweets, that is, unless she visited the kitchens or took tea at the vicarage, an occurrence of impressive regularity.

Emily was now licking her fingers in what appeared to be enraptured appreciation. The lemon tarts were a little too tart today, and the cakes a trifle dry, but it wasn't likely Emily would notice. A serving of stale bread sprinkled with sugar and a cup of tepid tea would likely garner her friend's effusive thanks. This, at least, was one situation in which her friend was entirely predictable. Sophie knew that if she waited patiently, Emily's thoughts would eventually come around and refocus themselves on whatever it was that had spurred her apparently eventful rush to the vicarage on such a dreary day.

Moments later, Emily sat back with a wide grin, folded her hands over her surprisingly slender stomach and closed her eyes in contentment. "I really must learn to tolerate Beatrice long enough to take tea at home," she said drowsily.

"It's true she can be a bit hard to take in large doses," Sophie agreed with a smile, "but she means well."

"I don't believe that phrase has ever been uttered by the person who is subjected to the behavior it describes," Emily offered for consideration. "*You* do not have the misfortune of being the object of her constant reform. It's maddening."

"True, but I do think she genuinely cares for you and wants you to be happy."

"Perhaps," Emily conceded with a frown.

"Now," Sophie prodded, "Here is your opportunity."

Emily could only stare blankly, not having the slightest clue what Sophie was talking about.

"To reveal the 'unbelievable', 'inconceivable' details of your day," Sophie reminded her, and then added, "Really, Emily, don't you know there are highwaymen about? You shouldn't be out riding alone until..."

She broke off as Emily bolted upright, her eyes flying open. "Heavens!" she gasped, "I'd quite forgotten."

"I believe the tea tray may have had something to do

with it," Sophie murmured.

Emily merely raised her brow and the end of her mouth in a well-practiced smirk.

"Anytime you're ready," Sophie said.

"Just so long as that moment coincides with your being ready?" Emily inquired. "If you'll recall, I was ready some fifteen minutes ago."

"Speaking of that, what took you so long abovestairs? From the look of you, you weren't all that fastidious with your appearance—although what little you did do is certainly a huge improvement."

Thinking quickly, Emily said, "Once I'd wrapped myself in your soft, warm blanket, I didn't want to come out. The cold water in the basin wasn't at all appealing."

"So…you wrapped your *filthy* self in my nice, clean blanket? You were supposed to wash first—I believe I made that very clear! Then what? Did you roll about on my newly washed linens and use my underthings to wipe away the mud?" Sophie inquired wryly.

"I don't think I'll answer that," Emily answered primly, tilting her chin up and pursing her lips.

"I can't tell you how that reassures me."

"Since you'll obviously not be put off, I'll tell you what has happened to me today," said Emily, changing the subject.

"You are *too* kind," Sophie murmured.

Ready to launch into what was sure to be an incomprehensible mish-mash of information, Emily paused a moment to determine how best to explain everything that had occurred. Chronological order would no doubt work best.

"I met the most infuriating man—" she blurted, tossing order out the window.

"Another one?" Sophie said dryly, clearly not at all impressed.

Emily smirked and continued without comment.

"He knocked me from my horse." Absently, Emily rubbed her bruised hip.

"Causing you to slip ignominiously into the mud?"

Sophie guessed.

"He neither offered to apologize nor to assist me,"

"You probably demanded the first and disallowed the second."

"He suggested I was at fault and further, incapable of handling Gypsy."

"You put him firmly in his place," Sophie assumed, nodding slowly and lifting her tea cup for a sip.

"No, but I will," Emily grinned, "I challenged him to a race."

Sophie spit the mouthful back into her cup.

"You *what*?!?"

Emily's eyes widened slightly at her friend's uncharacteristically poor manners, but she repeated herself.

"I challenged him to a race. On horseback," she added rather ridiculously. "You needn't worry—I shall win."

"That's not what worries me."

"Oh? What exactly has you looking at me as if I've lost my mind?"

"I fear you've lost your mind!"

"Sophie—"

"How could you be such a ninny? Have you no care for your reputation? No shame? No concern over the possibility that this 'infuriating' stranger just might be a highwayman? I would imagine such a quality would be enormously fitting in that line of work."

"Shall I answer your questions individually—other than the ninny question, which I refuse to dignify," Emily said, a trifle irritated. "No, apparently not, and no. One, my reputation is no longer a concern. Two, I hardly see what I have to be ashamed of, especially if I win. And three, I considered and discarded the possibility that he might actually be the highwayman. Happy now?"

"Guess," Sophie demanded, frowning disapprovingly as she snapped her cup down on the saucer, lowered the china, and kept silent.

"You're angry—"

"Good…" Sophie prompted as she might a dull-witted child.

"But I can't begin to guess why."

"No…you wouldn't. Dare I ask, is this all of it? Will there be any more shocking surprises, or did you somehow manage to spend the balance of the day with a modicum of dignity?"

"Really, Sophie!" Emily exclaimed, "How utterly rude."

"That, as I am certain you are aware, is not an answer. So there is something else? You might as well tell me." Quite suddenly, Sophie gasped and drew her head back, eyes wide. "I just realized… Perhaps you should tell me why your reputation is no longer a concern, because I am already assuming the worst."

Emily rolled her eyes and pursed her lips.

"It's not the worst, is it?" Sophie asked worriedly, quite obviously willing Emily to answer in the negative.

"That would depend on your point of view," Emily offered vaguely.

Sophie attempted a stern glare, but the concern in her eyes betrayed her intent.

"I've not been ravished, if that's what you're thinking, but eventually I will be." Emily tilted her head, pressed her lips together, and raised her eyebrows slightly, waiting for Sophie's reaction.

"What do you mean?" Sophie whispered, confused and horrified at once.

"My father has finally succumbed to Beatrice's blatant and incessant intimations that I should be married. I'm to be betrothed to her odious cousin, Mr. Desmond Richly, unless I can find a suitable alternative in one month's time."

Sophie blinked several times, swallowed suddenly, and nearly choked. The teacup she was holding threatened to topple onto the rug at their feet.

"I can see we finally agree on something. *This* is a matter for concern." Giving Sophie a look of mild reproof, Emily took a deep breath to elaborate. Sophie carefully put her tea cup down and resumed listening intently.

"I can't tell you how I've agonized over this predicament—"

"When did this happen?" Sophie demanded.

"After luncheon," Emily admitted.

"So…you've agonized for what? An hour?" Sophie prodded sarcastically.

"Two," Emily answered haughtily, not at all amused.

"Then by all means, please keep the details of that excruciating period to yourself."

Emily had found that it was better to ignore Sophie when she was behaving in such a manner, so instead of responding to her friend's barbs, she merely continued with her dismal news.

"I am being forced into an unwanted marriage—"

"That's not at all uncommon," Sophie reminded her.

"*Do you mind?!* This conversation would move along much more smoothly if you endeavored to show a little compassion."

"Pardon me." Sophie made certain the words dripped with sarcasm.

"Thank you. May I continue?"

"Please," Sophie encouraged, gesturing expansively with her arm.

"I'm to wed the most offensive gentleman to which I believe I have ever been introduced. The only way to escape that abhorrent eventuality is for me to somehow garner an alternate proposal before the engagement ball to be held in one month's time. Now I ask you, what is worse than that?"

Sophie opened her mouth to answer, but Emily quickly forestalled her, "Don't answer that. This is certainly bad enough."

Sophie nodded in concession.

"Any thoughts? I was really hoping to settle this matter this afternoon."

Faced with Sophie's expression of disbelief, she elaborated. "I need a plan. To ride home without one would be a triumph for Beatrice, and *that*, I'm afraid, I simply cannot allow."

"Em, you're being a ninny."

"Evidently, but given the day I've had, I believe I'm

entitled. So…?"

With great anticipation, Emily waited for Sophie to briskly present the solution that she herself had somehow managed to overlook. It was probably too much to hope that Sophie could think of a way to avoid engagement, wedding, and husband altogether, but that didn't stop her from leaning eagerly forward to hear what sage advice her friend would offer.

"So…I suppose I must offer my congratulations. Condolences would be unnecessarily pessimistic. You may well find that the two of you will manage together quite tolerably."

"Do you really think so?" Emily asked suspiciously, unable to school her features into anything other than a distasteful scrunch.

"Of course not!"

"Then why would you say so?"

"To be polite." Sophie toasted her with her teacup and took a dainty sip.

"Sophie, you are making no sense!"

"Consider then that my comments are based entirely on my expectation of your behavior, which in fact, often makes very little sense."

"That's outrageously vague."

"Very well," Sophie allowed, nodding once, "I can only assume you'll fritter the month away railing against your abhorrent situation and refuse to even consider any other gentlemen because such behavior would be admitting to yourself that you will in fact shortly be married."

"Haven't I just admitted it?" Emily asked, thoroughly exasperated.

"To me, yes. To yourself, I rather doubt it."

Before Emily could interrupt, she continued, "You were hoping to 'settle' this matter today so you wouldn't have to think about it any further, correct?"

A second passed in tense silence before Emily admitted in an embarrassed mumble, "The thought had occurred to me."

"Ignoring the inevitable won't change it, Em. But…"

Sophie continued, looking pointedly at her now petulant friend, "If you're willing to accept the reality you will face a month from now…" She trailed off, waiting for Emily's response.

"If that is a requirement, then very well."

"Then I'll certainly do my best to help you find an acceptable alternative from whom a proposal might prove forthcoming."

"Thank you, Sophie," Emily promptly answered, both gratitude and relief evident in her voice. Sophie smiled back encouragingly.

"I did wonder, just a little bit, whether Richly would be so utterly awful." With raised eyebrows, Emily let the unspoken question hang in the air between them.

"He would."

"Wait a moment, Sophie. Perhaps it wouldn't be so bad. If we agreed to stay away from each other: live apart, ignore one another, and consent not to meddle in each other's affairs, it might not be so bad. I wouldn't have to change so very much."

The last was said with such valiant sadness that Sophie rose from her chair and crossed to sit next to Emily on the sofa, taking her friend's hand in her own.

"Wouldn't you? You'd be consigning yourself to a travesty of marriage, tying yourself to a man who has only managed to inspire your intense dislike, and abandoning the possibility of ever achieving your hopes and dreams."

Emily looked up from their joined hands into Sophie's eyes.

"If you're considering that course, the only explanation is that you've already changed a great deal."

Smiling slightly at her friend, Emily said, "You're right, of course, I can't imagine what I was thinking of."

"Besides, you can't predict how any man will react once he's well and truly married. Perhaps any one of them would allow you to continue reasonably as you are."

"And perhaps this is all a very clever jest," Emily said grimly. "Let's cling to blind hope."

Ignoring her, Sophie suggested, "I think you should

view Richly as a wart. He'll only become more irritating and unsightly the longer he's allowed to linger."

"A better comparison there could not possibly be," Emily agreed appreciatively.

Emily took a deep expunging breath and, ever so slowly, felt the tension begin to slide away. Things would be all right now.

"So, are you ready to start?" Sophie asked.

"Yes." Emily could honestly admit she was.

"Good. Have you considered the obvious?" Sophie suggested pragmatically, wasting no time in dissecting the problem that had already plagued Emily for the aforementioned two hours. "Why don't you simply choose one of the suitors you've recently refused?"

Emily's only answer was to wrinkle her nose in distaste.

"Were each of them so utterly unacceptable?"

Emily didn't answer, instead holding her features unattractively in place with the intention that they convey her opinion. Sophie frowned sternly upon her.

"I think you need to approach this task by comparing each gentleman to Mr. Richly. After all, each suitor you reject, for whatever reason, brings you one step closer to a union with him."

Emily closed her eyes and hung her head, the picture of surrender. Finally she nodded her agreement.

"Why don't we try to come up with a list of possibilities and go from there."

"Fair enough," Emily grumbled.

"Excellent. I feel certain we'll find you a match in no time."

Sophie hurried over to the small writing desk in the corner and sat down. She pulled out a fresh sheet of parchment and dipped her quill in the ink pot.

"Let's see," she began crisply in her best lecturing voice. "What about Sir William Fitzhugh?"

Emily could see that her approval was not going to be required, as Sophie was already busily writing his name on the blank page.

Emily groaned.

"What do you find so obviously objectionable?" Sophie asked with a frown when she caught Emily rolling her eyes. "He's completely suitable." To prove her point, she quickly added a few notes next to Sir William's name, speaking them aloud for Emily's benefit: "Widower, small fortune, avid huntsman."

Emily parried, "Old, tight-fisted, single-minded, boring. It's been said he treats his hounds with more affection than he did his late wife."

"Oh, really, Emily. I'm sure that was just a spiteful rumor. I know for a fact that he's taken an interest in you, and he *is* looking to remarry. He has yet to produce an heir and—"

Not caring to hear any more, Emily closed her eyes and raised her hand, hoping her friend would show mercy.

"Sophie, I don't know about you, but I could never suffer the pressure of that man's smacking wet lips against my own, to say nothing of the other, er…more delicate, aspects of marriage. More than once he's trapped me into a private conversation while devouring the remains of some carcass or other. Probably something his precious hounds dragged in. The way his tongue flicks out to catch any escaping pieces is more than I can stand."

"Are you quite through?"

"Each time," Emily continued wonderingly, eyes staring sightless into the distance, "I was held mesmerized until he'd finished—I was just somehow unable to look away. But I am sure my interest was simply that of one faced with the grotesque and unusual."

An exasperated smile slipped out before Sophie could prevent it.

"Well, I'm going to leave him on the list anyway. He may look considerably better a fortnight from now when your time is running out and marriage to Mr. Richly is your only option. If it'll appease you I'll add a note next to his name: 'hearty appetite'."

"How about 'ravenous boar'," Emily quipped with a grin, "He'd probably be pleased with such a comparison."

Sophie ignored her. "Let's see now. Even you can't

have anything contrary to say about Lord Percival Rushton. It's said he's avidly searching for a young wife to provide him with an heir. And his reputation is impeccable."

Emily considered for a moment. "Cold," she finally concluded. "Looking for nothing more than a well-mannered breeder. In fact, I'd venture to say that every name you can come up with is only looking to marry in order to produce the requisite heir, giving no thought to the possibility of a union based on love, mutual respect, or friendship. If I must be trapped into marriage, I would have at least one of those three. Therein, my dear Sophie, lies the problem."

Not wanting to argue, and not even sure she could deny Emily's claim, Sophie continued, "All right, how about Lord Simon Heath? I understand he was quite a favorite last season."

"Rake." And then in disbelief, "Really, Sophie, even you must see that."

Rapidly losing patience, Sophie tried again, but through clenched teeth, "Viscount Aberly?   He has quite a commanding presence."

"He's also an arrogant, insufferable clod. I dislike men of his sort in general but him in particular. It's as if he feels that his title and fortune are enough to have any young lady swooning in his presence.   He doesn't even deign to introduce himself, assuming his reputation precedes him. Really, his pomposity knows no bounds."

She paused to gulp down some tea.

"I would venture to guess that everything he sees is overlaid with a view of his own nose, so busy is he looking down upon all of us."

"Emily," Sophie said with an exasperated huff, "I fail to see how you plan to avoid marriage to Mr. Richly if you're going to reject everyone out of hand. Just whom do you plan to persuade into a hasty engagement?   You've summarily rejected most of the eligible gentlemen in the area. And you're limited to their number, I am afraid, since you refused the seasons your father offered the past few years.   We don't have the luxury of an extensive list of eligible names from which to choose that we might have had were you introduced during a season. Not to mention that we are not, at present, anywhere near London—there are only so many gentlemen within your reach here."

"Well, that can't be helped. There simply *must* be someone else," Emily declared with unflagging determination.

She rose and began pacing but was only able to take a few steps in any given direction due to the surprising amount of furniture Sophie had managed to stuff into the cozy little room. After narrowly avoiding a collision with the reading lamp perched on the tiny table beside the sofa, she turned to Sophie with a blank stare and a flicker of fear.

Was it possible that even her friend's capable mind wouldn't be able to help her emerge unscathed from this ordeal?

Since reaching the vicarage, she'd felt wholly relieved and at ease. But uncertainty had finally intruded, and her optimism was faltering. Was it ridiculously naïve to believe there was someone worthy of this search? Someone within her reach who was searching also. Someone who would consider themselves fortunate to have found her.

She truly hoped not.

"Are you sure there is no one else you can think of?" she entreated.

Sophie sighed. "Let me think. Were there any other possibilities at the dance held by Sir William last week? You certainly had your share of admirers."

"No, none that would suit," Emily said with a frown.

Sophie sighed and looked thoughtfully up at her friend. Telling herself that Emily would eventually find out anyway, she decided she might as well be the one to impart the news. Hopefully it would be met with no more than passing interest.

"Well," she faltered, "perhaps you will meet someone dashing at the...ah...Willoughsby ball."

Emily forgot her own dilemma for a moment and peered at Sophie more closely. All evidence of Sophie's exasperation had disappeared, and in its place was...

awkwardness? Was it possible after all that Sophie did indeed have a gentleman friend who would likely be in attendance?

"Perhaps," agreed Emily cautiously, watching her friend for any sign of a clue. "But more than likely this ball will be the same as all others of recent memory in which Beatrice quickly drinks too much ratafia and then confides to anyone who will listen of Father's political influence and shrewd investment decisions."

Reaching across to the tea tray, Emily snatched up a tiny morsel of scone and popped it into her mouth.

"As you know, I use the term 'confides' quite loosely, as she is almost always hoarse the day after from trying to whisper with all available throat and lung capacity." Sophie didn't even bother to return a knowing smile. Shaking her head in bafflement over both her stepmother and her best friend, Emily casually inquired, "Just out of curiosity, why are the Willoughsbys holding a ball? Aren't they still mourning the death of Lord Willoughsby?"

"I'm surprised you haven't heard, " Sophie said primly, pleating her skirts between precise fingers, "The ball will celebrate Colin's return from the Continent. He's inherited the title, of course, and will soon be taking up residence, so I expect the ball has been planned as a means for him to become reacquainted with the local gentry."

"Colin?! Colin's finally come home?" Emily exclaimed with pleasure, clapping her hands together. "What fun! I wonder that I haven't heard of it before now… Oh I do so hate being ill—it's as if the world passes you by. Well no matter. It'll certainly be a treat to see him again." She smiled to herself, clearly delighted with the news.

Gifted with the reaction she was hoping for, Sophie breathed a little sigh of relief and waited for Emily to plunge once again into further discussion of her latest, and thus far most serious, predicament. Busily tidying her already immaculate escritoire, she kept her head averted and so missed seeing Emily staring at her quizzically. Coincidentally, she looked up just as Emily was struck by the full import of Colin's timely return, her puzzlement over

Sophie's strange behavior abruptly forgotten.

Realizing her optimism had been premature, Sophie faced Emily and waited for the inevitable. She watched helplessly as comprehension slowly dawned on Emily's face and hoped she could keep despair from descending upon her own. When Emily finally did speak, it was with complete confidence and relief.

"I would like to respectfully request that you promptly and noisily dispose of that abysmal list! Our work is done. Colin is the one! I didn't know what I was looking for, but now I do, and he's precisely right. Well, he *was* anyway, and I daresay he hasn't changed all that much. What's more, I'd wager I've a good chance to lure a proposal out of him."

Halting her giddy monologue, she glanced over at Sophie who had remained silent.

"Don't you agree that he's ideal prey for this husband hunt?" She giggled and wasn't certain whether it was at the silliness of her words or simply blissful relief. "The only prey worth catching, as far as I can tell."

In full swing now and oblivious to Sophie's reluctance to agree, she twirled, swishing her skirts around her, before finally collapsing on the sofa. As Emily sighed contentedly, Sophie turned quietly away to face the wall behind her desk.

A moment later, Emily's enthusiasm was back in full force.

"Just when I was beginning to despair, you once again came to the rescue," Emily praised, rushing forward to lean a hug over Sophie's back and plant a grateful kiss on her cheek.

"You are, and always will be, the best of friends!"

She was so caught up in her own good fortune that she didn't notice Sophie's stiff posture, and she was utterly unaware of the bleak look that paled her friend's usually warm countenance.

"Well, I won't keep you any longer," Emily continued brightly. "The weather has let up, and I need to make sure I'm home in time to restore my appearance before a chance encounter with Beatrice or my father. Although, right now,

I feel so relieved that I think I could even tolerate a combined lecture on the perils of riding alone, the carelessness of forgetting to wear a riding hat, and the indecency of issuing bold challenges to strange men."

"If it's all right with you," she continued, "I'll leave my gown to dry and wear yours home. I promise not to muddy it. Please say goodbye to your father for me. Tell him I'll be happy to listen to a lecture on his latest acquisitions another time." She fled the room calling "Thank you again, Sophie."

Sophie sighed heavily and laid her head on the desk. "What are best friends for?" she whispered.

She was still at her writing table when the maid came in nearly an hour later to light the evening's lamps and start a fire in the grate.

* * *

Emily decided that her leisurely return to Sinclair House could not have possibly been more different than her erratic ride in the opposite direction just hours earlier. And, as such, she thought, it couldn't have been more pleasant. Her dialogue with the stranger could not be lumped in with a frantic, impulsive journey to regain presence of mind. It was in a class by itself, and she was looking forward to dissecting and examining it separately. But for now, she, like the weather, had resumed a semblance of calm.

The wind had quickly blown the foul weather off to the north, leaving the countryside washed clean and sparkling in the last rays of sunlight before dusk. The air was crisp and fresh, and she was comfortable, if not entirely presentable, in her borrowed gown with her hair brushed free of snarls and stray leaves.

Most importantly, she felt relieved.

Faced with her father's unexpected ultimatum, she had been nervously cognizant of her own responsibility in securing her future happiness but uncertain just how to go about it. She'd felt helpless and a little afraid of what lay ahead. Now she could at least claim a modicum of control over the situation. It was to be expected that the nervousness hadn't disappeared, but it had most definitely changed. Tense anticipation had replaced nervous desperation and was vastly preferable to her way of thinking.

Sophie was truly a godsend—without her Emily would undoubtedly be swirling deeper into a void of confusion and uncertainty. She was grateful to instead feel relatively calm and content. What an immense relief to still have someone on whom she could depend.

She didn't want to think about how disappointed she was with her father or how furious over her stepmother's intrusion. She preferred instead to content herself with the knowledge that she had found a way to avoid the travesty of a marriage to Mr. Desmond Richly.

With luck Colin would still be the same man she had known so many years ago, and as such, demand no unwelcome sacrifices of her.

This was, of course, assuming he was willing to marry her.

She was optimistic that her chances were good. After all, as a young girl she had idolized Colin, and he had adored her.

She wasn't silly enough to pretend there might be a chance he still did but, rather, hopeful that he would appreciate her as she was now.

For she had most definitely changed—she'd been a young girl, and now she was a woman. No longer was she interested in a hero; she simply wanted someone who would respect her decisions and opinions. Mutual affection was almost a certainty given the past they had shared. Something more than that would be a glorious surprise, but she could manage to content herself without it.

Fate, and Sophie of course, could very well take credit for bringing them together, but with luck, Colin would still find a reason to adore her, perhaps an even better one than before.

As her horse slowly found its way home, Emily recalled their childhood adventures and realized how different her

life would have been if Colin had remained at home in the
years following her mother's death. If her father had not
been so mired in grief when Colin had left for the Continent,
he probably would have made arrangements for a future
betrothal.

So many years had passed in his absence. By now, they
would surely have been married with at least one babe in the
nursery. Well, she concluded, things had merely been
delayed a few years, that was all. She and Colin would
simply pick up where they had left off.

The proud gates of Sinclair House loomed in the
distance, heralding the unwelcome reminder that she was
riding alone at twilight against her father's wishes, in a
gown not her own. She was going to have to find a way to
sneak up to her room unobserved or risk one of her
stepmother's long-winded lectures, towards which she was
no longer feeling so indulgent.

Worse yet would be to fall victim to her father's stern
but silent disapproval. It saddened her to realize that after
today she no longer felt certain that the affectionate
relationship they had once shared could ever be repaired.

As she emptied her mind of that disturbing possibility,
another took its place.

She'd remembered.

A crumbling headstone etched with a warning from
beyond the grave.

> *Choices are no longer mine;*
> *they're now all left to you.*
> *I pray you'll make the right ones*
> *before your time is through.*

It couldn't be! She and Sophie had giggled over that
inscription many times, but this time it was no laughing
matter. As a note from a suitor, it was depressingly morbid.
Unless…it was a warning and from someone else entirely.
Could her first suspicion have indeed been correct? Was
Sophie being blackmailed? Had her belief that she'd soon
share the soil with Sir Humphrey Wellingsworth, author of

the disturbingly all-purpose sentiment, inspired her unwilling participation?

But what of the date?

Suddenly, she knew. It was so simple now that she had figured it out. The note alluded to a meeting and specified time and place. 'Specified' was perhaps a bit optimistic when referred to the time—it could easily signify any time within a twenty-four hour period. But the place was now obvious. Sophie planned to meet someone in the graveyard sometime today, most probably tonight, for really, what nefarious deeds were likely to be conducted bold as brass in full view of the vicarage windows?

Windows that would be shut tight with curtains at nightfall, concealing the shadows that weren't likely to be innocent.

Was it possible that Sophie could have agreed to meet a respectable person in such a place at such a time, or was it more likely that her liaison was with someone who had given her no choice in the matter? She truly hoped Sophie was simply up to mischief—not to mention previously unplumbed depths of daring—and not in any kind of danger. Yet she worried that that was not at all the case.

It seemed the matter was far more worthy of her attention than avoiding a harmless, albeit irritating, lecture. So as she slowed her horse to a walk, she began to consider what should be done.

After a moment she decided there was simply nothing for it. After dinner she'd plead a headache, ride out a second time, and hope she wasn't too late.

Having just recently come into possession of a pair of coarse brown breeches, a simple white shirt, and a concealing woolen vest and cap, she gleefully decided this occasion most definitely warranted their maiden use, so to speak.

All of it had been hidden beneath her woolens in the bottom drawer of her wardrobe, and she had been restlessly awaiting the perfect opportunity. Thanks to Sophie, tonight was to be the night.

Emily was never one to bother much with details,

preferring instead to improvise as the situation demanded.
Consequently, the extent of her preparation and planning for
the night ahead had begun and ended with her decisions to
plead a headache and disguise herself as a young man.

The rest, she assumed, would work itself out.

Almost home, Emily smiled to herself and considered
how crowded her life had suddenly become. Her father's
ultimatum had demanded a personal quest, and she was now
optimistic that matters would resolve themselves quite
satisfactorily. A smugly handsome stranger had turned an
unexpected encounter into a thrilling adventure with still
more to come. And now this. Sophie's predicament was
fraught with peril (very probably from Sophie herself once it
became obvious that Emily had been eavesdropping) and
just as close to her heart as her own life-altering dilemma.

She believed herself equal to all three tasks. The first
she'd deal with out of necessity, the second, out of sheer
delight, and the third, out of friendship. Ironically it was the
second one, the singularly trivial one, that seemed to loom
with importance in her mind.

4

"...I have decided to forgive Penelope Hartford her oversight in neglecting to invite us to her supper party. Lord and Lady Chesterwood were attacked by highwaymen as they returned home for the evening—on the very road we would have been traveling! The effect this will have on dear Penelope's reputation remains to be seen..."

LETTER FROM LADY BEATRICE SINCLAIR TO MR. DESMOND RICHLY
22 OCTOBER 1818

Sophie wasn't quite sure how it had happened, but then she never was. Once again she'd allowed herself to be trampled by Emily's whirlwind. She felt like a shadow whenever her friend was around—always behaving as expected, content to simply go along. None of it was Emily's fault; if anything, she owed her friend a debt of gratitude for virtually every shimmering moment of excitement that had occurred over the course of their friendship. Things just always seemed to *happen* to Emily—why couldn't they, just once, happen to her instead?

A little voice inside her answered that question promptly with a well-rehearsed answer: I am a vicar's daughter, and I have a duty to behave accordingly and uphold a certain level of dignity and decorum. She was content, she reminded herself, with her life as it was. She would keep house for her father as long as she was needed.

Her dreams of marriage and a family of her own were certainly within her grasp. After all, her looks were passable, perhaps even favored by some, and she certainly understood the management of a household. She was even resigned to the intimacies of the marriage bed, knowing they would, with luck, conceive the babies she so much desired. There was but one impediment to the delightful dream. Love. She refused to marry without it. Her practical nature had warned that imposing such a condition put marriage all but out of reach, but she had been unable to shake her heart's determination. The dream had remained intact despite all arguments. Until today.

Today her best friend had unknowingly dispersed those nebulous dreams with one rash decision. She had decided to marry Colin Willoughsby. Admittedly, Emily had yet to receive a proposal, but even Sophie could see that such a detail was insignificant. Emily and Colin were ideally suited, at least in the ways society believed mattered most. Emily was the daughter of a peer and had been groomed for marriage to a wealthy, titled gentleman. Perhaps the grooming should have been performed with a firmer hand, but the task had been completed nonetheless. Sure to be agreeable to the idea, Colin would propose, and announcements would be printed and sent, as far away as London. Most definitely to London if Lady Sinclair had any say in the matter. The banns would be posted, and the wedding would take place without either bride or groom ever knowing that Sophie Penrose harbored a heavy heart.

She had known the pair of them since childhood, and while Colin had been years older than they, he had spent countless afternoons in their company. Emily had just set out on her path to becoming an incorrigible hoyden, and Colin had readily encouraged her. Emily had always been delighted to participate in any scheme he cared to dream up. Contrarily, she herself had behaved demurely, the perfect young lady. Her decorum had done her little good—it had certainly not escaped her notice that her presence in the threesome was utterly unnecessary.

To her credit, Emily had tried endlessly to encourage her participation in their many reckless and, more often than not, ridiculous antics, and Colin had always been ready with a smile or a few kind words no matter what she had decided.

Which had of course been, "You two go along without me."

Before long, it had been painfully obvious that Emily had stolen not only Colin's attention, but his heart as well. Not romantically, more as a younger sister really, but it hadn't mattered. Her own young heart had been jealous and, after a time, quite distressed to realize she had fallen in love with a man she would never have and yet wanted so painfully much.

Colin had been the perfect gentleman: kind, compassionate, and courageous. Add to that his golden curls and bright blue eyes, and he had been quite simply perfect. Then he had gone—left for the Continent, and there had been no one since to take his place in her heart or thoughts. She had remained foolishly hopeful—for his return, for their reunion, and for a happily ever after.

She'd had plenty of time to daydream over him, before and since. Having spent many an afternoon watching he and Emily together, she'd often wished she could have been a different person. Someone who wasn't constrained by personal circumstance. Someone who could laugh at life instead of just moving sensibly through it. Someone who didn't insist on a tidy appearance, didn't care a fig for her reputation, and didn't feel compelled to lecture. Someone who demanded more than the life of a perfect young lady.

Well, she had never been that someone, and what had it gained her? The man she had dreamed about for longer than she could remember was going to marry her best friend. And neither of them knew—would ever know—just how much she would hurt.

Perhaps she needed to make a change before it really was too late. Before she grew to be a dried up old spinster, regretting her dull and lonely marriage to respectability. Instead of waiting for something to happen *to* her, why couldn't she make things happen for herself?

She could start by going along with a few of Emily's tamer suggestions. Heaven help her if she did.

No—dash it all! She would very well help herself. Starting tonight.

When the tingling glow started inside of her, it was

foreign and unexpected. But as she felt something start to unfurl, she knew. Having waited in dark dormancy for so long, the bit of daring that was tucked inside of her was finally ready to bloom—she could feel it already in the smile that played at her lips. And at long last, she was ready to let it.

Within reason of course, she amended, nodding primly.

As soon as the lamps were snuffed and her father had retired for the evening, innocently assuming his daughter had also, she was going to sneak into the cemetery and have an adventure of her own. Even without Emily to push and prod her along. It could be dangerous…it was likely to be exciting…and what was foremost on her mind? What to wear and how to keep it from getting dirty.

Perhaps she really was hopeless.

* * *

Not for the first time in her life, Sophie wished that she'd been born a man. It certainly would have made things easier. For example, here she was traipsing around the cemetery in the middle of the night wearing nothing but a flimsy white cotton nightrail, her warmest cloak, and a serviceable pair of old boots. It would have been much simpler to pull on a pair of breeches and top boots, sparing no consideration for the ill-effects they might suffer as a result of the afternoon's thunderstorm. As it was, she was having quite a bit of difficulty keeping her skirts from the sludge while avoiding the worst of the puddles. So far she'd managed to confine most of it to her boots, but she worried that the morning would reveal a heavy layer of caked mud that would commemorate this folly for days to come.

As she hitched her cloak a few inches higher, it immediately triggered thoughts of impropriety, and her fingers sagged a little as she glanced unnecessarily around. Resolute in her newfound courage, she pulled her fingers back up and added another inch for good measure. Now anyone who cared to look could see how daring and determined she was. Except that she didn't want anyone to see her. She didn't want anyone at all to know she was here when in fact here she was, her stretch of exposed leg no doubt glowing in the moonlight. Best to cover it as much as possible and save the bold display for a more worthy cause.

She supposed it was her imagination that the path seemed a trifle dimmer when her skirts were finally lowered, but the warmth and relief were most definitely real. Now with only the light of the moon to guide her, she stumbled over a crumbling gravestone and only just caught herself from falling.

"Sorry, Mrs. Pettiford," she whispered apologetically to the small stone monument, giving it a little pat.

Righting herself quickly, she hurried towards the church. It was nigh on midnight, and she'd be lucky if she wasn't already too late. The clock would soon tick through the last minutes of the day, and the date specified on the note would be left behind. Part of her wished she could let it slide uneventfully by, but the other part was determined that she'd be on time and find that for which she'd come.

After a quick inspection of the grounds, she decided that the thick hedgerow bordering the churchyard would do nicely. Shadows there were deep and dark, and should provide adequate camouflage. At least she hoped they would.

Reaching the shelter of the hedge, she crouched down, grimacing at the mud stains on her good cloak. She poked her head through the bushes and settled down to wait, and wonder at her own foolishness. She couldn't think how she'd persuaded herself into thinking that this was the best course of action. It certainly wasn't something a sane and rational person would do. It was more like something Emily would do. With a sigh she realized that was exactly what she thought she wanted. But was it? Why did she feel so confounded?

"Well, it appears I'm either early or late and with no way to tell which."

The unexpected muttering so close beside her startled Sophie so much it was a wonder she managed to avoid shrieking. Jerking her head out of the bushes and scraping her neck in the process, she looked to either side, expecting to see the origin of the voice. She didn't. Yet before she had time to ponder that, the voice spoke again.

"I doubt I'll see much of anything from here," came the grumbled assessment.

Suddenly Sophie knew exactly to whom that voice belonged, and she couldn't believe her ears. It couldn't be—truly it couldn't. Here she stood, well squatted really, on the brink of newfound daring, and who should be quite obviously hidden right around the corner of the hedge but Emily? Her best friend whose audaciousness knew virtually no bounds. She couldn't think of a more discouraging development. Nor a more suspicious one.

She slowly and silently extricated herself from her own hiding place and tiptoed down and around the hedge to confront the intruder.

What she saw had her biting back an exclamation of disbelief. A wiggling bottom clearly outlined in breeches was on display for anyone who might happen by. Someone, Sophie concluded, needed to talk some sense into the other end of this ninny before they were both discovered and their reputations ruined. Apparently the task fell to her—what a surprise. There was no question it was indecent for a young lady to be lurking in the cemetery in her nightrail, but it was scandalous for one to be sneaking about clad in snug breeches.

She debated giving the exposed backside a sound whack with one of the twigs lying close by but reluctantly changed her mind. It would probably result in a loud yelp, and she didn't dare risk it. She leaned in, getting as close as possible. Emily didn't scare easily.

"Delightful to see you as usual, Em." she whispered.

Emily lurched backwards, flung her arms out to find purchase, found nothing as Sophie shirked away, and sat down heavily in the only puddle in sight.

"Arghhh!" she groaned, gingerly easing herself out of the puddle. She shook her head in disgust. "Unbelievable! Two mud puddles in one day!"

"Do be quiet!" Sophie whispered furiously. "What if

someone were to hear you?"

Emily narrowed her eyes and then calmly hissed out a rational response, "I daresay that's something you should have considered before you snuck up on me."

Sophie had to admit that Emily had a point, but she wasn't about to concede it.

"Perhaps I was so startled by the sight of your bobbing bottom that I momentarily forgot myself," she caustically challenged.

Sparing a tentative glance at her friend, Emily supposed now was not a good time to ask her friend's opinion of her disguise. Sophie's irritation was readily apparent in the pinch between her brows and her tightly crossed arms.

"Would you care to explain what exactly you are doing dressed in that ridiculous costume," Sophie inquired dryly. "Surely you do not believe yourself disguised?" She stared pointedly, eyebrows now raised.

"Of course I'm disguised! I doubt even you would have recognized me if my voice hadn't given me away."

Sophie stared at her silently, her expression unreadable, before replying, "Most young men cannot claim such a bountiful bosom, Em. Not to mention the fact that your hair is falling down well past your shoulders."

Emily glanced down at her chest and then reached her hands up to stuff strands of hair back beneath the cap.

"Well, if you hadn't startled me right into the only puddle in the vicinity, I'd likely look a fair sight more authentic. With more practice, I'll just make sure everything is bound more tightly." She offered her friend a conciliatory smile, but it was ignored as Sophie turned away.

Sophie did her best to stalk back to her own hiding place. Admittedly it was difficult while bent enough at the waist and knees to keep her head sufficiently below the level of the hedge. She thought it best to refrain from any further discussion.

Emily wasn't about to be hampered by that decision.

"Come now, Sophie. Everything improves with practice. You simply didn't give me much time."

Emily blanched at her careless admission to snooping and quickly decided it best to continue talking in an attempt to distract Sophie's attention.

"Even though *you* cleverly saw through my disguise—"

Faced with Sophie's withering gaze, Emily hurried on, "There is no reason to think a stranger would be so observant. After all, I've donned all the necessary garments right down to the foul-smelling cap. If I keep my shoulders slumped and my head down, my odor alone should vouch for my disguise. Take a whiff of me, you'll see."

"Shhhhhh!"

Emily ignored her friend's demand for silence but kept her tone to a hush as she changed subjects, realizing it was fruitless to pretend there was any other explanation for her presence. What other reason could she possibly have for being in the cemetery tonight except the real one?

"May I ask what exactly *you* are doing hiding in the bushes? I'd venture a guess that whatever rendezvous you had in mind is doomed to failure with you lurking back here with me."

"Will you keep your voice down?" Sophie hissed. Then as an afterthought: "What rendezvous? What exactly do you think you are doing here, Emily?"

The snap of a twig effectively silenced any further conversation. Sophie grabbed Emily's wrist and yanked her down behind the hedge. They waited in tense silence for several moments before they heard the slap and suck of boots stomping around the headstones.

"Sum'un' 'ere?" came a high-pitched nervous voice off to their left.

Sophie couldn't see to whom the disembodied voice belonged and didn't dare move to get a better look. Emily couldn't see a thing but the back of Sophie's head. She considered rising slowly to peer over the top of the hedge, but Sophie had a vise-like grip on her wrist. She doubted she'd be able to wrench it free without quite a bit of noisy, not to mention painful, effort.

"You're late." The deep, cultured voice belonged to someone clearly used to giving orders and just as used to having them followed—a gentleman. The harshness underlying the simple words spoke volumes of the implications if ever they were not.

When did he arrive? Sophie wondered. Hopefully it hadn't been in time to overhear her exchange with Emily. She risked a peek but in vain. A dark shadow in the general shape of a man was visible in the shade of the hemlock tree near the garden, but the only thing she could clearly make out was the gleam from his highly polished top boots. Emily had been right, she thought disgustedly. This was the wrong hiding place from which to see anything. Still, any closer could have been dangerous. At least they could hear. Really, that should be enough.

"I can only assume that your tardiness implies success," the steely voice continued.

The late arrival had shifted into Sophie's line of vision. He was small and wiry with dark hair and close-set, beady eyes. She thought he looked remarkably like a large shabbily dressed rat. He appeared to be shuffling his feet, no doubt getting them very muddy indeed, and crushing the brim of his pathetic felt hat. Even at this distance, and with only the few words spoken, it was obvious he was terrified of the man in the shadows.

"Beggin' yer pardon, milord," he said with a tremor, "but there were a mite o' trouble."

"What's he talking about?" This from Emily who was doing her best to remain patient.

Sophie waved her into silence.

"I fail to see how there could have been a problem, Sneeves," the voice in the shadows said icily. "I gave you specific directions as to time and place. All that was required of you was to fire your gun into the air and relieve the passengers of their valuables. A simpleton could have done it. If that were not the case, you would not be in my employ."

Sophie and Emily gasped in unison.

"Highwaymen!" Emily hissed excitedly in her ear. "Sophie, we have to do something! Can you see them? Do you recognize them? Let's try to get closer."

Sophie whipped around with her finger to her lips and a stern look in her eyes. The last thing they needed was to be discovered by these villains. Thankfully, Emily quieted without any further encouragement and leaned closer to hear the rest of the conversation.

"Well, 'twas like this, milord," squeaked the man called Sneeves sheepishly. "The carriage passed by at the spot just as you'd said, but I weren't told to expect no other rider."

Sophie could only assume the second man's patience was worn as thin as her own when she heard the brittle anger in his voice.

"*What other rider?* You're not making sense, man."

"T'were a gentleman, milord. Thot for a moment as how 'e may 'av been after the blunt 'imself. But 'e was followin' the carriage a mite too close if you get my meanin'. An' when 'e called to the groom I knew fer sure that they was travelin' together. So I held back and let 'em pass. I could tell that 'e'd've put up a fight, that 'un."

"You incompetent fool!" the man in the shadows hissed furiously, slashing an arm through the air to punctuate his anger. His hand held a riding crop, and it whistled in warning, causing the henchman to take a fearful step back. "You were armed, were you not? You should have dealt with him."

"Aye, milord," Sneeves whimpered.

"I will not tolerate incompetence. Is that clear? You will either do your job, or I will find someone who is not quite so squeamish. And bear in mind that his first task will be to dispose of you, for you must realize that I cannot afford to leave any loose ends."

"Aye, milord," Sneeves assured him quickly. "Won't 'appen again, milord."

"On that we can agree. I will grant you one final chance to redeem yourself, but if you fail me again…"

The menacing silence was far worse than any consequences spoken aloud. Sneeves clenched his tightly wound hat, mangling it even further. Sophie supposed it would never be recognizable as anything resembling a hat again.

Apparently satisfied that his inept companion was sufficiently frightened, the man in the shadows continued tersely.

"There will be a carriage traveling the London road in two days time. It will carry a lady and gentleman and the lady's maid. None of them will give you any trouble...at least they had better not. Collect the usual from their persons, but be sure to relieve the maid of the jewelry case she will no doubt be carrying—it will most certainly contain a fortune in gems. We will meet here again at midnight. I've found a certain satisfaction in using this rundown old cemetery as a meeting point for our evenings' work. So close to the vicarage that no one, least of all that bumbling vicar or his prudish daughter, would ever suspect."

As the villain chuckled, Sophie nearly bolted upright in outrage at the boastful confession. Emily found her friend's wrist just in time to prevent her head from lurching above the hedge and assuredly revealing their presence. Abruptly, the man's humor faded, and he continued with his instructions.

"This little adventure will be our last...at least for a time. I find these midnight rendezvous damned inconvenient and melodramatic. And as you've no doubt concluded on your own, I've a strong desire to be rid of you. I leave it to you to determine whether or not the arrangement will be permanent. Fair enough?"

Sneeves recognized the last as the ominous dismissal it was and tossed off a nervous reply, "Yes, milord. Er...no, milord. Er..."

"Fool! Get out of my sight!"

The flickering of the whip through the air had Sneeves jumping back in fear. Likely the sting hadn't landed, or they'd have heard his pained yelp, but suddenly he was moving, quick as a shadow, stumbling over the gravestones in his need to escape. Sophie watched his ghostly figure disappear into the swirling mist and then looked quickly back to the hemlock.

The man was gone from the shadows.

With a feeling of uneasiness, she hurriedly scanned the

graveyard—no one. She couldn't think where he could have disappeared to so quickly, and she couldn't have been more irritated with herself. She should have had more sense than to focus her attention on the man called Sneeves. He, at least, was predictable. The other was an unknown, and as such, considerably more dangerous. And here they were, crouched in a darkened cemetery, alone, with him lurking about somewhere. He could be anywhere.

It was probably a good idea to remain hidden for a few more minutes just in case. She didn't even want to imagine the consequences if they were discovered.

She turned to whisper her plan to Emily but found herself once again looking at her friend's rear end. Emily was standing now, leaning into the hedge, no doubt squinting for any further signs of the two men. Sophie closed her eyes, prayed for patience, tolerance, tact, and anything else that would help her though the unavoidable discussion that would shortly be upon her.

"Maybe now you'll consider finding another, less dangerous spot for your midnight meetings," Emily chided. "Clearly, there's already a nasty bit of business being conducted here."

It had begun. And already Sophie was lost and wanting to escape.

Faced with Sophie's blank look Emily continued. "Where is the man you were to meet?"

"What man?"

"The man whose identity you're keeping secret..." Emily gasped and clapped a hand over her mouth, "Sophie! He isn't the gentleman we just overheard is he? That man's a highwayman, for heaven's sake, not to mention thoroughly ill-mannered. You can't possibly get yourself involved with a criminal and expect me to stand by and do nothing."

"I'm *not* involved with him. What *are* you talking about?"

"Well, when he referred to you as 'prudish', I was given to think for a moment," Emily lectured in the face of Sophie's unamused, very nearly belligerent, stare. "It wasn't said in a flattering way, although I personally see nothing at all wrong with such a quality. While not a likely comment for a suitor, it seems rather appropriate coming from a churlish scoundrel who has not been given full cooperation. And, of course, there is the fact that you never stepped out of the bushes. So...in conclusion...I've decided that you do not at all fancy that shadowy gentleman, and neither are you involved in any villainous pastimes. As such," she finished on a puff of breath, "I haven't the slightest clue as to what you are doing out here."

"Brilliant, Emily. Absolutely brilliant," Sophie drawled giving her companion a hard stare.

"Really, Sophie. You cannot possibly hope to remain secretive about this now," Emily said dryly. "If I had to guess, I'd say you were out here wearing nothing but your nightrail beneath that cloak." She paused and stared pointedly at her friend. The moonlight lent a pearly glow to the pink stain that had risen to Sophie's cheeks.

"As I suspected. As such I can only assume that you were to meet a gentleman with whom you have become somewhat...er...amorous. If that is true, then surely your nightrail is inappropriate—considerably more so than my breeches, wouldn't you say? At least I needn't worry over chilly air swirling up around my bare legs." Giving Sophie a self-satisfied smile, she added, "Rather silly to be skittish about the matter now, wouldn't you agree?"

Sophie's wide-eyed astonishment spurred Emily to reach for her friend's hand and continue in a gentler tone. "Come now, Sophie, we're best friends. Tell me—you can trust me."

Sophie snatched her hand away in annoyance.

"Emily, where in the world did you get the idea that I might be lurking about for a lover's tryst, or worse, bandying words with churlish scoundrels? Does it occur to you that such behavior is a trifle out of character? Is that why you're here? Were you hoping merely to eavesdrop, or did you plan to play the heroine? Or perhaps you were concerned for my reputation and resolved to prevent anything more familiar than a chaste kiss? Why in heaven would you have imagined I would have welcomed your interfering presence?"

Faced with Sophie's angry words, Emily was suddenly uncomfortable, "Well—" Put like that the whole thing sounded ridiculous.

"Ahh. I am coming to understand why it took you so long to dress this afternoon. You shamelessly riffled through my things, read a bit of private correspondence that I know for certain was hidden beneath my mother's silver mirror, and then wondered what to do about it. How long did it take you—to decide, I mean?"

Sophie skewered her, a glint of moon sparkling sharply in each eye.

When Emily's pale face turned a dull red, Sophie didn't wait for an answer.

"How could you, Em? Am I not entitled to a little privacy? This may surprise you, but I have secrets. Secrets I want to keep. In other words, I don't expect you to go prowling about in an attempt to unearth them. I daresay you wouldn't find them worth the effort. Leave them for me, and go about your own, surely much more exciting, business."

Emily winced as Sophie spoke her final words, more than a little shocked. Certainly she was used to her friend's mild reprimands and resigned disapproval, but this was different. This concerned their friendship and made Emily wonder over its continuity. What could she say to such a confession? What kind of secrets were so sensitive that you kept them from your best friend, yet so important that they caused such an emotional outburst. With perfect clarity she recalled the moment earlier in the day that she had looked through the parlour door at her friend and wondered what lay beneath the surface. Now she wondered anew.

Stalling, she looked down at her clothes and straightened them merely out of habit. She stopped almost immediately and dropped her hands when she realized that she was calling attention to her appearance and its blatant reminder that she had intruded on her friend's privacy. Facing Sophie's interpretation of events and her obvious distress was tremendously lowering. But in truth, she hadn't come tonight for herself but for Sophie. The lure of adventure was always strong but not as strong as friendship. She wanted, at least, to remind Sophie of that.

Emily tucked a few more escaped strands sloppily back beneath the filthy cap and then fidgeted with her fingernails, not wishing to take her friend's hand, only to be rejected a second time.

"Dearest," she tried tentatively, "Of course you are entitled to your privacy. But please know that as your friend, I'll always be interested in your life. If you want secrets, keep them, but if you wish to confide in me, I'll do my best to graciously listen to anything you have to say."

"Thank you, Emily," Sophie said softly, now seemingly a bit embarrassed over her outburst.

"I wouldn't dream of meddling in a situation you wish kept private."

Sophie raised her eyebrow and forced Emily to quickly amend her statement.

"Again."

Sophie's forgiving grin was a relief, but Emily couldn't help but feel that something was now lost between them, that their friendship wouldn't be quite the same again. She didn't wish to dwell on it just now.

"I'm sorry about tonight and the note—I truly am. I saw it on your dressing table—you know you really didn't do such a good job of hiding it—" Forestalled by Sophie's exasperated expression, she changed tactics, "But, really it should have been enough. Anyway, I saw it, and my curiosity was piqued by the fact that it wasn't your handwriting. I read it, and admittedly that was wrong, but it was done out of concern for you. Mostly," she amended, cringing slightly.

"Why would you think there was any reason for concern?"

"I don't know. I suppose I didn't really have a legitimate reason," Emily admitted. "I was just surprised to see the note in such intimate surroundings. It seemed so out of place amidst your brushes and ribbons that I was intrigued. But once I looked, I was most definitely concerned."

"Why?" Sophie inquired in obvious disbelief.

"Because absolutely nothing about it was normal. I didn't recognize the epitaph at first, so it seemed cryptic, threatening, and teasing all at once. I imagined you were involved with seedy characters, being blackmailed into dark deeds, and then I thought perhaps you were hiding a secret romance and that the gentleman was completely unsuitable. Either way I decided you needed my help. It wasn't until I was riding home that I realized the origin of the quote, and then it all seemed even more mysterious."

"I see," Sophie allowed with the barest acceptance.

Emily dropped her gaze and busied herself scuffing some of the mud caked over the top of her boot. Allowing a couple of seconds to pass, she peeked at her friend from beneath lowered lashes and spoke again into the silence.

"I have to admit to being a little hurt as well. Such an important, exciting development in your life—for whatever it was, I knew it was that—and you hadn't seen fit to share it with me. I suppose a part of me simply wanted to be involved. Please don't be angry. It was all a misunderstanding, and I truly am sorry."

Sophie sighed heavily. "Very well, you're forgiven. I can never stay mad at you for any length of time anyway," she said with a wry smile.

"Good," Emily said briskly, but she then bit her lip and looked slightly embarrassed and uncertain.

Sophie wanted nothing more than to return to the vicarage and common sense, but she could almost hear the warring voices in her friend's head. She wondered why Emily even bothered with the formality of trying to talk herself out of her innate nosiness and was expecting the question long before it was asked.

"So…what exactly *are* you doing out here?" Emily wondered aloud. When Sophie didn't immediately answer, she hurriedly continued, "You don't have to tell me if you don't want to, but I'd be delighted to hear full details if it's something you'd like to talk over."

Sophie smiled. Poor Emily. Avid curiosity paired with awkward uncertainty was clearly taking its toll. Sophie held her smile in place and waited a few more seconds. One, two, three...

"Come, Sophie, please!" Emily begged, unable to help herself.

"Oh all right. If you must know..." When Emily nodded to indicate that indeed she must, Sophie continued. "I found the note when I was going through my father's coat pockets."

"Your father—?!"

Sophie held up her hand, silently insisting that Emily refrain from further interruptions. "Sometimes he leaves his sermon notes in his pockets, so I always check them. When I found the message, naturally I assumed the worst...that he must have mistakenly gotten involved with smugglers or other distasteful persons in the course of his research. I thought it best to confirm my fears and see for myself who was out here. Father was already in bed when I snuck out, but being as he's quite forgetful, I gave the detail only passing consideration. It wasn't until I saw the highwaymen that I realized what had happened."

Having completed her narrative, Sophie was puzzled by Emily's expectant face.

Emily waited a beat but couldn't restrain herself any longer. "Well, *what had happened*?"

"Isn't it obvious? One of the two villains here tonight accidentally dropped the note somewhere about. My father picked it up, recognized the epitaph, tucked it into his pocket, and promptly forgot about it."

"That does sound logical. I certainly don't believe your father is involved with the two men here tonight. And I should have known better than to suggest that you were—of all the ridiculous notions. You, my dear, would never do something so utterly out of character. I don't know what I was thinking."

Sophie was suddenly very tired.

"Well, now that I know you're not involved," Emily continued excitedly, "all that is left is to devise a plan to trap these thieves."

Sophie rolled her eyes and yawned. "You're right, Em. Such a simple task, I think I'll leave it for tomorrow. Right now, I'm going home to remove these muddy boots and sink into bed. I've had enough of this folly for one evening."

"Sophie, be serious!" Emily implored. "A successful ambush requires careful planning. Especially since our quarry will be armed and we won't." Her brow wrinkled in thought. "On second thought," she said slowly, "perhaps I can—"

"Don't even think about it! We're not going to ambush anyone, most certainly not a highwayman. We'll simply report the matter to the proper authorities and let them handle it. Now, if you don't mind, I'm going home." She started to leave but then turned back to add, "Do be careful riding back, Em."

"But—"

"Emily, I am not going to discuss it any further tonight."

"But, Sophie—"

"Probably not tomorrow either, but definitely not tonight." And with that, she hoisted her skirts up two full inches and stomped off in the direction of the vicarage.

Emily could only stare after her.

* * *

Sometime between the lonely hours of midnight and dawn, before she finally fell into a fitful sleep, Sophie came to a long overdue decision. It had come on the heels of her resolution to break free of the confines of expectations. Her own, and others.

It was time she focused a bit of attention and a measure of effort on herself. Surely with planning, a practical approach, and fierce determination, she could get what *she* wanted, just this once.

And what she wanted was Colin.

Deep down, she didn't believe that Emily really did.

She realized the arrogance of the presumption but found

that, interestingly enough, it didn't trouble her overmuch. In truth, she was perversely proud of the utter absence of guilt such a self-serving opinion would normally have engendered. Perhaps she was destined for a single dauntless crusade in her quiet life. If so, she was determined that this would be it.

Having spent years considering, imagining, hoping what a life with Colin might be like, she found it difficult to believe that Emily's decision, within minutes of hearing of his return, might be based on anything more substantial than fond relief. Emily had snatched at his memory as she might the last bit of cake on the tea tray. And if she were to venture a guess, Sophie would further suppose that her friend's replete satisfaction with her newfound hero would be equally as fleeting.

Suffice it to say they both wanted him but for entirely different reasons. While Sophie longed for the perfect lifelong companion, Emily sought an immediate and tolerable replacement for someone else. Emily clung to a golden memory while she herself was anxious to share a no-less dazzling future.

She knew that she would be utterly content as Colin's helpmate. It would make her blissfully happy to support his endeavors and manage his home, to share his interests and build a nursery. More than anything she wanted simply to be his wife and the mother of his children, and she was as convinced of her own success in that role as she was of her friend's certain failure. Emily would never be content with such a tame existence.

But solely a difference in temperaments would not have been enough to have her daringly thwarting Emily's intentions. It was the stark reality that she was frustratingly, embarrassingly, almost painfully in love with the man they both sought that she felt tipped the scales in her favor. She had waited a long time, perhaps too long, and she would not waste this one last opportunity. She would not sit idly by while Emily cajoled him into a convenient marriage.

She had a plan for Colin. And it didn't include Emily.

Having discovered a shared interest with her father,

Colin was bound to be visiting rather frequently—it would be natural for her to share the conversation and camaraderie of old acquaintances, now amateur scholars. She would discreetly reminisce over their common past, relishing every shared day in the present while insinuating herself into his thoughts of the future. Soon he would realize how comfortable and rewarding their life together could be.

Certainly it would not be a dramatic or impetuous courtship—there was even a chance that the subtlety of her method may preclude it from even being labeled as such—but having been forced to take matters into her own hands, it was the best she could manage. The comfort and safety in waiting had disappeared, and in its place had come desperation and the need for a modest amount of deception.

Emily couldn't know what she was planning. Being as she herself was planning to embark on the identical task of luring a proposal from Colin, Sophie didn't imagine that divulging her own plans could come to any good. Emily would only end up getting hurt. Either that or she would. Best to keep her little secret and see what would come of her intentions.

She had a plan for Emily as well. One that quite obviously would not involve Colin. The plan itself was simple, but truly she had no idea how to go about implementing it.

Emily merely needed to be distracted by a more suitable match. The sooner the better. But how she, a vicar's daughter, was expected to unearth a selection of eligible gentlemen who had not yet been considered and deemed unsuitable by her overly dramatic best friend was indeed a quandary. Still, utter bafflement wasn't about to steer her from her course. She was much determined on the success of a plan that would ensure Colin was left unencumbered and vulnerable to her plans to entice him herself.

The thrilling admission sent her heart rate speeding just as her entire body stilled in tense expectation. She could admit it. After all, it hardly seemed productive to delude herself and pretend otherwise.

So with a liberating feeling of release she pushed the bed

linens from her chin to her waist, unclenched her grip along the edge, and allowed the rush of excitement to wash over her just as thoroughly as the chill air swirling about the room.

She was planning a seduction.   Heaven help her…Please!

Lying in the darkness, she stared at the cracks in the ceiling with a secret little smile until, able to stand it no longer, she shivered with delight, threw the covers over her head, and muffled a squeal of delight that would have shocked all who knew her.

Huddled in inky silence, she was content indeed to realize that a daring bit of spontaneity might not be so out of reach for her after all. She curled into herself, hugging her cozy secret; she then closed her eyes and dreamed she'd shortly be holding the man himself.

Her last thought before she fell exhausted into sleep was to hope that no one would be hurt by her actions. Except perhaps Mr. Richly—he could jolly well fend for himself.

5

"...Lord Colin Willoughsby is recently home from the Continent, and there's to be a ball held in his honor... you simply must attend as our guest! We shall give Emily no choice but to realize her good fortune..."

LETTER FROM LADY BEATRICE SINCLAIR TO MR. DESMOND RICHLY
27 OCTOBER 1818

"So you see, Emily dear," Lady Sinclair concluded, touching each corner of her pursed lips with the starched point of her embroidered linen napkin, "Dear Desmond is *quite* utterly suitable and matchless in every respect." Her ladyship twittered at the dual meaning of her words before prodding Emily a bit further. "He may not be titled, my dear, but he is a prince of a man, and for reasons of his own, he has chosen you. What's more, your father and I both agree that the two of you will deal together quite nicely."

Emily bit back a groan. 'Dear Desmond' was a toad and hadn't a hope of changing into anything remotely resembling a prince. Given the choice, she'd much prefer to live out her days with a frog on her pillow than 'Dear Desmond'. Ten frogs.

That reality aside, if her stepmother used the word 'suitable' one more time, there was a very good possibility that she would scream. She'd simply be unable to stop herself. So far this morning she'd been subjected to a dreadfully dull cataloguing of Mr. Richly's 'suitable' qualities and an incredibly boring history of his imminently 'suitable' ancestors, with particular emphasis on Lady

Sinclair's side of the family, which was of course slightly more suitable than the other. It was all just a little more than Emily could stand first thing in the morning, and she saw little chance of a reprieve in the near future.

Yet she'd willingly suffer through it every day of her life if it meant avoiding 'Disagreeable Desmond'.

Emily was suddenly struck by how vastly different her life was now compared to the delightfully contented life she'd once known. No one truly understood her, and it seemed no one truly wished to. They preferred instead that she conform.

Her mother had never wished that, but her mother was long gone.

When her mother had died unexpectedly in a carriage accident nine years ago, Emily had been lost, and her father had been lonely and defenseless. After two years of floundering grief, they were just managing to find their feet again. But it was too late. Beatrice Sheridan had jammed her foot in the door and refused to budge. After a time, her father had just resigned himself to marriage. Beatrice had been only too delighted to assume the title of Lady Sinclair and equally appreciative of what she viewed as its attendant responsibilities. The effects of her father's surrender had been extremely far reaching.

Having spent two years mired in numbing loneliness, unconcerned with food, fashion, or ladylike pursuits, Emily had been deemed by the new Lady Sinclair to be in desperate need of guidance. Emily had rallied at once, and Beatrice had preened as proudly as a peacock, utterly unaware of the real reason for the change. Rather than subject herself to her stepmother's company and its attendant tutelage, Emily had healed herself quickly and quietly.

Now facing a tragedy of a different sort, namely the possibility of a marriage to 'Despicable Desmond', Emily was no better equipped to defend against her stepmother's tactics—sarcasm, she'd found, had very little effect on the woman. Nonetheless, she was determined to thwart them all. She would strive to avoid the garrulous companionship and unsolicited advice whenever possible and sacrifice whenever she must, namely whenever she cared to dine.

Deciding that she was sufficiently hungry this morning to merit the sacrifice, she vigorously forked up a bit of tomato, fastened a brave smile on her face, and determined to keep silent. Her ladyship would not be at all appreciative of anything she had to say right now, and she didn't need the woman tattling to her father. Or he might rescind his offer that she may find a preferred alternative to 'Dreadful Desmond'. Luckily, Lady Sinclair didn't appear to require any type of response at all.

"And I simply don't understand," her stepmother continued purposefully, vigorously waving a piece of toast in the air to help make her point, "why you insist on this nonsense of trying to find a husband on your own when your father and I have already found one for you. One, I might add, who is unquestionably suitable."

Emily shifted away from the toast and tried to explain why she was not at all thrilled with the idea of being wedded to 'Dratted Desmond' without referring to him as such.

"As I've said, Beatrice, I hardly know Mr. Richly. We've met only once, and to be honest—"

"Rubbish!" Lady Sinclair said petulantly, literally waving Emily's concerns aside with her attendant corner of toast.

The footman who had moved forward to refill her ladyship's chocolate appeared unconcerned. Or perhaps it was all in a day's work.

Thoroughly exasperated, Emily turned her eyes back to her breakfast. When Beatrice's silence spanned longer than two seconds, Emily looked up to see her stepmother carefully watching her slather a slice of toast with a generous helping of current jam. Apparently the sight was sufficiently distracting as to encourage her to abandon the train of her original conversation. Perhaps she assumed her stepdaughter was readying her own weapon. The possibility nearly had Emily giggling.

"Careful with the jam, dear. I've noticed it's especially

drippy this morning, and you wouldn't wish to spill any on your gown." Ah, so this had been the matter requiring her stepmother's immediate attention—the danger of a spill.

Emily merely stared, wondering if she should mention the sticky blob already clinging to her stepmother's own curls. She decided instead to have a bit of fun.

"Certainly not," she agreed in apparent self-righteousness. "To do so would no doubt attract the unwanted attentions of a host of hungry gentlemen."

Lady Sinclair looked up from her breakfast with a cautious look of horror in her eyes but kept silent.

Emily however, pressed ruthlessly onward, "Just imagine the scandal that could attach itself to such an innocent accident, simply because every man in the vicinity wanted a sniff, or worse yet, a taste of me." She offered her stepmother an appreciative smile, "How could I ever manage without your constant diligence and sound advice?"

Lady Sinclair, who never seemed able to recognize the sarcasm that liberally laced all of her conversations with Emily, remained uncharacteristically speechless for a moment.

"*Well!*...How could...?....Er...yes...quite so."

The transition from shock to curiosity to self-righteousness was a sight to behold. Thoroughly amused, Emily kept her smile well tucked back.

Unfortunately, Lady Sinclair was quick to recover and resume their original discussion.

"I needed only one meeting with your father," she proclaimed importantly, "before I decided to marry him. And Dear Desmond is so highly suitable, a second meeting would be a waste of time unless it was to result in an announcement being sent to the London papers."

She lifted her eyebrows and speared Emily with the unspoken question—apparently her ladyship would promptly arrange a second meeting if Emily would abandon her ridiculous search.

Emily felt her mouth and eyebrows turn downwards, unmistakably conveying her grim rejection of such an idea, but she felt compelled to further impress her opinion on her stepmother.

"I agree. An utter waste of time."

Lady Sinclair snorted delicately and continued unconvinced, "I assure you, my dear, you won't find a better match."

"An unwittingly harsh set-down for all gentlemen," Emily muttered under her breath.

"I beg your pardon?" Lady Sinclair asked suspiciously. "Really Emily, you shouldn't talk with your mouth full. Most unladylike."

"Too true," Emily said around a bite of egg.

Thankfully at that moment, Lord Sinclair came in to breakfast, and Emily smoothly slid the subject matter around to horses. As expected, her stepmother had nothing to contribute, so by the time Emily excused herself and headed for the stables, all thoughts of 'Dismal Desmond' had agreeably slid away from her.

Gypsy seemed as anxious to escape as she, so as soon as Emily offered up the sugar wafers pilfered from the kitchen, pocketing the carrots for a later shared snack, they were on their way back to the vicarage with the intent to remind Sophie of the importance of opportunity.

Today she consciously turned Gypsy toward the forest and the shortcut she'd taken the day before. Yesterday's storm was little more than a memory this morning, the only signs of it being a few scattered puddles fancifully edged in sparkling sunlight, with the cloudless sky cheerfully reflected back from their depths. When she reached the spot where she had fallen from her horse, Emily slowed Gypsy to a halt, delighting in the warm sunlight filtering through the showy foliage and across her face.

She'd lain awake for hours last night, her thoughts darting from one subject to the next until she was mentally exhausted and tired of the whole mess. So it was hardly surprising that when she had finally succumbed to sleep, her dreams had been invaded by a dashing and dangerous highwayman with the face of her seductive stranger from the woods. It really wasn't perfectly clear who had ambushed whom, but their meeting had played out in this very spot.

Her thoughts had very obviously been tangled, that was all. She knew with utter certainty that her stranger was not the same man she had barely managed to overhear in the graveyard. The steely voiced gentleman who'd lingered in shadow had hinted at evil deeds indeed, while the delectably drenched stranger she'd cornered in the midst of yesterday's storm had had a different type of wickedness in mind. She didn't trouble to wonder over the assessment, just accepted it with confident certainty. She couldn't afford to spare the stranger another conscious thought—she'd allowed him too many already. What was worse, she could do nothing of his bold invasion of her subconscious.

In her dream the thunderstorm had returned, and she had fallen from her horse—there was indignity even in dreams. But rather than frown upon her from an imperious height, her mysterious stranger had quickly dismounted, and without a word (a crucial detail), had lifted her easily in his arms. She'd stared intently up into his teasing, knowing eyes, astonished to find herself hoping he'd dip his head to kiss her. And further shocked to realize she herself was contemplating whether it would be too outrageous and objectionable for her to act on her own. All she would have to do would be to reach up, place her hand on the back of his neck, and draw his mouth down to hers.

Her decision came quickly, and heedlessly, she acted upon it, twining her arms around his neck and pulling him close, until his mouth was but inches from hers and his breath fanned hot on her recently moistened lips. She relaxed in his arms and waited to be kissed, waited to kiss back. And then, at the absolute worst possible moment, she woke up. Once again in a puddle, and wanting only to curse her bad luck.

The humiliating truth was that in the course of her rather tumultuous dreams, she had somehow managed to tumble out of bed, sufficiently bumping the bedside table to upend the pitcher of water left there each night. So there she had sat, quite ignominiously in its contents. She had hastily changed her nightgown, praying her maid hadn't heard a thing, and had wondered for the first time whether she ever talked in her sleep. Her reaction to this man had left her feeling uncertain and gauche, so she most certainly did not wish to explain it. She didn't even know if she could. Still, avoiding it would be very nearly impossible with the stain on her cheeks and the confession in her eyes.

The dream had been so unexpectedly appealing as to be disturbing. Even now, wide awake and in full control of her thoughts, she didn't find the thought of such a kiss as objectionable as she might have found ten minutes in many other gentlemen's company. Nothing could have shocked her more. She simply couldn't understand it. What was it about him? Was it the delight of surprise in coming across him? The thrill of possibility he signified? Or perhaps the lure of seduction he promised? None seemed accurate.

Whatever it was eluded her, remaining just out of reach. Coincidentally, the same could be said of her common sense, she thought, thoroughly exasperated. At the rate she was going, she would be lucky to avoid another collision and one of yesterday's leftover puddles. She needed to pay attention.

Emily shook her head a bit reluctantly to clear it of his image and then smiled as an idea occurred to her. If her thoughts and dreams were going to be occupied by a man, it really should be Colin. She would simply replace the image of her dark-haired stranger with Colin's golden visage and then let her imagination wander.

She spent the remainder of the ride trying to conjure an image of Colin holding her in his arms and kissing her passionately. Unfortunately, she couldn't seem to envision anything more than a companionable squeeze around her shoulders and a friendly kiss on the cheek.

How odd, Emily thought, frowning in puzzlement. It must be because she still saw him through a child's eyes. When they renewed their acquaintance she would most certainly be able to marshal her thoughts towards a more amorous embrace. Perhaps she should call on him, hint and nudge him along in the direction of a match between them, even allow him to steal a kiss. With a bit of luck, she could very well come away with a willing fiancé, an easy mind, and time to spare before her engagement. Time she could use to concentrate on other, more exciting tasks.

Such as the thrilling ambush she now planned. Not to mention the race she had every intention of winning at week's end. While she was certain to enjoy the challenge of worthy competition, not to mention the spoils of victory, in truth she was more excitedly anticipating a bit of verbal sparring. Further, she was confident her stranger would be happy to oblige her. Just as she'd decided to oblige him with a kiss, should it become necessary. And with a prickle of guilt, she admitted, perhaps even if it was not.

She wouldn't consider it now; she would just wait and see and not make up her mind until then. Otherwise she'd be thinking of nothing but him for days to come. She supposed it would also be wise, before they met again, to cease referring to him in the possessive sense. He was not hers now, nor would he ever be. The adventure would be hers, and that alone. And perhaps that one kiss.

Adventure was hers at last, with even a bit to spare. And that which proved to be most exciting of all, she'd stumbled over quite by accident—and had already received a stinging reprimand for her efforts. She wasn't about to allow Sophie's disapproval keep her from seeing this through to the end. With a bit of luck, two nights hence would see the highwaymen apprehended and her a heroine. Time couldn't fly fast enough, as long as she didn't think of the consequences facing her at month's end.

She could now boast of her first exhilarating escapade masquerading as a man. Silently to herself, of course, but boast she could. The breeches had been even more liberating than she had expected. And worth every bit of censure she had endured from her best friend. She would most certainly wear them again, and to even greater success than some eavesdropping, a mud puddle, and a thorough down dressing.

She would wear them for an ambush and perhaps even convince Sophie to do the same.

Sophie's emphatic refusal to involve herself in Emily's

latest plan was, for once, not the slightest bit disappointing or discouraging. Emily felt only relief at the comforting glimpse of Sophie's sensible self amidst otherwise inscrutable behavior. Besides, she was certain she could conscript her compassionate friend for such a noble cause.

Although after last night, she was forced to concede that she really wasn't too certain of anything at all as far as Sophie was concerned. Other than the fact that she thoroughly disapproved of her best friend wearing breeches. And snooping and sharing secrets and planning an ambush and issuing challenges to strange gentlemen…

Perhaps the trouble was that Sophie disapproved of her.

She truly hoped that was not it. She couldn't deal with such an horrendous possibility right now—she needed at least one friend on which she could depend.

Determined not to think about it, she decided to deal with Sophie as she normally would have. Much as usual, she would be trying to convince Sophie to do something she really didn't wish to do. Or perhaps truly *did* want to do but wouldn't allow herself to try. She'd root for the latter. It was her only chance. And she'd slated the entire morning for the task.

To think…highwaymen meeting and planning their next robbery just out of earshot of Sophie's bedroom window. And Sophie content to ignore the opportunity!

Truly unbelievable.

Shaking her head a bit at the wonder of it, Emily rode the last bit of the journey at a gallop. As she neared the vicarage, she was surprised to find herself almost regretting the need to stop and even the task ahead of her. She'd much rather continue her ride and pretend she had nothing more serious to concern her today than faerie mischief.

Riding around to the side of the building, she noticed an unfamiliar horse tethered near the garden gate. Wondering to whom it belonged, Emily drew her mare alongside. She dismounted gracefully, albeit inappropriately as she had, of course, been riding astride, and set about tethering her horse.

Giving Gypsy a final pat and half the carrots from her

pocket, she turned to inspect the other visitor.

"Who might you be, my lovely?" she inquired of the glossy grey gelding who preened, with the sunlight dancing across his back. Emily smoothed her hand along the horse's neck and smiled into the bright eye that patiently stared back, silently, politely conveying that he was fully aware that the remainder of the carrots nestled in Emily's pocket were for him.

"Very well, you deserve them," Emily conceded chuckling. She fished out the remainder, glanced quickly, guiltily around, and then offered the treat before turning to open the garden gate.

She smiled when she noticed Sophie's boots sitting primly beside the backdoor. They were caked in mud to the ankle.

Emily did remember to knock first, but when Sophie didn't immediately answer, she did as she had always done and simply pushed open the door and walked in, stepping into the long, narrow hall at the back of the house. The vicar always worked at his studies in the hours before lunch, and the visitor was most assuredly closeted away with him, so Emily felt confident of finding Sophie alone. Walking quickly down the hall, she removed her riding hat and pulled off her gloves, laying both on a recently polished but worn cherrywood table that would have long ago been relegated to the attics at Sinclair House.

That could be said of just about everything in the cozy vicarage, but Emily loved it all.

With Sophie's diligent and loving touches, it was no wonder she spent so many contented hours here, subjecting herself to regular discussions of ancient civilizations, tolerating Sophie's mild and well-meant scoldings, and partaking of superb tea and cakes. She felt welcome here, or had, until last evening.

Still, she and Sophie had been friends a very long time, and she was determined not to think about the awkwardness and tension between them. So seeing the parlour door open, she strode gamely in that direction, launching into a discussion of the subject foremost on her mind.

"Sophie!" she announced, marching purposefully through the door, "It is now tomorrow, and we have matters to discuss..." Emily's voice died slowly away as she became aware of the cozy tableau in front of her.

There was Sophie, the perfect hostess, gracefully presiding over tea in a freshly pressed morning gown of palest violet, with her blonde hair pinned up neatly, bound by a violet satin ribbon. Faced with such pristine perfection, Emily glanced regretfully down at her own worn riding habit, more than a little wrinkled from her ride, and her fingers itched to tuck away the stray curls she knew must be escaping from her loosely plaited coronet of braids.

Vicar Penrose was sitting next to his daughter, dapper this morning in a blue and white striped waistcoat, his collar slightly askew. His round cheeks were slightly flushed and his white hair standing all on end. Such dishevelment was invariably caused by excited fingers, and on the occasions she managed to witness its onset, Emily always felt rather ruffled herself. Seeing his downy tufts in such endearing disarray always brought a smile to her face, a mild prelude to the infectious excitement he all but insisted be shared. Its source today was likely the array of journals and maps that covered every inch of the table and left little room for tea or, quite obviously, her own intentions for the remainder of the morning.

It hardly mattered. With her next indrawn breath, her thoughts scattered, and those intentions were all but forgotten. The other visitor to the vicarage today was not closeted away as she had predicted.

It was this person, seated on Sophie's other side, apparently an *invited* guest, who had Emily's heart racing with trepidation and excitement. She would have known Colin anywhere. This was an older, more mature Colin, to be sure, but it was unmistakably her childhood hero.

His hair was no longer the flaxen blond she remembered, rather more of a burnished gold. And the curls that had once been the cause of a surfeit of teasing had relaxed into gentle waves. His eyes, though still piercingly blue, seemed deeper, perhaps due to the fringe of long dark lashes now framing them. His once rosy cheeks had sharpened around well-defined cheekbones and were now bronzed dark by the sun. Any suspicion that the fun-loving child had disappeared completely was dispelled with the first hint of that easily recognizable, unapologetically mischievous smile.

It seemed the beautiful youth had become a devastatingly handsome man, and she suspected his talent for teasing had effortlessly transitioned through flattery and smoothly on to flirtation, no doubt earning him the label of 'rake'. For one as handsome and charming as he, it would rarely be used disparagingly.

The object of Emily's attention seemed slightly shocked, whether by her unexpected appearance, or her less than decorous entrance, she couldn't be certain, but still he managed to rise quickly, balancing his teacup. The vicar took considerably longer to find his feet, leaning heavily on the sofa, and almost upending his tea in the process. Both men bowed politely.

"Emily! I hadn't expected to see you as yet, but you are, as always, a delightful surprise," Colin said. He looked quickly around for a place to set his teacup, found nowhere suitable, and so stepped forward awkwardly holding onto it. He reached for her hand, grinned at her over it, and finally brought it to his lips. "By the sound of matters, you haven't changed a bit. Seeing you, I almost feel I've not been away at all—I assure you that is a most refreshing welcome home."

Wondering why she was flustered—she made a very firm point of *never* being flustered around a man—she struggled to think of something to say. Something witty, something memorable.

"I don't believe we've been introduced, sir. Although…you do slightly resemble the childhood friend who taught me to ride—I do hope you're more accomplished than he." Emily offered him a confident smile.

Colin kept hold of her hand and stared into her eyes, clearly amused.

"Apparently not, at least as far as you're concerned." His lips curved then in a slow, teasing smile, and she waited. There were no flutterings. She was even holding her breath and concentrating to make sure she wouldn't miss them. And then the moment passed as her hostess intruded.

"Emily," Sophie said quickly, "we weren't expecting you. You didn't tell me you'd be calling this morning."

Emily gave her a puzzled look. Why ever would Sophie have expected her to announce her intention to visit when she never had before?

"Well, I…" she began haltingly.

"Just a lucky coincidence I suppose," Sophie interrupted, smiling brightly. "Your timing is perfect as usual. As you can see, we're having tea and the spice cake you like so much. I'm not sure there is enough on the tray to assuage your appetite, but we'll make do."

Sophie was very nearly babbling, and her smile seemed etched in place. Not to mention the fact that her teasing had felt more like a carefully aimed barb.

Emily nodded dumbly, not sure how to respond.

Blessedly, the vicar was the same as always. He peered at her owlishly over the rims of his round little spectacles, looking for all the world like a good-natured old elf.

"Emily, my dear girl, sit down, sit down," he told the teapot.

"There's no need to be shy," he continued amiably when Emily seemed hesitant. "Surely you haven't forgotten young Colin Willoughsby. He's titled now, heir to his dear departed father, but you'll see, my dear, he's hardly changed a bit. Isn't that right, my boy?" he asked, looking expectantly at Colin's teacup.

"Er, no sir, hardly a bit," Colin replied with an amused smile.

"Quite so. And what's more," the vicar continued, addressing the table before him enthusiastically, "he's admitted to a keen interest in ancient civilizations. So you see, you and he have a great deal in common."

At Colin's look of surprise, he continued. "Emily has always been vastly interested in my studies. Haven't you, my dear?"

The bite of cake Emily had just popped into her mouth lodged dry in her throat at the question, and she was forced to endure an embarrassing fit of coughing before she could manage to speak.

"Well I…" she stammered helplessly. She couldn't be sure, but she thought she heard Sophie snicker.

Colin turned to look at Emily as if he'd just discovered a delightful surprise.

"So you too have succumbed to the lure of discovery, the thrill of piecing together a bit of ancient history? I must say that surprises me. I wouldn't have imagined studies of the past could have held your interest. You always seemed so wrapped up in the adventures of the moment. It appears you are a veritable enigma. What do you judge the most interesting period of study—I certainly wouldn't venture to *guess* the answer to that question."

Neither would I if you weren't insisting. Faced with Colin's intent curiosity, she knew she'd need to come up with something. But what could she possibly say? Other than to admit that she considered it all the same period— history.

At Sophie's urging, and simply to be polite, she had pretended interest in Vicar Penrose's discussions countless times over the years. But she'd only paid enough attention to make sure she nodded in the right places and supplied a "how interesting" whenever it seemed to be expected. To admit absolute ignorance now would not only make her look a fool, it would most assuredly disappoint the man who had treated her as a daughter for so many years. Such a consequence was unacceptable.

"Emily?" Three faces were looking at her expectantly. Sophie's lips, she noticed, were twisted slightly with wry amusement.

"What? Oh yes, my…favorite…period." She looked at the vicar, desperately trying to remember any snippet of information that wouldn't make her look completely ignorant. He smiled back encouragingly.

Suddenly she had it, and she had to force herself not to

rush to answer.

"I must confess to being slightly overwhelmed by all the fascinating details of each and every one, so much so that it is difficult to choose a single one." She could see Sophie's smile widen out of the corner of her eye. "But since you insist, I will confess that my study of Ancient Greece tends to occupy far more of my time than that of any of the other civilizations." She adored Greek mythology and had read the volumes in her father's library countless times.

"Indeed," Colin said with interest, nodding slowly.

She smiled back, proud of herself for avoiding an outright lie. She didn't allow herself to glance gloatingly over at her friend but still didn't miss Sophie's dramatic eye roll.

"What is it specifically that interests you?" Colin asked innocently.

Good heavens! It was to be a veritable inquisition!

"Their gods and goddesses. I'm of the opinion that a culture willing to endow its female gods with equal power, confident they'll wield it wisely, is one worthy of further study. I am confident that one day modern society will be so enlightened."

No longer so self-conscious, Emily reached for a second square of cake. With her eyes focused on the tea tray, she was oblivious to Colin's raised eyebrows and Sophie's warning darts.

"Artemis has always been my favorite. Goddess of the hunt and the moon... It must be wonderful to enjoy such freedom and independence, not bound by society's rules, not answering to any man."

"I believe she is also the goddess of chastity," Colin said quietly, keeping his eyes on his teacup.

"Of course," Emily smirked, "Forgive my oversight in mentioning it. Are you of the widely held opinion that a woman's reputation is her most commendable virtue? For your sake, I sincerely hope not."

Silence descended on the room, and each teacup was quickly put to use.

Emily bit her lip and wished she'd had the sense to stop

talking. Sophie was well used to her complaints regarding the restrictions placed on women in modern society, and the vicar was oblivious. But what if she had ruined her chances with Colin over a few careless words? She sat silently with head bowed until Sophie's father broke the silence.

"So you must be extremely fond of the friezes," Vicar Penrose told the pot of scarlet cyclamen to her left.

Emily's momentary relief promptly deserted her as she puzzled over the seemingly arbitrary question. Before she had managed an answer, Sophie forestalled her.

"You are indeed, aren't you, Emily? The Greeks often incorporated these sculptured bands in their architecture, but I would venture to guess that the ones depicting their gods and goddesses are of most interest in your studies. Am I correct?"

Emily wondered if anyone else had heard the pause before Sophie's reference to her 'studies' but decided she couldn't complain after her friend had graciously come to her rescue.

"Of course," she smoothly agreed. "Do you suppose 'friezes' were thusly named because their subjects are forever frozen in time?"

She had thought it a valid question, but Colin's and the vicar's chuckle suggested otherwise.

"I believe the word is derived from the French word for 'fringe'," Sophie offered modestly. "The bands are used as decorative embellishment, and often appear to be hanging from the cornice of a structure, suspended above its columns."

Her father and Colin both nodded their amused assent.

"Ahhh," Emily answered in apparent understanding but, in fact, without a clue.

"It might be easier," Vicar Penrose told her elbow, "to demonstrate the word's origin with the use of some sketches." Turning his attention to the table in front of him he continued, "Now where would those be?" He tipped his gaze down to look through his glasses and began sifting through the pile of notebooks positioned in front of him.

"I suspect you'll find what you're looking for in Volume

III, Father."

"Volume III, eh?" The vicar quickly found the specified volume by the neatly penned marking on the spine. Emily noted it was in Sophie's handwriting. "Ah, yes. Discovery and Examination of Antiquities of Ancient Greece."

The vicar beamed in his daughter's direction. "Right as usual, my dear." He turned and spoke conspiratorially to Colin's shoulder. "Don't know how I'd manage without her. Lucky for me, no gentleman has yet to snatch her away. But it won't be long before one realizes just what a treasure she is."

"A sharp intellect is a dangerous quality in a woman," Colin said teasingly, "especially when paired with beauty." The last was said with utter sincerity.

Sophie coloured prettily, clearly uncomfortable as the subject of discussion, but pleased with Colin's compliment. Emily was irritated. As much with Colin's narrow-minded comment as with her own jealousy over not being the target of his compliment. But she could think of absolutely nothing to say, so she sat in silence.

As the vicar perused the journal he'd laid on his lap, seemingly engrossed in its contents, Sophie and Colin steered the conversation away from the Ancient Greeks. Emily had no recourse but to listen and wish she'd backed straight away out the parlour door.

"Have you been to see the Rosetta Stone in the British Museum?" Sophie shyly questioned.

"No, I regret I have not yet had the pleasure," he answered, smiling at her. "But as soon as I have matters a bit more settled here, I plan to remedy the lack of opportunity. Have you seen it?"

"No," Sophie said, simultaneously regretful and reverent.

"Then perhaps you and your father would like to accompany me on a trip to London to see it." Almost as an afterthought, he glanced over at Emily and added, "You would be more than welcome to join us, Emily."

A reply clearly wasn't expected—Colin had already turned his attention back to Sophie.

"I'm sure Father would be as appreciative of the company and opportunity as I." Sophie replied, pink-cheeked.

"I didn't realize you were interested in antiquities as well, Sophie," Colin said.

"Not to the extent of my father, of course. But I do find all the new discoveries fascinating. At present I'm reading *Travels in Upper and Lower Egypt* by Dominique Vivant, Baron de Denon. Do you know it?"

"I've just finished with it! I found it enormously engrossing."

"Oh, I know precisely what you mean," Sophie said with fervor. "How exciting it must have been to be a part of Napoleon's expedition into Egypt."

They beamed at each other in companionable silence until Emily felt slightly nauseated.

"Have you found what you were looking for, Vicar Penrose?" Emily inquired loudly, looking back and forth between Colin and the vicar in an attempt to ascertain the success of her attempt at distraction.

Colin's eyes slid away from Sophie, and Emily tried to catch her friend's eye. Her efforts were met with subtle rebuff as Sophie's gaze turned downward, seemingly mesmerized by her interlocking fingers held primly in her lap. Caught off guard by the evasion, Emily was forced to acknowledge that the usually cozy vicarage had this afternoon become a confusing labyrinth.

"Ah, yes. Here we are," Vicar Penrose finally answered, "Rather than sketch the friezes here, I have merely referenced a series of other journals I have in my collection. I'll just go and find them. Won't take me but a minute or two."

As the vicar slowly creaked to his feet, both Colin and Sophie stood as well, offering to help.

"Well then, if you wouldn't mind, my boy, I'd appreciate the help. Sophie could no doubt use a break from all this." The vicar's hand swept out in front of him, and Emily had the distinct suspicion that he was not referring specifically to his research but rather her entire life at the vicarage.

She couldn't help but wonder if Sophie's father intended to pursue a match between Colin and his daughter. If so, the situation could hardly get any messier.

Or perhaps it could.

Sophie had moved up alongside her but was keeping her eyes determinedly averted. It wasn't until Emily happened to glance down, and notice a long thin stain trailing down the side of her skirts that she was able to deduce why. Raising her eyes once more, she took in Sophie's now-empty teacup, and then her friend's slightly apologetic face.

Realization came swiftly—Sophie intended to extricate her from the discussion before matters got considerably worse. And they would, she was certain, if left unchecked. Resigned but appreciative, Emily glanced back to the two gentlemen as they moved towards the door, smiled slightly, and waited to be saved. She was determined to return very shortly and steer the conversation down a less precarious path.

"Oh, Emily, your gown!" Sophie gasped in what Emily would concede was a fair showing of mock dismay. Both Colin and the vicar turned to see what had caused such a reaction.

"Bad luck, it seems," returned Emily, now seeing that the excess tea had moved rather efficiently on to her boots. She decided the small puddle forming on the floor was Sophie's due.

"Quickly, before the stain sets." Taking firm hold of Emily's elbow, Sophie began to pull her toward the stairs. "Please excuse us, gentlemen," added the ever-gracious hostess.

"I bid you good luck," Colin joked, grinning at Sophie and giving Emily a wink.

"I may very well need it," Emily managed to reply before Sophie yanked her from the room. For the second time in two days her skirts dripped a trail up the stairs to Sophie's room.

"How very inventive, Sophie," Emily praised once the door had been closed behind them. "Although I must say

I'm surprised you chose a tact that was bound to prove so messy."

"I'm sorry," Sophie apologized ruefully, helping Emily out of the soiled gown. "The idea had obvious shortcomings, but you seemed to be floundering so miserably that I decided to sacrifice. You can be thankful none spilled on your bodice."

"As can you," Emily said pointedly, her words muffled by the dress being pulled over her head. "Seeing as you successfully managed to spirit me away from an uncomfortable situation, it would surely be ungracious of me to comment on my new one—trapped in your room without a suitable gown in which to escape."

Wearing nothing but her chemise, she tossed a look in Sophie's direction that was ignored. She then flung herself back onto the bed, rolled over onto her stomach, and rested her chin on her hand. "As long as we're here…" she began, smiling wickedly, "Shall we discuss tonight's ambush?"

"I'd prefer not," Sophie dismissed, pouring water from the pitcher beside the bed over a clean cloth. Emily's reaction being that of someone ready and willing to commence a tedious battle of wills, Sophie promptly reconsidered, choosing to launch an initial attack.

"You cannot simply decide to ambush highwaymen. It's utterly absurd." Giving Emily a withering look, she sat down at her dressing table with the gown in her lap and began to rub gently at the tea stain.

"It is *not* absurd," Emily declared with feeling, "We have an obligation to see that these villains are apprehended before they strike again."

Sophie groaned.

"Besides, I doubt we'll soon have another such exciting opportunity," Emily continued, her spirits undampened.

At Sophie's comical frown, Emily insisted, "You can't pretend you didn't feel even the tiniest thrill last night in the cemetery."

Sophie dropped her hands to her lap and stared, wide-eyed and exasperated, at her friend.

"What I felt was a chill. But luckily, that discomfort

was tempered by fear, foolishness, and utter disbelief at my own regrettable decisions."

She raised the dress again but then paused and sighed heavily as she slowly lowered it again.

"While I applaud your enthusiasm and sense of duty, Em, I can neither condone nor participate in your scheme to apprehend a couple of highwaymen."

"Come, Sophie, I need you in this. It'll take two of us if my plan's to work."

Sophie raised a quizzical brow. "What plan?" she asked skeptically.

"Well," Emily hedged, flushing slightly, "I haven't yet worked out every last detail, but I assure you, you are instrumental in the plan's eventual success."

"What a coincidence. I am instrumental to the success of my plan as well. Shall I reveal the details to you?" Not waiting for a response that would surely be negative, Sophie continued, "I plan to distract you from your dangerous intentions with a tray of tea and ginger scones, notify the authorities, and then forget the matter entirely."

Sophie noticed the mutinous line of her friend's lips and hoped she had put an end to the discussion of ambushing highwaymen.

"I can't imagine what I was thinking to go haring off to the cemetery in the middle of the night." She glanced up at Emily, this time with an affectionate smile. "I think perhaps I've allowed you too much influence over my life."

"Sophie, please. It couldn't be more perfectly planned. You *saw* the highwaymen!" Then, as an afterthought, "You *did* see them, didn't you?"

Warring thoughts momentarily kept Sophie from answering. If she answered honestly, she'd have no choice but to listen to Emily's plans to pursue an ill-fated ambush. Her other choice was to conceal the truth from her friend—to lie. And while she had already decided such behavior might be a necessary evil in carrying out her plan for Colin, she was determined to keep it from invading the rest of her life. She rather doubted it would make a difference either way. So she nodded as she clarified.

"Only one of them. The other one, the gentleman, stayed hidden in shadow throughout their meeting. Remind me again why this is not a matter for the authorities. For heaven's sake, Emily, don't think you are playing the part of heroine in one of your novels—this is *real*."

"Of course it is real," Emily sniffed, resigned to her friend's ability to see right through her. "And I will tell you why you would not wish to leave the matter to the authorities. We cannot very easily divulge what we know without revealing how we came about the information, now can we? I am not concerned for my reputation," Emily pressed on ruthlessly, "but, I can only assume that you would not prefer it be common knowledge that you were lurking about the cemetery in the middle of the night."

Emily tilted her head innocently as she added the final touch, "It's sure to come out that you were dressed only in your nightrail. And how would that look? The vicar's daughter and all?"

As Sophie blanched, Emily bit her lip to keep her smile tucked back.

"There simply must be a way to allow the authorities to handle the matter without involving ourselves. Surely between the two of us, we can come up with a solution."

After barely a moment's pause, Sophie believed she had determined the best course of action.

"We can reveal everything in an anonymous letter. It's the perfect solution! The authorities will have the information as completely as we can provide it, our involvement will be kept secret, and *they* can plan and carry out the ambush. Then they'll conveniently be on hand to arrest the villains."

It was quite obvious that Emily was opposed to the suggestion.

Now thoroughly exasperated, Sophie continued on, "Em, you seem unwilling to recognize the possibility for danger. Last night we *chanced* to come upon highwaymen. You are now proposing that we arrange an excursion with the purpose of apprehending them. Most definitely not. I will not even for one moment consider participating in such a dangerous scheme, and I will be forced to go to your father if you insist on continuing with this plan by yourself."

Sophie truly regretted having to resort to blackmail, but she needed Emily to take the matter seriously. This was dangerous business, not merely the adventure her impulsive friend believed it to be. From the sound of things, unless that scoundrel Sneeves met with success, there was going to be trouble for him. The man in the shadows had made that abundantly clear. Sneeves would undoubtedly do whatever it took to prevent the dire consequences that threatened to befall him if he failed a second time. She needed Emily's promise that she wouldn't try anything foolish like attempting to apprehend an armed highwayman on her own.

Emily was well used to listening patiently as Sophie raised her characteristic objections to whatever grand scheme Emily had planned. She had been fully prepared to wait them out. She had not been prepared for the devious turn of her friend's mind.

Sophie had never before resorted to intimidation, or blackmail for that matter, but Emily didn't think for one moment that her friend was bluffing. Apparently Sophie was very strongly opposed to this adventure.

Bad luck that she herself was just as strongly in favor and, in all likelihood, far more devious.

"All right," Emily sighed in what she hoped passed for a dejected tone, "if you feel so strongly about it, we'll turn the matter over to the authorities and have done with it. I must say that I think we could have handled it ourselves, but you've made your point—it would definitely be dangerous. And there are certainly enough other things going on for me to relinquish the role of heroine for a time. But your concession must then be a promise to participate in the next adventure that falls into our laps. And," she added with an impish smile, "you must do so wearing breeches."

Although surprised by Emily's ready capitulation, Sophie wasn't the slightest bit suspicious. Rather, she had to admit to a certain admiration for her friend's ingeniousness. In exchange for graciously bowing out of the ambush, Emily was demanding Sophie's costumed participation in the next escapade. It was to be a sacrifice for both of them. Despite her misgivings, Sophie considered Emily's offer the best solution.

"Very well," she said briskly, "then that's settled. I assume that was all you wished to discuss with me?"

Emily thought of her dream, her mysterious stranger, and the awkwardness she felt towards Colin. But as she looked at Sophie's expectant face, she couldn't bring herself to discuss any of it. She would just need to come up with some solutions on her own for once, without her best friend's help.

"Um…yes," she said hedging, "that was all. But let me just confirm that I have your agreement. You, Sophia Penrose, a vicar's daughter consistently above reproach, will procure a pair of breeches and wear them for the next adventure I deem worthy?"

Sophie sighed in resignation. "If that is what is required for you to abandon your plans for tomorrow night, then yes I agree."

"Hooray!" Emily rolled onto her back and clapped her hands together gleefully. "You needn't worry—I'll make sure the occasion is truly deserving. Oooh, I can hardly wait."

Both were quiet for a moment, each lost in her own vastly different thoughts, but Emily soon rolled over and resumed their discussion.

"Oh, and don't trouble yourself over the authorities—I'll have Father notify them as soon as possible. Remaining anonymous will not be possible if I involve Father, but he doesn't have to know how we came into possession of the information. I will embellish the truth a trifle and leave out all incriminating details. Father simply need know that you found a note in the vicar's pockets outlining plans for a highwayman's ambush."

Emily raised her eyebrows and edged up the corner of her mouth, "What do you think? It's a compromise of sorts."

"Mostly by you, which you'll admit is out of character. I have to say, I'm surprised at your willingness to abandon your plans—what there were of them, anyway."

"It's true I believe this be a lost opportunity, but at least with my father's influence we'll sooner be rid of the villains. Heaven knows I'm anxious to be allowed the freedom to ride unescorted."

At Sophie's raised eyebrow she added, "Obviously I have continued to ride unescorted, but that doesn't mean I'm not eager for permission. It's irritating to have to worry over getting caught. Speaking of getting caught, how can I best steer the discussion belowstairs away from artifacts and ruins? And apparently friezes as well," she added as an afterthought, her brow furrowed in thought.

Sophie thought it best to intercede. "Perhaps it would be best if you instead made a graceful exit."

"I suppose. That will at least give me a bit of time to decide what to do if the topic should come up in the future." She continued on, mumbling to herself, "But, what reason can I give for leaving so abruptly?"

"A soiled gown? A prior engagement? The fact that you're bored senseless and know absolutely nothing about the subject matter?"

Sophie's little poke went unnoticed as Emily pounced on her second suggestion.

"I have it," Emily announced wryly, "The perfect solution—morning tea with Beatrice. Ironic isn't it that the day she fails to invite me is the day I need the excuse? I shall go and wish myself somewhere else."

"Ahhh, so it's to be the truth. So simple and yet so often ignored. Perhaps this will be a new beginning for you. Hmmm?"

"I daresay not. Honesty is most often fraught with pitfalls. Today I am willing to accept it as the perfect solution simply because nothing else has presented itself."

If Emily saw Sophie's dramatic eyeroll or heard her exasperated sigh, she didn't acknowledge it.

"Well," she said, walking briskly to the door, "Shall we?" She was turning the knob in her hand when Sophie raised an eyebrow and lifted the rumpled gown in her lap.

Emily released the knob as if burnt and jumped back,

looking down at herself clad only in a chemise.

"Gracious! Just imagine the consequences of that single oblivious moment. Had I somehow managed to slip out of your house unnoticed, the hue and cry that would have been raised at Sinclair House is more than I can bear to consider. Between Prissy and Beatrice, my ears would have been ringing for days." Shaking her head in appalled silence, she suddenly paused to cut her eyes over to her friend. "Do you think your father would even have noticed?"

"Odds would have been in your favor," Sophie allowed dryly.

"It's possible Colin would have been equally oblivious if he really is as interested in the past as he seems."

"True enough, Em, but perhaps it would be better not to test that theory."

Sophie smiled indulgently and stood to help her friend to dress.

"I know I never invite you, Sophie," Emily said with some chagrin, "Largely because I'm never there myself. But you are always more than welcome to come to tea with me at home. Lady Sinclair believes you to be a steadying feminine influence on me and would no doubt delight in discussing the extensive efforts the two of you have been expending on my behalf. Would you care to come with me?"

"No," Sophie said quietly, busily doing up the buttons at the back of Emily's gown, "I think I'll stay here in case my father or Colin requires anything. But thank you for the invitation. Perhaps another day?"

Emily frowned at her friend's reserved politeness, helpless as another wave of isolation washed over her. For the moment, she was glad to have her back to Sophie. The position afforded her a little privacy to hide her reaction to her friend's words as well as the thoughts currently swirling through her mind. Something was definitely going on in Sophie's life, and she couldn't understand why her friend didn't wish to confide in her.

Had she really become so self-absorbed that Sophie didn't even want to bother? Emily didn't want to believe it, but still she couldn't help wonder whether the balance of friendship was significantly weighted in her favor. Vowing to do better, she forced a little brightness into her tone, waiting as Sophie retied the chocolate brown sash around the waist of her cornflower blue gown.

"Well, I certainly can't say I blame you. It's really the last place I'd choose to spend my afternoon. A soliloquy from Beatrice is inevitable, but whether she will choose to speak to Mr. Richly's unquestionable suitability or the extensive preparations for the celebratory ball is anyone's guess."

Sophie heard the sarcasm in her friend's voice turn to melancholy and steeled herself against it as Emily continued speaking.

"I wish I didn't have to go myself, but I think it might be best this way. Finished?" She turned her head to look back over her shoulder at her friend. Seeing the nod, and feeling the straightening of her skirts, she turned back to smooth the front of the dress. "Good. Now shall we?" She paused as she again reached the door and turned back to face her friend.

"You're sure there is nothing you wish to discuss with me? You don't seem at all yourself. Is anything wrong?"

"No," Sophie said with a sigh, "nothing at all. I'm just anxious over Father's excitement and exertions. Colin's newfound interest in ancient civilizations was a delightful surprise for him, and he's determined to discuss his studies as much as possible during each of Colin's visits. I just want to make sure he isn't tiring himself."

Apparently a little white lie wasn't as troubling as she thought it would be. She didn't even feel a twinge of guilt, and the fib had rolled smoothly off her tongue.

"All right," Emily said hesitantly, "but you'd tell me if there was anything bothering you, wouldn't you?"

"Of course I would," Sophie continued the lie, "Just as you'd tell me the same."

"Exactly so," Emily answered with a sticky lump in her throat.

The two friends smiled warmly, if a bit guiltily, at each

other as they linked arms and proceeded to descend the stairs.

As they stepped through the doorway of the parlour, it was obvious the two men were in close consort, speaking quietly, almost reverently. The back of the sofa hid all but a thatch of white hair bent towards a mane of golden waves. Sophie discreetly cleared her throat.

Both heads turned in unison at the interruption, and Colin helped the vicar to his feet.

"I apologize for disturbing you," Sophie said politely, "but I wanted to let you know that Emily has remembered a promised engagement with her stepmother. She's expected back at Sinclair House immediately and won't be able to continue to…er…take part in this morning's discussion."

Colin glanced at the vicar to assure himself that the older man was steady on his feet and then promptly stepped around the couch towards the pair in the doorway. He smiled before taking Emily's hand.

"Bored you already, have I?" Colin teased.

Caught utterly off guard, Emily stood mute before him.

"I imagine you've had plenty of opportunity to hear most of this before, but I confess, I'm quite fascinated with the vicar's vast collection of journals and sketches. So much has been discovered, and so much still remains, waiting to be unearthed."

"Indeed," Emily allowed.

"Are you certain your excuse to escape is not a contrived one?" he asked, feigning seriousness.

Emily could only assume several moments passed in silence as she and Sophie both stared blankly back at him.

Truly, she wanted to blurt out that it was indeed but knew she couldn't. Beyond that, her mind had frozen, and she wondered absurdly if she was to be caught in a lie. Crossing her fingers behind her back, she spoke.

"Why on earth would I wish to escape your company so soon after it's been restored to me? Truly, I wish the circumstances were such that I could stay." As her eyes slid over Sophie's face, it seemed the smile held in place there tightened a fraction, but she didn't puzzle over it, merely shifted her eyes back to Colin. Touching a hand to her brow, and then curving it around to the back of her neck, she confided, "Although, I suppose I'm lucky to have the reprieve—not expecting to see you, I didn't trouble the slightest bit over my appearance."

"Well, it wouldn't have made a bit of difference. You're as lovely as ever. I'm not sure how it happened, but you've grown even more beautiful than you were as a child."

Emily coloured slightly but smiled knowingly. "I wouldn't have believed it possible, but your skill with flattery has far surpassed even my memory of it."

Colin grinned, and Emily caught another glimpse of the boy she remembered. She indulged herself with a quiet sigh of relief before she realized he was speaking to her.

"I'd planned to call on you and your father, but with the myriad estate matters that needed attention, I just haven't had the opportunity. I'm looking forward to the pleasure of meeting your stepmother—it seems she's quite well known throughout the countryside."

Needing a moment to consider exactly how to respond to such an opening, Emily tucked her tongue in her cheek and smiled at him. And became immediately distracted.

Colin was every bit as well-formed as her mysterious stranger, she thought with some satisfaction. He was tall—taller than she had remembered, and where he had been wiry in youth, he was now solid. Wide shoulders filled his coat without need of padding, and she had seen the muscles of his legs tighten with masculine strength as he moved. Yet his touch had been gentle, almost reverent.

The stranger in the woods had been more imposing—taller, harder, darker, and certainly more dangerous.

Utterly exasperated, Emily wasn't in the mood to ponder why her traitorous mind persisted in these unwanted comparisons. Colin was respectable, familiar, and dear. So why was she so intent on comparing him to someone she hadn't even really met and didn't much care to know? It was a mystery, to be sure, and one that she was not particularly enthusiastic to solve.

Her eyes rapidly refocused on Colin, who was watching

her expectantly, and she realized that he was still awaiting her response.

"Of course we'd be delighted to have you visit," she assured him hurriedly, hoping he hadn't said anything more while she was lost in thought. "You and my father no doubt have much to discuss, and my stepmother will, of course, be charmed. However, consider yourself duly warned. You will most certainly be cajoled into holding Lady Priscilla on your lap."

"I beg your pardon," Colin asked.

"Prissy is her ladyship's rather termagant terrier. The dog has assumed the task of judging any and all visitors to Sinclair House. If Prissy likes you, you can do no wrong. If she doesn't, well, you'll see…" Emily smiled impishly and added impulsively, "Oh, it's so good to see you!"

"Then perhaps I could call on you tomorrow? I must meet with my estate manager in the morning, but I'll be finished by midday. Might I persuade you to accompany me on a ride about the countryside? You can show me all that's changed since I've been gone."

"That sounds perfect. Then I'll tell my father and stepmother to expect you for tea?"

"Wonderful. Until tomorrow then."

"Until tomorrow," she agreed smiling. Delighted with the arrangement and Colin as well, she turned to Sophie, who appeared to be clenching her teeth rather ferociously.

"Sophie are you all right?" she asked with concern. "You look a little pale."

"Of course," Sophie replied with forced cheerfulness. She couldn't very well tell Emily that seeing she and Colin together, holding hands, was harder than she had expected it to be. "I'm fine, really."

So assured, Emily patted her friend's arm, thanked her for tea, and assured her that she could find her own way out. She then hurried down the hall, slowing her pace to snatch up her hat and gloves from the hall table before darting out the back door into the garden.

The second horse grazed lazily beside Gypsy, but as Emily came forward, he turned his head to look at her and

straightened, as if sensing he was about to be judged and
determined to show himself well.

Colin's gelding was certainly a beauty, but Emily
decided she would choose the stranger's horse over this one
any day. Like the stranger himself, his horse had been
disdainful, arrogant, dark, and dangerous. This one was
amenable, gentle, and friendly. Tame.

And therein lay the difference, Emily realized. Given
her inability to escape the pull of her dark stranger, even in
dreams, she apparently desired excitement over
contentment, danger over security, and the devil over the
angel. Or she imagined she did.

It hardly mattered. There wasn't the slightest possibility
of a future with the stranger. Still, she realized she'd like
the matter resolved all the same. She wasn't at all content
with the way her thoughts had been tending for the last
twenty-four hours.

Perhaps she simply needed a bit of daring, a bit of
danger. An adventure that allowed for more participation
than just eavesdropping. After all, she'd been doing that
since she was a child. Admittedly she had not had the
luxury of breeches, but she had always thought of them
more as a means to an end rather than the high point itself.
Ambushing a pair of highwaymen was serious business
indeed, and she imagined that afterwards, regardless of her
success or failure, she'd view a great many things in a
different light entirely. It was now but a day away.

Tomorrow night would shake away the errant thoughts,
and she could be sensible again. She would be resolute
where Colin was concerned rather than ambivalent, and her
thoughts would no longer stray to where they had no
purpose. Best to be optimistic, but if by some chance she
was unsuccessful in sloughing away the thrill the stranger
continued to inspire, a second meeting with the man was
sure to put her off. She would no longer be able to gloss
over his unpleasantness. He would just be another pompous
man, and she would be glad to strike him down a notch.

Satisfied, she moved towards Gypsy, and noticed that
Colin's horse was still holding her in its gentle gaze. It was

almost as if he had read her thoughts and was lamenting her decision.

"A pity you don't agree," Emily tossed at the horse.

A timely snort seemed to be its answer.

"I'll have my adventure, mind you. It could very well be my last chance, and I don't intend to let it slip away untested. Being male, you couldn't possibly understand."

* * *

"What a delightful surprise, Emily dear," Lady Sinclair gushed. "We rarely have a chance to talk, just the three of us. Isn't that right, Lady Priscilla?"

Emily wrinkled her nose in distaste as her stepmother turned to touch noses with her pet. Apparently Prissy had been elevated in status to distinguished guest and was now allowed the dubious privilege of sitting on the sofa beside her ladyship. Emily suspected this new distinction might be due to the lack of any other guests for tea and couldn't help but feel a stirring of pity for her stepmother. But a second look at Prissy and the charitable thought all but dissolved. The dog was showing tiny sharp white teeth and licking her lips menacingly.

Emily wanted to snarl right back at her. Instead she pointedly ignored the little beast as Lady Sinclair began what would no doubt be a very long-winded opinion.

"Emily dear, you really should try not to be so forgetful. Lady Priscilla and I always take our morning tea at precisely half past ten, yet you seem incapable of remembering that. How do you think you'll be able to manage a household if you cannot keep to schedules and remember appointments?"

Prissy appeared to sneeze, but it was possible that she had simply been nodding and snorting loudly in agreement.

"I suppose I'll simply have to do better," Emily answered humbly, darting her eyes at the tea tray in a not-so-subtle hint.

She wondered whether it would be impolite to reach for one of the pastries before Lady Sinclair offered. Oddly, it seemed her ladyship was in no hurry to partake of the tray's offering and was, in fact, warming to her subject.

"Dear Desmond will no doubt be irritated if you are inattentive to his needs. And my dear, it's best to not irritate your husband. If you do, they feel compelled to lecture and criticize, tiresome in itself, but worse, it mistakenly gives them the idea that they are in charge when that is clearly not the case."

Coming from any other lady, such comments would have struck Emily as very forward-thinking, but knowing her stepmother as she did, she wasn't the slightest bit impressed. Beatrice most definitely held sway over her "charges", namely the running of Sinclair House and the upkeep of the Sinclair reputation, but Emily was determined not to be bound by similar shortsightedness.

She considered informing her stepmother that she emphatically refused to marry 'Dear Desmond', let alone worry about his needs, but wisely refrained.

Instead she watched expectantly as Lady Sinclair chose a trio of wafer-thin biscuits from the tray and arranged them on a plate. Emily held out her hand to accept the plate and was taken aback when her stepmother offered it to Prissy. Emily gasped and let her hand fall, then watched in disbelief as Prissy sniffed the offering, tossed her a look of triumph, and then nibbled the treats slowly. Tauntingly. Emily narrowed her eyes at the pair of them but kept silent.

"I plan to do my best to help you, my dear," her stepmother announced, selecting a biscuit for herself and taking a bite. "I have decided to guide you in the art of manners and household management."

Emily raised her brows in disbelief. *Manners?!* The woman had served her pet before her own stepdaughter. Even now she remained seemingly oblivious to Emily's blank stare as she alternately nibbled and sipped. Emily opened her mouth to protest her stepmother's ridiculous suggestion, but Lady Sinclair waved her hand in dismissal of the unspoken objection.

"I know, I know, my dear. I'm sure your dear mother advised you on such matters, but it's been some time since your instruction, and I'm sure your memory could use a little refreshing."

She certainly could use a little refreshing, Emily thought caustically, her stomach growling. She turned to glare at Prissy, who licked her lips loudly and gave Emily a superior smile.

While she deliberated on what The Beatrice Sinclair School of Manners and Household Management might entail, her stepmother absently poured a cup of tea and handed it across to Emily. She neglected to offer cream, sugar, or lemon, but luckily Emily liked it well enough without as long as it was strong and hot. As no accompaniment appeared to be coming her way in the foreseeable future, she slowly sipped her tea, and wondered how to avoid this training her stepmother so wanted to provide.

"You must not think that I am in any way disparaging your dear mama by suggesting a bit of further instruction," Lady Sinclair said, reaching for another biscuit. "I'm sure that whatever I might suggest will only serve to remind you of the things that she has already taught. And of course, your mother did not have the pleasure of knowing Dear Desmond. You'll find that I can give you a few specific hints as to how to go on with your new husband."

Tea with her stepmother was turning out to be even more of a trial than Emily had believed possible. She was about to ignore the rules of etiquette, rise, and fix her own plate, when Lady Sinclair stared across at her with a little frown.

"No biscuits today, Emily? You really should try one. Cook has gotten them so light and thin and crisp, we can indulge in twice as many! Isn't that right, Lady Priscilla? That's mama's angel." She went on to make, in Emily's opinion, exceedingly obnoxious kissing noises in the dog's direction. Irritated beyond manners, Emily reached across Prissy and helped herself to a quantity of crispy biscuits. It went unnoticed as her stepmother continued to talk about her plans for Emily's instruction.

She herself was happily occupied nibbling and sipping when she finally remembered Colin and their arrangement that he come to tea the next day. *That* would surely divert her stepmother's attention.

"How thoughtless of me," she began, brushing the crumbs from her fingers, "I don't know how I could have forgotten to mention it. I was at the vicarage earlier, visiting with Sophie and her father, and you won't believe who was there before me. Lord Colin Willoughsby."

Her stepmother's eyes snapped immediately up, focusing sharply on hers, and Emily struggled to contain a crow of triumph. With deceptive calm, Beatrice lowered her forgotten biscuit back to her plate (a rare occurrence indeed) and took up her teacup.

"Indeed?" It was spoken as a question, and Emily understood she was now supposed to furnish full details. As expected, her stepmother's attention had been fully drawn by this tidbit of news. Drawn, that is, away from herself.

"As you know," Emily began smoothly, happy to impart the news that would momentarily silence her stepmother, "Lord Henry Willoughsby died recently, and his son Colin, who had been commissioned in the army for some years, has returned to assume the title. There's to be a ball in his honor, but surely you are aware of that." Beatrice kept silent, and Emily bit her lip, knowing the gossip mill would be ground tirelessly for full details later. Finally ready to add the crowning touch, she revealed all.

"Being an old friend of the family, Colin was anxious to call on us. So, I invited him for tea tomorrow. He expressed considerable excitement over the prospect of meeting you. I hope that won't be any trouble…"

Barely suppressing the urge to giggle, Emily raised her own teacup to shield her twitching lips as her stepmother carefully put hers down in order to properly dust away the collection of crumbs now adorning her person. Prissy apparently got a noseful, and sneezed quite messily, before jumping off of the sofa in disgust.

Or, Emily supposed, her disgruntled exit might instead be a reaction to the prospect of visitors to tea a second day in a row. Emily smugly believed a little competition would do the little priss a world of good.

"Trouble? Don't be ridiculous! Perhaps your first lesson should be that wealthy, titled gentlemen do not cause trouble—it is, quite simply, beneath them," Lady Sinclair informed her reproachfully. That bit of wisdom imparted, Beatrice was no longer able to suppress her barely veiled excitement. Pursed lips curled up at the edges, frown lines disappeared, eyes sparkled, and cheeks pinked with anticipation.

"We shall be delighted to have him and will do whatever we must to prepare on such short notice. We must make sure your dear father is available for tea tomorrow. He's often too busy, and that's to be expected. After all, he is without a doubt the most respected, most important man in the county. But he'll no doubt make himself available for an old friend. Perhaps I should discuss the menu with Cook. She won't be pleased, but these are special circumstances, as I'm sure you agree. We must uphold the reputation of Sinclair House, and to do so, what better than an incomparable tea tray? Let's see now. What shall we serve? Watercress sandwiches? A selection of iced cakes? I'm rather partial to the ones spread with raspberry preserves. And I do so love meringues…"

Emily listened with half an ear as her stepmother rambled on about culinary possibilities. She'd been expecting such a response and took the opportunity it afforded to thoroughly enjoy her plate of pastries and a second cup of tea, nodding every now and then to give the impression that she was listening intently.

She was just finishing her tea when she became aware of the uncharacteristic silence. Reluctantly she looked up to see her stepmother staring into space, brow furrowed. Suddenly her visage cleared, and she turned towards Emily, her eyes bright with determination and a superior smile playing about her lips. Emily groaned silently and resumed eating, hoping to once again be ignored. It didn't work.

"Emily, my dear, I've just been struck by an idea," Beatrice announced proudly.

Heaven help us all.

"Tomorrow's tea offers the perfect opportunity for you

to begin your training in earnest. You must accompany me to meet with Cook this very afternoon. Such a task will readily demonstrate how to deal with kitchen staff. You will also come away with exquisite instruction on how to plan an afternoon tea so that it is simple but elegant, light but restorative."

There must be a legitimate sounding reason that she couldn't do that. What exactly could it be? She needed a reason Beatrice would consider acceptable—no easy task.

"I cannot think of a more enjoyable or informative manner in which to spend the afternoon," she began hesitantly, "However, I…ahhh…promised Mrs. Tattenham that I would read some letters she has recently received from her relations in Kent."

It was a standing arrangement between Emily and the old woman, although Emily had not planned to fulfill the obligation today. But why not?

Perhaps she had overlooked the simplicity of honesty. Or, at the very least, the sense in actually carrying out the fibs she was obliged to tell.

Desirous of a quick escape, Emily added, "In fact, I do believe I am late already. I'd best be on my way…?" At times like these she wondered if it were possible to will someone to respond in the manner you wished them to.

"Oh, very well." Beatrice shooed her away with some disappointment.

But as Emily turned to go, her ladyship began talking in earnest. "There is so much I need to impress upon you, and time is so very short. We simply must begin spending our days together. It is disappointing that we cannot start your lessons today, but perhaps that's best. Tomorrow's tea promises to be an important event, and we've been given little notice. I'll need to work a miracle."

And remember not to neglect the appetites of the human guests…

After several minutes of animated muttering on the subject of what to serve, her stepmother finally noticed Emily's expectant look and waved her hand in dismissal. "Oh for heaven's sake, go. But don't run, my dear. Ladies never run.

As an afterthought, Emily scooped up the biscuits remaining on the tray and wrapped them in a napkin, tossing a quick explanation to her stepmother. "I'll just take these for Mrs. Tattenham—you know how she loves Cook's biscuits."

Inevitably, Beatrice was calling after her as she hurried through the door. "Make certain a groom accompanies you!"

Biting back an oath, Emily hurried upstairs, inordinately grateful to finally be alone again.

6

"...I am confident the highwayman will soon be apprehended. After all, the Willoughsby ball is only days away, and surely the villain would not dare interfere with such a grand event..."

LETTER FROM LADY BEATRICE SINCLAIR TO MR. DESMOND RICHLY
27 OCTOBER 1818

Fighting acute impatience, Emily checked the clock for the sixth time in as many minutes. She couldn't believe it was nearly time. Her second chance at adventure was about to commence.

Walking to the cheval glass in the corner, she examined her appearance with a critical eye and decided she could definitely pass for a boy if she hunched over and kept her head down. She had bound her breasts much more tightly this time, making it more than a little painful to breathe too deeply, and had braided her hair tightly and pinned it up under the filthy wool cap. She was ready.

Emily sighed as a definite grumble issued forth from her empty stomach. She had decided to plead a headache in order to skip dinner and remain in her room to get ready, but she was beginning to regret the decision. She happened to know Cook had made plum pudding for dessert. If these nighttime excursions were going to require that she miss the most substantive meal of the day, Emily thought grumpily, she was going to have to weigh her priorities. She would need to see what her sacrifice netted her this evening.

While the 'gentleman highwayman' had been obligingly forthcoming with details of the carriage occupants—right down to the jewel box—he had been frustratingly stingy in revealing its schedule or location. Perhaps Sneeves would need to guess as she would. Likely he wouldn't venture out before twilight. She assumed he'd crawl out of his hole under cover of darkness to attempt a bit of cowardly thievery. With luck the pair of them would be routed this very evening. If only she was certain of the planned location of the hold-up. The London road passed through a dense stand of trees not far from the vicarage graveyard. She supposed it was a likely and convenient spot for Sneeves to conceal himself, but still she wished she had more definitive details. All she could do at this point was hide amid those trees until something happened. Or wait while nothing did.

She was away with almost disappointing ease—it appeared she could have walked boldly through the front hall without anyone noticing. So much for careful planning and precise timing.

It was a relief to set her horse to gallop. The chilly wind enveloped her in its tingly cloak, and her heartbeat caught in her throat. The sun had gone down moments ago, and taken with it every bit of the day's warmth and certainty—the evening was alive with mystery, and she was anxious to meet its challenge. She felt wonderful—alert, excited, and just the tiniest bit nervous. Simply perfect.

Now that was enough. She would have time later to relive each thrilling detail; right now she needed to concentrate on the task ahead of her. She needed her eyes to search the shadows and her ears to sift through the night's whispers in order to be certain she was alone, and likely to remain so. While it would be disastrously inconvenient to be followed by someone in her father's employ, it could very well prove deadly if she was intercepted by the highwayman himself.

With only her vest and cap for warmth, Emily wondered if her sudden bout of shivering was attributable to the evening chill or fear of the evening's possible outcome. Either way, it had her shaking steadily over the course of her journey.

Luckily, she met no one and was soon well hidden in a thicket of trees with her horse tethered and silent a few yards away. There was nothing to do now but wait.

* * *

Sophie was thinking the very same.

She'd been pouring the tea her father preferred after dinner when she'd heard a horse's unexpected approach. Wondering over it as she laid a thin slice of lemon in each of two cups, and added a single sugar wafer to her own, she was startled to hear a tentative knock on the door. Obviously her father was as curious as she, for he shuffled out of his library in order to answer the door himself. Hearing the voice of the visitor, Sophie cringed and cheered at once, luckily all without an audience. She was thrilled over the unexpected opportunity to spend a bit of time with Colin but regretful that she'd not have an opportunity to neaten her appearance. No sooner had she raised her hands to smooth over her hair and tuck away any escaped strands than she heard approaching footsteps, her cue to snatch them right back down again. The two men had found her busily attending the tea tray.

Two cozy hours had now passed, and her father was beginning to tire. Sophie felt the slightest bit devious for waiting out his resigned apologies and trip up to bed. Yet that didn't stop her from desperately hoping that Colin wouldn't leave before it happened. Perhaps it would be best if she gave her father a nudge before he fell face down into the dusty tome he was perusing and startled himself awake with a fit of coughing.

Just as she was to offer her tentative suggestion, Sophie glanced over at Colin and chanced to see him gazing at her in a curious fashion. Words caught in her throat, and giddy confusion swirled inside her, bumping thoughts of her father casually aside. When she finally recovered, puzzling moments had passed, and she was forestalled once again, this time by her father.

"Ahem." His throat sounded dry, and apparently it was,

for he took one last sip of tea before continuing. The snap of cup on saucer was startling in the quiet room, but her father appeared not to notice. "I do believe I am bound for my bed. I've a need to rest up before you visit us again, my dear boy."

Colin smiled easily, "Thank you, sir, for an enlightening evening. It's been quite a time since I've enjoyed one quite as much."

"Then perhaps it is time to find yourself a wife, my boy," the vicar answered, with a pointed look at Colin and a matching one aimed at his daughter. He then rose slowly and padded towards the parlour door. Sophie rose to kiss him on the cheek as he passed, determined to keep her opinions of his lack of subtlety to herself.

"Goodnight, Father. Pleasant dreams. I will take care of Colin."

"That, my dear, is my fondest wish," he whispered awfully loudly. Without turning around, Sophie knew Colin had heard the words and now felt her heart start its nervous beat.

"Shame on you," she whispered back, conscious of her volume and without any heat in her words.

Closing her eyes on his mischievous smile, she waited until she heard him cross the threshold and leave them alone. Then she turned back to her guest. And felt her heart sink a bit as he rose to leave.

"I should best be off as well. Otherwise I'm bound to drop off to sleep right here, and then you'd have to deal with me in the morning as well."

Although wishing she could echo her father's sentiment that that was *her* fondest wish, she decided against it, supposing she'd not get away with it as easily as he'd managed.

"I'm certain you wouldn't be all that much trouble."

"I can't decide whether to take that as a compliment or consider it a challenge," he teased, his eyes crinkling at the edges and his mouth quirked up a bit at the corners.

"Do both," Sophie boldly suggested, hoping he didn't notice her heartbeat racing at her throat.

All at once he was gazing at her in the same curious manner he had just moments before. She couldn't decide whether to be encouraged or frustrated.

"Perhaps I will do that," he finally conceded with a quiet nod.

As he moved to the door, she turned to proceed him out, but he caught her elbow. The shock of his touch jolted through her, but she didn't snatch her arm away. Instead she lifted her eyes to his in time to see their purposeful descent. His lips fit over hers, smooth and cool, but he allowed them only one caress before he withdrew.

"You are hard to resist, Sweet Sophie."

He almost looked apologetic, and Sophie wondered whether it was for himself or her. She supposed it wouldn't be appropriate to demand, "Don't!" before fisting her hands in the lapels of his coat to yank him back down again. And while that was a pity, it couldn't be helped. She wasn't a strumpet, for heaven's sakes. She'd already flirted with him, although not quite so boldly as her father. All things considered, the man had had enough to deal with for one evening.

Touching her lips, she pivoted on her heels and led the way into the hall, her eyes glancing over everything in sight. She could barely keep still, and it wasn't until she had bid him goodnight and closed and locked the door behind him that she let herself react as she wished to.

* * *

If any of his London acquaintances could see him now, walking his horse through the Devon countryside in the near-darkness, it would undoubtedly confirm their belief that he was a trifle eccentric. As being labeled eccentric apparently afforded a little more freedom than was typical in polite society, the descriptor was just fine with Brand.

He had spent an exhausting two days in his father's tedious company before realizing that the old man was not even close to loosening his grip on mortality. In fact, he had a reasonable suspicion that the earl had faked the spell that had spurred the summons. His excuse? As it had been so eloquently phrased by the old man himself, he had wanted only to request that his son grant a "dying man's last wish". In other words, he wanted Brand to find himself a wife and begin working on his nursery. Well, Brand thought, he'd be damned if he was going to fall for that ruse—even after his father *was* dead.

Realizing the summons was nothing more than another effort on the earl's part to gain control of his son's life, Brand had bid his father adieu and quickly arranged to depart his family's seat in Cornwall and return to Devon and the easy comfort of Colin's home. He'd taken his time on the return journey, stopping twice to water his horse and quench his own thirst. Since he was now within an hour of his destination, and confident of his safety despite the encroaching dark, he had decided to complete the journey on foot, giving his stallion some well-deserved rest. If he met with any trouble, his greatcoat concealed two pistols, primed and loaded.

Ever cautious, Brand remained alert even while he let his mind wander to a feisty auburn-haired beauty and their dawn appointment in four days time. He certainly couldn't claim it was the first time in the last two days that his thoughts had taken such a turn. Never had he imagined he would so eagerly anticipate a duel. Admittedly, this duel was not of the typical sort, but a duel it assuredly was. And he was sure that the spirited hoyden who had challenged him would readily agree.

Although Brand felt confident that he would emerge victorious, if he willingly admitted it to himself, he didn't even care who won or lost. For some reason, he simply wanted to see her again, a fact which Brand found exceedingly odd, as he knew nothing of her. Well, that wasn't entirely true. He knew she was headstrong, argumentative, fiery, and lovely. Although she had been wet and dirty from the storm and her fall, it hadn't been enough to disguise her beauty, unadorned as it was except by nature.

The mud and leaves clinging to her hadn't disguised a

thing. Her skin had glowed like pearls, flushed more with life than cold, and tracks of freckles had run across her nose. Eyes the color of sapphires had blazed at him, as sharp and deep as the gemstone itself. He'd seen several smiles from her, each more intriguing than the last. All had been at his expense. He'd not yet enjoyed the pleasure of her laugh and was looking forward to the chance of luring one out of her.

And then their had been that stringy, sodden, mess of hair...a mesmerizing fire-gold underneath. He was certain he had never seen hair quite that color.

Brand allowed that she would never be labeled a beauty by society's standards. To their critical, prejudiced eyes, her hair would simply be seen as unfashionably red. Her complexion would be said to be too rosy, her lips too full, her disposition too animated, and her manner too daring.

He grinned and realized it was no wonder he had become obsessed with her and no reason he should avoid the harmless bit of flirtation she provoked. He'd quickly convinced himself that she could not possibly be married. No man would allow his wife to ride about in such a fashion, a temptation to all who came upon her. Still, he knew he shouldn't trifle with her—shouldn't even be considering it—but it was too late. In truth only a few moments had passed before he had decided to kiss her. Probably it had been as soon as she'd spoken to him in such a daring manner. She hadn't cared a wit for his title or his fortune—hadn't even known of their existence—but likely would not have cared if she had. His attraction had been immediate.

So as long as he was willing to risk her temper, he could see no reason not to proceed. He smiled in anticipation and then in amusement as he predicted her initial reaction to such a liberty. With luck he would catch her off guard. It would be more pleasant all around if she decided to enjoy it as much as he planned to.

His musings were cut short by the realization that he was rapidly approaching a band of trees. The ribbon of road disappeared shortly past the towering elms standing sentry to a dark threshold. He'd heard mention of highwaymen in the area and thought it best to err on the side of caution. Slipping his free hand into the deep pocket of his greatcoat, he rested it on the handle of his pistol. His horse darted a look back at him, so he rubbed his hand along the stallion's neck. Seeing no warning signs of trouble to come, he let his mind drift while his body remained on alert.

Neither of them had volunteered a name. It was an unprecedented turn of events as far as he was concerned. Everywhere he went, whether he wished them to or not, ladies and gentlemen both were intent upon introducing themselves. Ladies especially. But not her, not here. He was in Devon now, and apparently things were a far sight different. He may very well stay longer than he'd intended.

He wondered whether he could arrange another meeting with his bold and mysterious miss after the race. She was bound to be angry and embarrassed over a loss, wanting only to see the back of him. Perhaps Colin knew her and could be persuaded to arrange a formal introduction.

Suddenly he heard it. The barest of whispers. Someone or something had moved in the trees off to his right. He kept walking lest he rouse suspicion, and although he didn't hear anything further, he decided it wouldn't hurt to move along and then double back to investigate.

* * *

Emily had to admit to being extremely uncomfortable. The air was raw, and the wind carried a sting, making her long for her cozy bed and a warm cup of chocolate. The dratted breeches were itchy, the stench of her cap was nearly intolerable, and she had already been squatting for the better part of an hour. Add to that the fact that her feet were stuck in the mud—again—and it was turning out to be quite a disappointing evening.

The thunderstorm of two days ago had apparently drenched this shady band of trees quite thoroughly. While the water was mostly gone, the ground itself was like a bog, sucking at everything that ventured across it. The tips of Emily's boots kept disappearing from view, and she had been amusing herself by attempting to retrieve them as silently as possible.

Thoroughly disgusted, she wondered whether all adventures demanded patience, tolerance, and tedious time spent in unpleasant surroundings. If so, she wasn't at all certain she was cut out for further adventuring. Wasn't anything ever going to happen?

Seeing a long, thin branch lying a little away from her and assuming it had likely been as much a victim of the storm as she had, she reached for it and began scratching marks in the muddy landscape that surrounded her. Her inclination to produce her own name whenever presented with a writing implement was as strong as any other young lady's, and it wasn't long before she began spelling out her given name, adding gaudy flourishes to amuse herself.

Just as she began to add her surname, she was reminded of her surroundings, and spared a moment to glance curiously about, not at all expecting to see anything she'd not seen two minutes ago. Proven correct, she returned the branch to her less-than-pristine page just where she'd started the curving stroke of an 'S'. A mischievous thought teased and taunted her into pulling her writing implement diagonally down to form a 'W'. Smiling with intent, she added the other letters, gracing the final 'y' with a flourish to match the one in 'Emily'.

Emily Willoughsby. Em-i-ly Will-oughs-by. Something about it didn't sound quite right, but she couldn't quite determine what it was exactly. It seemed the sort of name children would chant as part of a silly rhyme. She puzzled over it a moment longer before a glance down informed her that it was once again time to extricate her boots. Apparently this was as exciting as the evening was likely to get. As she balanced herself on her right foot in order to pull her left free of the sludge, she inadvertently leaned on the twig she held in her right hand, causing it to splinter with what seemed a crackle of dread. Closing her eyes tightly and clenching her teeth, she prayed that at this very moment she was alone in the dark.

She strained her ears, trying to hear over the frantic

beating of her heart, and heard nothing. Much relieved, she relaxed and gently laid the crutch away from her as she moved her foot to an untried location.

Just then she heard it—at long last—the familiar sounds of a horse, walking slowly. She scanned the trees for visitors to her dismal hiding place, but her eyes didn't alight on anything unexpected for a long, tense moment. Finally, the forms of a horse and its companion took shape before her eyes, and she blinked to be certain she hadn't imagined them. Shadows were everywhere, leaning over and stretching out—it was now dark enough such that she could barely discern the silhouettes moving casually through the darkening forest. Seemingly they hadn't a care.

Could this possibly be the highwayman? Surely not, unless this Sneeves truly was incompetent. Emily almost felt a touch of sympathy for his steely voiced accomplice.

Having been deprived of the opportunity to get a look at Sneeves in the cemetery, hidden as she was behind Sophie, she could only assume that this was not he. That high-pitched, whining voice simply could not belong to this man. This was a gentleman, one who carried himself confidently, with an air of command. Evidently he was also a fool— didn't he know better than to be wandering about in the dark—through a boggy forest!? Even if he was unaware that highwaymen were lurking about, he really should have more sense. Well, she would keep her eye on him, if nothing else, for his own safety.

Not that she could provide him with much assistance if the need arose. Any demands or threats she might have cause to make were, in effect, quite empty. She truly hoped Sneeves hadn't the courage to call her bluff.

She had no bullets, and a pistol wasn't much use without them.

When she'd snuck the gun from her father's study, she hadn't for a moment considered that it might not be loaded. Stupid carelessness. If only she'd spared a moment to check, and then another to load the bullets! The way the evening was tending, she could have easily spared the time for dinner as well. And now she wished she had.

Tearing her gaze from the intruder, of whom she was irrationally envious simply because he was moving, she focused on freeing her other boot. Her irritation with herself and her impatience with the evening thus far caused her to pull a bit too forcefully. Quite unexpectedly, her boot came free of its muddy encasement and had her flailing to recover. The best she could manage was to roll sideways, holding her breath with nerves. As the man and his horse continued their slow progress through the trees and out of sight, she let her breath out slowly with immeasurable relief. She checked her boots and steadied herself on what she prayed was firmer ground. It could be a long wait.

A quarter of an hour later she could stand no more. The muscles in her legs were cramped and sore, her boots had sunken into the quagmire once again, and she was thoroughly bored. She decided she could risk the noise that would result if she stood, stretched, and moved to check on Gypsy. After all, it appeared the trees were deserted.

And why shouldn't they be? No one else was foolish enough to loiter about in this gloomy section of forest waiting for, it would seem, nothing at all.

With a grimace of pain, she slowly rose to her full height, surprised at how weak and numb her legs felt as a result of all that crouching. Her hands, one clutching the pistol, hung limply at her sides as she stretched her neck. Even knowing it wasn't loaded, she felt comforted by its heavy weight in her hand. Besides, she'd bluffed her way out of some tricky situations in her life—perhaps they'd all been practice for this.

The quietly voiced words no more than a foot behind her had her jerking her hands up, raising the pistol to a firing position.

"Toss the gun away from you and turn around."

Emily was so startled by the fact that someone had managed to sneak up behind her that she failed to grasp the words. She whipped around and began to extend her arm, her index finger clenched tightly on the gun's trigger. The new arrival lashed out at the pistol and easily knocked it from her grip, leaving her hand throbbing. He threw himself heavily against her, and her weakened legs immediately gave way so that he landed on top of her. Emily felt the breath whoosh out of her under his crushing weight, and unable to help it, she moaned in pain.

Emily soon found that trying to extricate herself from her assailant was going to be no small task, especially as he had pinned her arms. After a few desperate moments of writhing and bucking, she admitted it was no use. He was simply too big. He didn't even appear to be expending any energy controlling her frantic movements. Realizing the futility in continuing to struggle, she stopped and looked up into his face. And simply stared as her mouth went dry.

If pain wasn't pulsing through her body and wetness creeping through her clothes, she might have believed she was dreaming again. But this was no dream—this was cruel reality. Her stranger, it seemed, was destined to have yet another victory over her, this one even more ignominious than the first.

What is he doing here?

Emily wondered if she'd been wrong. She hadn't believed it possible that this man was the owner of the cruel voice she had overheard, arranging the hold-ups and hissing out orders, but perhaps it had just been wishful thinking. The possibility now loomed before her, nearly as depressing as her apparent failure as a heroine. She determinedly pushed her suspicion aside to focus on something over which she still had some measure of control.

At all costs, she must keep her identity a secret. Even a flicker of recognition and she could very well be in big trouble. It was true that she had never revealed her name to him, but surely he could find out who she was without much trouble. He struck her as being extremely thorough and efficient, not to mention utterly unsympathetic. She determinedly tried to keep her expression blank and innocent, then added a bit of sullen so as to be convincing as a boy.

"What the devil do you think you're doing, boy?" he demanded. His voice was harsh and belittling, and it irritated Emily to no end.

Before she could prevent herself, she responded in kind.
"It is certainly no business of yours!"

Emily closed her eyes and wished that she could sink
fully into the mud. Why hadn't she troubled to disguise her
voice or even altered her speech to match that of a
stableboy?

Drat! Drat! Drat!

The brute was lying on top of her now, and so she had
plenty of time to notice the disbelieving recognition in his
eyes before she shut her own. Remaining silent, and hoping
that she would disappear—or he would—she was unprepared
when he reached up and plucked her cap off. She felt a few
escaped curls spill out around her face.

"I thought so!" he said sharply. "What the devil are you
doing out here?"

"I don't really think that's any of your concern," Emily
said curtly. "Now do you think you might consider getting
off of me? You're rather heavy."

He shifted his weight but continued to pin her down. He
even had the nerve to grin at her! She gritted her teeth and
kept silent.

Clearly amused, he spoke again, "Might I say that you
are looking just as beautiful as the last time our paths
crossed? No one wears mud quite so appealingly as you
do."

Emily scowled, truly wishing she had the use of her
hands.

"May I get up?" she bit out.

"Not until you explain what you're doing out here, in the
middle of nowhere, dressed as a boy, and brandishing a
pistol. You aren't by any chance a highwayman are you?"
he asked soberly, eyebrows raised.

"Certainly not," she answered contemptuously, "I did,
however, assume *you* might be one."

He appeared willing to ignore the implication. "Well, if
you're not out here for some nefarious purpose, then why
were you hiding? And how might you explain your
unconventional mode of dress?" he asked, eyeing her snug
breeches with a lazy smile.

Emily felt colour flood her face.

"There's no time to explain," she snapped irritably, "we might be overheard. You've already managed to make enough noise to reveal our presence to anyone in the vicinity."

She tried to shift away from him, tried to pull her hands from his grasp, but it was hopeless and exhausting.

"On the contrary. We've plenty of time and appear to be quite conveniently alone. And I must say, *I'm* not the least bit uncomfortable."

Emily bit her lip to kept silent, wishing she could bite his instead.

The thought had her tensing in embarrassment and her eyes roaming everywhere, anywhere so that they not meet his. Her next thought, if it was possible, was equally as shocking. She suddenly realized that if she really wanted to, she could kiss him, right this very minute. His face was positioned right above hers, and she guessed she could lean up just enough for their lips to touch before he realized what her intentions were. But then she'd be at his mercy, and she couldn't imagine what to expect of such an eventuality.

Part of her wished she was brave enough to risk it, and the other part was appalled she'd even considered it. Still, she spent another moment doing just that. Once again, this time because of near-darkness, she was unable to discern the true color of his hair, but she could see that he was in need of a shave. Reflecting the moonlight, his teeth were straight and white and possessed of an almost predatory glow. She shivered, and when her eyes flicked up to his, she saw that he knew precisely what she considered. Now deceptively black with a bit of gilt at the edges, his eyes taunted her, tempted her further. Until nervously, she tore her wide-eyed gaze away from his mesmerizing one to puff out a breath of almost feverish resolve.

She couldn't do it. It would only stroke his ego, and she couldn't be responsible for such an eventuality. That, and she had to admit to being a bit skittish over the matter.

From the corner of her eye, she saw him smile, but his apparent amusement couldn't conceal the fact that his muscles had tensed along with her own and now relaxed, just as hers did.

She needed to dislodge him and get away. Particularly as he had an extraordinarily annoying habit of reading her thoughts. Absolutely nothing good could come of this. Faced with a standoff between them, she would most certainly lose. He appeared to be enjoying himself immensely, fully aware that he was interrupting her plans and content to do so. She would need to concede at least a modicum of control. Although, lying as she was in the mud beneath him, she wondered if she could be considered to have even that much remaining to her.

"Very well," Emily said stiffly. She had closed her eyes, knowing that to look at him would only make matters more difficult. For she had been correct about at least one thing: face to face, he really was intolerable. And yet, she grudgingly admitted, she liked him still. It was perverse.

Amazingly, the weight of his hands lifted from hers the moment her eyes shuttered closed. She felt his knees tighten their hold on her sides but didn't open her eyes. Perhaps he thought she was ever-so-gradually falling victim to his questionable brand of charm. She would pretend it was so and bide her time. As she massaged her bruised wrists above her, she answered him.

"I don't know if you are aware," she continued slowly and evenly, avoiding his eyes, "but we've had several attacks by a highwayman in the area recently, and I have good reason to believe that there will be another attack tonight on this patch of road. So, if you'll be good enough to get off of me and be on your merry way, I can retrieve my pistol and return to my post."

"Surely you're not serious?"

She faced him with a hard, silent stare, expecting it would be sufficiently convincing.

"Let me see if I understand correctly. You thought to disguise yourself, hide among the trees, and ambush the unsuspecting fellow with what is undoubtedly an empty pistol?"

Emily's features settled into a mutinous look, and she

kept her thoughts (and curses) to herself. Still, she was unable to avoid clenching her fists.

"You realize that highwaymen are armed, don't you? How else would you suppose they could expect their victims' compliance? *Is* your pistol loaded?" he inquired lazily, glancing at her threatening gesture with apparently very little concern.

Emily moved her gaze back to his.

"No," she said tightly, "I was in a hurry. What made you assume that it wasn't?"

"If it was, I'd have a bullet hole attesting to your inexpert handling. First horses and now firearms." He shook his head in disbelief. "Do you even know how to fire a pistol?"

"Certainly," she bristled, fiercely angry over his accusations of her ineptitude and now desperately wishing to send her fist into his smug-lipped jaw. Instead she answered tightly, "If you'd care to loan me a pistol and act as target, I can demonstrate."

He ignored her suggestion.

"Ahhh…a mark in your favor. Well then, as I'm going to have to stay here and confirm that you're telling the truth, I believe I should at least have your name."

At once, Emily recalled with sickly clarity that her name was written not three feet from her. Worse, she'd foolishly paired her given name with the surname she imagined would soon be hers. He *couldn't* see it—he absolutely mustn't. It would be horrid if he were to discover her true identity but considerably worse to have him privy to her plans to catch a husband.

Glancing back into his eyes, she could see he was much determined on an answer. She let her eyes roam, seemingly pensive, over the trees that surrounded them, trying to determine where precisely she was situated with respect to the treacherous mud markings. With any luck she was directly atop them, and his weight was smearing them into oblivion.

Seeing her discarded twig very nearly within reach of her left hand had her heartbeat speeding in her chest. A reaction she desperately hoped he hadn't noticed. She needed to think. What were her options? Lure him from the subject matter—extremely unlikely—or claw her fingers through the mud surrounding them to erase all evidence— chancy and somewhat maniacal. Neither sounded particularly worthy solutions, but with him lying heavily on top of her, there was very little she could do. Even the ultimate distraction of a wanton kiss didn't seem feasible. Eventually they'd have to get up, and who knew what would happen before 'eventually' finally occurred. She simply wasn't bold enough to find out.

"Hello? You've not forgotten me, have you? Is it that you need a bit of encouragement?" The dratted man seemed to be relishing her uneasiness.

"No, I will tell you," she assured him, stalling for time. She swept her eyelashes down shyly and stole a surreptitious glance to her left. It was there. At least she thought it was. But she'd have to reach a bit, and in truth she wasn't sure she could manage it before he realized her intent.

Deciding it was now or never, she lunged, nails down in a clawing grip, as she bucked up with her hips. After less than two seconds of indiscriminate scratching, his hands grappled with hers and, too quickly, pinned them back to the ground above her head. Oddly, he appeared not the slightest bit concerned with their intentions. It seemed it was the reaction of her lower body that had intrigued him. As he brought his face down close to hers, she could see anger and heat whirling about in his eyes, but his voice was deceptively calm.

"Encouragement it is then. Though I would have you remember that you are merely postponing the inevitable. I intend to have your name, but if you'd prefer to dally, it would be my pleasure to oblige you."

He waited until he was certain she understood the dual meaning of his words before revealing a feral smile, much intent on claiming her lips.

"Wait!" The demand felt as if it had clawed its way out of her throat, surfacing only as a whisper. Her body was still tingling from its scandalous press against the solid line of his, and she wasn't at all ready for further indecencies with this man. Her heartbeat roared in her ears, and her breath came with difficulty. She needed a minute to recover but rather doubted a lifetime would be sufficient.

"Now," he commanded, his eyes hard and unwavering.

What could she say? Her mind groped for anything while her eyes stared into the hypnotic depths of his.

And then she had it. The evening was turning out to be dangerous indeed but not in the manner she would have expected. At least luck seemed to be with her.

"Emma Breton," she blurted, borrowing the name of the heroine in the novel she was reading. She thought the false name extremely fitting as it was similar to her own but just barely hinting at her true identity. By assuming the heroine's name, she could almost forget the difficulties that kept interfering in her own adventures. Some very irritating difficulties. She fervently hoped that this man did not have a fondness for the enormously popular novels she favored. Something told her that that, at least, was something she need not worry over.

"At last an introduction, Miss Breton. For some reason, I feel as if we've already moved well beyond this point." He looked pointedly down at her beneath him. "Brandon Davenport, once again at your service." He tipped his head to the side and nodded once courteously.

Emily rolled her eyes.

"My…ah…*friends* call me Brand."

"Then you will no doubt understand why I do not. I'm charmed of course," Emily said with a sardonic smile. "Forgive me if I don't rise and offer my hand."

"Don't bother," he said unnecessarily. "Is it Miss Breton? Or are you married?"

"Not that it's any business of yours," Emily said primly, "But I'm not."

"Hmm. Your tongue is no doubt sharper than most men would care to handle."

"If the men of my acquaintance are unable to appreciate a bit of challenging repartee in a woman, whose fault is it but their own? Rather than being pitied for my unmarried state, I should be congratulated on avoiding a life of boredom in the company of any one of them."

He laughed, and she immediately shushed him, glancing around as much as possible from her prostrate position. Recognizing her concern, he magnanimously leveraged himself upwards and used the advantage of his position to survey the area. Seeing no one, he shook his head and then once again settled himself beside her, keeping a firm grip on her wrists and pulling them above her head.

"Is this really necessary?" she asked acerbically.

"That depends, Miss Emma Breton. If I release you, what will you do? Strike out at me? Try to escape? I assume your horse is tethered somewhere nearby. Is it the same large animal you had such difficulty handling on our first encounter?"

He knew the effect his jibe would have and had made it purposefully to rile her. As soon as the words were out of his mouth, Brand tightened his grip on her wrists and shifted his weight towards her. It was not a moment too soon.

Pushed beyond tolerance, Emily tried once again to shake free of his grasp. He had best hold tight, she thought furiously, because she was going to bloody his lip as soon as she was able. After a moment she recognized that her efforts were fruitless and retaliated in the only way possible.

"Bastard," she hissed.

"Not in the literal sense but undoubtedly in every other way," he agreed with a laugh.

She glowered in indignation, and he acknowledged his bad behavior.

"My apologies. That wasn't well done of me."

Emily huffed out a breath of air and turned her face away from him.

"Come now, Emma," he said companionably, "May I call you, Emma?"

"Certainly not."

Darting her eyes away from his, much intent on biting away the smile that fought to show itself, she decided that the entire evening's absurdity felt like a dream. She wished she dare giggle. Here she was, thoroughly compromised—there was a man on top of her, for heaven's sake—having just pressed herself scandalously up against his hard length, and her companion was doing his apparent best to cling to propriety. He probably considered they were now intimately acquainted, and she supposed, in a way, she did as well. The realization had her amusement dropping away. In its place came tense wariness.

"Shall we call a truce until our dawn appointment? That is, if you are still determined to go through with it…"

He hadn't meant the last words as a taunt but was not surprised when they were delivered as one. Irrationally, he wanted to incite her to reckless behavior. He wanted to see her lips purse and her eyes snap in challenge. Most of all, he wanted to see the color rise to her cheeks and bloom there. But there were other ways to get that becoming heat to stain her skin, and he was looking forward to trying a different tactic.

"As you seem so sure of yourself, perhaps you'd care to settle a wager on our race?" He issued the question with a definite note of challenge that he knew she would be unable to ignore.

"Gladly, Mr. Davenport," Emily said with smug confidence, relieved to be distracted from her thoughts.

"Brand."

Emily ignored him and announced her demand. "If I win, you must apologize for your rude remarks calling my abilities into question, admit that I am the superior rider, and…allow me to ride your stallion—alone." She smiled coolly.

"Very well. And if I win…I should like a kiss. And, my dear, you must follow through with this one."

Damn the man! He had known precisely where her thoughts had been tending.

Emily could feel the heat in her cheeks and was glad of the darkness. He had found his mark. Now it was her turn to parry. As they had long ago left appropriate behavior behind, she felt no qualms over looking him steadily in the eye, smiling slightly, and speaking her mind.

"I wouldn't have expected it—your disguise as an insufferable clod is impeccable—but now it has become clear to me. You are, beneath it all, a rake."

She spoke the words with amused contempt.

"There are times I wish I were."

"And other times that you are honest with yourself?"

"My dear, the trouble with condemning an innocent man is that it gives him an excuse for bad behavior."

Before Emily could issue the sharp retort ready on her tongue, his lips were claiming hers.

It was as if every uncomplimentary thought he had inspired in her was recklessly launched away with a sizzle on the air. The barest second later, each exploded to create a dazzling fireworks display. She couldn't think, other than to wish quite desperately that she wasn't so damnably constrained.

Even so, she wasn't so much of a ninny as to allow such an opportunity slip through her fingers. This was not the time to quibble over his presumption. He at least had been bold enough to act. She would just relish the moment and kiss him back as best she could.

She was shocked to realize that she would be content if this alone was to be the evening's adventure. For now at least the waiting was over. She closed her eyes and tried to forget how awful she looked and smelled, willed him not to notice.

Already her mind was blurring, and her breath was ragged in her throat. As he pulled away slightly, her heart stuttered, and she wanted only to pull him back. But it seemed he'd retreated as much as he'd intended, and his breath now fanned hot on her lips. Without thinking, she snuck her tongue out to lick over her lips. To taste him and feel the same shivery sensation once again. His eyes darkened but still seemed to glint enchantingly above her, like lanterns in the dark.

When his tongue began its slow slide over the seam of her lips, her eyes flew open, and she saw that he was watching her intently. Evidently he had forgotten what had come before as easily as she and was now waiting for

invitation. Keeping her eyes locked with his, she opened for
him, gasped with the pleasure of it, and then allowed her
eyelids to flicker closed once again.

Just as she began to relax slightly, she felt him ease his
grip on her wrists. His fingers still encircled her, but she
was certain it wasn't with the thought to restrain. Although
she ached to touch him, she didn't wish to pull her hands
free of their bonds, and so decided instead to tentatively
extend the tip of her tongue for an exploration of her own.

She never got the chance. Abruptly, and quite
disappointingly, he pulled away from her and clapped a
hand over her mouth.

Emily felt as though she'd been doused with icy water.
As soon as she'd recovered from the shock of it, she was
seething.

The beast! He'd been toying with her the entire time!
And she'd been…what? Eager, enthralled certainly, but
something else besides? She truly hoped not, because she
didn't wish anything to interfere with her plan to punish him
for such perfectly rakish behavior. Until the opportunity
arose, she would pretend herself as unaffected as he
appeared to be.

She turned to look at the enemy. He was crouched
beside her head staring into the darkness. No doubt at the
carriage she now heard making its rumbling way towards
them. A carriage he had heard seconds before her. As he
turned to look down at her, she had no doubt he could see
the chagrin plainly in her face. Would he assume it was due
to her wanton behavior or the fact that he'd distracted her
sufficiently to have her missing the tell-tale signs of an
approaching carriage? He tossed her a grin and inched up
his eyebrow in an impudent manner. Obviously he
suspected the latter, and he was right again.

Piqued, she looked away and tried to extricate herself
from the sludge. When it became obvious that she needed
his assistance, she accepted it…with very little grace. She
knew she looked a mess, coated in mud and floundering
clumsily with embarrassment. And there he was, composed,
and self-assured. Emily gritted her teeth against the

injustice of it but knew it was the least of her concerns. The remainder of this evening's adventure was about to unfold. She could only hope she could manage to keep her wits about her from now on.

Irritated to be retrieving her hat after his careless toss of it, she jammed it on her head and hurriedly tucked a few loose and muddy strands of hair back up into it, marveling that it had gotten even filthier than before. Deciding silent indifference would be the best way to handle her companion, she refused to give him the satisfaction of further complaints and instead turned her attention to the matter of finding her father's pistol. Relieved to once again have its weight in her hand, she gripped it tightly before stepping back towards her original hiding place and Brand. She used his nickname grudgingly, even in her thoughts.

"Can you see anything?" she whispered, careful to keep her voice even.

Brand shook his head, gesturing for her to keep silent. He then stepped away from her, closer to the road.

Eyes scanning the darkening trees, Emily crept slowly forward, straining for a better look. Feeling his eyes on her, she turned and was surprised to realize that she was standing much too close to him. His face was now only inches from her own, and she found herself staring at his lips, remembering their kiss. She slowly lifted her eyes to meet his and imagined for a moment that she caught a glimpse of something more than unrepentant desire lurking there. Unsteady once again, she turned her gaze towards the road and moved away from him, forcing herself to focus on the task at hand.

A fine mist had descended at some point during Emily's lonely vigil, and it now blurred the glow from the carriage lamps so that they resembled giant fireflies. They offered little aid to the shafts of moonlight that filtered through the leafy canopy. The shadows were great inky puddles that alternately swallowed and teasingly exposed, and shapes shifted continuously. In unfamiliar territory, the horses were moving cautiously—the perfect target for a highwayman.

Waiting and watching silently, Emily and her unexpected evening companion trained their eyes on the slow progress of the coach. She held her breath in anticipation and sensed from the line of his body that he also waited with tense readiness. Nothing happened until the horses were nearly even with their hiding place. Then suddenly a figure on horseback slid like a shadow from the trees opposite and rode swiftly to the center of the path, immediately behind the carriage.

Emily realized that even without the cover of approaching darkness, the rider's identity would have remained a mystery. Even Sophie would have been unable to confirm that this was indeed the man she had seen in the graveyard. His eyes were hidden deep in the shadow of his hat, and he wore a black cloth over the lower portion of his face. His body was made shapeless by a swirling cape. However, there was no mistaking the object he held aloft in his right hand. Emily thought his finger looked to be wrapped quite convincingly over the trigger of his pistol.

"Halt! Stand and deliver."

The words seemed to echo through the trees and fade into nervous silence.

The carriage slowed amid some blustering from the box, and the masked rider raised his pistol, leveling it at the coachman's back.

Emily had known that this was going to happen but could barely suppress her outrage over the cowardly injustice. She might very well have jumped from the trees and rashly revealed her presence if Brand had not immediately and quite easily restrained her, clapping his rough hand over her mouth. Without taking his eyes off the highwayman, he ordered softly, "Wait."

Even knowing as she did that he was right, Emily glared at him, furious with his high-handedness. *Who did the man think he was?* Here finally was her chance to step into the role of anonymous heroine, and she was saddled with an irritating male poised to countermand her every move, before she could even make one.

He had probably thought to ravish her thoughts with a

skillful kiss and then smoothly usurp control of the situation while she wondered, utterly oblivious, at the implications and consequences of allowing him such a liberty. If he thought she would be so easily distracted or routed, he was sadly mistaken. She wasn't about to waste precious time daydreaming over what would never be.

There would be plenty of time for that later.

To his credit, his little plan might have worked if their kiss hadn't been interrupted. But it had been, most disappointingly. Another missed opportunity. She couldn't think about that now—it was much too distracting. Where he was concerned, she only had a single intention. Before the evening was finished, she would make bloody sure that he didn't underestimate her ever again. If 'ever' was to encompass only four more days, then so be it. At least she would have made her point.

Realizing that he would refuse to release her until he was sure of her compliance, she nodded her assent. As he loosened his fingers, she considered biting one of them but then thought better of it and instead jerked her head free, elbowing him sharply in the ribs. He didn't make a sound but grabbed the offending elbow and held it tightly against her as he wrapped his other arm around her back and held her immobile beside him.

No one had yet emerged from the carriage, and the coachman seemed to be making quite a project of steadying the horses and climbing down off the box. When it seemed he was finally ready to heed the villain's demands, he shocked them all.

Emily and Brand watched in disbelief as the coachman swung around brandishing a pistol of his own. Without pausing to take aim, he fired in the general direction of the highwayman's voice, apparently hoping for a lucky shot.

The bullet strayed from its intended target, embedding itself in the trunk of one of the trees lining the road. And yet the highwayman reeled back as if struck. His horse responded similarly, rearing and plunging, but unlike its rider, chose not to keep silent, instead whinnying loudly at the offense.

The carriage horses were inciting each other to reckless behavior, and the coachman was forced to scramble back up onto the box to calm them. Amid the chaos, he was defenseless against the second shot fired. The villain had easily managed to steady his horse and had promptly leveled his own pistol, firing just as the coachman had turned in sudden, fearful awareness.

With a howl of pain, the coachman released his grip on the reins to clamp a hand to his shoulder. Already edgy, the horses caught the metallic scent of blood on the whisper of wind and began snorting and stomping in nervousness and fear, poised to bolt.

"See to the horses and then to the coachman if you can manage it."

The murmured order came curtly as Brand released her, but it was clear he was waiting for her acquiescence.

Emily wavered, clearly wishing for a more exciting role in the night's adventure, and was immediately ashamed of herself for even hesitating to provide assistance to the injured man. She snapped out her answer.

"Of course I can manage it. But I suggest that you don't underestimate that villain in your rush to be a hero. He's desperate and no doubt unpredictable."

She disappeared through the trees before Brand could question her parting comment.

As he moved forward, closing the distance between himself and the masked rider, he remained well concealed by the cover of trees. When the highwayman spoke again, Brand heard the quaver in the man's voice and knew Emily had been right.

"Right, then. Now step down—all of ye—an' don't be forgettin' yer valu'bles. Gun's got 'nother bullet, so ye'd best be keepin' that in mind."

As the carriage door swung smartly open, revealing an elderly gentleman formally attired, Emily watched Brand nudge his horse forward as he cocked his pistol.

"Toss down your gun," he demanded. "I am armed, and I assure you, I am a crack shot."

Both the highwayman and his intended victim started at

the unexpected, disembodied voice, but neither immediately acknowledged the mysterious presence.

With his back deliberately turned, the villain pivoted his aim from coachman to passenger, quite clearly nervous of the pair of them. Sparing only seconds of contemptuous attention for the incompetent thief, the gentleman from the carriage soon squinted in Brand's direction, trying to distinguish the voice from the shadows. Sensing no further threat in front of him or perhaps simply resigned to the inevitable, the highwayman, at long last, jerkily brought his pistol around to the new arrival.

"If you think your luck will hold long enough to disarm me and gather these peoples' valuables," Brand said with authority, "then you are mistaken. My valet is currently tending to the coachman, and he is armed as well. Don't risk it. My advice is to abandon this evening's obviously ill-fated deed and content yourself with the wages allotted for a respectable day's work."

Emily opened her mouth to protest but, with considerable effort, kept silent. She would wait, but if Davenport let this scoundrel scurry back to his hole with naught but a warning, she would see that he received the tongue-lashing he well deserved. And next time, she would handle matters herself.

After a moment's consideration, the villain's shoulders slumped in defeat, and with a muffled curse, he tossed his pistol to the ground. Brand strode forward, pocketing one of his own pistols to lift the discarded one. He gestured for the man to dismount just as the old gentleman, apparently confident that the danger had passed, stepped down from his carriage and turned to assist the other passengers.

Before addressing the coach's occupants, Brand called out to Emily.

"Breton, how do you fare?"

Grateful that he did not plan to give her away, Emily answered gruffly.

"Just a flesh wound, sir. I'll need to bind it up, but it'll heal right 'nuf."

After helping the coachman to a sitting position, she rose

awkwardly and faced the group before her, which consisted of the elderly gentleman, a middle-aged lady, and her maid. They all stared politely at her, and she suddenly wondered if perhaps her disguise was as inadequate as Sophie had indicated.

Apparently pleased with her competent handling of the tasks he had assigned her, Brand nodded in approval before turning his attention to the coachman to inquire about some rope. He was told it was kept in the storage compartment under the box, so while he kept his pistol trained on their now cowering captive, he nodded to Emily to fetch it. She assumed she'd find the supplies necessary to bandage the coachman's wound located conveniently in the same place. As she moved to comply, Brand addressed the occupants of the coach.

"I suggest we leave our captive bound and gagged and allow him to fend for himself for the remainder of the night. I'll report the incident and his whereabouts to the authorities in the morning. Any objections?"

The gentleman cleared his throat and stepped forward.

"No objections, although it's considerably more lenient than he deserves. I am Lord Haversham and this is my wife, Lady Penelope. We greatly appreciate your assistance with this unfortunate incident and will remain in your debt. If I can ever be of assistance, do not hesitate to call upon me."

When he turned his attention to Emily, she slumped a little in the face of his studied perusal.

"And you, young man, if you find yourself in need of a new position, you have only to inquire at Haversham House. With your considerable talents, I'd be delighted to have you in my employ. I'm sure my coachman would agree."

Brand spared a glance for the coachman and was amused to see that he was indeed nodding his agreement.

Emily barely caught herself before executing a gracious curtsy, instead deciding a tug on the brim of her cap would be the expected response. She didn't dare look in Brand's direction, for she was sure to see his eyes lit with amusement and a teasing smile about his lips. It seemed everything she did amused him.

"Yes, milord. Thank ye, milord."

When Lord Haversham turned his attention back to Brand, Emily was free to take a good look at the highwaymen's targets. Both lord and lady were dressed simply for traveling, but even in the near-darkness, Emily was able to make out the fineness of their clothes. Lady Penelope was wearing no jewelry save a single ring on the third finger of her gloved left hand. The setting held a rather large stone, and Emily assumed it was her wedding ring. The lady's maid, who had not spoken, nor been spoken to, was standing close beside her ladyship, wearing a rather fine traveling gown herself. She was clutching what was no doubt the aforementioned jewel case tightly to her bosom.

The 'gentleman' from the cemetery had known what he was about or, more accurately, what this incompetent standing here before them was about. If the attack had been successful, Emily had no doubt the two would have made away with a fortune. Just as she was certain it would not have been evenly divided between them.

"Foolish to travel after dark," Lord Haversham was admitting ruefully, "but we decided to press on as we are only a short distance from our journey's end. We go to Clifton Manor, Lord Colin Willoughsby's estate."

Emily's eyes widened at that revelation, but she was even more shocked by Brand's reply.

"I'm headed there myself. I'm Lord Brandon Davenport, Viscount Ashwood. Lord Willoughsby and I served together on the Continent for a time."

Emily thought she would expire from the injustice. Not only was the brute a viscount, so by rights, she should be calling him 'my lord', but he was a personal friend of Colin's, a fact which would make it nearly impossible for her to keep her identity a secret from him. Lord Davenport would, of course, attend the Willoughsby ball, and it was simply too much to hope for that she would be able to avoid him the entire evening. Add to that the probability that Colin would insist on introducing them, and she hadn't a chance.

And how exactly was she to behave knowing that her thoughts and dreams were ruled by the friend of her intended fiancé? She'd kissed him for heaven's sake! And worse, she didn't regret it. Not one little bit.

Sinful, sinful, sinful!

Lord Haversham gestured to his wife, standing silent and composed by his side, and answered, "My wife is Lady Willoughsby's sister. We're traveling from London to pay our respects to the Lords Willoughsby, past and present. We'll plan to stay on for the ball a few days hence." Lady Haversham nodded her head and curtsied, adding her thanks to her husband's.

Bowing slightly to the ladies, Brand continued in a competent manner, "I suggest that you allow my groom to handle the reins for you while I stay behind to deal with this villain. Your coachman really should be examined by a physician."

"Agreed. My thanks again." The old man's voice was gravelly, and Emily found herself thinking it was probably the result of too many cheroots. "I look forward to sharing a glass of the excellent French brandy that the Willoughsbys keep well-stocked."

With these parting words, he assisted his wife and her maid back up into the carriage before spryly vaulting up himself. After ascertaining that the coachman preferred the open air to the comfort of the coach, Emily gently helped him up onto the box. Although disappointed that she wasn't to be the one left to deal with the villain, she was thankful at least for the reprieve from Brand's disconcerting company. She had just taken up the reins in preparation for their departure, when Brand addressed her tersely.

"A word, Breton?"

Close to seething over his high and mighty manner, Emily took her time getting down from the box and making her way towards him. A slight smile lifted the corners of his lips in mocking salute. Conscious of the watchful eye of Sneeves, Emily wondered how much he would reveal.

"Well done. Your command of a situation never fails to impress me."

Emily's eyes narrowed at the veiled references as she gracefully accepted the seemingly well-meant compliment.

"Thank ye, milord."

"After I'm through here, I'll ride to Clifton Manor with all speed. Wait for me in the stables."

Emily heard the hint of steel in his voice and saw him raise his eyebrows in challenge. Oh, how she wanted to toss her defiance in his face, wanted nothing more than to tell him exactly what she thought of him and his bullying tactics, but she didn't dare. She needed him to keep her secret.

"Yes, milord," she answered with a nod before turning on her heel to stalk back towards the carriage. She glanced back as she moved the horses down the road at a rapid clip; he was standing staring after her with his gun still leveled at Sneeves.

She truly hoped he wasn't a highwayman.

* * *

As soon as the carriage was out of sight, Brand turned to his captive, ready to begin the inquisition.

"Perhaps you'd be more comfortable removing your mask?" he drawled.

The villain recognized that he'd not been given an option, but an order, and slowly reached up to untie the strings that held the piece of cloth in place. He turned slightly away from Brand, keeping his head lowered.

"Come now," Brand invited, "you gambled and lost. Surely you recognized that possibility and are prepared to pay the penalty? Show yourself." He gestured casually with his pistol for added emphasis.

The man dragged his hat off his head, gripped its brim with both hands and held it in front of him. Shaking and silent, he turned slowly, reluctantly lifting his eyes to meet Brand's. After one glance at his imposing captor, he crushed his hat in a fearsome grip and quickly lowered his gaze.

Not believing for an instant that this man had the

cunning required of a successful highwayman, Brand assumed he must be working under the direction of another. His objective now was to either force or cajole his captive into revealing the other man's name in order to prevent continued attacks. Otherwise this lackey would simply be replaced, and there was every chance that the replacement would meet with more success. It was almost impossible that he not.

Brand suspected he would find his task relatively simple. His captive's face hinted at a weak nature, and his eyes were shifting back and forth, a clue, Brand supposed, that the man was anxious to lever the blame away from himself. He decided to start with an easy question.

"What's your name?"

His captive merely shuffled his feet and gripped his hat tighter.

"Perhaps you didn't hear me," Brand said, raising the pistol level with the man's chest. "I asked for your name."

"Sneeves, milord."

"There. Now we're acquainted. Surely you aren't the only one to blame for this debacle, are you, Sneeves?" Brand asked in a deceptively casual voice. "Someone put you up to it, didn't they? Someone who knew that there would be a carriage traveling this road tonight. Come now…don't you think the others deserve to be punished as well? Better to spread it around, wouldn't you say? Instead of having it all fall on your head?"

When Sneeves failed to answer, he continued.

"If you alone are responsible for this attack, there is every chance you will be hanged. You wounded a man and threatened the lives of several members of the peerage, including the heir to an earldom. Add to that my account of events, and you haven't a chance. Unless…"

Brand paused, waiting for the man to look up at him once again.

"Unless you'd care to reveal the identity of your associates?" He raised his eyebrows questioningly, waiting.

Sneeves dropped his eyes to the ground to watch his nervously shuffling feet. It seemed he was thinking. Brand wasn't certain how long this might take, just as he wasn't certain how long he could trust the delectably unpredictable Miss Breton to wait. The thought of her loitering about in the Willoughsby stables, dressed as she was, had him scowling.

"Make your choice, man," he said impatiently, using his pistol again to punctuate his offer. " I haven't got all night."

The man spoke quickly, almost whining.

"Don't know 'is name—never even got a look at 'im—but 'e's a gennelman, its sure I am o' that. 'E sends round a note tellin' me when to meet 'im. Always meet in the graveyard—'e gives the orders, I does me best and meets 'im afterwards. Was to meet 'im tonight at midnight, but I s'pose there'd be no chance o' that?" He looked expectantly at Brand.

Brand considered his options. He could escort Emma home with a few words of warning and then wait in the darkness of the cemetery himself. Or he could allow the second highwayman to wait in vain. Both choices promised a certain measure of satisfaction but not as much as the alternative. He would allow this sniveling incompetent to keep the prearranged meeting and thus use him to unmask the man giving orders. There stood a risk that the evening's failure could inspire murderous intentions towards the man before him, but Brand couldn't work himself up to any measure of concern. Consequences would likely be the same with or without his interference.

An idea had taken root in his mind, as fitting as it was unexpected. And Brand, eager to be away, made his decision with a devious smirk playing about his lips. He would put his father's title, reputation, and wealth to use, but not in any way in which they were intended.

The very idea that a mere two hours ago he'd been congratulating himself on remaining uninvolved in anything more serious than a dawn appointment now seemed preposterous. The audacious miss claiming to be Emma Breton could be held accountable for this evening's development as well. Really, the woman was a menace, he thought with a smile. He would deal with her later; it would be his pleasure.

Right now Brand simply needed to insure the cooperation of the man who stood cowering before him, oddly defiant. Shouldn't be too difficult. Once presented with the options, he was confident that regrets would not hinder the smooth transfer of loyalties. He offered his captive the choice.

"I'll let you decide, Sneeves. You can either meet your associate as planned, follow my instructions, and be paid for an honest night's work, or I will tie you to a tree and leave you to the mercy of the magistrate or whatever finds you first." Brand made a show of examining his pistol with some interest for several seconds before raising his eyes to capture the other man's hunted gaze. "What's your decision?"

Sneeves scratched his head with some uncertainty but was unable to hide his fear when he confessed.

"Warned me 'bout 'nother botched job, 'e did. Said as how he couldn't 'ford loose ends. If I go an' meet 'im, 'e'll know, won't 'e, 'an grin while 'e's putting a bullet right thru me."

"Simply assure him that you were lucky to get away with your life. You weren't expecting additional armed men, were you? Well, surely he will commend your common sense—you preserved your anonymity for another, more fortuitous hold-up."

Brand spoke sardonically but was sure the tone was lost on his new apprentice.

"If you say so, milord." Sneeves was clearly not convinced and appeared even more frightened than when faced with the authorities and the possibility of hanging.

"Believe me, men who conceal themselves in shadow and allow others to take the risks rarely have the nerve required to kill a man."

Brand felt a trifle guilty at offering up the falsehood as a means to ensure the other man's cooperation. But not enough that it bothered him.

Sneeves appeared to be considering.

"What would you have me do, milord?"

Brand's words had apparently succeeded in reassuring the man as he was no longer quivering and had posed the question boldly, mashing his hat back onto his head.

Brand lowered the pistol and took a few steps away from the man now in his employ.

"I would like you to keep your meeting in the cemetery and convince your associate that, despite this night's failure, you are aware of an even more profitable target that will soon present itself."

Brand turned and walked back towards Sneeves, staring into his glittering eyes.

"Tell him the Earl of Chase will be traveling this road tomorrow night on his way to Clifton Manor. Tell him you have heard rumors that he travels in great luxury and that a successful attack will more than compensate for the missed opportunity tonight."

"'E'll know of it before I tell 'im, you can be sure o' that. 'E was prob'ly plannin' to give me the partic'lars tonight. But I'll tell 'im if that be what you want."

"Ahhh, but also tell him that the earl always travels with two armed outriders to ensure that his valuables are well-protected. Convince him that you are not equipped to handle such a job alone. After tonight, he can scarcely argue, now can he?"

"S'pose not."

Brand suspected that this had not been the fellow's first bungled job.

"Good. Do you think you can handle that?"

"I'll do me best, milord."

"Oh, and one more thing. Tell him this information came straight from the earl's own son and heir. Tell him he is a friend of Lord Colin Willoughsby and was getting soaked in the taproom of the village pub and so revealed a bit more than he ought."

Sneeves had visibly braced himself to hear the instructions. The rigid line of the man's body put Brand in mind of one long exposed nerve. The fear of possible consequences pulsing through him must be disturbingly real indeed, Brand allowed. Uncertain why he felt any sympathy for the man but resigned to the absurdity that he did, Brand fabricated a final bit of information to be conveyed. He knew a bit of reassurance, no matter how misguided, was likely to work to his own advantage.

Brand spoke calmly and firmly, "Tell him you have a bit of extra information that will insure your success, but don't reveal it until you are in place, awaiting the carriage. When he presses you, you should confide that one of the outriders always rides off near the journey's end to make ready for the carriage's arrival."

Sneeves nodded, a bit more comfortable until Brand warned, "While he would not dare risk shooting you here where the shot would likely be heard, showing your cards too soon could very well be the death of your partnership. So to speak."

An involuntary shudder ran through the man in front of him, and his eyes now looked hunted. Brand supposed it meant he'd understood the veiled innuendo. Excellent.

He hoped the man would heed his warning, but either way, he was well satisfied that he had done his best to protect him. With a nod of encouragement, he stepped forward to return the pistol before issuing a final warning.

"If you are not successful in luring your associate tomorrow night, I will track you down myself, hand you bodily over to the magistrate, and leave you to a punishment you deserve. If you do your job effectively, I will pay you for your assistance and expect you never to involve yourself in any such devious and cowardly plots again. Is that clear?"

"Well 'nuff, milord."

"Good."

With a final nod, Brand turned his back on the hireling and retreated into the forest to fetch his stallion and Emma's mare and, at long last, return to Clifton for yet another confrontation.

* * *

Emily waited in the shadows just outside the stable

doors.   Impatience had funneled itself into restless movement, and so she paced. Her irritation over Brand's blithe   interference   and   domineering   manner   had transformed itself into the anger that seemed to rise easily to the surface at each of their encounters. She couldn't explain her vehement reaction to him. After all, time and again, he had proven himself a typical male, cut from the same chafing fabric as all the others. Why had she thought him different?

Because he was a dark and mysterious stranger? That must be it—she had put her faith in him simply because he was a stranger. It was optimistic and naïve and obviously misplaced.

The fact that he happened to be disturbingly handsome had had nothing whatever to do with it. It would merely have been a side benefit if he had, in fact, been someone worthy of her attention.

Disappointingly,   the   realization   that   he   was   as overriding a male as any of her acquaintance, and as such, thoroughly useless, had squelched any possibilities there may have been between them. As soon as he had seen through her disguise and realized she was not a man, his attitude towards her had changed dramatically.   For heaven's sake, within seconds of the revelation, he had kissed her as if she were some silly tavern wench!

Although, in his defense, perhaps he thought she was. She had certainly made no attempt to disabuse that notion. But even so, did that give him the right to pin her down and have his way with her? Well, things hadn't gone quite that far, but who knows what could have happened if the noise of the carriage hadn't stopped them.

Perhaps she had encouraged him—slightly—but that was only after he had already put his lips on hers. And why shouldn't she encourage him?

If he was going to take advantage, she may as well indulge a few of her own curiosities. The gentlemen of her acquaintance had certainly not inspired her to explore the intimacies possible with the opposite sex. Some had convinced her that there was nothing whatsoever worth exploring and others had quite simply repulsed her. But Brand's kiss (she supposed there was no harm in calling him that in her thoughts) had left her with a wonderful mix of impressions. It had left her feeling reckless, shameless, and senseless but also quivery and blissfully content...for a fleeting moment. It had both comforted and excited her at once. In fact, she realized with a shiver, it continued to do so even now. Perhaps the shiver she felt was simply due to the icy cold wind. Either that or it was apprehension at the reality that she may forgive him almost anything for the memory of that kiss.

With considerable effort, she attempted to ignore the tumultuous feelings his kiss had inspired and focus on the evening's other revelations. The mysterious viscount had simply assumed command, then taken what appeared to be a sinful amount of pleasure in lording each and every little victory over her. It wasn't as if she had even wanted his assistance, let alone requested or needed it.

She had had the situation well in hand. Well enough anyway. And then he had arrived and begun ordering her about as if she were a servant. What was worse, she had actually had to act the part! The man was infuriating, but she doubted he was incompetent. He had no doubt handled matters quite satisfactorily without her. The knowledge left her with a desire to simply go home and brood.

At the sound of hoofbeats rapidly approaching, Emily peered from the shadows and immediately recognized her stranger, who, she supposed, was no longer so much of one. Astride his own stallion and leading Gypsy, he looked like a hero, worthy of a homecoming. She looked, she knew, like a stable rat. Silently cursing him, Emily hurried forward to retrieve her horse, preferring to relinquish her own angry words if it meant avoiding a confrontation between them.

He apparently was not content with such an expeditious arrangement and so held Gypsy's reins out of her reach as he dismounted. Emily watched in irritation as he tethered both animals to an ancient oak whose leafy branches smothered the area in deep shadows, cloaking them in privacy.

"I'd like a moment, Miss Breton," Brand stated in a clipped tone.

"Perhaps another time," Emily answered prettily. "I really should be getting home. My thanks for retrieving my mare."

She stepped forward to snatch her horse's reins but was easily thwarted when Brand sidestepped directly into her path. She knew that if she was going to escape without unleashing her temper, she would either need to get around him or convince him to move out of her way. Neither looked to be an easy task. His gaze appeared unyielding, and his body would no doubt be even more difficult to dislodge.

Sighing deeply, Emily stepped back and raised contemptuous eyes to his.

"I see you're not adverse to using coercion to get your way. Very well then. What is it you wish to discuss?"

Her tone had his eyes narrowing in irritation, but he refused to be drawn. He crossed his arms over his chest and snaked his eyes over her disguise.

"What exactly did you think you were doing out there tonight? Did you think it was some sort of game—dressing up and playing at ambush? For God's sake, woman, that was a real highwayman! Your gun wasn't even loaded. What did you expect to do—throw it at him? I would have thought you'd have more sense, but the more I learn about you, the more I wonder why I should have arrived at that conclusion."

Unable to maintain her façade of disinterest and quiet dignity any longer, Emily rounded on him.

"How dare you presume to lecture me! I had the situation well under control before you arrived and began issuing orders. I am not yours to command, *my lord*!"

The last was spoken with an unmistakable sneer, and she couldn't bring herself to care. Brand stepped forward unexpectedly and grasped Emily's upper arms in a brutal grip. She knew instinctively that his intention was not to cause pain but to rivet her attention. Knowing this, she was as angry by his presumption as by the certainty that she'd have new bruises in the morning. A few more to the tally; it seemed to be the price of adventure.

The condemnation that had risen in her throat at such familiar handling slid back down as a frisson of awareness raced through her body. A glance at his face glossed her pride with the knowledge that he had felt something too, however unwanted it had been for both of them. Anxious to break the contact between them, she stepped back jerkily, wrenching her arms free. She rubbed them, as much to soothe her muscles as to distract her troubled mind. Still reeling from her reaction, and wondering over his, she was barely aware of his softly spoken words.

"Listen to me, my little hoyden. You may consider this fair warning. Your days of adventuring in this manner are now over." Acknowledging her furious scowl, he asked, "Do you have any idea what you look like? I must have been insane to have believed for even an instant that you were a boy. Those breeches certainly don't leave anything to the imagination."

He shuddered visibly and misinterpreted the shock of outrage reflected in her eyes.

"You needn't worry; the villain will be duly punished, in time. And if you persist with these nighttime escapades, I'll make sure you are as well. I will expose you, and you needn't worry that I'll feel the slightest bit of remorse. While it's bound to be damaging to your reputation, such an eventuality is hardly worth mentioning compared to the danger you could face at the hands of unscrupulous men. I can only assume that your father is unaware of your evening's exploits and that he would indeed disapprove?"

Nerves prickled under her skin, but Emily leveled him with a cool, hard glare.

"My 'nighttime escapades' will never be your concern, my lord. And until they cease to be entertaining, I've no intention of calling them to a halt. They've thus far been most enlightening as well, providing me with information I very much doubt you have at your disposal."

"Try me," Brand drawled.

"Excellent tactics, my lord. Evidently you imagine that

I'll heedlessly accept any challenge you issue, even at my own expense. So sorry, but I'm afraid I'll have to decline your offer. Now if you'll kindly allow me my horse?"

"Try me," Brand repeated, a smile still on his lips. "If you are in possession of a piece of information that continues to elude me, I will take you on as an even partner."

Interest sparked, and Emily was certain he could see it. But suspicion remained.

"What prevents you from lying—telling me you already know, when in fact you do not?"

"My word."

She scoffed but then looked him in the eye and quickly sobered. He wouldn't deceive her—of that much, she was convinced.

"Very well then, there are two of them," she offered, smiling thinly.

"I assume the number refers to highwaymen?" At her nod he prompted, "Try again," and lazily crossed his arms over his chest.

She gaped at him but then popped her mouth shut. Apparently Sneeves had talked.

"They rendezvous in the graveyard, steps from the vicarage gate," she tried.

He looked slightly bored.

"At midnight," she tossed in desperately.

The insufferable oaf turned his gaze to the ground, almost as if he was embarrassed for her. In actuality, he was probably hiding a smirk. *Damn him.*

"So you've nothing new at all." It was a statement, not a question. "Your name for instance? Your *real* name perhaps."

"Nothing else I'm willing to tell," she answered childishly, "Miss Breton will suit just fine."

"Then it appears your involvement in this matter has come to a tidy end." He tossed the words off in dismissal.

"Do not mistake the matter, my lord," Emily ground out, "You have absolutely no power over me."

"Come now, I think we both know that that is simply

untrue."

Emily gaped at him for the second time in as many minutes and was rendered momentarily speechless at his innuendo. It was difficult to watch as his smile turned devilishly smug, but she didn't look away.

Brand's eyebrows lifted in sardonic amusement as he pressed his advantage.

"When you've recovered, perhaps you'd like to tell me how you came to discover that there is someone else involved in these hold-ups."

"Perhaps you'd be good enough to give me back my horse."

Emily slitted her eyes and pressed her lips together in a mutinous line. Then, for good measure, she crossed her arms beneath her breasts silently daring him to touch her again. This time she would not hesitate to slap the amused arrogance from his face.

So they waited. Brand stood alert but relaxed. He kept his eyes on Emily and reserved his movements to settling the horses. Emily was only able to maintain her defiant stance for the space of a minute before she hissed out a breath and began to pace with restless energy.

Damn him! Must he always be so utterly smug? Not even Beatrice vexes me as thoroughly as he does, and it's not for lack of trying.

Brand waited in silence as the seconds passed. Despite their short acquaintance, he was confident he could read her irritated silence and expressive features accurately—she was planning something, very likely something devious. His best guess was that she was trying to determine how best to outwit him. He could only hope that her dealings with him thus far would have demonstrated that he wasn't likely to be duped. If so, perhaps she was hoping to bargain.

Show your cards, love.

Emily was determined not to give in too quickly to the patiently penetrating gaze he had leveled in her direction. She would make him wait just a bit longer and savor the exhilarating feeling of power over him...however fleeting.

However she quickly tired of the game, realizing it was

punishing her as well. The sooner they reached agreement, the sooner she could be enjoying her soft warm bed. Considering the bruises, the hunger, and the fatigue, she was almost ready to abandon the whole business of adventuring in favor of her comfortable, if unexciting, existence. Almost, but not quite.

When she turned to face him, her hands perched regally on gently rounded hips, Brand couldn't seem to wrench his gaze away. He hadn't noticed them before, but her hands were graceful, slim and pale. Yet settled fiercely against her worn and dirty breeches, they looked perfectly at home. She was as intriguing as she was irritating.

There was no question that she was a lady, although her actions so far belied that fact. He wasn't sure if his mouth was watering or not, but it was a close thing. How was it that this infuriating little firebrand could so easily distract him from the task at hand, no matter what it might be? With difficulty, he wrenched his gaze upward and found that she was watching him steadily and a bit contemptuously, her eyes lit with challenge.

"I'm willing to reveal the information I have on these villains on one condition," Emily said pertly.

"I shudder to think what that might be."

Emily made a face at him. "I expect to play a role in their ultimate capture. A role other than that of ostler and nursemaid."

"You don't say."

"Allow me to clarify," she said, stepping forward slowly. "If you would like the benefit of the information I have uncovered, then you must promise that our...association will remain a secret. Believe me, I will find a way to remain involved with or without your assistance. I assure you that I'm well able to handle myself, whether you choose to believe it or not."

"On that last score, I've yet to come to any conclusions."

She didn't speak. Probably didn't trust herself, Brand thought in some amusement. He was torn himself. He didn't wish to involve or endanger her further, but he felt it important to know just how she had uncovered the details of the night's hold-up. And while he was of the opinion that a father should know how his daughter was spending her evenings, he really didn't care for the task of playing informant. One more night. Then he would make sure her adventuring was finished for good. If he accepted her compromise, he could keep an eye on her himself, assign her an insignificant task, and thereby insure she was kept safe. Otherwise, unless he planned to make good on his none-too-appealing threat, he must simply resign himself to the fact that she would act rashly on her own and possibly endanger herself further.

"Very well," he allowed with a nod of his head. "Tell me how you came to discover that there was to be a hold-up this evening. And how you seem to know there are two men involved when only one was present tonight."

"First I want your word. I can only assume your sense of honor will demand you keep it." She let the last words trail off in silent question.

"You have it, as long as I have yours that you will follow my orders without question and without complaint." One eyebrow arched up, waiting for her answer.

Seeing no other choice, she nodded her head sharply and scowled before surrendering her information. She told him everything she remembered about the midnight rendezvous in the cemetery but refused to divulge her reason for being there, thereby keeping Sophie's participation a secret. Brand shook his head once, seemingly in disbelief, but accepted her narrative without question. When she was finished, he revealed his provisional plans for a second ambush.

Although momentarily speechless with disbelief, Emily quickly broke her silence.

"You would lecture me on the foolishness of ambushing a single highwayman only to draw the attack of two?" she demanded huffily. "One of whom, I might add, we had already captured. Forgive me, but your judgment appears highly questionable, and I'm not certain that I can, in good conscience, allow you to remain in charge."

Brand snapped back derisively, "I don't think I asked for

your opinion or your approval. But that aside, perhaps I didn't clarify one key point. *I* will be armed with two loaded pistols."

Knowing she could not logically argue, she lifted her chin and chose instead to respond with cold dignity.

"I already conceded the flaw in my preparations," she answered tightly before deciding to poke him right back. "Surely you do not wish to embarrass me, *my lord*. I really shouldn't have to remind you that a true gentleman would refrain from mentioning my error in judgment. Don't you agree?"

"Of course. You have my apologies. We shall not discuss it again—you have my word," he conceded gracefully.

Emily smiled to herself at the concession until he spoke again.

"Let's try to avoid any other such 'errors in judgment', or we may both end up dead." He raised his eyebrows to draw her agreement but tempered the subtle taunt with a quirk about his lips.

She should have known. Clearly he was not a man who was going to allow her to taunt and bully him into agreement. She had to admit to a grudging respect. Add that to the ever-present irritation and unwelcome attraction, and her reaction to him certainly included a strange mix of emotions.

She looked him directly in the eye, smiled ever so slightly and answered, "Rest assured that I'll be better prepared tomorrow night."

"One would hope. You will serve as our element of surprise. I cannot think of a job for which you are better suited. I will need you to keep out of sight, well hidden in the trees. As soon as the second villain shows himself, keep your *loaded* pistol trained on him, and be prepared to shoot on my signal. Even *you* cannot argue that I am entrusting you with what could very well be the most critical element of the entire strategy."

"Clearly." Emily had softened her voice, causing Brand to stand very still, watching her with narrowed eyes. "And as it is such a pivotal role, I do not wish to bungle it. I will gladly be content with a task more suited to what we agree is my limited experience."

He was so startled by her rapid change in demeanor that he was temporarily at a loss to answer her.

She winged one eyebrow up and then trampled his attempt to recover as, all pretense gone, she spoke briskly and confidently, "I will either ride as one of the outriders, yours to command, or I will ride alone, answering only to myself. The choice is yours."

She was challenging him to deny her. Brand cursed fluently and ran a hand through his dark tousled hair. At long last he agreed, grudgingly impressed with her courage and determination, irritated by the same. Add to that his frustrated amusement over her willingness and ability to use whatever means necessary to get her way, and he wasn't at all sure what to think of her.

"Very well, but you'd best remember our agreement. You're to follow my orders to the last detail. And you're to remember that it is not a game and that it will definitely be dangerous."

At his capitulation, her whole face lit up, and she spoke excitedly, teasingly, "Aye, milord."

His expression softened slightly as he looked down at her, small and delicate despite her best attempts to appear otherwise. As the smile suffused her face, it was plainly obvious that she was a beautiful young lady merely searching for a little excitement. Tucked into both breeches and cap, spattered with mud, she could barely contain her excitement. She was pleased with herself and, amazingly, him as well. Brand was, quite simply, charmed.

"Come along, *Emma*, we'd best get you home. We'll meet here tomorrow at dusk—you may wear your breeches." He followed the words with a slow grin.

He moved forward to help her mount, and she graciously accepted his assistance, using his cupped hand to boost herself into the saddle. But as soon as she had gained her balance, Emily lifted her boot from his hands to center it over his chest and then pushed with all her strength. Brand was sent staggering backwards, more from shock at her audacity than the actual shove. He landed with a thud against the stable wall, provoking a disgruntled snort from the adjacent stall.

Confounded by the woman and suddenly more than a little weary, Brand stayed on his backside as she turned her mare and looked over her shoulder at him with a slow grin of her own.

"Don't trouble yourself to escort me, my lord."

As she turned away, her cap slid to the side, demanding she catch hold of it before it was lost. No longer confined, her hair caught on the wind, steadily working itself free of its pins. The lights from the stable illuminated the silky mass, turning it into a shimmering lick of flame, until she moved beyond the reaches of the lamp glow, leaving him staring after her. Still, he was able to see her hair flying out behind her for several long moments, glinting softly in the moonlight, before both horse and rider were enveloped in darkness.

7

"...I have just heard! The Earl of Chase is to be in attendance at the Willoughsby ball! The favor of a reply was surely preferred long before this...tis too late now even to bother with a modiste."

LETTER FROM LADY BEATRICE SINCLAIR TO MR. DESMOND RICHLY
28 OCTOBER 1818

 Emily was loath to admit it, even to herself, but she was a little anxious over spending the afternoon with Colin.

This was the man she had nagged and bossed incessantly as a girl, the one who had treated her as an equal, despite her misfortune of having been born female. He was the one who had taught her to ride and swim, taught her so well in fact, that she'd bested him at each skill long before he had decided to leave.

He had departed for the Continent with glorious dreams of victory for Britain, and she had been left behind to awkwardly settle into life as a young lady. It had not been easy. In fact to this day she had still not settled into the role expected of her. But she *had* made concessions— compromises with which no one was content. Thinking back, she remembered her time spent as Colin's surrogate younger brother as infinitely preferable.

She thought gloomily of all the years they had spent apart and wondered whether things could ever be the same between them. It seemed like the lost time was a vast, invisible barrier they must find a way to topple.

The euphoria she had felt over a nasty problem neatly solved had quickly passed, and in its wake had come nervousness. She had realized with a shock that if events proceeded just as she had convinced herself she wished them to, Colin would be her husband, not simply her friend. On the surface, such an end to her desperate predicament wasn't at all troubling. What bothered her was the fact that she no longer knew enough about him to understand how much things would have to change. Certainly she loved him—there was no question—but would she ever fall *in* love with him? And if not, would fond friendship be enough for either of them?

She felt as if she'd been set adrift with no map or compass to guide her. Her intentions now seemed fraught with uncertainties. Colin had seemed an island oasis beckoning her through a storm-tossed sea crowded with hideous sea monsters. How depressing that marriage to any gentlemen of her acquaintance could fit so easily into that metaphor.

A likeness of Sir William rose up before her, complete with tentacles and rows of pointy teeth hung with ropy saliva. It really was quite amazing how true to life it seemed. She allowed herself another moment to indulge in the silly imagery before turning her thoughts to more serious matters.

Sophie's revelation that Colin had finally returned had set off the very feelings that the mention of his name always had—just knowing he was back had eased her mind. He had always been able to soothe her hurts and steady her thoughts, and she had naïvely assumed he still could. If she kept her thoughts of him confined to memories, she was content with the choice she had made, but when her mind strayed to the future, she couldn't help but question the prudence of her decision.

As a child she had resolved never to marry unless it was for love. Despite her searching, love had remained elusive, never within her grasp. So, with considerable regret, she had resigned herself to life as a spinster and tried to embrace the advantages such a life had to offer. Now she was being forced into a hasty engagement, and she knew well that love simply didn't comply with ultimatums or keep to any kind of schedule. She was trapped. Now it seemed she faced a scavenger hunt—she must find someone with as many desirable qualities as possible before time simply ran out.

A twinge of guilt deep in her stomach offered up a disturbing question.

Was she being fair to Colin?

Placing her hand over her fidgety middle, she reminded herself that from society's viewpoint she was quite a good catch. She was, after all, an heiress, and most anyone she might choose to wed stood to benefit significantly from a connection with her father. Colin especially, given that his estate adjoined her father's. Add to that her passable looks—some would even call her pretty despite her unfortunate coloring—and her presumed ability to conceive and mother a child, and she was every man's dream, however hollow that reality made their minds and her heart.

It was lowering to realize that no man of her acquaintance—other than Colin—had ever troubled to truly get to know her. And even he had only known her as a child. Ironically, polite society's absurd guidelines for marriage may very well work to her advantage. As long as she met all the requirements for a wife, it was unlikely her husband-to-be would notice or care that she was offering loyalty in place of love. She wondered if Colin would be the exception.

The proposed arrangement seemed to resonate with hollow finality. But what could she do? She wasn't in love with anyone. And there was no one who seemed preferable to Colin. Her thoughts shifted slightly, but she ignored the way they were tending. It would be utterly ridiculous to allow herself to consider Lord Brand Davenport as a husband. He was an impossible alternative. If she thought she was nervous and uncertain now, how would she feel facing a life of exasperation and frustration with an arrogant scoundrel such as he? She refused to think of it.

She needed to concentrate her thoughts on Colin and pretend Brand existed only for a bit of adventure in the darkness. Her eyes widened at the wicked insinuation of her thoughts, and she raised her hands to cool her suddenly heated cheeks.

Blowing out a calming breath of air, she held her hands in front of her, palms out, and focused. She needed to decide how to conduct herself during her afternoon with Colin. Perhaps she should simply pretend that their courtship had already begun. That way she could avoid an awkward beginning and just move straight to the comfort of companionship. If she was lucky, he too would be relieved with her presumption. Or agreeable to it at the very least.

Perfect. She would be flirtatious but not overly so. She would be…interested. Simply a longtime friend, eager to hear about his time on the Continent. That was true after all, so it shouldn't be too difficult to carry out. She could treat him as a dashing hero, come to rescue her from a hideous fate (there was considerable truth in that as well). Truly, that should be easy enough. She was prepared to be sensible. She could be content without love, and certainly without romance.

She just wished desperately that she didn't have to be.

Thinking back to the criteria she had long ago laid out for a husband, she had to admit that she wasn't yet certain that Colin met any of them. Still, he was caring, charming, and extremely handsome as well. Perhaps she couldn't hope to do any better. Unless she somehow managed to fall in love.

A dark, enticing image of the smug and overbearing Lord Davenport rose once again to overshadow her thoughts. This time she let herself escape to daydreams. He played well the part of swashbuckling adventurer, and yet he didn't seem too keen on applauding her step outside the bounds of propriety—he'd made his opinion of breeches quite clear, and he was likely a strong advocate of the sidesaddle as well. She had to admit, though, that he was possessed of a wicked sense of humor, abundant charm, and a presence that sent her heart fluttering… Based on her list, he was, quite simply, as close as she had ever come to finding the man of her dreams—the perfect husband.

Bloody deceptive list!

She couldn't think about this right now. She needed to

keep herself focused on a potential relationship with Colin, not a nonexistent one with Lord Davenport. Shaking her head a bit to clear it, she closed her eyes and straightened her shoulders to stiffen her resolve.

If she could simply remember Colin as a friend and not think of him as a husband, perhaps she could ease this tight ball of nerves that seemed to have settled in her stomach. After all, she couldn't spend the afternoon alone with him in this state of mind, forever second-guessing her motives. Today would be the perfect opportunity to subtly bring his thoughts around to a union between them—she needed to take advantage of it. Best to let him think they already had an understanding.

Taking several deep, calming breaths, Emily moved to look into the cheval glass and assess her appearance. She looked the perfect young miss, dressed smartly as she was in her most formal riding dress. Both skirt and jacket were a deep navy and trimmed *a la militaire.* As soon as Emily had seen it finished, she'd been delighted. The shiny gold buttons, frogging, and epaulettes raised her spirits each time she wore it. A thin strip of crimson ribbon bordered the edge of the up-turned collar, ran alongside the line of buttons down the front of the jacket, and also along the side seams of the skirt. She had decided against wearing the neat little hat that had been ordered to match, instead having Bess pin her hair up tightly in an elegant chignon.

With a dusting of powder to subdue the freckles that seemed to have multiplied over the summer months, she was ready. But rather than descend the stairs and chance a meeting with her stepmother, she chose to remain abovestairs until she was summoned. The solitude would allow her a chance to consider this night's adventure and, if she was honest with herself, her next meeting with Brand.

* * *

"Well, at least she left us a few moments to spare before tea."

Emily spoke wryly, commenting on her stepmother's

success in detaining them for the better part of an hour merely exchanging pleasantries. It was clear to Emily that all other discussion was to be reserved for this afternoon's grand event: tea. Even as she and Colin stepped outside, heading for the stables, she was certain Lady Sinclair was paying a visit to the kitchens to assure herself that all was as it should be.

"She's charming," Colin offered generously, "and she is clearly fond of you. I expect it was difficult for you when your father married again, but I assume you were relieved he made such a fortuitous choice." He paused and turned to her with concern in his eyes. "I was never able to tell you how sorry I was about your mother. She was a great beauty, in possession of the gentlest nature, and understandably adored throughout the countryside. You are so like her." He smiled at her tenderly, and she hurried to correct him, uncomfortable with both the comparison and his demeanor.

Was it possible that he was flirting with her? Could he also be planning to go on as if their courtship was a fait accompli? *How very odd—but serendipitous indeed!*

"Thank you for the kind words, but they are misplaced. My mother was a wonderful woman, and she taught me a great deal, but we were never even remotely alike. When I was younger, she tried everything to divert my interest from horses and estate work to more feminine pursuits such as needlework and household management. But eventually she recognized the futility of her actions and let me be, as much as possible, for better or worse. I will never be the lady that she was, nor will I ever be perfectly lovely as she was." Emily tipped her head down and stared at the riding gloves in her hands. "I still miss her greatly, but I have moved past the loss."

Neither spoke as one of the stable boys helped Emily to don Gypsy with the unfamiliar sidesaddle. Emily allowed Colin to assist her into the awkward seat and then watched enviously as he swiftly mounted his own horse. She imagined it was too early still to test his reaction to the sight of her riding astride. Time would tell, she knew.

"I have to admit to being at least partially to blame for

your rebellious nature." He spoke soberly but was clearly holding back a smile. "After all, I let you charm your way into tagging along each time I discovered a new pursuit. I should have known better, but at such a tender age, I didn't realize the consequences of such negligence. And there was the added distraction that I was delighted to be a hero in someone's eyes—no matter that it was a school girl nearly ten years younger."

Emily decided to forgive him his words and remind him of his success as a mentor.

"The only consequence that need concern you is the fact that I was able to outride you when you left, and I'll wager I can still. A race to the pond? Normally I'd insist that the loser wade into the water, but it's sure to be frigid in this weather."

"Em, I hardly think it appropriate for us to be racing about the countryside. After all, you are a young woman now, not some schoolroom miss. Have a care for your reputation."

Disappointed, but undesirous of starting an argument between them, Emily resigned herself to riding sedately alongside him. She was no longer in the mood to flirt. After a few moments of tense silence, Colin spoke again.

"If you were indeed the hoyden you imply, your pastimes must have altered significantly as the years passed. I assume you have since discovered that needlework and household management are not the punishments you once believed them to be?"

Emily was so irritated by his words that she refrained from speaking for several seconds. When she was certain she would not snap at him, she answered tightly.

"I cannot speak intelligently on needlework as I have never taken it up seriously. As to household management, I did what was required of me until Beatrice assumed the tasks. I think I performed competently, and the staff was of immense help, but I prefer to spend my time helping my father on estate matters and tenant concerns. He has come to accept my seemingly unnatural proclivity towards those pursuits and allows me to help him regularly. I can only hope for such lenience in a husband."

She turned to face him, lifting her chin with uncharacteristic haughtiness. He had already been watching her and was now frowning at both her words and demeanor. The next several minutes were spent in stiff silence.

Emily felt as if they had reached an impasse. Their brief conversation had disoriented her. She was confused, dismayed, and more than a little hurt. How could he have changed so much? It seemed a distinct possibility that she would be once again tossed back into the sea of uncertainty...desperately fishing for the least unappetizing of its inhabitants.

She simply didn't think she could live with Colin's obvious and outspoken disapproval, friendship or no. If his comments thus far were a fair indication, his opinions matched those of every other gentleman whom she had already rejected. Were there no men who would accept and respect her as she was? It was simply too depressing to contemplate that she might actually end up married to any one of them. It might as well be Richly.

Suddenly she felt overwhelmingly cold. The crisp autumn wind that had moments ago gone unnoticed was now a nagging reminder that she should have brought a shawl. Still, she rather doubted its enveloping warmth would have dispelled the stark chill of loneliness.

A vivid memory of Brand as he had accused her of being a highwayman sparked a light inside her. As she immersed herself in thoughts of their shared adventure, the glow spread until she felt warm and settled again. She conveniently and momentarily chose to forget his bullying manner, instead remembering simply that he had accepted and trusted her.

Oddly, it was her conflicted thoughts of Brand that had been keeping her mind occupied and distracted from the disappointing reality her life had suddenly become. It was impossible to shut him out, especially as he seemed to have commanded a most compelling role in her life of late. 'Compelling' she thought, was a perfect descriptor, offering the dual meaning of significant and imperious. She'd recognized evidence of his high-handedness immediately; it had taken a bit more time to admit that he was to become considerably more to her than just a distraction.

Still, she wasn't about to admit it to him. To do so would paste a smugly satisfied smile on his face and make their dealings together quite intolerable indeed. Right up until he was gone from her life.

She frowned, wishing she could hold back the days. Before long her adventuring would be over, Brand would have disappeared from whence he'd come, and she'd be trapped into making a final, fateful decision. And then…she'd be married.

The arrogant, teasing smile and dark, disturbing gaze of Lord Brand Davenport shifted tauntingly through her thoughts yet again. She felt oddly as though he was daring her to consider the idea, the possibility.

Of what?! Committing herself to a life of seething frustration, knowing always that she was a source of endless amusement to him, truly subservient to him, even by law?

Impossible.

She couldn't marry him—she didn't even know him! She paused a moment to consider before conceding that she probably knew him quite a bit better than most other gentlemen of her acquaintance. She had spent more time with him than with almost any of them, and she hadn't once been bored. Incensed, yes. Bored, no.

Maybe the idea wasn't as ridiculous as she'd originally thought. She supposed she should consider the possibility. With her face scrunched into a grimace, she tried but couldn't get past the idea that she might need to persuade him, convince *him* to marry *her*. Huffing out a breath, she imagined it would be immensely lowering. She could picture him already, smug smile in place, a single eyebrow raised. She shivered at the thought. She simply couldn't do it. If it came to that, she would find a way to convince him it had all been his idea. Men, she knew, liked to believe they were in complete control of every situation, and for once, she would be delighted to overlook the character flaw.

Despite the grudging addition of another possible

candidate in her search for a suitable husband, Emily wasn't the slightest bit cheered. Marriage to Lord Brand Davenport seemed so far-fetched that she didn't want to consider it too seriously just yet. Beyond that, she didn't yet know him well enough to assess the life she'd be choosing for herself. Best to see how things fared with Colin for the remainder of the afternoon. Although the way things had progressed thus far, she might not even be speaking civilly to him by teatime. She chided herself for such a foolish notion—she could behave herself for a single afternoon.

She rode the next few moments enjoying the bite in the air and the countryside spread out before her, wondering what the next few weeks would bring.

Would she have to nudge Brand into offering for her? Did she even want to?

Stranger things had happened, she admitted. Disturbing things. She would never understand how Devious Desmond had been found suitable! Such a gross error in judgment was uncharacteristic of her father. Perhaps he had confused Richly with some other gentleman, she allowed. Or perhaps he had chosen someone he imagined would take her to task for her unladylike behavior. She truly hoped he hadn't pawned the task onto someone else simply because he didn't want to deal with it—or her—himself.

She desperately needed an escape, but there was nowhere she could go. The best she could do right now was to spend her spare time with Brand. He, at least, let her forget. If it were simply a matter of Brand's irresistible adventuring versus Colin's dependable companionship, the choice would have been easy. But it wasn't.

"Emily?" Colin's voice was a mix of concern and uncertainty.

She very nearly slid off her horse. Having completely forgotten that she was not alone, Colin's interruption came as a startling surprise. Reading confusion in the downward tilt of his brows and puzzlement in his soft eyes, she wondered how long she'd been silent. Judging by their whereabouts and the relatively slow gait of the horses, it had been for some time.

Immediately contrite, she found herself hoping quite desperately that neither of them would be hurt in the days to come. He had been so dear to her, but he was no longer that same young man. She would cherish what had been and focus on getting to know the man he had become. Perhaps she had judged him too quickly. She truly hoped so.

"Forgive me. My mind wandered off, and I must confess to being a bit chilly. Would you mind if we started back? It's no doubt almost teatime, and we do not want to be late, I assure you."

"Of course," Colin acceded vaguely. Emily thought he looked as if he wanted to speak further but couldn't bring himself to do so. So she waited, uncomfortable and uncertain. To put them both at ease, she hummed softly as they rode, a tune they had known as children.

As they crested the hill to the west of her family's estate, Colin reached across to gently take hold of Gypsy's reins, tugging both horses to a halt. He sat quietly, looking down at the strips of leather in his hands for several seconds before raising his eyes to Emily's puzzled face.

"Em...I hope I didn't offend you. It was certainly not my intention—"

She hurried to reassure him, hoping her words would help them regain their once-easy companionship.

"Of course not! You are in no way to blame for my ill manners. It is simply that the disapproving nature of some recent suitors has left me more than a little irritated. Your teasing comments on appropriate lady's pastimes merely reminded me." She smiled fondly at him. "It seems I'm unable to find a gentleman who's willing to exercise a bit of tolerance with regard to his wife. I merely wish to continue the work I have grown to love. Riding about the grounds, conversing with tenants, working with the horses, perhaps even learning a bit about the crops. Is such behavior really as outrageous as they all seem to think?"

She already knew the answer to her question; the question was, did he?

"Well..."

He seemed tentative, and she sympathized with him

even as she determined to have his honest answer. An answer that was critical to the most important decision she may ever make.

"Men are creatures of habit, Em. They are comfortable with the world as they have known it, and they are not anxious to see it change too significantly or too quickly. I daresay their displeasure over your pastimes is more a reflection of themselves than of you. You are intelligent, curious, and independent, all admirable qualities certainly, but they may be viewed as threatening by gentlemen who are looking merely for a simple life with a sweet-tempered wife."

Colin again looked down at his hands, seemingly with regret. Emily's eyes never wavered from his face as he continued, but they darkened to the color of an ocean storm, and her mouth hardened into a pale thin line.

"When a gentleman decides to marry, it is typically because he is ready to settle down, be cared for, and fill a nursery. He wants assurance that the bride he chooses will be able to manage his household, care for his children, and share companionable evenings. He does not wish to chase after a wife who goes haring off at the slightest hint of adventure. Surely you can understand that."

It sounded to Emily as if Colin was describing a bride he could see clearly in his thoughts—one possessed of a great many qualities that she herself was not. Was it possible that he was hinting at the changes that would be required of her? Well, she wasn't at all certain she was willing to make them. Suddenly the unfairness of her situation flooded over her. It was as if she was back where she started—frustrated with all men but needing to choose one among them. She couldn't seem to stop the bitterness of her words or tone.

"Certainly I understand. Men desire to cling to a lifestyle that levers them above women without any expenditure of effort. Many are not forced to prove anything to themselves or others, instead allowing the coincidence of birth to define their lives. They are distrustful, and perhaps even fearful, of any woman who is willing to openly challenge their opinions or position, and for that they are undeserving of respect. These men are unenlightened and self-serving, and I hope I never need accept one as a husband. Does that answer your question?"

Her entire speech was spoken softly and prettily, and Emily knew she had startled and confused him. Emotions passed over his face but were not voiced. He was clearly floundering, probably wondering what to say to the woman he realized he no longer knew. Yet Emily couldn't bring herself to an apology. Instead she tipped her chin up a bit, gritted her teeth, and waited, wishing for both of them that they need not sit through tea with her stepmother.

"Shall we?" Emily asked politely after another moment of silence had passed. She knew not what her companion was thinking, but she was suddenly too weary to care.

Colin sighed and visibly collected himself. "Of course."

Emily reached for Gypsy's reins, and as Colin relinquished them, their fingers intertwined and instinctively they clung. Looking into the other's eyes, both remembered the friends they had been, mourned the time they had lost, and vowed to renew the friendship that had once been so important to them.

When the moment passed, they rode silently back. Both were dreading the impending repast.

* * *

It scarcely seemed possible, but here she sat, for the second day in a row, taking tea with Prissy and her stepmother. Would wonders never cease? She could but hope that Beatrice wouldn't be stingy today, except perhaps with her conversation.

Lady Sinclair had chosen to preside over the occasion wearing a rose satin gown trimmed at the throat, wrists, bodice, and hem with an abundance of lace. She had further adorned her bodice with a creamy white rose from the gardens and added a ribbon edged with satin rosebuds to her upswept hair. Her appearance and behavior put Emily in mind of a well-rehearsed, costumed performance. One in which the actress was inordinately pleased with herself and desirous of showing herself to the best advantage.

Once everyone was comfortably seated, Lady Sinclair cleared her throat to draw her guests' attention. Having successfully riveted them, she then lifted a handled silver bell that had been sitting alone on the tea tray and rang it for precisely three seconds.

Emily and her father looked at each other in confusion, and Colin appeared bewildered. Lady Sinclair smiled widely as the butler led a procession of downstairs maids into the room, each holding a tray of delicacies before her. Performance, indeed, Emily thought, rolling her eyes.

She immediately regretted her ungracious (and thankfully unnoticed) reaction when she realized the selection spread out before her. The apple scones smelled heavenly and thus were probably still warm, the little squares of cake arranged prettily on the best Sinclair china were filled generously with her favorite lemon curd, and the gooseberry tarts looked almost too good to eat. Almost.

Utterly delighted by the selection, Emily beamed at her stepmother.

Bravo, Beatrice!

Emily fully planned to sample one of each. At a minimum. What better way to offer her congratulations to Beatrice on such a splendid success?

Her intentions had the added benefit of excusing her participation in as much conversation as she wished. As long as she kept her mouth full, she had little doubt that her stepmother would refrain from speaking to her for fear she might answer with the food still in her mouth. Beatrice's strict adherence to 'proper' behavior was, she conceded, occasionally quite useful.

Beatrice, giddily presiding over tea from her favored position on the sofa, had begun to pour before Emily happened to notice the empty space on the cushion beside her ladyship. Prissy, it seemed, had been relegated to the floor. Herself seated in a Louis XV armchair, quite comfortably upholstered in patterned rose silk, Emily smirked in the dog's direction. The slow scowl she received in return was delightfully ignored.

Colin sat on a matching chair opposite her, and her father, who had arrived a few moments late and been rewarded with a silent reprimand, sat on the sofa opposite his wife, rounding out the party. It was a cozy little group, Emily thought. Other than the fact that everyone was attempting to avoid joining the conversation her stepmother was valiantly carrying on alone.

Her father had greeted Colin warmly and spent the first few moments after his arrival questioning him about his time on the Continent. But his wife had interrupted so frequently, intent upon changing the subject, that finally both men had given up and decided it was easier to simply wait silently for their tea.

As tea was graciously handed around and everyone filled their plates, Emily couldn't help but wonder whether she had been foolish to avoid this afternoon repast for so long. Her stepmother really wasn't all that bad. In fact, she obviously took tea as seriously as her stepdaughter.

With perfect timing, Beatrice renewed Emily's vow to stay away in the future.

"Edward and I have decided that it is time for Emily to marry. She is no longer a young girl, indeed far from it, and we really don't wish her to be relegated to society's unfortunate "shelf" of spinsters. She simply needs to find a man who will appreciate her somewhat...er...frivolous nature."

Lady Sinclair smiled fondly at her stepdaughter, and Emily forced herself to smile politely back.

"Beatrice, please," her father urged, shaking his head gently.

"I do not find Emily to be at all frivolous," Colin countered, "rather quite the opposite. She knows what she wants, and she determinedly sets about trying to get it."

Colin would always be a treasured friend, even if they weren't meant to marry. Emily smiled gratefully and kept silent.

"If only her priorities were aligned with those of other young ladies of her class." Lady Sinclair sighed heavily before continuing, "Emily *has* improved considerably with my influence over the past few years. After her poor mother died, she was left without adequate feminine influence until I arrived to take matters firmly in hand. I can tell you, we had our work cut out for us." She took a dainty sip of tea and barely finished swallowing before adding, "And we still have much more to do."

Emily groaned, Colin smiled, and Lord Sinclair heaved a massive sigh, apparently unwilling to interfere any further.

"I understand that you yourself are unmarried, Lord Willoughsby." Colin nodded. "Your military career gave you somewhat of a reprieve," Beatrice generously allowed, "but now that you're back and settling in to Clifton Manor, you will, of course, be looking for a bride."

Pausing again to take another sip of tea and a bite of gooseberry tart, her ladyship was either unaware that a bevy of crust crumbs had tumbled down the front of her dress, or she felt that it was not a sufficient catastrophe to deter her from such enticing subject matter.

"Allow me to assist you in your search, my lord," she said. "I'm acquainted with a great many young ladies in the area, each of whom would be simply delighted to have you so much as look in her direction. You are quite a catch, after all. I pride myself on the ability to accurately assess a person's character, and I can tell you that I much approve of yours—you understand what is important. You're not a rake are you?"

Beatrice speared him with a look of avid interest.

Emily thought she heard an embarrassed, softly muttered curse from her father's direction in the seconds before Colin replied.

"Indeed not, Lady Sinclair." Despite her father's embarrassment, Colin appeared to be somewhat amused.

"And Emily? What is your opinion of our dashing Lord Willoughsby? I ask because you are a young lady yourself, no matter that you seem to believe otherwise."

"My opinion?" Emily said, suddenly eager for the chance to poke her stepmother right back. "I think Lord Willoughsby is a divine catch. I'd even let him charm away my fortune."

Colin sputtered into his teacup, trying to hold back a laugh.

"Really, Emily! That is quite enough. You will embarrass poor Lord Willoughsby."

Lady Sinclair herself huffed in embarrassment.

"Oh, but he is most definitely not *poor*. You, of all people, must be in possession of that most pertinent detail."

Lord Sinclair chuckled quietly, shaking his head. Colin caught her eye and managed to wink without Beatrice noticing, and Emily smiled contentedly, delighted to feel comfortable again with her father and childhood friend.

Beatrice smiled, but her eyes frowned. "Emily is fond of teasing and very clever. Perhaps too much so for her own good. When she marries, I suspect she may very well find the adjustments required of her a bit difficult."

Lord Sinclair and Colin both saw the light go out of Emily's eyes and immediately sobered. As Lady Sinclair finished her tart and reached for a morsel of cake, she mistakenly assumed the silence was contemplative, rather than exasperated and embarrassed.

"Now Lord Willoughsby, I will, of course, be in attendance at the ball in your honor a few days hence. It will be my pleasure to introduce you to the marriageable young ladies."

"Beatrice," Lord Sinclair said sharply, "That is not—"

"'Tis likely," Emily interrupted, "that he'll manage to distinguish the married ladies from the unmarried quite on his own."

"Oh dear." Heaving a great sigh, Lady Sinclair pronounced to the room, "There is still so much work I've yet to do with you, my dear."

And so many excuses I've yet to devise…

Behaving as if much put upon, Lady Sinclair carefully set her cup back in the saucer and spoke quite seriously.

"This is hardly the setting to discuss these matters, but as Emily has difficulty remembering our sessions, and as Lord Willoughsby is, after all, an old friend of the family, I can see no harm in it. Make certain to pay close attention, my lord." And with a pointed aside to her stepdaughter, "You too, Emily, would be wise to pay heed."

Lady Sinclair immediately turned her attention back to Lord Willoughsby and so was not aware of Emily's childish, but silent, response.

"I've no doubt you'll find my advice extremely relevant to your search for a suitable wife. You have been away for quite some time…"

And absolutely nothing has changed—gentlemen still expect the ridiculous, and ladies continue to tolerate their whims.

Emily suspected such an interruption would not be well received.

No one spoke. Everyone stared at her ladyship in cringing disbelief. She acknowledged the silence as curious anticipation and took a deep breath before speaking slowly and concisely.

"In order to determine the suitability of a match, one must consider a great many things. The young lady's social standing…preferably she moves in the same circles, but if not, she must at least be above reproach."

The enumeration, it would seem, was to be marked by a separate finger per item, each individually ticked off by her ladyship's thumb.

"Her family's foibles, faults, and failings…you must be cautious and determinedly avoid a union that would bring about unfavorable associations or, worse, untoward gossip!"

Her ladyship was so insistent on this piece of advice that she paused to allow the information to sink in.

"Absolutely never to be forgotten are the benefits the union will bring. Is her dowry satisfactory? Will the alignment of her family and yours be beneficial? You must think not only of yourself but of your heirs as well."

She stopped once again as if to prompt Colin's nod of understanding. Emily noted that he hastily offered it.

"Of critical importance is the young lady's manner and, ultimately, her behavior…was she brought up as a lady, and does she understand the responsibilities she will face as a wife and hostess?"

Stopping in her narrative to glance pointedly at Emily,

her thumb pressed firmly against her now very pink little finger, she then stared in turn at her other unwilling pupils to convince herself that she still held their attention.

Realizing she had exhausted the available fingers on one hand, she lowered it demurely to her lap.

"Although not necessary, it is helpful to have a certain rapport with your chosen bride. In that way, you can be certain you will not have difficulty with, ah, other aspects of the marriage."

The last served to embarrass her ladyship so thoroughly that she stopped speaking and took several rather large gulps of tea while keeping her eyes focused on her cup's rapidly draining contents.

Feeling a response was expected of him, Colin awkwardly filled the silence.

"I've no doubt that you are correct, Lady Sinclair. I understand that there are many things to consider when choosing a wife, and I will do my best to keep all of your recommendations in mind."

"You need not worry, Lord Willoughsby. I will happily offer you my dedicated assistance. As you are recently returned to the area and unmarried, I feel an obligation to assist you in whatever way I can."

"You are very kind," Colin answered.

It was with considerable effort that Emily kept silent as her stepmother proceeded to continue Colin's instruction in all manner of things. Her irritation with her stepmother was once again back in full force. Emily took the opportunity to finish the selections on her plate uninterrupted and let her thoughts wander. Perhaps Colin would be a fellow pupil at The Beatrice Sinclair School of Manners and Household Management. It would serve him right, she thought, remembering their earlier conversation.

8

"...I should hope the scoundrels who have been plaguing the area with their masked maraudings would not dare approach the Earl's traveling coach. His title really should insulate him from such antics, don't you agree?"

LETTER FROM LADY BEATRICE SINCLAIR TO MR. DESMOND RICHLY
28 OCTOBER 1818

Tea had ended later than usual, and having consumed what might politely be termed a generous amount, Emily was hardly surprised to be nursing a stomachache. While the discomfort had afforded her the perfect excuse to skip going down to dinner, it had also garnered her a lecture on moderation. She felt she had succumbed quite gracefully all things, her stepmother specifically, considered. Blissfully alone now, she was once again in high spirits, eagerly anticipating the night ahead and what would be her second adventure.

She doubted she would need as much time to don her disguise as she had the previous night but was pleased to have the extra minutes to purge her thoughts of Beatrice and Colin, deadlines and consequences. So replete, if a bit queasy, with tea and its many accompaniments, she sat down at her vanity to let her thoughts wander. She was hardly surprised and in truth a bit delighted that they tended in the direction of the kiss she had shared with Brand. She may as well get used to it. As she unpinned her hair, she let her mind imagine what exactly she would do if given another opportunity to repeat the experience this evening.

Plenty, apparently. When she pulled herself almost reluctantly back to the present, she found herself faced with a shameless wanton. Reflected in the glass, her own face was flushed with excitement and—dare she admit it— desire. Her lips were moist, her eyes clouded, and her hair loose, the tips of it reaching just past her bosom. Rather than being shocked, she hugged her scandalous little secret to herself and delighted in the heady anticipation of planning a minor seduction. Grinning at her appearance, she realized she had somehow managed to brush her hair smooth without paying the task the slightest attention. How very efficient of her.

As she began the painful process of pinning it all tightly to her head, she marveled that she'd spent a quarter of an hour daydreaming over a man.

She promptly convinced herself that it didn't mean anything beyond the fact that she was curious and desirous of new experiences, most especially pleasant ones. Or perhaps she was just desirous of him period. Quite surprisingly, she could accept even that; she simply did not wish to confuse a little flirtation with anything more serious. She was not in love with him by any means. *Heaven forbid!* She was simply enjoying herself, much as she imagined he was himself.

She would be married before long, and it was unlikely she would welcome any amorous behavior at all from her husband. Although…if she somehow ended up marrying Brand, there was every possibility that she would feel differently. But at this point, such a turn of events was extremely far-fetched. It didn't even bear considering. Besides, she didn't want to forego any kisses just because there was a possibility, albeit extremely slim, that she might one day have access to as many as she pleased…

Her eyes widened and then lit with secret delight as the implications of that very possibility churned through her head. She lifted a hand to cover her mouth as if the secret might otherwise seep out and just stared back at herself, enthralled.

Remembering the unfortunate necessity she now faced

in judging every gentleman of her acquaintance, she knew she would need to credit Brand for his latest show of worthiness. It wouldn't change the fact that she would feel guilty doing so. The very idea that her choice of a husband might hinge on something so…unladylike was almost sinful in its appeal. Lost in pleasant speculation, she admitted it was a pity one couldn't base one's whole marriage on the thrill of desire, the glow of passion. Then she wondered more seriously…*could one*? It wasn't something she could even dare to consider right now—it would be far too distracting. She could, however, deal with the prospect of one more kiss, particularly one that might present itself this very evening.

She wanted one more chance to feel the pin-pricks of desire Brand had inspired the last time he had kissed her. She longed for one more chance to discover what would have come next if they hadn't been interrupted. She needed one final chance to kiss him back, to explore and experiment on her own, to let herself be swept away, if not by love then at least by a whisper of romance.

Time was running out—she just wanted one more chance. At everything.

The trouble was, 'everything' now seemed to involve Brand. Quite ironically, he embodied everything that was pleasant in her life, despite being relatively unpleasant himself. Yet, the explanation was simple: with him there were no expectations, only a plethora of irritations. The latter could be overlooked, at least temporarily.

Somehow their paths had crossed such that he was now intimately involved in her adventures and unavoidably insinuated into her memories. Memories that would need to hold her for a lifetime—she would remember him forever whether she married him or not. He had invaded her thoughts and her life, and oddly enough, she couldn't convince herself to mind.

But that didn't necessarily mean she wanted to marry him. In fact, it was unlikely she would ever see him again after the Willoughsby ball. Such an eventuality rose up before her, bleak in the extreme, and so she consigned it to the rapidly growing list of subjects she preferred not to think about.

When she realized she had frittered away almost all of her time daydreaming, she was thoroughly irritated with herself. If she was late, she could only imagine the superior smirk and disapproving words she would be forced to endure, and she would not be able to say a single word in her own defense. He would be completely justified.

Luckily, at some point during her mind's wanderings, she had managed to change out of her dress and into the now infamous breeches and shirt. Slipping on the vest and donning the wretched cap, she was ready, with scarcely a moment to spare. Standing in front of the full-length wardrobe mirror, she turned herself this way and that to make sure there was no sign of Miss Emily Sinclair. Convinced her disguise was adequate, she stepped confidently away from the glass.

Her escape was identical to the previous night's, and the ease with which she accomplished it only contributed to her unabashed delight. As she rode away from the lights of Sinclair House, she tilted her face back to watch the stars wink on in the deepening sky.

To her, twilight had always seemed the perfect time for secrets—the fading light could reveal or conceal on a whim, and the world seemed to be holding it's breath, waiting for darkness and shadow, waiting, it seemed, for opportunity. As she herself had waited for exactly that, it seemed fitting that she would grasp it at such a time. Who would be revealed tonight, she wondered? She prayed it would not be her—she needed to ensure that her identity remained a secret, even from Brand. She rode the rest of the way in silence wondering if he would ever know who she really was.

As she neared Clifton Manor, she slowed Gypsy to a walk and then smoothly dismounted, walking the rest of the way in the silence of deepening shadow. When it became apparent that she had arrived first, she allowed herself a moment to relax. She wasn't particularly proud of the fact that she had been anxiously holding her breath like a child waiting to be scolded and so rubbed her forearms rather vigorously against the encroaching chill. When the wind that had been buffeting her back suddenly stilled, she knew, and turned to find him looking down at her in grim resignation.

"Still convinced that you wish to go through with this?" He reached out and cupped her chin almost tenderly, "Be assured, I won't think any less of you if you don't. In fact, I will applaud your common sense."

Irritated with herself once again for letting him get so close undetected, and annoyed that he would bother with the question, she shook herself free of his touch and clipped out her answer.

"Your concern for my well-being is heartwarming indeed, but, I assure you, your opinion couldn't matter less." She offered him a bland smile, "Shall we?"

As she turned away from him, he grabbed her upper arm in a stern grip. She turned back, a scathing retort on her lips, but he interrupted in a hard, commanding tone.

"See that you remember our agreement. You are to follow my orders. No exceptions."

She nodded curtly and shook her arm free. As she mounted Gypsy unassisted, Brand had already resumed his teasing manner.

"I confess that I'm beginning to get used to the idea of you wearing breeches. In fact, it's very possible that your choice of dress could be the evening's sole redeeming quality."

Brand swung smoothly into the saddle and turned his stallion in the direction they were headed. Back into the muddy darkness of the forest. Before kneeing her mare to follow, Emily watched his retreating figure with narrowed eyes.

"Insufferable man," she muttered before ascertaining that it was dark enough that a grudging smile would go unnoticed. Although she'd never admit it, she was secretly pleased that he no longer seemed offended or outraged over her choice of garments. She had been right in thinking he had potential.

* * *

Certainly Sophie had felt foolish, but she'd also been inordinately proud of herself. Venturing out into the cemetery nigh on midnight three nights ago should have hovered at the forefront of her mind for days to come. But it hadn't. Shortly after conceding that her first ever adventure had, in fact, been the slightest bit exciting, Sophie could unashamedly admit that she wouldn't soon be ready for the next one. Fond reminisces of her one-time escapade had gone almost completely out of her mind.

She truly doubted the same could be said of her thrill-seeking best friend. It wasn't every day that Emily had the opportunity to ambush a pair of highwaymen, just as it wasn't everyday that she herself resorted to blackmail. She prayed that for once Emily was behaving with decorum and displaying a modicum of good sense. It had thus far remained a mystery whether the silly widgeon had decided to heed the lure of adventure or the threat of blackmail.

More than a day had passed since she had spoken to Emily—a veritable eternity given her friend's tendency to drop by unexpectedly. Not to mention the latest predicament in which she now found herself—the sporting 'husband-hunt'. As a result, Sophie's nerves were beginning to fray. Surely if anything had happened, she would have heard by now…she should really interpret no news as the triumph of good sense.

If Emily had indeed broken her promise, Sophie would know soon enough. Emily wasn't one for keeping secrets. She wanted to share everything—the excitement, the drama, the swirl of emotions, and inevitably, the responsibility. Over the years, Sophie had delighted in letting her. It wasn't as if anything of interest had been going on in her own life.

But now it was. Now she clung to a morsel of possibility, a long-savored wish, a delicious secret of her own. And nothing had ever been more important.

Now she was willing to risk everything. Colin had

finally returned, and she had every intention of marrying him. And judging from the seductive promise he'd offered her last night, to say nothing of the stirring kiss, she had every chance of success.

Smiling at the thrilling possibility, Sophie pushed Emily and her questionable conduct from her mind, determined not to spare her another thought for the remainder of this evening. Her efforts were better focused on devising a way to encourage Colin to kiss her again or, barring that, working up the courage to kiss him herself.

The object of her thoughts was sitting directly in front of her, just as he'd been for the better part of an hour. The majority of that time had found him deep in conversation with her father. Colin had returned to the vicarage for the second evening in a row. He'd mentioned a houseguest, an old friend, but had then hinted at unexplained evening absences. His mother's sister and her husband were also currently in residence, but they preferred to spend the evening at cards with Lady Willoughsby. Having no interest in rounding out a foursome, Colin had escaped, and had admitted with a chuckle to having no idea as to the identity of the poor fellow who had been selected to take his place.

Sophie was much determined on drawing and holding the man's interest and so much appreciated the opportunity to do so.

A few moments ago the maid had come in with tea and biscuits, filling the companionable silence with the clink of china and silver. Now she could hear the tell-tale sounds of her father shuffling back to the parlour from his library. This evening was shaping up precisely as yesterday's had, and that was just fine with her. She'd lost count of the number of times her father had gone in search of a singular piece he believed required immediate examination. Ironically, the fetched artifact soon paled in significance to another and so spurred him on to further search. Sophie cared not. Her father seemed content, and she and Colin had spent the time dancing around the implications of last evening's timid seduction.

"Here it is, my boy," her father announced, proudly staring down at the specimen he carried. "Took a bit longer to find than I expected. I'd set it aside so as not to misplace it."

The endearing irony was lost on her father.

"It's a tricky thing," allowed Colin, sitting forward on his seat in anticipation.

She was unable to resist tipping up the corners of her mouth as she watched Colin with her father. The reality of the man was more perfect even than the conjured one of her dreams. She could almost imagine that God had bestowed His blessing upon her and her intentions. She and Colin had renewed their long-dormant friendship, they'd all been delighted to discover that Colin and her father shared a passion for antiquities and ancient civilizations, Colin had appeared at the vicarage two nights in a row, and perhaps most noteworthy of all, Emily had been uncharacteristically absent. All that was missing was a declaration of love and a proposal. But she was content to wait—for now.

"I was certain that *this* was the piece, but I do believe there is another that may better demonstrate my theory. Although…one cannot deny that this is also a very interesting piece…"

"Indeed," Colin answered promptly. "Why don't we spend a few moments discussing it before you fetch the next one? Perhaps over another cup of tea?"

"Oh, why, yes of course. That would be fine." As her father settled himself onto the sofa beside Colin, she heard him wheeze out a tired breath. Sophie watched him for a moment before letting her eyes settle briefly on Colin.

The man hadn't a prayer. Sophie planned to do whatever it took to ensure that she could look forward to many more evenings as cozy as this. And many more nights preoccupied with pastimes that involved only her and Colin.

As she set aside her needlework to freshen the cups of tea, Sophie settled an innocent expression on her face and began planning how to best to entice Colin to further seduction this very evening.

* * *

Emily caught up with Brand quickly and suggested that they review the details of the plan.

"I have sent word to my father requesting the use of his carriage. It's scheduled to pass through our strip of trees at nightfall. There will be a coachman but no passengers. We are to be the outriders. We shall wait at the edge of the trees and move to flank the carriage as it passes. It is unlikely our villains plan to attack precipitately as the road is exposed and the risk much greater. If necessary, however, we will change tactics." Eyeing Emily as she nodded, he added, "Let me rephrase. *I* will change tactics; *you* will simply carry on as planned—implicitly following any instructions I issue."

Emily smiled blandly in response.

"Last chance, now. Are you truly certain you wish to go through with this?"

Emily remained silent, staring back at him.

"Are you armed?"

She tilted her head to the side and raised her eyebrows a fraction.

"A pistol?" he prompted after getting no reply.

"Two."

"Loaded?"

"I'd be happy to give you a demonstration."

"That's my girl."

"I find it is impossible not to dislike you rather intensely," she muttered.

As they approached the band of trees, Brand warned her against further conversation with a pointed glance and a single shake of his head. He signaled her to follow him into its darkening shelter.

It quickly became evident that they were alone. It was either that or accept the fact that someone else was lurking silently with them in the dark. Emily preferred to believe that they were setting a trap, rather than walking blindly into one, and so assured herself that they would be ready and watching when anyone else eventually arrived. Content for the moment, Emily left Brand to the task of vigilance and snatched the rare opportunity to watch him unobserved. Chance had generously afforded her a bit of remaining light with which to render the deed.

She realized with delighted surprise that the color of his hair was no longer a mystery. Having seen it drenched with rain at their first meeting and in the shadows of these same trees on their second, it had been impossible to tell with any certainty. Now, feet away from him in the rapidly encroaching darkness, she realized that his hair wasn't black, as she'd originally assumed, but a very deep brown. She also noticed, somewhat belatedly, that his normally tousled mane was held back in a tidy queue that left his face exposed to her scrutiny.

With his profile etched against the shadows beyond, his eyes appeared as chips of black stone, but those eyes had stared into hers just moments ago in waning light. And she'd been mesmerized—no matter how ridiculous it seemed, it was true. How often did one come across cool grey eyes warmed with flecks of gold? Not often enough, she had to admit.

Everything about this man made her feel conflicted. He was an enigma, everything she wanted and everything she didn't all at once. Rather than think about it, she decided she'd simply rather keep looking at him.

His nose was undeniably aristocratic, although it had a slight bend near the top that hinted at past violence. His mouth was different than any other man of her acquaintance. Instead of being thin and effeminate, wily, surly, or even determined, Brand's was honest. Even she didn't know how that was an appropriate description, but it was. Like it or not, she always seemed to know precisely what he was thinking.

He seemed to have the same talent where she was concerned. Perhaps her mouth was honest as well. At least up to a point. There were some things she truly hoped her mouth wasn't revealing…

* * *

Having assured himself that they were alone and concealed as much as possible, he gestured for Emily to move closer. As she leaned in to hear what final whispered advice her companion thought it wise to bestow, she felt suddenly trapped in his watchful gaze.

Brand's eyes raked her assessingly before he closed them briefly and shook his head. Emily could well imagine what he must be thinking. No doubt he was second-guessing his decision to allow her to tag along. Oddly enough she felt the tiniest bit sympathetic. This would certainly not be considered an appropriate pursuit for a young lady—but then she was no ordinary miss. She had waited for just such a thrilling opportunity her entire life, and this was her very last chance to grab hold of it. Faced with his grim expression, she tried to appear competent and encouraging. Judging by the edge in Brand's voice when he finally spoke, her attempts had been thoroughly unsuccessful.

"You are to ride on this side of the carriage. The highwayman approached from the trees on the opposite side last night so *I* will ride on that side. With any luck we will find that he is a creature of habit. We have no way of knowing where his partner will appear, if he deigns to show himself at all, so watch carefully!"

Emily nodded and waited patiently for him to complete his perusal. His eyes scanned her face but showed no expression. They then panned down to stare at the heavy pistol she held in a calm steady grip against her mare's back. His jaw hardened, and his eyes sharpened to chips of familiar black stone. She remained impassive, treating him as she might a bumblebee. If she didn't move, didn't flinch, perhaps he'd turn his attention to other matters and refrain from stinging her.

Finally he looked away and spoke almost off-handedly, "Hopefully it will pass unnoticed that we are not attired as outriders, most particularly the earl's."

It had certainly escaped *her* notice, Emily conceded, realizing that she hadn't spared a single thought or glance for what Brand was wearing. Looking now, she saw he wore much the same as she did, but rather than looking like a filthy, bedraggled stable boy, he succeeded in looking relaxed and capable in an open-necked white shirt, plain brown breeches, and serviceable boots. As she wondered if anything in life would ever be fair, she caught a particularly awful whiff of the foul smelling cap positioned right above her nose.

An involuntary shudder rippled through her body. Brand either didn't see it or chose to ignore it.

"Keep the reins to one hand, and hold your pistol with the other. Keep your finger on the trigger, and fire only if necessary. How's your aim?"

"Dead on," she answered waspishly, rapidly growing irritated with his lecturing manner.

"Not a bit of modesty. Lucky for you, I admire that."

He smirked resignedly before running a hand over his dark hair, which was now nearly black in the enveloping twilight. His neat queue had become slightly disheveled, and still he looked composed. She heard him curse again under his breath and silently agreed, certain their irritation arose from very different things entirely.

"Are you quite sure you can handle this?" he asked, apparently needing it confirmed one final time.

"Yes," she gritted out. "Now please stop treating me like an imbecile. I understand that you might be nervous over my abilities as you have had no opportunity to judge them, but I have not expressed doubts over yours. Kindly extend me the same courtesy. Now if that is all, I will take up my position and allow you to do the same."

She looked to him for approval, eyebrows raised in silent question. He nodded his acquiescence and turned his horse sharply to move away through the trees. She watched him pause several feet from the edge of the road before abandoning concealment to cross quickly before disappearing into the dense shelter on the opposite side.

So, this is it. There could be no arguments over whether this was indeed a real adventure. Filled with nervous anticipation she moved Gypsy as far forward as she dared, looped the reins around her left hand so that she had her right free to handle the gun. Now alone, she took a moment to relax her fingers and let the gun lie in her open palm. Sealing her lips and then closing her eyes, she breathed in the cold night air before tensing her grip firmly around the butt of the weapon. Watching intently, she slowly extended her finger and wrapped it over the trigger, glad to see her hands were steady.

She wasn't nervous, but she couldn't claim much eagerness either. Her accuracy was as good as she had claimed—Colin had capitulated easily and taught her when she was but thirteen—but she had never fired at a live target, had never wanted to. Still, she didn't imagine she would have any trouble, if it came to that. After all, these were villains who had already shot one man and apparently had no qualms over further violence. Yes, she would certainly be willing to pull the trigger. If it should become necessary.

With the pistol once again lying lightly across Gypsy's back, she settled down to wait once again. All this waiting could really put a person off further adventuring, she thought, more than a bit disgruntled. At least she didn't have to wait in Brand's company. He was bound to find some reason to lecture or reprimand, and she really wasn't in the mood for either just now.

She tilted her head back and breathed deeply once again, gulping in the air through parted lips. As the icy bite needled her throat, she barely contained the cough that wanted so desperately to escape. It was the damp swirling through the air that caused that bittersweet sting and the same damp that misted everything and infused the air with such a wondrous smell. She spared a moment to capture the memory before lowering her head with a smile still lingering on her lips. Her eyes immediately settled on Brand's, staring back at her from the trees opposite. She could barely see him, and yet his eyes seemed to draw her gaze.

Her smile dropped away as she straightened her spine and looked quickly away from him to regain her composure.

It seemed she was neither able to keep her thoughts, nor her eyes, away from him. Here she was, alone with him again this evening, her only chaperone being the very distance that separated them. It wasn't nearly far enough. She was too easily distracted by his disturbing presence, and her thoughts were not at all what they should be.

Emily determinedly brought her musings back to the ever-deepening shadows and continued to wait. She glanced upwards and could barely distinguish the slivers of rapidly darkening sky that outlined the canopy of leaves. Twilight would soon be swallowed up by nightfall, and then it would be almost impossible to discern the shapes moving amid the shelter of these trees. If memory served her, there would be no moon this evening, so it was bound to be as black as pitch. As she wondered whether Brand's omniscience extended to the lunar calendar and decided that it probably did, she heard the tell-tale sounds of an approaching team of horses. Placing a calming hand on Gypsy's neck, she tightened her grip on the pistol and strained her eyes and ears. And waited.

As the carriage neared their hiding places, Emily could hear the coachman urging the team to slow to a walk. She chanced to catch a sparkling glimpse mere seconds before they crossed into shadowy darkness. Even in the dimming light, Emily was certain that the conveyance was grander than any she had ever seen. It looked to be trimmed in gold and appeared to subtly shimmer in the glow from the carriage lanterns. A magnificent crest adorned the door of the carriage, evidence of both the rank and wealth of its owner. The interior of the coach, Emily noted, was concealed from curious eyes by dark velvet curtains.

The coachman was attired in a coat so dark its color was indistinguishable from the surroundings. His top hat, however, looked to be buff-colored and, reflected in lamp glow, served as a veritable beacon. The horses, Emily noted, were a matched set of chestnut bays and outfitted in the same color as the coachman. If the earl himself ever wore that color, she supposed they would *all* be a matched set. Holding back a guilty smile, she vowed to be more serious from now on.

As the carriage passed them at a leisurely pace, Emily moved smoothly to take up her position at the back of the coach. Brand emerged from the trees at precisely the same moment, and his movements mirrored her own, inspiring a burst of confidence within her. He met her eyes long enough to give her an encouraging nod before he brought his horse in line on the opposite side of the carriage.

Emily was tense but confident, and like Brand, she surveyed their surroundings carefully as they moved more deeply into the encroaching darkness. So much waiting…

They were almost halfway through the copse of trees, at its most secluded spot, when things began to happen quickly. Emily's memory flashed back to the previous night's hold-up. The attack had come in precisely the same location. Filing the information away, she forced her attention towards the figure that had detached itself from a dense cluster of trees to her left. It was impossible to tell in the darkness, but she was relatively certain that it was the same man, the turncoat. Apparently his role continued to be one of visibility—he would be the one issuing orders and making demands of others while his accomplice did the same of him. He would be the one who might be recognized, identified, and apprehended.

Emily almost felt a stirring of pity; he clearly wanted to be anywhere else. Then she ruthlessly shifted her thoughts and gaze away from the shadowy figure and quickly scanned the surrounding trees. There was no one else. A quick glance at Brand showed her that his search too had come up empty.

"Halt! Stand and deliver. I'll have yer pistols first," came a familiar and clearly flustered voice.

Oh for heaven's sake. Emily didn't believe he sounded even remotely confident of his orders being followed. But as expected, the coachman drew the team to a halt and made to get down from his perch. Both Emily and Brand held themselves still, opting neither to take aim nor relinquish their weapons, instead waiting to see how events would unfold. The wait ended quickly as the coachman raised up a beefy hand holding a large pistol. As the firearm was aimed and leveled at the frightened but determined fellow who had dared draw a halt to the earl's carriage, Emily felt her breath catch in her throat. It was as if the stage had been set to reenact the disturbing farce of last evening.

Abruptly, she wondered what the 'gentleman' highwayman must think if he was indeed watching from a secluded hiding place. No doubt he was incensed, she thought with a smirk. For the second time in as many days, demands were being met with defiance rather than compliance. As he had yet to put in an appearance, she could only assume he didn't plan to. He was probably cursing his luck and his incompetent partner as well, but she felt only relief that there would most likely be no shots fired here tonight.

The expectation of danger that had tensed her back and shoulders began to ebb slowly away. Now she relaxed slightly, relieved she would not need to fire her father's pistol. The highwayman they now faced was here at Brand's direction, and the other, the one for which they had set this trap, appeared notably absent.

So much for her adventuring. In truth it was the coachmen who were having adventures; she had merely gotten the delightful opportunity to wait about in the muck and the dark for the chance to watch as they had them. From now on, perhaps she would simply stick to her novels. Those she could enjoy in the warmth of her own bedroom where a cup of chocolate was always within easy reach. It seemed she was quite eager indeed to consign her daring evening escapades to the past—she was ready to be off and out of her wretched disguise. She was even hoping she might have a bit of time to read tonight before weariness overtook her. If things here could be finished up quickly…

As the coachman broke the silence and her concentration as well, she jerked her gaze back towards him.

"I'll see ye swingin' by your neck or buried six feet under fer darin' to call a halt to the Earl o' Chase's carriage."

Full of swaggering bluster, the coachman fired without

bothering to steady his aim. The thunderous explosion was deafening and had the carriage horses plunging heedlessly in fright. The coachman had had neither the good sense to come fully down off the box, nor to take a firm hold of the reins, and so he found himself lurching backwards and then lunging forward to grasp hold of the loose strips of leather. Within seconds, he had managed to calm and quiet the pair, only to glance up and realize that his shot had gone wide, and the highwayman's pistol now held aim at his heart. He glanced sideways towards his outriders before returning his wide-eyed gaze to the villain's unsteady hand.

As the shot echoed through the trees, Emily had watched, wide-eyed, as Sneeves seemed to shrink even further into himself, waiting perhaps for the pain of injury and then simply for the deafening noise to die away. With the return of the tense, watchful silence, it was clear he was not angry, rather he seemed resigned to have cheated death once again. Reluctantly, he drew his own pistol, tossed an apologetic look in Brand's direction and a fearful one in Emily's, and then took half-hearted aim at the coachman.

Not comfortable depending on Sneeves' questionable loyalty, Emily clenched her trigger finger and leveled her pistol at his. She was confident her aim was true enough to knock the gun cleanly away, but if, by chance, lack of practice had put her off a bit, she certainly wouldn't feel guilty. In her opinion, the man could use a little nick of pain. It just might nudge him out of the stupor that had him playing highwayman and causing trouble in this quiet corner of England.

Emily darted a glance at Brand, a subtle acknowledgment of her agreement to follow orders. In her defense, he hadn't issued any orders, and her heartbeat drummed nervously, hoping he remembered that. As she kept a watchful eye on both Brand and her target, she soon saw Brand tip his head in apparent acquiescence and released the breath she hadn't even realized she'd been holding. She'd noticed the rigid line of Brand's body and imagined she could make out the white of his knuckles as they tensed over the handle of his own pistol. Still she remained unfazed, assuming he'd yielded to her silent request so that he might focus his own weapon and attention on the true, and still blind, threat. She would do her best to handle the courageous incompetent. Viewed in that manner, it was no wonder this pair of highwaymen was destined to failure.

Of the opinion that further waiting was needless if not outright dangerous, Emily looked calmly down the gleaming barrel of her father's pistol and quietly cocked the weapon. She kept her knees tight to Gypsy's side and held the reins tautly in her left hand while smoothly stroking the horse's neck. Much to the dismay of Colin, who had taken every opportunity to insist that she delay in firing, Emily had always fired immediately upon sighting her target. A quick assessment assured her that this situation certainly warranted no change in tactics, so she eagerly took the shot. She felt a surge of pride and a measure of relief when she realized that her bullet had indeed found its mark.

Both emotions were immediately and forcibly subdued by pain. As she watched her bullet knock the gun from her target's already-limp fingers, she felt a fire rage through her arm.

The arm that had fired the pistol so calmly, so confidently, so dispassionately was now being punished. If this was her conscience expressing its disapproval, it had apparently been appalled by her actions. Or maybe it was God's intention to show her how the fires of hell would feel if she continued to stand in judgment of others. Thoroughly confused, she used her left arm to steady Gypsy while allowing her right arm to recover. She spoke soft, soothing words, but she had no idea what she said or whom she spoke to, Gypsy or herself.

Brand's voice broke through her litany as if calling from a great distance.

"Breton! Breton—are you all right?"

Was he angry with her? The very idea seemed absurd, especially after she had knocked the man's gun cleanly away.

She tore her gaze away from the still smoking firearm,

lying limply in her open palm on the edge of the saddle, to stare at Brand. He was speaking to her but apparently couldn't bring himself to look at her as his eyes darted everywhere, frequently skimming over her, but quickly moving on. He had sidestepped his horse away from the carriage and away from her.

"Of course I'm all right," she answered waspishly. *Was it possible he was referring to the strange reaction she had had to the gunshot?* Curiosity got the better of her. "Why are you asking?" Her voice sounded oddly husky to her own ears.

"Because you've just been shot!"

It was the first time she had heard his voice raised in anger. Apparently she had finally managed to ruffle his control, and it appeared to have taken very little effort. She would have smiled, but nothing seemed amusing, so instead she simply watched as he spared one final glance for the threatening shadows and then started back towards her, cursing fluently.

Through a fog of pain and a haze of confusion, the testy words he had fired in her direction finally registered. *Shot? But that was absurd!* Eager to correct him, she made a point of looking down at herself in a cursory, dismissive fashion. It was as she moved her eyes upwards along her arm that she saw the dark stain spreading over the filthy white shirt.

Shock had her mind reeling.

How did this happen? Only one shot was fired—from my own pistol. It stings…it burns…it hurts like the very devil. I desperately wish to curse, and I want very much to cry, but first I need to get away. It will be hell if he sees me this way…

Never again will I believe what I read in novels. There is no hero riding to my rescue. Only an ill-mannered, ill-tempered beast of a man is coming, no doubt solely to reprimand me. I just wish to lie down and be left alone.

* * *

"Bloody hell!" Brand struggled to control his stallion as the shot roared through the silence. He hadn't thought she would actually fire—he'd only nodded to indicate she should keep up appearances.

What the devil had she been thinking!?

He'd known Sneeves' actions would need to appear convincing, but he'd assumed the man was smart enough to gauge the situation. After all, Sneeves was now in his employ and had been threatened with arrest if events didn't go as planned. Even if it had become necessary to fire on them, Brand had expected the requisite shot to go wide. Apparently Emma hadn't been so trusting.

Damnation!

Surprised at the panic that had flared up in his chest, he fought for calm and control in both himself and his mount. It seemed an eternity before he was able to finally subdue the horse, but it was in fact only a matter of seconds. Amid the chaos that had descended on this deceptively innocent spot, he raked his eyes over the dense foliage searching for signs of the second highwayman. When he was convinced he searched in vain, he spared a hopeful glance for Sneeves. The man seemed shaken but was, by all appearances, unharmed. He was also unarmed and obviously uncertain over what he should do next.

Emma had been as good as her word, Brand conceded, more than a little bit proud of her. He turned to offer her a smile and nod of approval, but instead of the smug smirk he was anticipating, he was struck by the pallor of her face as it seemed to glow in the darkness. She appeared confused and was quietly murmuring something to her horse or herself. He noticed her firing arm lying almost reverently against her horse's back, and when the beast turned slightly, he could see the blood.

Shock held him immobile before he angrily shook away the useless emotion. Emma was injured, and the only explanation could be that the elusive highwayman had been watching them, waiting for an opportunity, taking it when Emma herself had fired her own weapon. Now Brand couldn't know whether danger still hovered. And as such, he could not and would not go to her. He had never been ruled by emotions, and he determined not to be this evening, no matter how desperate he felt. Such a lapse in control was dangerous and could very well be deadly. Knowing this, he gritted his teeth, raised both of his pistols, and purposefully stepped his horse away from the carriage and its restricted visibility...and away from Emma as well. Then he swept his gaze over everything, searching the trees for a movement, a flicker, anything.

Damnation! Where was the bloody moon?

Each time he allowed his eyes to roam back to her, his stomach clenched, each hand gripped its pistol even tighter, and his conscience berated him anew. She looked so fragile now, sitting astride her horse, a pretend stable boy. She was composed but apparently unable to hold herself completely upright. The slight slump in her posture was the only outward sign that she was in pain but even it was too much to bear. He felt completely responsible for this debacle, perhaps because no one else seemed to claim responsibility for this mischievous sprite. He should never have allowed her to accompany him when danger was almost inevitable. Ridiculous as it was, he had not wanted to disappoint her. Now she was injured, and he was the only one to tend her wound. But he couldn't—not yet.

He would though, whether she deigned to let him or not.

He called out to her a few times to make sure she was alert, unable to believe he had his wits well enough about him to remember to call her by the surname she had given him. His eyes and attention remained focused on the trees and the darkness that had settled in between. Finally he heard what he'd been waiting for—the sound of a horse moving away through the trees to his right. Needing to be certain, he waited several long seconds before tossing Sneeves a nod of dismissal, pocketing his pistols, and hurrying to Emma's side.

9

"...it seems the Earl will not be in attendance after all, which is odd indeed as I heard tell that his carriage was seen in the vicinity...But no matter, we will certainly make due without him—I understand his heir is in residence at the Willoughsby estate."

LETTER FROM LADY BEATRICE SINCLAIR TO MR. DESMOND RICHLY
30 OCTOBER 1818

Brand released some of his pent-up emotion by roaring a string of curses at the villains and himself. He would have liked to pursue the cowardly bastard who had done this to Emma, but it was a risk he was unwilling to take. No matter how daring or self-sufficient she might presume herself, nothing could have prepared her for such an experience tonight. He would relish punishing the man who had inflicted injury so carelessly and so damn cowardly. But right now she needed all his attention. Whether she could admit it or not, she would need him, just as he needed to stay with her.

Having interpreted Brand's unspoken consent, Sneeves spared only a moment to glance over at Emma with apparent regret before he turned his horse towards the trees and escape.

The coachman, climbing purposefully down from the box, had just reached the ground as the scoundrel turned his horse, urged him to speed, and promptly disappeared into the surrounding trees. Adding his colorful curse to Brand's, he bent to palm the abandoned gun.

"Thot we 'ad 'em, milord, when the young lad shot 'is

pistol clean away. Who would 'av guessed there'd be a second one 'idin' in the trees—nasty bit 'o work." The man shook his head over the injustice while turning the recovered pistol in his hands. "Not likely we'll ever catch 'em now that the second one's made off through the trees. I could follow 'em, but I'd have little chance with no moon an' no direction."

"A little faith, Bristol. The one you fired on is working for me, at least temporarily."

"A highwayman, milord? You're involved in this business?"

At Brand's quelling glare, Bristol hurried to make amends.

"Beg yer pardon, milord, should 'av known such as you'd never get involved in such nasty work. Wot exactly was he to do, milord?"

"Help me lure and catch the 'nasty bit 'o work'," Brand replied, thoroughly exasperated.

"Ah, yes, milord," Bristol answered with a comprehending nod. Leaning in slightly, he added, "If I might make a suggestion, milord?" No doubt seeing the impatience in Brand's eyes as he slowly turned back to hear the unsolicited advice, the coachman spoke hurriedly, "A bit more blunt might find you a more capable fellow."

"Interesting. So, if my father were to increase your wages, your aim might improve?" Brand narrowed his eyes at the man and then spun away, unwilling to hold to the charade of master-servant tactics while more important matters awaited.

The blustering erupted from behind him. "No, milord. Shouldn't think so, that is. Temper got the better o' me, an' that ain't no excuse. Won't 'appen again. Beggin' your pardon, of course, milord."

"You did fine, Bristol," Brand assured him, eager to call a halt to the idle prattle, "I appreciate the assistance. Give me a minute here, and we'll get our heroic lad into the carriage. Can you manage a blanket and a bit of brandy? Well, I daresay more than just a bit. I could use a tumbler full myself."

"Forgot meself for a moment—should 'av asked ye sooner. How does the young lad fare—winged, was he? He looks right 'nuff, if a bit sluggish, but we can't very well blame him for that now, can we?" Bristol was shuffling about, clearly uncomfortable and wishing to put himself to work.

"It should be no trouble to set him to rights—I'll handle the task myself in the carriage. No doctors, Bristol. Understood?" Brand added a touch of steel to his dismissive tone, determined that the coachman understand just how imperative it was that no one know what had happened.

Bristol nodded and then went about following orders. Brand immediately turned his attention back to Emma. He moved up alongside of her and covered her hands with his own, working her tangled fingers free of the thin strips of leather. The horses eyed each other, but both were well-trained enough to keep relatively still.

His cursory inspection of the wound revealed that the ball was still lodged in her shoulder—he would need to remove it. The task shouldn't be difficult as it had been a clean shot, unlikely even to have nipped the bone. Enough blood had been spilled to drench her entire upper arm and part of her chest, but it looked as if she had been able to stem the flow by keeping relatively still. Her shirt would be unsalvageable—no loss there—but her shoulder should heal nicely. His conscience would not be so lucky.

He might as well prepare himself for a healthy measure of unpleasantness. This was undoubtedly only the first phase of the punishment that God would mete out for his irresponsibility with regard to this woman.

Whatever else there was in store, he knew he deserved it.

He shifted his eyes from her shoulder to her face to gauge her condition. Although slightly bleary-eyed, she was gazing at him expectantly now that awareness had taken a slippery hold. She continued to cling tightly to her horse's reins, whether for composure or the comfort they afforded her he wasn't certain.

By God, but he was proud of her.

When Brand was confident that Gypsy understood the change of command, he put his arm gently around Emma's waist. As soon as he did, she leaned into him and turned her face up to his. The tense silence he maintained must have caused her a bit of apprehension, for when she finally spoke her voice was quietly pleading.

"Please don't blame me for this—I truly can't bear a lecture right now. This really wasn't my fault."

"Hush, love. Of course it wasn't. Your aim was perfect. It appears our second highwayman is even more cowardly, and thus more elusive, than we had originally thought."

Emma winced, and he quickly relaxed fingers that had tightened with rage.

"You cannot ride home…" As she turned towards him and opened her mouth to protest, he wisely amended his statement. "I've no doubts that you could handle the ride home and perhaps even manage to bind the wound on your own, but I'd prefer it if you didn't." She made to protest a second time, but he cut her off, "Let us pretend, just for tonight, that you are a frivolous miss whose charms run to giggling and inane chatter. You might even try batting your eyelashes if you wish me to pay particular attention."

Looking at her, he wasn't sure which emotion flitting across her face was the one she would decide upon. Exasperation… contempt… amusement… resignation. When he saw signs of the latter, he decided to press his advantage.

"Emma," he said quietly, "you cannot slay every dragon on your own." She looked away from him and bit her lip as he continued speaking. "Besides, this was entirely my fault."

He was surprised to hear her answer primly and promptly, "I agree."

A grin stole over his face, and he cupped her chin and lifted it slightly until her eyes met his. Slowly he moved his thumb along the crescent-shaped recess between her lips and chin.

"Then let me help you."

As she gazed into his eyes, almost overcome with numbing pain and weariness, she realized that she trusted him enough to relax into his care. She nodded, closed her eyes slightly, and answered with a mysterious whisper, "You may soon wish you never offered."

Puzzled, but unwilling to press her into further explanation, he called to Bristol to take both sets of reins and tie them to the rear of the carriage.

"I'll ride inside with her...er...him," he stuttered, furious with himself for slipping. "I don't want him to lose consciousness." It was so absurd to think of her as a 'him' that he could barely bring himself to utter the word.

Contenting himself that the man could navigate through the inky darkness to Clifton Manor, Brand decided to leave everything but Emma in the coachman's capable hands.

As Bristol moved forward to take the reins, nodding in agreement or simple servility—it really didn't matter which—Brand pulled Emma across his lap and carefully dismounted. He had expected her to weigh little more than a feather, but it seemed he had been mistaken yet again. Miss Emma Breton would surely delight in knowing that she had surprised him once more. She was tightly built, with plenty of muscle under all of those gentle curves, and as she turned slightly in his arms, he was forcibly reminded of her innocence and his lack of it. Brand gritted his teeth and looked away from her towards his father's unsuspecting coachman.

If Bristol found Brand's method of tending to a young man strange, he didn't mention it but, rather, kept his attention focused on calming the unfamiliar horses. Brand would have expected nothing less. Consistently above reproach, the earl's servants retained their positions as long as they understood that their job was simply to follow orders. Opinions were generally frowned upon—a fact that Bristol had apparently forgotten amidst the evening's excitement—and gossip was forbidden. The same rules had also applied to Brand, but he'd decided early on not to conform.

As he settled Emma on the carriage seat, he was, for

once, thankful that his father had insisted on the deep, plush velvet upholstery and decadent proportions. It would all ensure that Emma was as comfortable as possible until the moment came that she was very uncomfortable indeed. For now, however, she was turned on her side and curled into herself, her eyelids fluttering as she fought sleep. He would need to keep her awake for a time to be sure she didn't lose consciousness, but he would give her and himself a couple moments of peacefulness first.

Glancing at the seat across from her, he saw that Bristol had set out a soft wool blanket, a full bottle of French brandy, and a crystal tumbler. Despite his father's unwavering support of the British army, the old earl had continued to support local smuggling. It was one of a very few matters on which father and son saw eye to eye.

Brand splashed some of the spirit into the glass as he heard Bristol urging the horses to move on. He downed the contents in one swallow and then regretted the heedless decision as the fiery liquid shot straight to his belly. He was reminded that he hadn't eaten and wasn't likely to anytime soon. He needed to be careful. Much as he wanted to, he couldn't drink himself into a stupor. He needed his wits about him and his hands steady. It would be a tricky thing as he'd still need to drink enough to get the job done. Pouring a couple more swallows for himself, he sat with his forearms resting on his knees. He spared a moment to lower his head and close his eyes. Then he took a deep, calming breath before raising his head and opening them once more. What he saw had the breath catching in his throat.

Bristol had managed to light the two small carriage lamps his father had insisted be mounted inside the carriage in order to allow himself sufficient illumination for reading. Brand knew the sparkle in the air that surrounded them was caused by the light glinting off the mist now swirling through the space, but looking at Emma, it was difficult to remain sensible.

For the moment her eyes were closed, so he gifted himself with one long look at her. The faerie, it seemed, had reappeared. And while he knew that the beauty that lay before him was real, he was almost tempted to believe she was a figment of his imagination.

What other young lady of his acquaintance would behave this way? Planning ambushes, dressing as a boy, riding astride, and mocking him with his title? Each time he was with her, she managed to surprise and shock him just a bit more, almost as if that alone was her intention. One thing was for certain: she was not willing to conform to some preconceived ideal merely for his benefit, nor, most probably, for any man's. He found he respected her rebelliousness—it reminded him of his own—and enjoyed her company immensely.

She was too pale, which was to be expected with the shock and blood loss, but otherwise her skin was flawless. Rather than believe the sprinkling of freckles across her nose marred her complexion, he thought they only made her more lovely, more real. The blue tinged skin below her eyes hinted at missed sleep—he knew it would only be worse by morning. Her eyelids flickered as thoughts criss-crossed in her mind, and long, light lashes fringed over, nearly to her cheekbones. Her lips were slightly chapped and parted. They didn't look nearly as appealing as they had felt when he had carelessly tossed away common sense to kiss her. Yet even now, amidst the pain, her lips turned up slightly as if holding back some wonderful secret. She looked innocent, fragile, and to his critical eye, bruised.

From the corner of his eye he noticed a few burnished strands of her glorious hair struggling to escape their confinement beneath that hideous cap. Leaning forward to remove the offensive article, he had to applaud their valiant effort. The mass was pinned so tightly he was certain it must be painful for her. But he would need to leave it for now; he couldn't risk letting it loose. He didn't know whose help he may yet be forced to rely upon, and he didn't wish it known that a gently bred young lady had been involved in this evening's exploits. In fact, he didn't want to believe it himself.

He dipped his head and found himself staring at the cap he still held in his hand. He couldn't bear the sight of it.

Without it she wouldn't have had a hope of participating in the past nights' adventures, and in truth she couldn't have fooled anyone if they'd had cause to take a second look. He seriously considered tossing it from the carriage as they rolled through the trees but then thought better of it. Still, he needed to do something with it—the thing was appalling. He reached under his own seat and pulled open one of the drawers hidden beneath. Wool blankets. The next drawer contained a safe and a few of his father's books. He smiled, thinking of his father's reaction, before tossing the wretched thing in and slamming the drawer shut.

Wincing at the noise, he guiltily turned back to see Emma's eyes blinking slowly once again. He was able to excuse his thoughtlessness with the reminder that it was better that she not fall asleep just yet. Taking another gulp from his glass, Brand tried to convince himself that he was almost ready.

He stole another look at her cap of red-gold hair. It almost seemed to beckon him, glowing as it was in the muted light of the candles. He wished that he could unpin it himself and watch as she was transformed from fresh-faced pixie to beautiful woman. The yearning was utterly unexpected—he had never wished for such a thing before. His mistresses, when he had sought them, had all been in varying states of undress. None of them had ever had their hair pinned up. None of them had ever companioned him outside of their own bedrooms. He had never wished them to.

Giving it a moment's consideration, he expected he'd thoroughly enjoy the task of undoing a woman's hair. As well as the opportunity to simply delve his fingers into it uninhibited. In fact, he conceded, it was bound to be incredibly arousing, transforming a socially acceptable coiffure into a private fantasy saved for one man alone...

Amazingly, as he'd imagined this arousing diversion, his mind hadn't chosen to share it with any one of the many mistresses he had enjoyed over the years or even the new one he had been considering. He was surprised to realize that he was no longer even able to picture their faces.

Instead a gamine face, pale in moonlight, merged his thoughts with reality, and he found himself once again staring at Emma as she quietly suffered. He shouldn't be allowing himself to think of such things, not now. Even far away from this place and its memories, it wouldn't be appropriate, and it most certainly wasn't now. He needed to keep himself detached so he could do his job.

But he still had a bit of brandy and a couple of minutes to spare...

Her auburn hair gleamed as he reached out to touch it. He stayed his hand mere inches from her and watched her eyes flicker open, clouded with interrupted dreams. Eyes he once thought simply a vibrant blue now informed him he'd been mistaken. Their color seemed to shift and change endlessly. The longer he looked at them, the more he wished to. A stormy blue, he finally decided, swirled with touches of green. They fit her perfectly.

He was startled when she smiled at him, a full, honest smile touched with sleepiness. He wasn't ready for the ripple of desire that coursed through him before ending with a tug deep in his belly. He wasn't certain he was ready for anything with regard to this woman.

It was almost as if she had woven a spell around him, and he was unable to act as anything other than a... *bumbling idiot*?!

"Bloody hell." He had suddenly remembered Colin's absurd prediction.

Emily winced at the vicious tone of the curse and saw him snatch his hand away from her as if burned. Whatever he'd been about to do was to remain a mystery, for the moment had most assuredly passed. That hand was now being put to rough use massaging his own temples.

When his fingers had completed their assault, ending with his eyes, he looked at her once more. As she lay watching him patiently, his eyes wandered over her body, which he belatedly realized he probably should have covered. Her chest looked almost as flat as a young boy's. Yet another deception. She must have bound her breasts rather tightly as well. Shaking his head slightly, knowing that he would soon need to remove the shirt and knowing too what it would cost him, he turned his gaze lower. Her breeches were tight, and the slightly rounded outline of her hips was undisguised in this silhouette.

"God, help me," he begged before downing the last swallow of brandy he'd decided to allow himself. He prayed it was enough.

Pouring a trickle for Emma and eyeing it longingly, he knelt in front of her and spoke softly.

"Emma. Come now. Let's get a bit of this brandy into you. We can wait a bit until it starts to take effect, but we need to get you bound up quickly."

Emily narrowed her eyes, wondering at his mercurial moods. She could only assume he was as dazed by recent events as she. When she put out her hand, silently requesting his help in sitting up, he offered it. When she was settled with her back against the cushions, he handed her the glass, and she allowed an impressive amount to flood her mouth. Emily felt the brandy slide down, biting at her throat, and was barely able to hold back her gasp of surprise. But as the sting wore quickly away, she felt herself slowly relax into its soothing warmth.

She smiled at Brand, as comfortable as she'd been in what seemed a very long time. Now, as her body fought sleep, her thoughts and emotions swirled in a frenzy of activity.

Seeing the transformation as color bloomed in her cheeks and awareness returned to her eyes, Brand spoke first, "Better?"

"Much, thank you," she agreed, handing him back the glass. "It was exactly what I needed."

Allowing himself to relax a little bit, Brand smiled back. "Me too, although I could have used a bit more." Concerned she might not have had enough to dull the pain, he offered her another swallow. When she refused, he felt obliged to remind her of what lay ahead of her.

"You're aware that the bullet is still lodged in your shoulder?" he asked gently. Wordlessly, she accepted the glass back, and he watched her sip more cautiously this time, swallow slowly, and then nod once. "So you must know that I'll have to remove it—there's no one else. Unless, that is, you wish to call your family doctor and have him tend to you?"

Her single raised eyebrow and curled lip answered that question.

"Thought not. As it stands, we don't have many options. Virtually none, as far as I can tell. Feel free to contradict or interrupt at any time you feel I'm speaking in error."

Her lips slowly curved up into a smile, and she raised her eyebrow a bit higher.

"Don't worry," she said huskily.

He matched his expression to hers, and they watched each other for a long moment in the candlelight.

"I propose that we both get a trifle drunk with this really superb brandy my father was generous enough to provide, and then I will remove the bullet."

"You cannot possibly be serious! While it might be wise for me to drink a bit extra for the pain, I can see no reason for you to do the same. As your patient, I can tell you that I will not let you touch me if I think that you are even the slightest bit foxed."

The very picture of shocked disbelief, she made to cross her arms but stopped as pain snaked through her, a bitter reminder. Wincing, she bit down on her lip and slitted her eyes at him.

"Calm down," Brand soothed, "before you do yourself further injury. I was only teasing, although I should warn you, I have drunk just enough to have me teetering the edge of sobriety."

She opened her mouth to protest, but he quickly held up his hand to halt the objection ready to fly off her tongue. He really didn't have the energy to fight with her this evening, and he very much doubted if she could spare it either. As such, he had no choice. If she persisted with her argumentative tendencies, he was simply going to have to start using a more direct method of cutting her off—a much more pleasant one.

When he realized that this new resolution only made him

anticipate her fiery outbursts, he nearly chuckled, certain that he would be able to test out his new tactic before much longer.

"I know what you must think of me." He spoke self-deprecatingly, but his teasing words belied his tone. " A gallant knight, riding to your rescue, ready to soothe your fears and tend your wounds."

Emily's chest clenched at the misguided truth of his words. Whether she wished to or not, that was exactly how she viewed him, and not because she'd been shot. He was an adventurous stranger who had arrived just in time to save her from a marriage of tedium. She just hadn't decided yet if she should let him.

Unwilling to show him the shock his words had given her, she snorted in feigned contempt.

He hid a smile, recognizing that he had done as he'd intended, distracting her with his teasing.

"Dauntless, fearless, courageous. All accurate descriptors, it is true, but there is an exception, as there must always be. Unfortunately, my Achilles heel just happens to be bloody wounds. I don't like to see them, touch them, or, by God, have them."

Emily burst out laughing as Brand shook his head in mock disgust, and he saw that she kept her smile after her laughter had subsided.

"I assure you, it's true, at least that last bit. But I have done it before, all of it, and no doubt I'll be forced to again, even after tonight. Not surprisingly, practice doesn't make it any easier." He saw that she was staring at him quite intently, but still she kept silent. "Perhaps now you'll understand why I need that brandy, swirling around inside me, bolstering my ego." You needn't worry," he continued seriously, "I can certainly handle the task of removing the bullet and binding the wound. Stitches would be another matter entirely, but we'll leave that for the doctor."

He'd noticed that she'd taken a few more sips of the brandy during his monologue, and he could see that the spirit was beginning to take its bold effect. When she spoke, her voice was husky and slow.

"A doctor is quite impossible—how could I possibly explain a gunshot wound?"

"A good question. One you might have considered before insisting on participating in this evening's debacle."

Now a pout had replaced her smile, but at least they weren't arguing.

"How long have you known the man?" Brand asked hopefully.

"What man?" she asked, thoroughly befuddled.

"Your family's doctor," Brand patiently reminded.

"Virtually my whole life, but he has never been my doctor—until quite recently anyway." Faced with Brand's puzzled, impatient gaze, she elaborated. "He has taken over the family practice now that his father cannot get about so easily. I have not yet had cause to be examined or tended by the young doctor."

"Damn. It was a long shot anyway."

"What on earth are you talking about?" Emily asked, sounding more tired than exasperated, and not appearing the slightest bit interested. Brand wondered if she noticed that her words had begun slurring together. When he answered her, he slowed his speech a bit so she'd be able to follow his words more easily.

"If the old man was still your doctor, he might have kept your secret. I have found that loyalty can be a strong motivator. No doubt he was fond of you—you were probably a sweet child."

Brand added the teasing poke to gauge the effect of the brandy through her reaction. He wondered how much longer he would have to wait until she was ready. By his calculations, they should be arriving at Clifton Manor in a matter of minutes. As she sat impassively waiting for him to finish, it was obvious his subtle taunt had gone unnoticed. She was ready.

"The son is a different matter altogether," he continued. "He will be trying to establish himself respectably in the area. Keeping a daughter's scandalous secret from her father, a man who no doubt holds prominence in the area, would not be a good way to go on. We'll need to think of something else."

When she spoke, it was with utter calm. "I have just decided I don't care for the man." She didn't add anything that would confirm or deny his suspicions regarding her family.

Then he had it—it was quite simple really, and the only risk was to her reputation. Something that no one at all seemed particularly concerned with. Admittedly his plan had a few flaws, but if she was finally willing to confide in him, it could very well come off with nary a hitch.

"Come now, why not tell me your name? We now share enough secrets that it almost seems ridiculous that I don't know that one."

"Please…I'm not really ready to discuss this," Emily informed him weakly, her head tipped down. Brand didn't need to see her eyes darting up at him from beneath her lashes to know he was being deceived. It appeared her caginess had gone undiminished despite the brandy. She would hide behind her injury if it would keep her secret.

Irritated but determined, Brand continued to press gently. "How exactly do you propose to get home this evening? And before you answer, let me remind you that even if I allowed it, which I most certainly wouldn't, you would never be able to make it home on your own. Have you already forgotten what you still have yet to face tonight, or are you simply unaware that you are teetering on the brink of becoming thoroughly foxed? I can assure you that when I have finished with you tonight, you will not be able to sit a horse."

As healthy color stained her cheeks, Brand realized that the last bit had not come out exactly as he had meant it. No matter. It would be worth the embarrassment she suffered if it opened her eyes to the dangers she faced if she continued with this blasted charade. Here she was, alone with him in a closed carriage, allowing him to ply her with spirits, and she wasn't exhibiting a single ounce of fear or even a jigger of uncertainty. Thus far he had only succumbed to inappropriate thoughts, but there were men she may encounter whose conscience would not balk at doing considerably more.

Emily's reply was stilted, almost as if she considered each word carefully to make certain it did not reveal anything she did not wish it to.

"Perhaps...your coachman...would be...kind enough... to...take me?" She wavered a moment, then seemed to decide on something before speaking again. "Of course...you would...have to promise..."

"Not to question him regarding his destination? I wouldn't dream of it—what would be the sport in that? When I determine your real name, it will be a victory fairly won."

He smiled at her then and granted the favor. "Very well. As it happens, your clandestine arrangement should suit my plan to get you examined by a discreet physician as well."

"How?" Emily asked, for once succinct in her reply.

"When I am satisfied that I have done all I can for you, Bristol will deposit you as close to your doorstep as is possible under the circumstances. Then tomorrow morning he will collect you at a prearranged spot. The earlier the better, although too early and your family will become suspicious. Shall we say nine 'o clock?"

Before she could respond, he added an afterthought, "I just realized that this entire plan hinges on your being able to dress yourself—in a traveling gown, with an injured shoulder—without assistance." Watching her closely for a reaction, he added, "Or perhaps you have a sympathetic and loyal lady's maid?"

"Why can I not dress like this?" she inquired politely, blinking.

"Why not indeed?" Brand replied, clearly exasperated. "If it were not for your condition, I would be justified in turning you over my knee for such a ridiculous question. However, given the circumstances, I will answer. First, and most importantly, it will be daylight. Second, you wouldn't fool anyone. Third, your shirt is drenched in blood, and to be honest, you smell quite foul. Forth, it would be difficult for me to explain the presence of a stable lad in my father's—"

"Fine," Emily interrupted, irritated with both him and herself. "I'll manage," she added when she saw he was going to repeat his original question. Then she pressed her lips firmly closed in a manner she knew resembled a pout.

"I will meet up with you near the same stretch of forest, for which I am bound to have many fond memories. I'm not sure my selection is wise as the place seems to upset even the best laid plans, but I'm not familiar enough with the area to suggest anywhere else."

Emma's eyebrows were raised in expectation of his next words, and her mouth was silent, so he continued.

"Then we will proceed to ride together to my family's country home in Cornwall, where you will be treated by my father's personal physician."

As he had revealed the last, Emma's eyebrows had rapidly fallen, causing her forehead to wrinkle inward. He had to wait for her to form a coherent objection, as she was thoroughly muddled by drink.

"Tis quite impossible. Even you must realize…cannot possibly make a journey…alone in your carriage. My reputation would be in tatters." The objection sounded ridiculous, even to her own ears, but she didn't retract it.

"My dear, if your reputation survives tonight's mischief, you have no cause for concern. After all, you are currently riding unescorted in a closed carriage with a man who has plied you with brandy and plans, in short order, to remove a good portion of your shirt." Watching her eyes widen, he was satisfied he had made his point. "Having just fallen victim to one of the consequences of such adventuring, you should be relieved that tomorrow promises a pleasant excursion between friends. Besides, I will be riding alongside the carriage, not within, so you will be safe from any unwanted advances."

Her eyes narrowed, and he assumed she'd taken offense to his sardonic assessment of events.

"I can handle your advances very well, thank you!"

It was the last response he would have expected, but he was delighted with it nonetheless. Sparing a moment to consider the implications, he curved his mouth from a disapproving line into a satisfied grin.

"We shall have to discuss that later then. Let us deal with the less enjoyable, but perhaps more important, issues first. I assume you are agreeable to making the journey I have just described?"

"Very well. Don't even know why I care—won't change anything. If my...reputation's to be in tatters, why not take...full advantage? Marriage will go ahead. Money...motivates...far better than loyalty. Believe me."

Silence hung thickly between them. Seemingly oblivious, Emily grabbed the glass from Brand, downed its contents in a single swallow, and then laid back down on her cushion. Brand watched her, utterly speechless, and it wasn't for some moments that he finally realized that he hadn't yet relaxed the hand from which she'd boldly snatched the drink.

Her admission a moment ago had surprised him. The fact that she hadn't condemned him for his forward behavior had managed to warm him more thoroughly than the brandy. This new confidence, however, put her previous one into an entirely different perspective, dispelled every bit of warmth he'd mustered, and left him feeling empty. He allowed, or rather hoped, that he might have misunderstood her. Given past experience with her, such a possibility was quite probable, but he couldn't think what else she could have meant by such statements.

"Would you care to elaborate—I'm not quite sure I understand."

She smiled a bit mistily, turned on her side to look up at him, and answered.

"Don't blame yourself. I think it tis the brandy. I'm having a bit of trouble myself."

Too preoccupied to correct her mistaken assumption, he instead demanded, "You plan to marry?"

"*I* didn't plan anything of the sort...no one seems the slightest bit interested in *my* opinion."

Running a hand roughly through his hair, Brand looked down at the carriage floor, not at all certain he could handle any more surprises this evening. Thankfully, he was able to shield his reaction with the curtain of hair that fell around his face. It seemed the ribbon holding his queue had finally come loose. Gifting himself with a moment to recover, Brand then took a deep breath, lifted his eyes to meet hers, and asked tightly, "When, may I ask, is the wedding?"

"I don't know why *you're* so angry—*you're* not the one getting married. Are you?"

She peered at him, puzzled now.

"No."

She smiled. "Good. I wish *I* didn't have to, but my father has insisted."

"Who?"

"Surely you…do not think I…would give you my…father's name—that would be…"

"Whom," Brand interrupted, speaking slowly and carefully, "does your father intend will be your husband?"

"Another secret, I'm afraid." She seemed strangely apologetic. "Besides…with luck, I won't…have to marry him. You see…I don't like him one bit."

"How, might I ask, do you plan to rid yourself of this unwanted fiancé?"

"Oh, he is not my fiancé," she returned blithely.

"Emma," Brand threatened warningly, "you are making no sense, and, I confess, my fingers are just itching to throttle you after everything you have put me through."

Emily tilted her head up as a matter of pride, but the shift didn't have the desired effect, lying as she was, prostrate on a carriage bench. Assuming she must look ridiculous and feeling a trifle indecent with her neck so exposed to his scrutiny, she rolled her eyes and lowered her head once more.

"You're free to go. I've not kidnapped you." Emily knew her words weren't at all funny, but she couldn't hold back the fit of giggles that overtook her.

Good God, but she was unpredictable! He wasn't at all certain how to deal with her, but he took comfort in the knowledge that no one else apparently knew how either.

"Do not be ridiculous, Emma." Brand wished he didn't sound so surly, but he couldn't help himself.

"Em," she corrected automatically, still smiling.

Brand knew the second she realized her slip. Slowly comprehension seeped through the brandy fog, and she knew. Her smile dropped away, and she stared at him, very obviously trying to gauge his reaction.

Brand kept his face impassive, determined not to gloat over the fact that she herself had given him a very important clue to her identity. 'Em' must indeed be her nickname, or else it wouldn't have slid so readily off her tongue when everything else was tripping or staggering off.

"Very well…*Em*…perhaps you'd care to confide the rest of the details of your father's plan to marry you off."

"There really isn't much more to tell," she protested, clearly not wanting to reveal anything more. He imagined she was now regretting that last gulp of brandy.

"Humor me," he insisted.

She stared at him a moment, seeming to consider, and then looked resigned to the inevitable.

"Very well," she sighed. "Three days ago, my father announced…most unceremoniously…that it was time…for me…to marry."

It was obvious that she was fighting to keep her eyes open—if they both fluttered closed, she compromised, letting one rest while dutifully pulling open the other. As it was, much of the conversation took place with her winking at him. Brand couldn't help but smile at her.

"In one month, I'm to be engaged…to an extremely…unsavory relation…of my…st'mother's. Of course I protested, and…now have…opportunity to find a replacement to his…appalling choice…before time is up."

"Many young ladies would consider you in a most envious position."

"I would too. If it weren't for…the fact…that all men…essentially the same. As it is… don't want a single one of them."

"How exactly did you reach that conclusion?"

"I judged…gennelmen of my 'quaintance…'gainst husband criteria…found them all lacking…in most 'portant one of all."

"Which one was that?" Brand asked, suddenly, inexplicably interested.

She looked at him conspiratorily, winking and blinking all the while.

"Must appreciate me—just as I am...don't want to stay home...occupied with ladies' pursuits. Want to do things...see things...not be...locked away...to breed heirs."

Brand coughed discreetly, hiding a smile, but he kept silent.

Apparently done with her explanation, Emily muttered her last words on the subject to herself, "I would have thought Colin would have realized that."

Brand's amusement quickly turned to awareness at the mention of his friend's name. *She knows Colin?* It was too much of a coincidence that she might be referring to a different Colin. Colin Willoughsby must indeed be a 'gentleman of her acquaintance' if she included him in her search for an acceptable husband. Obviously he too had disappointed her. Brand hoped his friend had not been hurt by her rejection. It was unlikely—Colin was, by reputation, something of a rake, willing to take pleasure where it was offered but ready to flee if anything more was demanded.

Certain that his friend had not suffered more than a sting to his pride, he found himself thoroughly relieved and easily convinced that she and Colin would not have suited...

Bloody hell!

Until this moment, he had forgotten Colin's recently revealed, utterly inexplicable desire to marry. Only politely interested at the time of the excited announcement, Brand now remembered that his friend had, in fact, already chosen a bride. After everything that had happened, the news had been pushed ruthlessly back into the recesses of his memory. Now Emma's casual mention of his friend's name had Colin's words flaring to the forefront.

Her name is Emily Sinclair and she is the daughter of Lord Edward Sinclair.

Emily...Emma...Em. By God, the mystery had been solved. The woman lying before him, drunk on brandy and patiently waiting for him to expose what was sure to be a tempting expanse of skin in order to deal with the highwayman's bullet that had lodged in her shoulder, was the only daughter of Lord Edward Sinclair. The woman that invaded his thoughts and inspired his fantasies, the woman he had kissed and had been looking forward to kissing again soon, was the lady Colin intended to marry, the one who had already rejected him.

Whatever he had been expecting, it hadn't been this. But never one to appreciate secrets—except his own, he was at least relieved her identity had finally been revealed. Perhaps now he could bring himself to behave as a true gentleman might.   Whereas before she had been an anonymous miss and gracious—or perhaps foolish—enough to pretend with him that each of them existed outside the strictures of society, now he knew exactly who she was, and the ruse was, at long last, over. He couldn't quite decide how he felt about her latest revelation, but it was, without a doubt, not what he wanted to feel.

Aware that he should refrain from further drink, but unable to restrain himself, he made to gulp from the glass Emily had proudly thrust back at him empty. Tossing the heavy tumbler aside, Brand reached for the bottle and took a long swallow. He felt the pricking sting behind his eyes and squinted tightly to keep them from watering. That was the last one, he promised himself. He had simply needed to clear his head—again.   Much more time spent with Emma—Emily—and he would end up a drunkard.

Watching Emily, her eyes fluttering once again between awareness and slumber, he presumed that any concerns she might have had had slid away. She was completely relaxed, and yet he felt a compelling urge to find out what it was she planned to do about her predicament. It didn't sound as if anyone of her acquaintance would suit, including Colin, so whom had she found to promise her a life of adventuring? For clearly, that was what she wanted.   Perhaps a highwayman would accommodate her, he thought ruefully. A highwayman in the guise of a gentleman—otherwise her father would never approve. *Good Lord. It couldn't be. She couldn't be hoping to ambush the 'gentleman highwayman' with the intention of luring him into marriage...could she? The possibility was outrageous, implausible, horrifying even, and yet it seemed a decision worthy of her reckless unpredictability. More than a little disturbed, he wondered if this was to be a lesson in revenge. God help her father.*

The more Brand thought on it, the more he believed her father's ultimatum had derived from self-preservation. Likely Emma's father was only an incident or two away from Bedlam, and this evening's business may very well speed his journey.

Deciding he really should have all the details despite not wanting them, Brand began gently to shake her awake.

"Emma...Em...I'll let you relax in a moment. First tell me who it is you plan to marry."

Groggily and somewhat grumpily, Emily answered unselfconsciously. "Well, I could very well change my mind," she warned pointedly, one eye closed, "But I'd thought...I might ask you." With that quiet announcement, she smiled blandly, blinked several times, and finally closed her eyes.

Brand knew he was staring at her, shocked to his boots, but he couldn't seem to help himself. He didn't know what to say, what to do, and for once with this woman, it didn't matter at all, for she had already drifted off, unaware of the reprieve she had granted.

Yet again she had managed to surprise him. No, that wasn't quite right. This time she had shocked, stunned, and confounded him with a single calmly uttered sentence. It didn't seem possible, but this final confidence was more startling than all the others. He really needed another swig of brandy, but he knew he couldn't risk it.

It was his own fault—he hadn't stopped nudging her, pressing her to reveal her secrets. It had perhaps been unscrupulous of him, but he couldn't bring himself to feel guilty. In truth he felt somewhat relieved—now at least he could try to act accordingly. What exactly that entailed he wasn't certain.

Moments away from Clifton Manor and the task that

loomed painful for both of them, Brand was struck with the unfamiliar and unwelcome feeling of uncertainty. There was a young lady lying virtually unconscious in his father's coach, and he had only just managed to unearth her true identity. She was Miss Emily Sinclair. Now he realized a part of him wished her identity had remained a mystery. When he hadn't known her real name he had been able to pretend that there were no consequences and that her reputation was of no concern. Now he knew it would be difficult for that feminine prize to come away from this debacle unscathed.

There were no excuses and no defense. It was true that they had both acted irresponsibly, but his conscience balked at laying the blame with her. She was young, after all, and a woman—she had simply wanted an adventure and hadn't known what to expect or the dangers she faced. He had allowed her participation, encouraged her to arm herself with what were surely her father's pistols, complemented her unconventional manner of dress, and nearly congratulated her on her admirable shooting ability. He should have forbidden her, should have kept his plans secret, should have done something, anything but this.

What had he been thinking?

Quite simply, he had not been.

He'd often been accused of being too cautious, too stodgy, too bloody careful. He'd prudently involved himself only in thoroughly researched, minimal risk ventures that promised considerable return on his investments. Further, he'd thus far managed to retain complete authority over matters in which he chose to involve himself. None of these admirable characteristics had served him in his dealings with Miss Emily Sinclair. And he had no reason to believe they would in the future.

She'd confounded him since the beginning.

He'd been amused that rather than stroking his ego, she'd preferred to poke at it instead. He'd been distracted by her companionship, exciting in its unpredictability. And he'd been astonished at her ability to stir up emotions that he had ruthlessly buried long ago. Quite simply, he had been, and continued to be, enthralled with her.

The difficulty was that they would soon part ways, and after their time spent together, it wasn't likely either of them would ever be the same. More troubling still was the fact that he would probably be responsible for wounding her a second time in the very near future. He couldn't marry her—he wouldn't marry anyone.

He just hoped like hell that he'd never be forced to convince her of that. There was a very real possibility that he might not be able to. He had first-hand knowledge of her stubbornness.

Brand glanced out the carriage window and watched as shadowy shapes rose up indistinguishable in every direction. Strange that he felt he could just as well have been watching the emotions shifting and swirling through his mind. He was staring blind as the carriage slowed.

A sharp rap on the carriage door had him surging to his feet and bumping his head on the ceiling. Bristol called quietly to him, "Milord? What is it ye wish me to do?"

Smothering the string of curses he wanted to howl into the night, he mustered his control and answered calmly.

"Where are we exactly?"

"Judgin' by the way the horses are fidgetin', I'd say the stables be right behind those trees." He indicated what appeared to be an enormous swaying shadow. Pinpricks of light poking through holes in the foliage suggested that the lamps remained lit at the Willoughsby stables.

"Perfect. I will have to remove the bullet and bind the wound, so I'm going to need you to stand watch. If anyone approaches, whistle. I'm not sure what we'll do then, but I'll save worrying about that until it actually becomes necessary. I'm going to need your knife, perhaps a bit of leather in case he comes to and needs to grapple with the pain, and some clean cloth."

As Bristol handed over his knife, he allowed his eyes to rake over the prone form a single time before shifting them away.

"The rest 'o what you'll be needin', you can find in there. 'Is lordship likes to be prepared." He nodded to indicate the other items could be found in one of the drawers Brand had already started to rifle through.

"I'll keep him as quiet as I can, but be ready just in case."

"Yes, milord." With that, Bristol closed the door and left Brand to get to work. He quickly gathered the necessary items and readied them on the empty carriage seat. Then, gritting his teeth, he set about cutting away as little of Emily's shirt as was possible to do the job adequately. The torn and swollen skin was now caked with dried blood, and the wound looked obscene to his steady gaze. He leaned in to speak to her but didn't know what to say, so he smoothed away the escaping strands of hair and kissed her fleetingly before setting to work.

He finished quickly, relieved she hadn't woken. He had winced at her first startled gasp and again with each discomforted moan that escaped her lips. Staring down at the pristine white bandage that now covered her injury, he knew he had to wake her in order to let Bristol drive her home.

He pulled out one of the extra blankets to cover her exposed arm and chest. He'd cut away only as much as he'd needed to, but it had been enough to see the tight band of fabric she had wrapped around her upper torso. While he cursed the entire length of it, both for the discomfort he was certain it inflicted, and the shame of letting such lovely breasts go unnoticed, he kept it in place. He needed to insure that her disguise remained intact for dealings with Bristol, but more, he was concerned that he simply couldn't handle a more intimate glimpse of her.

He suddenly realized. Bristol would deliver a stable lad this evening and collect a young lady tomorrow morning. Beyond caring, he decided that there was simply no way around the matter. *Let him sort it out.*

"Come, Emma. Wake up. We need to get you home and to sleep so you can be ready for Bristol to collect you in the morning."

Her eyes winked open, then clouded in pain and closed once again. As he watched, she bit her lip, fisted her hands, and slowly opened them again.

Smiling sleepily, her voice husky from the brandy, she finally spoke, "Can't think...but thank you.   Too embarrassing...see you...tomorrow."

Some of the tension holding his body rigid eased a little at her words. "I'm sorry, sweetheart," he answered quietly, unable to help himself. He kept from touching her though and quickly rallied, speaking the rest matter-of-factly. "The bullet came out cleanly, and you shouldn't need to worry over infection. We'll have to ask the doctor to be certain, but don't let it trouble you until then."

She nodded, her eyes slicked with unshed tears, and he couldn't help himself. He kissed her gently, a feather touch on her lips, and pulled back just a bit to give her instructions.

"I'll send Bristol to the door of the carriage. Give him directions to take you home." She nodded again, and he kissed her once more, hard and reckless, before turning to step out of the carriage. "Until tomorrow, fair maiden," he tossed back with an encouraging smile.

"Farewell...Sir Knight," she teased.

And then suddenly he was gone, and the doorway was filled with the ample silhouette of the coachman.

10

"...One would assume that with servants lurking in every corner, someone would be able to ascertain the whereabouts of my stepdaughter. Tis more difficult than it should be planning a wedding with the bride forever absent."

LETTER FROM LADY BEATRICE SINCLAIR TO MR. DESMOND RICHLY
29 OCTOBER 1818

When Emily had finally succeeded in struggling into her nightrail, it was already midnight. The clock standing in the front hall had chimed the hour just as she had slid under the covers. Now, a mere six hours later, she was awake again and feeling as if she had hardly slept at all. While she hadn't actually been tossing and turning—her shoulder had prevented that—she might as well have been. Her thoughts had replayed the evening's events over and over until she had no longer been certain of anything.

What had she revealed? Was she truly going to sneak away to Cornwall to be examined by Brand's father's doctor? Had she gotten drunk on brandy and made an utter fool of herself? How on earth had this happened?

Now, finally comfortable but for her headache, warm and cozy under the covers, she didn't want to get up, didn't want to face anything looming in her future. But she knew she must. Even though she had three hours before she would need to meet Bristol at the boundary of the Sinclair and Willoughsby estates, she knew it would barely be enough. Her morning ritual typically took her no more than ten minutes. Today she would be lucky to finish within the hour, for she didn't wish her maid's help—a bullet wound was surely too much temptation for even a discreet girl such as Bess. Then, of course, there was breakfast with her stepmother, and who knew how long that would take.

Somehow she managed to dress herself in a stylish riding gown, a slate blue wool trimmed in silver lace, but after a quarter of an hour's unsuccessful attempts to style her hair on her own, Emily conceded defeat and rang for Bess. Her maid's deft fingers quickly confined the thick unruly mass with surprisingly few pins and then showed Emily how to position and pin the jaunty grey top hat that had been selected to pair with the gown. Emily knew she'd never manage it but thanked Bess just the same.

Turning once, slowly, before her wardrobe mirror, she supposed she would have to do. She really wasn't dressed appropriately for traveling, but she couldn't very well arrive at the breakfast table in a traveling gown and announce that she was going on a lengthy excursion without invitation or permission. There would be questions enough as it was—she most definitely didn't want to encourage more of them than were necessary. She also did not wish to endure the ritual of changing gowns simply to uphold a charade. With all the trouble it had been, she may very well decide to sleep in this gown tonight.

Right now, however, she had other things to worry over. Would Beatrice suspect anything scandalous had occurred last evening? Would she wonder and inquire over her stepdaughter's painstaking movements? Would she be offended if an attempt to touch her stepdaughter was met with a scream of horror? Tucking back a smile, Emily turned from the mirror.

* * *

"Really, Emily, I hardly think such a fine riding gown is necessary for you to ride about in, even if you do plan on a visit to the vicarage. That gown was meant for riding sedately about the grounds with titled gentlemen—not that many opportunities for such excursions have arisen thus far, but one must always be optimistic." A frown now marred her ladyship's countenance, but it quickly disappeared in the face of said optimism, "But now that you are all but tidily engaged to dear Desmond, it will come to good use. He will, of course, expect you to present yourself to best advantage."

As her stepmother forked up a hearty mouthful of orange-glazed ham, Emily returned a mild smile that didn't reach her eyes and finished a bite of warm biscuit slathered with cherry jam. She poked her tongue from behind her lips pretending to lick away a few errant crumbs, inordinately cheered by the fact that Beatrice would remain unaware of her rather more impolite intention.

After a few moments of silence broken only by the sounds of china and silver, Lady Sinclair lowered her fork and heaved a sigh whose volume could have easily resulted in its being mistaken for a snort. "Oh, very well," she grudgingly conceded, and then, "If you could attempt to hold your skirts clear of the mud this time?"

"I'll give it my best effort," Emily agreed in the second between finishing one bite of biscuit and popping in the next rather inappropriately with her uninjured left hand.

"Emily."

Emily kept her attention focused on her plate, but after seconds passed in peaceful quiet, she risked a peek at her stepmother. Smothering a groan, she straightened her spine and slowly, painstakingly lowered her fork, politely responding to Beatrice's very obvious desire to have her attention.

"I'm sorry, I assumed you were finished."

"Not at all. I merely wanted to be certain I had your attention."

"What could possibly snatch my attention away from your riveting conversation," Emily asked sweetly, tilting her head slightly to counter the lilt of sarcasm in her voice.

What indeed? How about a nasty gunshot wound...an urgent husband hunt... revenge on a cowardly highwayman... the possibility of another kiss with Lord Brandon Davenport... a journey to the home of the Earl of

Chase… my breakfast…the movement of dust motes in the room…

"Quite so." Lady Sinclair was easily and conveniently mollified—a sprinkling of flattery and she would forgive almost anything.

"I have been wanting to discuss with you how it is quite the most absurd idea I have ever heard…"

As usual, Emily promptly tuned out her stepmother's steady stream of advice, gossip, and criticisms. As long as her stepdaughter appeared attentive, Beatrice was content. Questions were posed infrequently, and answers were rarely expected. All was well as long as Emily remembered to nod occasionally in apparent agreement.

Today she was unable to focus on anything other than the pain throbbing through her shoulder and down along her arm—the arm she must use to lift her fork and glass. Each bite was a challenge in and of itself, but she was determined to behave normally, at least as much as possible. Having just slowly, carefully lowered her cup to its saucer, she allowed herself a single glorious moment to relax, unclenching her teeth and breathing a sigh of fleeting relief.

"…that you should allow me to take care of the arrangements for the engagement ball."

Catching the tail end of her stepmother's comment, Emily looked up to give the obligatory nod and found her stepmother eyeing her encouragingly, eyebrows raised in question. Emily couldn't imagine what she could possibly be expecting and knew there was no way of knowing. She couldn't admit to not listening—that would be the completely wrong thing to do. She had found that, in general, honesty was not the best tact to use with Beatrice. She would simply have to hazard a guess based on the snippets she had heard.

Absurd idea… engagement ball. Surely there must have been something else, but she hadn't a clue what it was. As such, she had no choice but to wholeheartedly agree with the sentiment—an engagement ball *was* an absurd idea.

"Of course you are right, Beatrice," Emily said slowly, marveling that she was uttering the words.

"Oh! Well that's settled then." Her answer was very clearly the one Beatrice had been hoping for, evidence that it would also be one that she herself would soon regret. No doubt the moment she deduced what it was to which she had just agreed.

"Don't worry, dear, I think you'll find it's best this way. Please excuse me. I've much to see to."

Those ominous words were uttered as Beatrice abruptly stood, nearly upending her chair in the process. Emily frowned, puzzling over both words and actions, before finally noticing that Beatrice had left her breakfast unfinished.

Good heavens! What has just occurred here?

Cursing herself for such an ill-considered remark, it took her a moment to realize she was staring open-mouthed after her stepmother. She briefly considered racing after her and trying to subtly divine the truth but decided that even with an hour to spare, she had neither the time, nor the energy. And truly, right this minute, she didn't even wish to know.

She could barely deal with everything else right now; she didn't need to deal with Beatrice as well.

What she needed was a chance to lie down before she had to face the long hours trapped in the sumptuously oppressive carriage belonging to the Earl of Chase. Perhaps she could take one of her novels along to speed the journey.

At least that way she wouldn't have to think about the man riding right outside or what she faced at the journey's end.

* * *

Bristol had been precisely on time, and if he thought it at all strange that last night he had deposited a young man and this morning he was collecting a young lady, it didn't register on his face. She hadn't even had the wherewithal to consider that tiny but significant detail last night. It wouldn't have mattered—there was no other way.

Before climbing into the carriage, she'd darted her eyes around to ascertain that no one was watching. As Bristol closed the door behind her, she was content that her secret was safe. Leaning forward, she stretched the deep blue velvet curtains over the windows to ensure that it would remain so.

After a few moments, however, as the carriage slowed, she couldn't help risking a peek. As she had suspected, they were approaching the spot where Brand would join them.

The trees looked different in the daylight; the leaves even appeared to sparkle in invitation. They showed no signs of the danger and intrigue that lurked in their midst after nightfall. But she knew, only too well. Unconsciously, she reached up to gently cover her injury as she stared out at the bright autumn morning. Her view changed abruptly as Brand moved his horse even with the window. Glancing up to meet his eyes, she noted his raised eyebrow, silently asking after her injury. Suddenly and inexplicably shy, she bobbed her head slightly before lowering her eyes and dropping the curtain back into place.

Emily determined that she would shield her mind from thoughts of the man just as thoroughly as she had blocked her view of him. For as long as possible anyway. To that end she spent the first hour or so of the journey contemplating how she should behave when next she visited the vicarage.

What could she possibly say to Sophie?

She knew it would probably be best if she said very little. And oddly enough, she was quite content with that decision. If ever there was a time for keeping secrets from her prim and proper best friend, this was unquestionably it. Not only would Sophie disapprove of everything that had transpired, Emily feared that once subjected to her friend's chastisement, she herself would begin to further question her own motives and decisions. And that was something she most definitely did not care to do.

She had made her choices and accepted the consequences. For her, that was enough to make the whole mess worthwhile. Miss Emily Sinclair had had an adventure. She had disarmed a highwayman, been shot, gotten a trifle drunk, and shared a carriage alone with a gentleman stranger. And then there had been the small number of quite magnificently memorable kisses. She never would have expected that they'd be the most exciting aspect of the entire escapade. But then, there'd been a lot of surprises. Still, everything had been done with intent and fervor, and even though her shoulder throbbed and her head ached, she felt wonderful to know she had been through it all.

She'd been hurt and confused by Sophie's insistence that there were matters she wished kept secret. Now she understood. She had secrets of her own to keep.

That decided, Emily turned her attention away from Sophie, ignored its desire to veer towards Brand, and smartly pushed open her novel.

* * *

The moment she heard the carriage pull up, Sophie's nerves danced; she was nervous and yet delighted she had reason to be. The morning was crisp and clear, perfect weather to spend outdoors despite a few errant wisps of wind that had been tossing the shrubs about rather ferociously. She'd packed a picnic lunch and donned her prettiest gown, a pansy-purple trimmed with cotton lace, and then she'd waited, staring at herself in the mirror on her dressing table. Should she feel guilty? She wasn't certain whether she should or not, but she didn't. She wasn't deceiving anyone, for there wasn't anyone about to deceive; she hadn't seen Emily in days. Beyond that, she rather doubted Colin would have suggested the afternoon's pastime if he was intent on marriage to her best friend.

Perhaps he didn't know of her whereabouts either, and perhaps he didn't care. She was hoping both were true, but she wasn't going to worry over it. She would have a wonderful time and hope the afternoon inched her closer to a life full of them. So with a sure smile and a twinkle in her eye, Sophie stepped through the gate to be handed up into the chaise.

She and Colin settled on the grassy banks of the pond

edging the Sinclair and Willoughsby estates, spreading a
yellow woolen blanket to protect against mud and grass
stains. Kneeling gracefully, Sophie busied herself in laying
out her provisions while Colin, hair sparkling in the wind
and sun, lounged just as gracefully. He was propped up on
his elbow to watch her, fiddling with a yellowing blade of
grass, and Sophie couldn't think of more perfect scenery.

"I'm delighted I was able to lure you out, Sophie. My
luck in convincing you has never run strong." Sophie
glanced over at him and saw that he was staring right back,
an unsettling intensity firing his eyes.

"Well, as it's rather too cold for swimming, and I'm far
too old for much else you dreamed up once upon a time, I
decided I just might be safe."

"Is that what you wish to be? Safe?" His tone was
serious now, and Sophie set down a bag of oranges to settle
back on her heels and answer.

"Among other things." She'd decided to be purposefully
cryptic.

"What other things?" he asked quietly. Nerves skittered
up Sophie's spine and spread out over her skin as
gooseflesh.

"I wish to be happy," she admitted, shyly but firmly.

Colin took her hand and caressed it with his thumb,
"And what would make you happy, Sweet Sophie?"

Sophie desperately wanted to announce, "*You* would!"
but didn't. She couldn't. Such a declaration was beyond
her, beyond even her courageous new self. But she had to
say something.

"Love," she answered steadily, proud that her voice had
neither faded to a whisper, nor quavered with
embarrassment.

Colin was quiet for a beat, but his fingers had tightened
on hers, and Sophie couldn't interpret just what that meant.
Still, she was glad she had answered honestly no matter
what the outcome.

"Your father loves you a great deal," came a soft
reminder, "And I'd venture to guess that everyone who
knows you has found some reason or other to fall in love

with you."

Clenching her free hand into a fist and lifting her chin with a tilt of pride, she queried, "Have you?"

Apparently not the slightest bit startled by her question, he answered promptly, "Come down." He tugged at her hand persuasively. "I have a secret I wish to tell you."

Curious and only a trifle self-conscious, Sophie leaned down to him and turned her head slightly until her ear was on level with his mouth. Then his free hand was on her chin, shifting it back to face him. And then, quite suddenly, his lips claimed hers in a manner thrillingly out-of-place on a companionable afternoon.

Practical Sophie wanted to pull back with questions, but she was ignored by the new, slightly-more-daring Sophie who decided she was sufficiently reckless to indulge in a truly decadent kiss. Almost at once she heard a low rumble of laughter in Colin's throat, but it disappeared on the heels of a growl. Even Practical Sophie decided that the sound alone was sufficient encouragement, but first she profoundly wished to hear a few magic words. She would hold tight to decorum until she had a declaration of love and a proposal of marriage tucked away. And then...

Leveraging herself up over him, she sweetly requested them. "Do you plan to tell me then?"

"Tell you what?" He seemed dazed, and that was just perfect.

She leaned a little closer and watched as tendrils of her hair danced over his cheeks and forehead. "Your secret," she whispered.

Colin's eyes darkened with the realization that she was teasing him. He reached his arms up to spear his fingers through the hair at the base of her neck and curl his thumbs around her jaw.

"It is you, my devious miss. I don't believe I can get along without you. As it is, I'm barely managing now." He slipped his hands down and over her shoulders, caressing the length of her arms, catching hold of her fingers. Raising their joined hands to his lips, he carefully placed a kiss on her ring finger and then pulled his gaze up to hers. "I suspect I have your father's approval, but it matters not. I intend to ask you either way. Marry me, Sophie. Make me the happiest of men."

He was smiling at her, light-hearted, confident, and beautiful. Suddenly she was being offered her dreams. Almost. He'd not said *he'd* had reason to fall in love with her, and it was a glaring omission as far as she was concerned. Floundering now without reason, for she'd long imagined just such a scenario, with her love hanging unrequited between them, she let the moment escape her. The silence rolled over her and, horribly, Colin noticed.

"Please don't say no," he pleaded, tipping her chin up so that she'd have no choice but to look into his eyes. Arresting eyes, pools she could drown in if only she'd allow herself.

"I wouldn't dream of it," she assured him in a calm and pleasant voice. "Yes. Most definitely yes. Father will be delighted, particularly as he's likely to suppose that it was all his idea." Busying her hands repairing the damage the wind and impropriety had inflicted on her hair, Sophie hoped Colin couldn't see that her smile was forced. For truly she was happy. She just never should have said anything about love that was all. She would forget it and not let her poor judgment ruin the day for her. Scooting backwards, she pulled on her hands for Colin to release them.

He didn't. He yanked back, caught her off-balance, and had her falling over him again. When he was assured of her attention, he spoke with great seriousness, "I plan to make you very happy indeed, my sweet, for I plan to love you every day I have left to me. Will that suit you?"

Sophie felt a roaring in her ears that could have been the wind, her heartbeat, or simple magic. Everything she'd wished for was to be hers at last. All at once it felt as if layers of caked-on modesty, secrecy, and insecurity slid away from her. She was breathless with excitement, giddy with delight, and drowning with love as she reached up to shake loose the clip that held her hair demurely coiled. The wind was delighted to further her efforts, and soon her silky blonde locks were flying behind and around her like a cape. Her great adventure was upon her.

"Perfectly," Sophie enthused, not intending to let him up for lunch any time soon.

* * *

When she woke, she didn't know where she was or how long she had been there. It was dark and musty and thoroughly uncomfortable. And then she remembered. He had brought her here, left her here, and would soon be coming back for her. It was too soon—she needed time to think, time to decide what must be done. How much more must she suffer at this man's hands? Suddenly she heard him on the stair, coming inexorably closer, and as she watched, the door's handle slowly turned...

The carriage door flew open, having apparently succumbed to the fierce pummeling of a nipping wind (and the sharp twist of its handle).

Emily yelped and jerked backwards, accidentally dropping her book and painfully jarring her shoulder in the process. As she turned wide, startled eyes towards the opening, she was forced to squint into the rectangle of daylight now streaming into the darkened space. The groaning wind rowdily rippled through the pages of her discarded book.

When she realized who was standing there she let out a relieved breath and fleetingly closed her eyes against the pain and embarrassment. Holding her arm tightly against her side, she bent to snatch the book back from the floor and kept her eyes down, ostensibly to smooth the bent pages but, in truth, not wishing him to notice her discomfiture. She always imagined herself the heroine of any novel she happened to be reading and so tended to become overly engrossed. She now realized it had probably been unwise to bring her book along.

When Brand didn't speak, she did, eagerly wishing to break the silence and dispel his no-doubt vivid memory of her acting a complete ninny. Not to mention her own.

"Did you come to change places with me?" she asked hopefully.

"As tempting as that sounds, I'm afraid not. If you are done reading for the moment, you might be interested to know that at long last, we have arrived."

She looked beyond him through the door and could see rosy pink brick and classical columns rising upwards. Turning away from him, she pushed the curtain back from the opposite window and glimpsed a gravel drive lined with boxwood hedges, an open iron gate at its end. All in all, she rather thought the place looked extremely inviting. She was anxious to see what lay beyond the front door.

Brand waited while she gathered her belongings—she had brought a reticule large enough to hold her novel and a shawl to ward off drafts. And he waited some more while she tried to pin on her hat. Finally, damning propriety, he stilled her fingers and settled the hat atop her hair himself. He then circled her waist with his hands and lifted her easily down from the carriage.

"Welcome to Danenbury Hall, country seat of the Earl of Chase." She nodded, trying her best to recover from the tingling shiver she'd felt at being held so intimately.

A glance at Brand was enough to convince her that he had not been similarly affected. In fact, it seemed possible that he'd forgotten her presence entirely. His eyes had clouded, deepened, darkened as he continued to stare at his father's home. Quite obviously, he wished he were elsewhere. What a coincidence—so did she.

"Should we go in?" she asked hesitantly, not really wising to intrude upon his thoughts, "if only to get away from the chill?"

With a single raised eyebrow, he proceeded to answer in the most peculiar fashion, "What makes you think you will do better inside?" His enigmatic words hung bitter in the air, and Emily was, for once, at a loss for words. She laid a hesitant hand on the arm he held out to her, and they climbed the steps together.

"Do you think we will at least be offered tea and…er something to go with it? I confess that I am quite famished." She was whispering the last as they reached the top of the steps and the already open door of the Hall.

The butler greeted them with a stiff bow and held out his hand for Brand's hat, gloves, and greatcoat. Emily removed her pelisse, gloves, and hat and offered those as well.

"Kettering, may I present Miss Emma Breton."

While his words and tone seemed innocent and straightforward, Emily felt as if Brand's steady gaze was filled with innuendo. It was almost as if he knew who she was and was taunting her with the knowledge of it. But that couldn't be—could it? Not wanting to consider the possibility, she decided to ignore him.

"Welcome, Miss Breton. Please let me know if there is anything I may do to assist you."

Was it her imagination, or did Kettering now sound suspicious as well? She really didn't wish to deal with this right now...

Turning his attention back to Brand, the butler continued, "If it is suitable, my lord, a light luncheon is being set up in the sunroom. If you and Miss Breton would care to refresh yourselves, all will be in readiness when you return."

"Excellent. Thank you, Kettering," Brand nodded his approval.

"Shall I show Miss Breton to her room?"

"Yes, thank you," Emily interjected, anxious to be alone, even if the reprieve was to be short-lived.

She started off after the pristine-coated, rigid-backed servant, rolling her eyes slightly. As she looked slowly around her, she marveled at the truth of Brand's warning. As far as she could tell, chilliness pervaded every corner. Not a peep of sound issued forth from any direction, no gossip or chatter between servants going about their duties, no conversation or laughter from the house's residents. There were no fresh flowers and very little sunlight. What little there was, the heavy draperies were doing their very best to smother. Everything appeared pristine and in readiness. For what she wasn't certain until she realized it all reminded her of a tomb. It appeared that the Earl of

Chase had chosen to wait for death rather than bother with living.

When her curious perusal had brought her gaze back to Brand, she saw that he stood watching her. Abruptly he turned and strode purposefully towards the back of the house.

* * *

Emily was not impressed with extravagance; in fact, she would go so far as to say she was contemptuous of it as a general rule. She was appreciative of the comforts and luxuries that had been provided for her, but she could certainly make due without them. Her life would no doubt be harder, but it would almost certainly be more rewarding and exciting.

Ostentatious displays of wealth were prevalent everywhere, reaching from London all the way to her somewhat secluded corner of Devon. Such a shame really when the money could have been put to much better use.

Even with that opinion firmly etched in her mind, Emily was delighted with the room Kettering had labeled hers for the day. Clearly no expense had been spared—everything was exquisite, from the shiny walnut four-poster bed and its sunny yellow damask spread and chiffon canopy to the cream and celadon striped silk wallpaper, to the richly polished dresser adorned with a colorful, albeit empty, cachepot. With the curtains swept back, she couldn't help but be comfortable here—it was a cheery refuge in what seemed an otherwise dreary house.

Wishing to postpone for a few extra moments her return downstairs, she lingered over her toilette and performed it with difficulty. Her shoulder had kept up a pulsing, painful throb throughout the journey, and she was doing her best not to dwell on it. So she washed away the tedium of the journey with the tepid water left for that purpose and then contemplated her hair. The fact that it had loosened made her appear a bit more relaxed than she felt, but she supposed that was good. What mattered was that it held, for she'd never be able to repair it on her own.

Staring into the mirror, she reminded herself that she was an uninvited guest (for it was clear Brand did not live here and did not wish to), quite a distance from her home, and in the sole confidence of a man she barely knew. Best to be cautious.

She had already come to that conclusion where Brand was concerned, but still, it seemed that the more she knew of him, the more she wanted to know. His effect on her was utterly at odds with her typical reaction to the male of the species. Previous attempts by gentlemen to further her acquaintance had found her pasting a bland smile on her face while she silently wished herself anywhere else.

Then Brand had charged into her life, and she had found that, to her dismay, she didn't want to be anywhere else, and that her reaction to him was far from bland. Even time they'd spent apart had been filled with thoughts of him. Some thrilling, some infuriating, all of them distracting and inspiring. Truly, what more could she want?

Wasn't it safe to assume that he would take hold of her life in the same fashion that he had managed to take hold of her thoughts?

Wasn't today an indication? Here she was, virtually alone with him, sharing secrets and hoping there was more to come between them…more that *would* come if they were husband and wife.

Had she decided then? Truly made up her mind? She supposed she had—she'd just been afraid to admit it. Now she needed to consider matters sensibly—she needed to be clever enough to convince Brand that he'd come to the identical conclusion. While it was true he'd asked her if she was married, he hadn't seemed too interested in her reply. So either he was a confirmed bachelor, or he didn't think she was worth his attention. And yet she'd been worth his attention when the opportunity had arisen for a kiss…

She knew she should be offended but couldn't bring herself to it. She was, after all, guilty of the same thing. Besides, time was growing short. She'd been given an ultimatum, and she needed to act upon it.

God in heaven, she was going to have to flirt with him.

Surely that wasn't the only way. She didn't even know how to flirt—she had spent the sum of her adult years trying to avoid any behavior that might mistakenly be misconstrued as even the slightest bit flirtatious. Well, she could do it if it meant avoiding the likes of Mr. Desmond Richly. She would even go so far as to come right out and propose marriage herself if her original intention seemed doomed to failure and a union with Mr. Richly appeared otherwise inevitable. Likely her pride was to suffer a few difficult weeks.

* * *

Back downstairs again, Emily noticed that Brand seemed to be in an even crustier mood than when she had ventured up, convincing and cheering evidence that she wasn't to blame for his ill humor. She presumed it was his father who had gotten him so disgruntled, but she hadn't a clue as to how.

That made her wonder if she was to be introduced to the old earl. It wasn't as if Brand was trying to keep her presence here a secret. And yet he didn't seem particularly concerned with the proprieties. Perhaps he had warned his father of her temperament, and the old man had begged off meeting her. That hardly seemed fair. Brand's only gauge of her behavior was in their dramatic dealings with each other, and it had hardly been her best showing. At the time, she'd felt completely justified; now she simply felt a bit childish. She really shouldn't be surprised if he thought her something of a shrew.

Determined not to take offense at the presumed judgment, she decided she would go about convincing him otherwise and thereby set his mind at ease. She would be on her best behavior. As her intention was for Brand to shortly become her fiancé and the old earl eventually her father-in-law, it would be prudent if they could all deal tolerably well together.

On that note, she supposed now was as good a time as

any to begin the courtship…

She was given a seat across from Brand at the round table overlooking the Hall's gardens and became immediately distracted from her intentions. Finally, she was to have the enjoyment of a cup of tea. And judging from the table before her, quite a fortifying lunch as well. All in what was surely the only spot outside of her own bedroom that sunlight had been allowed to penetrate. She could almost forget the reason she was here…

She could also have easily ignored her companion, had she wished it. He was already doing his ready best of ignoring her, staring out the window with his brow furrowed and his mouth grim. She could have begun eating in earnest and consigned him the leftovers. But she didn't. She waited, eyeing the empty teacups, the steaming teapot, and the slices of lemon that themselves looked like little suns. Her eyes roamed over the sandwiches, the fruit, and the biscuits topped with sugary crust. Then her eyes lit on her own empty plate, and she lifted her eyes to Brand once more.

She had no choice but to interrupt him. With her shoulder as it was, she would never manage the teapot. Surely he would take pity on her.

"Shall we?" she asked quietly, politely, sweetly even.

He glanced up and stared at her for several long seconds.

Finally he gestured grandly towards of the tray. "Yes, of course. Please go ahead."

Emily cleared her throat delicately and waited. Her subtle hint was met with no reaction. Apparently she must be more direct in her approach.

She glanced surreptitiously around and noted that the door was wide open. It was possible that she heard the barest hint of a sniffle coming from that direction. Undoubtedly one of the lower servants had been dispatched by the uppers to unearth the story behind her utterly inappropriate visit. Best not to call him by his given name as that might be construed as excessive, even scandalous, familiarity.

Egad! Was Beatrice slowly but surely leaving her

mark?   Out, out, damn spot!

"Br—" She couldn't do it. She couldn't bring herself to call him by his given name. No doubt fear of prolonged enrollment in The Beatrice Sinclair School of Manners and Household Management was holding her back. She would deal with this later. "Lord Davenport?"

Still no answer.

Very well, it was unavoidable. The courtship would simply have to wait. She reached out with her left hand and selected a wafer of sugar. She then aimed and tossed it awkwardly in his direction. It bounced off the index finger he had resting along his upper lip, inspiring a measure of pride at her success.

She had startled him, she was certain, but if she hadn't been staring at him, she would never have known. He had blinked twice, but that was the only outward sign that he had even noticed her indiscretion. She was more than a little impressed with his unflinching control.

When he slowly turned his eyes to hers, they skewered her.

"*What* do you think you are doing?" he asked, clearly not amused.

She tried a shy smile, but he simply raised one eyebrow and held it, waiting.

Emily puffed out a breath and rolled her eyes, unable to continue the pretense. She knew she had much work ahead of her...

"I was attempting to get your attention. What has you so preoccupied?"

"Nothing," he answered giving his head one abrupt shake.

"It is very clearly something," she replied lightly.

He very slowly turned his head to gaze at her. "It is nothing," he returned precisely, "that need concern you."

She felt a delicious release in finding a reason to laugh. "*You* didn't accept that as an answer, if I recall, so I see no reason to either. Especially as it means I must forego a cup of tea."

Tilting her head in the direction of her shoulder to

remind him of her injury, she was pleased that her laugh had at least appeared to improve his mood.

"Of course. I'd forgotten. That hardly seems possible, does it?"

Rising, he lifted the teapot with aplomb and filled first her cup and then her plate from the selection laid out before them. Doing the same for himself, he resumed his seat. Neither spoke for several minutes as each enjoyed the warming comfort of the tea.

Emily let the unique brew slide over her tongue as she watched him watching her. As usual, he appeared a bit irritated, partly amused, and thoroughly resigned.

"What exactly is the plan?"

Brand slowly lowered his sandwich to his plate and made a point of finishing the food in his mouth before answering pointedly.

"After we have dispatched the remainder of these sandwiches, you will return to your room, and I will summon the doctor. Once he has completed his examination and assured you that you are on your way to an immediate recovery, we will be off again. A rather miserable day, all in all."

"What about your father?"

"What about him?" Brand queried, almost daring her to pursue the matter.

"Well, won't I be introduced to him?"

"Is there some reason that you wish to be?" he asked, slightly puzzled but clearly irritated at the direction of the conversation.

"I merely wish to adhere to the convention that dictates that one be introduced to one's host," she replied tipping her chin back a bit as she spoke.

"*You* are concerned with convention? I hesitate to call you a liar directly to your face, but, I can assure you, that did not come off as the slightest bit believable."

Ooooooh, but he was difficult!

"Believe whatever you wish. Just arrange the introduction. And while you are about it—is there anyone else here to whom I should make my curtsy?"

"I'm afraid you are going to have to deal with disappointment, and I am going to have to deal with your wretched temper as I plan on keeping you as far away from my father as possible."

Brand leveled her a hard stare, and Emily arrowed one right back.

Just as she opened her mouth to protest his imperious, and seemingly causeless, pronouncement, she realized they were no longer alone. Quickly swiveling her head to the right, she saw Kettering standing rigidly uncomfortable several steps inside the doorway.

"Your lordship?" he probed with quiet dignity.

"What is it, Kettering?"

"Your father has requested your presence, along with your guest, in his bedchamber, as soon as it is convenient."

Brand had not turned at the intrusion and so was still facing Emily, with his back to the door and the bearer of bad news. Emily saw him close his eyes, clench his fists, and whisper, "Bloody…damn…hell," before he opened his eyes again and looked across at her.

"Very well. Tell him we will come," he dismissed, his eyes never leaving Emily.

When Brand was certain Kettering had retreated, he smiled slightly, but his smile didn't come close to reaching his eyes.

"Well, it appears you've gotten what you wished for once again. Let us hope you come away all in one piece."

Emily wasn't quite sure what he meant by that, but it didn't sound at all good.

Still, she was not to be dissuaded from such an opportunity and so immediately following the summons, decided she was no longer hungry. So she carefully placed her partially eaten egg sandwich back on her plate and folded her hands in her lap.

Brand's mood had darkened considerably, so she supposed she was fortunate he had turned introspective once more. He was so absorbed in thought that it was hardly surprising that two full minutes passed before he noticed Emily sitting quietly, gazing at him expectantly as her hands worried over the lace cuff that extended past her jacket sleeve.

Heaving a massive sigh and glaring at her quite ferociously, he tossed down his own sandwich and rose. She shivered in reaction.

"I suppose we might as well be done with it." Assisting her to rise, he added, "Come along—you'll no doubt find this extremely amusing."

"It's not at all amusing. I think it's rather sad actually that you and your father do not deal well together."

She didn't quite meet his eyes as she said this, instead focusing intently on tidying her appearance as best as possible without use of a mirror.

"Our dealings with each other suit us both. What would have you believe otherwise?"

"It's quite obvious," she answered, with a self-satisfied tilt of her head.

"Indeed," he remarked calmly, and Emily was uncertain whether he was incensed or merely dismissive. But then he continued.

"I am delighted that one of us is in possession of enough insight into the other's life so as to make such presumptuous comments. Perhaps if you were more forthcoming with personal information, I'd be just as capable of drawing ignorant conclusions with regards to your life."

More than a little surprised at the fierceness of his response, she decided not to take offense and answered lightly, "Well, you have put me firmly in my place."

"You'll never stay there," he said ruefully.

"Of course not," she admitted, hoping to call a truce with a smile. Seeing the one he returned, she felt a familiar fluttering in her chest that only intensified as he placed his hand on the small of her back.

"You are never as good-humoured when matters don't go the way you intend," he reminded her, "Try to hang on to your manners for race day—I fully intend to spur your disappointment."

"I will promise you a winning smile, and it will be all the easier to bestow when Gypsy and I outride you."

Neither had let their eyes stray; they remained forward facing. It hardly mattered, for Emily felt his reaction. He tightened his fingers against her, demanding that she hold her breath to prevent its gasping out of her. She was still moderating each exhalation carefully when he raised his hand to knock at his father's bedchamber door. Abruptly, he dropped his hand from her waist, leaving her but a moment to soothe her strangled nerves.

"Come," demanded a craggy voice that sounded like it was beckoning from deep within a cave.

"I tried to spare you," Brand said wryly, glancing pityingly in Emily's direction. She elbowed him in response.

As they stepped into the room, Emily was astounded. The dimness prevalent throughout the rest of the house had not prepared her for the darkness she'd face here. Apparently her ears had not deceived her—she was indeed venturing into a cave. Curtains hung from the windows like shrouds, shutting out the day's light almost completely. The bed was canopied with what she presumed to be heavy velvet. The excess of fabric cascaded down the sides of bed so that its occupant was almost completely shielded from view. Her breath came a bit shallow in reaction to the mustiness layering the air.

She could barely make out the man who sat almost regally amid the gloom. The two gutted candles flickering on his bedside table cast distorted shadows all around him. His round head, topped as it was with downy white hair, looked oddly out of place, especially as it put her in mind of Vicar Penrose. Perhaps the earl too was a sweet old man, simply misunderstood.

"Now you're here, you might as well come closer. Get an eyeful yourself, and let me have one as well."

As she stepped forward, Emily noticed he hadn't been content to wait for a better view. He was already greedily raking his eyes over her and clearly not the slightest bit embarrassed to be doing so. He stopped his perusal to peer closely at her face, clearly hoping to guess her identity rather than have it revealed to him. As she was certain there would be no flicker of recognition, no triumphant discovery, she waited patiently for him to finish, offering up a blandly amused smile.

"Don't know you, and I'm reasonably certain I've never laid eyes on you before. My *memory* has never failed me," he announced proudly. "Can't say as much for my son and heir." As his gaze settled on Brand, the earl beetled his eyebrows over his faded grey eyes in obvious disapproval.

Brand stared down at the man, a brittle smile on his face, but he kept silent, apparently unperturbed by the veiled insult. Emily, however, was appalled.

"My lord, if I may offer my opinion?" Seeing his nod of acquiescence, she continued, "Surely such a comment is inappropriate in the company of a stranger. Especially one as unwarranted as I imagine that one to be."

"Emma—" Brand attempted, intending to ward her off.

"Oh, let her be!" the earl petulantly demanded, adjusting the blankets over himself. "Although now you have me curious over who you were hurrying to defend, me or yourself. Either way it would be well past time." Shaking his head dismissively, he added, "You may go and be about your business. I will have Kettering fetch her when we have finished what proves to be a very interesting conversation."

"You may count madness among the vast and varied symptoms of your illness," Brand jabbed, "if you believe that I will leave her here alone with you. She doesn't deserve such shabby treatment, although I've no doubt she could handle herself should you decide to mete it out."

As his father started to bluster and lever himself up off the mountain of pillows supporting his head and shoulders, Emily pushed out her hands, palms away from herself, warding off any further arguments from either of them.

"Enough!" she announced, eyeing each of them with disapproval. "I will stay and speak to you, my lord, but only because I wish to—not because you believe you can order me about as a servant."

Emily wondered fleetingly if he might possibly believe she was one. Interesting.

After tossing the bedridden earl a withering look, she

turned her attention to Brand, hoping to placate him without her words giving rise to yet another argument.

"It's fine. Truly. You've just said as much yourself. I don't plan on being cowed by a man I've never met and will probably never see again."

She paused for a moment, wondering at the truth of her words. If she did end up luring a proposal from Brand, she would most certainly see the old earl again. And if she did not, she was very afraid she would miss the both of them.

Brand was clearly unsupportive of the idea, but with a nod and a royal sweep of his arm, he exited the room with the warning, "As you wish…"

Watching him go, Emily inhaled a deep breath and turned back to her obscured companion. Whether his reason for confinement was real or imagined, she had yet to determine.

"Come closer. Biting isn't one of my symptoms…yet," he finished with a twinkle in his eye.

Emily imagined that perhaps her first impression had been correct—the old man was quite harmless. It appeared that he could boast of a clever, teasing soul, well-hidden as it was beneath a grumpy disposition.

"Sit here." He indicated a deep brocaded chair standing beside the bedside table to his right. Most probably his doctor's chair, she assumed.

Ignoring it, she stepped confidently towards the bed and perched along its edge beside him with apparent calm. She truly hoped he couldn't discern the uncertainty coursing through her.

The earl eyed her critically but then shrugged slightly and began his inquisition.

"Emma, is it?"

"Indeed it is," she answered smoothly. "Miss Emma Breton."

"Breton? Don't know the name, but right now, I'm not so curious about your ancestry as your intentions."

Emily pursed her lips and kept silent.

"So, you've trapped my son into marriage?"

"No," she said calmly, wondering if he could see she

was dancing around the truth of the matter.

Her answer had surprised him. Well that was something. Best to keep the upper hand for herself.

"But you plan to?"

"No."

"You have no aspirations towards marriage? The man's a viscount, you know. And when I finally decide to depart this life, he will be the next Earl of Chase."

"That is hardly a concern of mine."

"I see. It's a fortune you're after, is it?" he smiled smugly, delighted to have pegged her. He ignored her raised eyebrows. "Ashwood made his fortune, against my wishes, I'll have you know. Utter waste of time, seeing as he'll shortly inherit a more sizable one. You need have no worries on that score."

"I assure you I wasn't worried," she offered blandly, masking her surprise at the nature of their conversation. If anything, she'd been expecting to be warned off, not encouraged!

"So you are not planning to marry Ashwood?" the earl asked suspiciously.

"I did not say that," Emily returned primly.

"By God, woman, you could try the patience of a saint! What is it you are doing here?"

Taking pity on him, Emily decided to take him into her confidence. She was certain he would not reveal any of their conversation to Brand, and she wanted so desperately to talk to *someone*.

"I am here because yesterday a bullet was lodged in my shoulder."

At his raised eyebrows, she added, "Bit of bad luck."

"I see," he intoned, and she felt strangely as if he might.

"Your son was stuck with the nasty task of removing it, and if you must know, I am considering marrying him. Bear in mind the two are completely unrelated."

The earl leaned back further against his pillows and rubbed his chin thoughtfully. "Considering, eh? What's to consider?"

"Whether or not he will make a tolerable husband, of

course."

"And what exactly makes for a 'tolerable husband'?" he asked with raised eyebrows and a finger crossed over his lips.

"Many things," Emily answered sagely and somewhat mysteriously.

"Such as?" the earl pressed.

"I am not about to share the list I composed outlining desirable qualities in a husband," came her retort.

"Fair enough," he allowed. "Can you tell me how the boy is faring?"

"He far surpasses the competition. The only uncertainty I have is when I spend any time with him."

She had been serious, but, at the earl's loud guffaw, she allowed her lips, which had tightened with each successive question, to relax into a self-deprecating smile.

"You'll do," he huffed out between chuckles. "You'll do just fine."

Narrowing her eyes, she posed a question of her own.

"For someone who has very recently implied that his son has come as somewhat of a disappointment, it is very odd that you should be flaunting the man's recommendations and encouraging me to accept his suit, which is nonexistent, by the way."

"Bah!" He swatted the nonsensical reply at her with his curled palm. "Ashwood is a fine man, and he doesn't need me to tell him that. We deal together better with snipes and bickers."

"How do you know? I'd wager you've never attempted any other method." Emily knew she was being impertinent but decided she had very little to lose.

"'Tis too late now, we're both set in our ways. But I might be persuaded to change a bit for my grandsons."

He raised his eyebrows expectantly, but she refused to be bated.

"How forward thinking," she murmured and then added, "I can only assume you would be equally as doting with both grandsons and granddaughters." She hoped, in the darkness, he could not see her pink-cheeked reaction to the inappropriate train of conversation.

"Indeed I would," he allowed seriously before rubbing his hands together with undisguised anticipation. When he spoke again, it was utterly unexpected. "Is your plan to compromise him? To get caught alone with him so as to leave your reputation in tatters?"

He was apparently oblivious to her incredulity because he offered his assistance to the abhorrent plan. To which she recoiled in disapproving shock.

"Most certainly not!"

The old earl slumped a bit but seemed to be considering. "So, how exactly is it that you plan to trap him into marriage?"

"I don't. It really shouldn't be necessary."

"Well now, if you'd allow me to offer you a bit of advice? I think you'd be wise to reconsider, because he isn't likely to come willingly."

"What do you mean?" She was now more than a bit puzzled herself, and her nerves were beginning to fray. It was all made worse when he began to chuckle and shake his head slowly back and forth.

"He intends never to marry, is quite determined on it, in fact. Preposterous I know, particularly as he is heir to an earldom, but there you have it." Having revealed this tricky bit of information, he leaned forward and whispered conspiratorily, "So what do you intend to do about *that*?"

With this latest development ringing in her ears, her plan of hinting around and dropping subtle suggestions didn't seem too promising. Still it was all she had at the moment—that is until she resigned herself to proposing to him outright.

"Convince him, I suppose. Either that or outwit him"

He stared at her a moment before answering. "You'll be needing a bit of help then."

Rather overwhelmed by her entire discussion with this man, she listened wide-eyed and a bit warily as he quietly confided that it had been his own marriage that had set Brand on remaining a bachelor.

"Brand's mother and I were both possessed of

headstrong natures and quarrelsome tongues. We argued frequently and liked each other better for it. Still, a bit of decorum may have been well-advised. We were never concerned over keeping our disagreements private from our sons or our servants." He looked down at the bed linens before continuing, and Emily imagined the memories still stung. "When she died, quite suddenly of consumption, I know Brandon blamed me. The boy reminded me so much of his mother, I think I poked at him just to hold onto her memory. But he wasn't like her. There was no fight in him—he just stood rigid before me, his jaw tight with pride and dislike. And before long, he had closed himself off from me. And I from him."

Finished with his narrative, he looked up into her eyes, willing her to understand.

Emily could see the regret there as well as the pride he hoped would shield it.

"Now you know why we behave the way we do. Occasionally I summon him here under the guise of my worsening condition, for he would not come otherwise. We spend a bit of time bickering before he quickly departs again, but at least I'm reminded of better days."

At Emily's disapproving frown, he added, "While hardly doting, my son knows his duties. Otherwise he wouldn't come. My advice to you is not to disagree with him—save your arguments until after you're married. Otherwise you may well scare him away."

As they'd already managed to bicker enough to send him fleeting to the far corners of the world, Emily imagined she may very well be doomed to a life with Devious Desmond.

Although…he hadn't fled yet…

She much preferred to change the subject.

"You mentioned sons. I wasn't aware that Brand had a brother—where is he?"

"Dead. Murdered in a London alley. William was the rightful heir."

The words were spoken with such cold finality that Emily shivered, feeling horribly inept.

"I am truly sorry that the time you have spent with me

has caused so many painful memories to resurface. Perhaps it would be best if I find my own way back to the parlour."

Heeding his regretful nod, she covered his crinkly hands with one of her own and then rose and turned towards the door.

"Miss Breton?" She turned back. "We will indeed meet again."

Relieved to hear the teasing amusement in his voice, she answered in kind.

"I rather expect we will."

* * *

Her visit with the doctor had been uneventful and, strangely enough, slightly reaffirming. After performing a silent perusal of her wound, he had pronounced Brand's presence fortunate indeed and praised his efforts as impressively thorough. It had come as no surprise to her— she had made the same assessment of him herself. She, of course, had been referring to her life.

Despite her objection, the doctor had administered a bit of laudanum, and he'd pressed her into taking several packets for use in the coming days whenever the pain became unbearable. It was more likely the throbbing wound would simply serve to remind her of the ignominious end to her life of adventuring. She wouldn't dwell on it, wouldn't waste time thinking of it now. With little more than three weeks left until her engagement, she needed to take action. Having finally come to a decision about her future husband, she now needed to determine how best to ensnare him. With his father's advice undermining her original intentions, she held out little hope that it would be easy. More likely it would be a tricky task indeed.

As the carriage rumbled over the rutted road, gently buffeted by the wind, Emily sat alone inside, determined to distract herself from the uncomfortable twinges in her shoulder. She passed the time considering, thinking back over the few hours she had spent with Brand. Suddenly her eyes widened, her breath caught, and she sat motionless in awed wonder. She didn't know how much time passed as she stared sightless, seeing only memories—snatches of time they'd spent together.   Arguing and...kissing. Strangely enough, that was virtually all there'd been, but somehow it had been enough. As she breathed out a quiet sigh of acceptance, she acknowledged the truth of her heart's unexpected revelation.

She had fallen in love with him.

When had this happened? She could barely call to mind more than a few moments in his presence that an argument had not broken out between them. How had there been time amidst all that to fall in love? It was so sudden it was scarcely believable.

Despite her fondness for romantic novels, she found it difficult to accept how easily the heroines seemed to fall in love with the men who initially seemed the most intolerable. Now that it had happened to her, she felt just the same as the heroines described in the pages of her books. Foolish and reckless, giddy and secretive, snug in the knowledge that everything would work out just as it was meant to.

It simply must, for it was becoming distressingly evident that the alternative was now considerably more horrid than before. She promptly decided she did not wish to take any chances and vowed to do the asking herself. She would convince him; she would swallow her pride.

Better to do it sooner than later. Then it would be over with, and her mind and heart would be easy. But only if he said yes. If he said no, matters would get considerably more difficult—for both of them, she resolved grimly.

So for the remainder of the journey, Emily gave the matter considerable thought. She would ask him as soon as the carriage rolled to a stop, as soon as he opened the door for her. She would just blurt it out and wait and hope. If he refused her, she would simply convince him. And if that didn't work, she would find something with which to cosh him over the head in the hope of knocking some sense into his thick skull.

Minutes passed, miles passed. She wasn't sure where exactly she was, and it didn't matter unless they were close to their destination. She waited, too anxious to sleep, too fidgety to read, until finally she felt the horses slow.

It was time. She steeled herself for the task ahead of her, straightening her spine and tipping up her chin with confidence. Then watching the door, she clasped her fingers together and waited.

As it started to swing open, she gasped in a quick breath and blurted her proposal before pride and embarrassment trapped it inside her.

"Will you marry me?" She had closed her eyes at the last second before she had even caught a glimpse of him, so she wasn't at all expecting the reply she received.

"Gettin' leg-shackled is not fer the likes o' me, miss. Beggin' your pardon, of course. Perhaps 'is lordship would suit ye."

Bristol stood in the open doorway, oblivious to her mortification, and, by all appearances, the misunderstanding as well. Either way, he apparently expected a reply before he'd leave her to wallow in embarrassment.

"Perhaps you're right," she answered, her voice barely above a whisper.

Nodding approvingly, he added, " 'Is lordship sends 'is apologies. 'E rode on ahead to Clifton Manor. Pressin' business of some sort. Says 'e'll find ye at the ball."

The ball? Good grief! Lady Willoughsby's ball was to be held tomorrow evening—how could she have forgotten? She had been dreading it ever since she had learned Brand's identity. And now, here he was taunting her with the very real possibility of exposure. What utter nerve!

"Thank you, Bristol. I apologize if my comments made you uncomfortable." She couldn't believe she felt compelled to utter those words.

Bristol waved his hand dismissively. "Don't you worry about it none, miss."

If this was the sort of incident she could expect as an effect of the laudanum, she would not be swallowing one bit more.

A certain individual will suffer dearly for this outrageously humiliating debacle!

"Will you be all right on yer own, miss?"

"I shall be fine, Bristol. Thank you for your concern."

With that, she stepped from the carriage and started off in the direction of Sinclair House, her home for just a little longer.

11

"...Something is amiss, of that I am certain. What exactly it is has thus far managed to allude me. No one seems able to offer the tiniest bit of useful information..."

LETTER FROM LADY BEATRICE SINCLAIR TO MR. DESMOND RICHLY
29 OCTOBER 1818

Emily had just turned onto the lane that led nowhere but the vicarage, but her thoughts had preceded her by some time. They'd long been occupied—quite uselessly—in wishing she was not expected today. Certainly no one was aware that she intended to visit today, but that ignorance in no way eliminated the necessity of a visit. Three days would be assessed as a lengthy and suspicious absence, and an explanation would certainly be expected.

She didn't have one as yet but was hoping she'd soon think of something.

It was troubling not to be arriving prepared but better than to shirk the obligation altogether. That could spell dire consequences indeed if Sophie happened to visit Sinclair House wondering where she'd been. Best to handle matters her own way.

Deciding the distraction of good manners was the ideal way to begin, she rapped sharply on the door. And felt the brisk tattoo in her chest as well.

The door swung open just as she'd exhaled her steadying breath.

"Hello." She offered the greeting with wide, darting eyes and a smile that began with pressed lips and ended with a slight curve at either end.

"Hello," Sophie answered, smiling before her eyes slid away.

Easily able to recognize suspicious behavior in others, having made good use of much of it herself, Emily couldn't help but wonder, *Is she hiding something too?*

In the silence that separated them, it registered that Sophie was dressed to go out. And not in a gown she would use to go shopping or casually visiting. If Emily remembered correctly, this was her friend's best gown and finest pelisse. *Where could she be going? Or where had she been?*

Emily wasn't the slightest bit anxious for another lecture, so for now, she was content to allow Sophie to keep her secret. That didn't preclude her from speculating on what could have caused Sophie's manners to slip. For here she was, still standing outside, without the slightest clue as to whether she was to be invited in or not.

She would have loved to stay a bit and discover why.

Yet Sophie, by some strange coincidence, in seeking an escape of her own, was offering Emily one as well. Relief swamped her. Luck, chance, perhaps even a miracle, had saved her from revealing everything. Faced with Sophie's accomplished interrogation tactics, she very likely would have been unable to avoid it. Now she needn't lie to her best friend, and better still, she needn't get caught at it. She was holding her breath in tense excitement.

"I can't stay long," she announced in a rush of words.

"I'm going out." Sophie's words came out on a single breath, the first one overlapping Emily's last.

"Really?" they both replied simultaneously, each separately puzzled.

"Where are you going?" inquired Emily, unable to help herself.

"I've been invited to take tea with Lady Willoughsby," Sophie answered, seemingly listening to the sound of her words.

"I see," Emily answered slowly. But she didn't, not at all.

"Where are *you* going," Sophie queried her friend.

"Tea also. I have discovered that Beatrice is not so bad in small doses," Emily answered. *If you don't mind swallowing the spoon along with the medicine.*

"Better late than never," Sophie teased.

"I suppose."

"Well then," Sophie prodded briskly, "no doubt we should both be off." Then she paused and peered closely at her friend. "Now you have me curious. Why did you ride all the way over here if you had arranged to take tea with Lady Sinclair?"

Sophie would have made a brilliant spy.

But right now she didn't find the knowledge the slightest bit impressive. *What to do? What to do?* She couldn't very well confess her intention of allaying suspicions by making an appearance. *But what could she say?*

"I…was out riding and…wanted to ease your mind on the matter of the highwaymen," she improvised. "Father has informed me that while they have not yet been apprehended, the authorities are confident of their imminent capture." The lie slid easily off her tongue.

"Excellent." Sophie answered, apparently not the slightest bit curious for details.

"Yes, isn't it," Emily agreed nodding. "We shall have to plan a visit when we each have more time to spare. Although…what there'll be to discuss, I'm sure I can't say. Nothing out of the ordinary going on around here, that's for certain."

Horrid, horrid, horrid! When would she learn to hush up? Less was better when you were trying to keep a secret. Sophie had that lesson locked up right and tight, and here she was babbling on and on. If someone didn't stop her, she might very well make a full confession here on the doorstep.

"I'm sure we'll find something—we always do."

Sophie was actually closing the door on her!

Emily sincerely hoped she wasn't gawking.

"I'll look for you tomorrow at the ball," Emily waved, stepping back. But suddenly noticing a small green spot on the skirt of Sophie's purple gown, she innocently brought it to her friend's attention. "You've a stain on your skirt, Sophie. It looks to me like it might be a grass stain, but that's rather unlikely, isn't it?"

Startled, Sophie glanced quickly down at her skirt before backing slowly into the house and waving an awkward goodbye.

Baffled but relieved, Emily set off at a comfortable gallop. She truly hoped Sophie would soon realize that secrets weren't nearly as thrilling as they seemed when you didn't have them.

* * *

Having dismissed her maid, Emily stood in front of the full-length mirror, examining herself from every angle. She had known she would wear her sea green silk. It was her newest gown, and she could anticipate no other occasion for which she might wear it, except perhaps her own engagement ball, and she most certainly did not wish to waste such a dress on Detestable Desmond. If it should come to that.

She had hoped to know by now exactly what the future held for her, but the great debacle of the previous afternoon had prevented such peace of mind. Only a few days ago she hadn't felt as if time was any concern.

As Sophie had predicted, she hadn't wanted to consider the finality of marriage or even the disillusionment of engagement and so had spared few thoughts for the rapidly approaching deadline. Now all she could think of was how many hours had passed and even now were passing away from her. She hadn't much time left. She would need to give the matter of proposing (this time to the right man) some serious thought. But not tonight.

Tonight she would meet him as Miss Emily Sinclair and pray that he didn't recognize her as the wicked-tongued and wounded Miss Emma Breton. Such a daring plan would have been all but unattainable was it not for Lady Willoughsby's rather unorthodox decision regarding appropriate dress for this evening's ball.

It seemed Lady Willoughsby had thoughtfully considered and come to the conclusion (no one knew just how) that a masquerade ball would be the best way to combine the gaiety she felt over Colin's return with the solemnity of her husband's recent death.

Emily wondered if her stepmother had had anything to do with that unaccountably odd decision. It certainly sounded like something the new Lady Sinclair would have suggested. If so, Emily owed her stepmother a debt of gratitude. Who would have guessed that such a thoroughly nonsensical idea would be the absolute perfect solution to her problem?

All invited guests had been requested to wear a plain black domino over their formal evening finery, a concession to the late Lord Willoughsby's passing. Masks, she understood, were permitted but not required. *She* would most definitely wear one. Yesterday's journey had been revealing indeed—Brand had seen her undisguised, which meant all that stood between her and exposure was a thin layer of black satin. She fully intended to cover as much of her body as was acceptable.

To cover such a beautiful gown was truly a shame but a small concession indeed to the anonymity it would afford her, at least as far as Brand was concerned. Aware that her hair alone could very possibly give her away, she'd asked Bess to arrange her blazing mane tight against her head. She fully intended to keep her hood up throughout the evening. While she didn't imagine the ensemble would set her off to best advantage, she merely hoped it would be sufficiently concealing.

She was content to be her own—and only—admirer and so lingered another moment before the mirror.

The gown, while being simply cut, was really quite stunning. Its square neckline was perhaps a trifle too revealing, but it hardly mattered now. With her future looming, uncertain and inescapable, what could it hurt? After all, she would be married soon and wouldn't have to worry over rakish gazes or leering stares unless they belonged to her husband. As such, she could see no reason not to be a little daring while she still had the chance. Besides, the domino would hide a portion of her décolletage.

Luckily the gown had been fashioned with the cooler seasons in mind. It had long, fitted sleeves, slightly puffed at the shoulder, and it would conceal her wound quite adequately. Bess had asked about the bandage and had accepted her fibbed confession of a riding accident with no more than a tisk of disapproval. But could she manage to keep her secret from the milling throng of the ballroom, or, trickier still, a dancing partner?

Time would most certainly tell. Still she was relieved to have the extra concealment afforded by the domino. Yet another advantage of the evening's certain-to-be-gossiped-over dress requirements.

Emily raised a hand to run her fingers along the bumpy row of tiny seed pearls that decorated the gown's bodice. A crusting of pearls also adorned the gown's hem and edged the sleeves at her wrists, making the fabric a bit heavy and inexplicably giving her a feeling of security. Additional pearls had also been meticulously handsewn in an intricately swirling design on the skirt.

The color and design of the gown put Emily in mind of the ocean, misty and soft, swirling and deep. She added that last descriptor merely in reference to the neckline. And if the gown was the ocean, what was she except a mermaid, bathed in mystery? At least for tonight.

Usually she didn't much care one way or another which gown she wore, and she would certainly never be called vain, but she had to admit a certain fondness for this gown and a modest appreciation for her own appearance while wearing it. The shimmery color reflected itself in her eyes, changing their color from a murky blue to a mysterious sea green that was as unique as it was fitting. After all, whether anyone realized it or not, she was a bit of an enigma.

That was rather the point, wasn't it? That no one knew.

Well, no one but Brand knew of her adventurous side (even Sophie had no idea of the lengths to which she had gone), and Brand would never recognize her, disguised as the well-behaved daughter of Lord Sinclair. In truth, she was having difficulty recognizing herself.

Her hair was braided tightly in perhaps not the most flattering style, but she rather hoped, the safest. She had even given in to a modicum of vanity and decided to dust the slightest bit of powder over the freckles scattered over her nose and cheeks. Now she wasn't certain she needed to. Peering more closely at her reflection in the mirror, she noticed that her usual pale complexion had been transformed. No doubt the dress again. Her cheeks each looked as creamy soft as rose petals, and her freckles almost seemed nonexistent. She smiled slightly, replacing the powder, and instead smoothed her hands over the front of her gown and shook the creases from her skirt. With her mother's short rope of pearls at her throat, she felt an unexpected surge of feminine confidence.

Excellent. She would certainly need it tonight.

Reaching for her domino, she wrapped it around herself with a swirl of satin. Having asked Bess to tie the mask on earlier, she had merely slipped it off over her head while she finished getting ready. Now lifting the black mask by its silk strings, she fumbled a bit but, at long last, eased it back into position. Nodding to herself in the mirror, she quickly turned away, wishing to hold tightly to that image of herself, satisfied, self-assured, and *disguised*.

The evening awaited, and there was no telling what it might demand of her.

* * *

Brand noticed her the moment she entered the ballroom and recognized her instantly. He couldn't really say how. Her hair and the upper portion of her face were concealed, and her mouth was not arranged in any of the positions he had come to know so well. Her smile was forced and came off looking brittle while her eyes quite obviously searched for someone.

He didn't consider it the slightest bit arrogant to believe with utter confidence that it was he she sought. Apparently her thoughts were as affected as his own.

If he had been close enough to her to look into her eyes, her secret would have been laid bare instantly. No one else had eyes like hers. So full of secret mischief. At times they were transparent and a window into her mind and soul. At others they were shuttered, and the swirl of her thoughts remained a mystery. He would know them anywhere.

She would no doubt be disappointed that her domino and mask had not kept her secret.

He himself wore the requisite domino but no mask. He'd debated wearing the bit of cloth that would shield his face but found he rather preferred to taunt Miss Emma Breton with his presence.

There had never been any doubt in his mind that he would expose her tonight. But in truth he hadn't expected to find quite so much of her already exposed.

On anyone else the gown would have been the height of fashion, but on her it was scandalous. He found himself unable to tear his gaze away from all that white skin. It started at the base of her neck and plunged recklessly down until, by the grace of God, the rest was swallowed up by her tightly fitted bodice.

He had seen her in the rain, her dress clinging to every curve, and he had ripped away a portion of her shirt and bandaged her bare skin when she'd been injured, but this wasn't at all the same. This was almost indecent. As he watched, mesmerized, a host of gentlemen approached her. He very seriously doubted it was because, like he, they recognized her eyes. His mouth settled into a grim line, but as a few of these new admirers had the audacity to stare at the magnificent display, his expression deepened into a scowl.

He remained utterly distracted by her as he stood, trapped by manners in a dreadfully dull conversation with the local squire. His tortured sensibilities were newly appalled each time he chanced to flick his eyes back over the man, a concession to his unceasing chatter. Brand had absolutely no idea what the man had found to eat that closely resembled a dead squirrel, but whatever it was had quite turned his own stomach.

"Hosted a dance myself some weeks back. Not as grand as this, mind you, but I can tell you the hounds and I provided a right fine dinner. I expect you're curious as to what that might have included, eh?"

The man, whose name Brand suddenly remembered had been Fitzhugh, was now licking slippery fingers and nodding encouragingly.

"Of course," he managed, gesturing expansively.

"Just let me finish this morsel."

Amused and disgusted both, Brand noticed that the man needed both hands to manage the 'morsel'.

"Fitzhugh! Glad to see you are enjoying the buffet. Mother added a few surprises for those as adventurous as yourself."

Relief at last in the form of his old friend.

"Davenport. Managing to enjoy yourself at this staid country dance?"

"Best not let your mother hear your description of the evening's entertainment, Willoughsby, or she may realize she had no cause for celebration after all."

Colin's laugh rang out, causing several guests to turn in their direction. Seeing it was the prodigal son, they smiled indulgently and resumed their conversations.

"Could you spare a moment?" Colin asked, tongue very obviously in cheek, "There are a few people to whom I would introduce you."

"Fitzhugh?" Brand inquired politely.

The man waved him away with the remains of the sad carcass before adding, "I'll run you to ground a bit later, Davenport."

Resolving that indeed he would not, Brand stepped determinedly away with Colin.

"My thanks. Did you imagine me in dire circumstances and desperately in need of aid, or did you truly wish to introduce me?" Brand inquired wryly.

"Fitzhugh is full of bluster, I'll grant you, but otherwise he's harmless."

"If you manage to avoid the spittle," Brand conceded,

making a point of wiping his chin and forehead rather vigorously.

Colin tried for a stern expression. "Consider him a reprieve from our marriageable young ladies and their pushy mamas. I can only assume it hasn't escaped your notice that *something* has managed to hold them at bay?"

"Fair enough," Brand chuckled, willing to concede the point. "Who is it you wish me to meet? Someone whose conversation recommends them? Or perhaps their beauty?" he added with newfound interest.

"Both," Colin easily admitted. "And it is two someones. One is my partner for the next dance, and the other can be yours."

"Is mine married?" Brand asked suspiciously.

"No, but she may soon be," Colin offered with a cheeky grin.

Brand warily hoped he was not about to be introduced to Miss Emily Sinclair. For if Colin still had intentions in that direction, Brand feared his friend was in for quite a disappointment. He himself hadn't any intentions where she was concerned, and yet she left *him* feeling oddly disgruntled all the same.

Brand was nervously considering this as they circled the ballroom in search of their partners. Consequently, he was unaware that they had slowed to a halt until he turned to see two ladies standing before him. A lovely blond stranger, unmasked and unhooded, stood beside Emily who was all but covered in black satin. All but her bosom.

He spared a fleeting thought for how very seductive she looked but let it slither away for the time being.

As his gaze locked with hers, he was certain she was aware that the domino hid nothing.

"Lord Brandon Davenport, Miss Emily Sinclair, please consider this an introduction." Colin smiled almost indulgently on each of them in turn.

Brand neither heard nor saw any indication that Colin was the least bit infatuated with Miss Sinclair. That either meant he'd come to his senses or that he was a cagey fellow indeed. Brand was sufficiently relieved as to applaud his good sense, realizing he himself had not fared quite so well in the face of this particular lady's rather unique charms.

"Sinclair, did you say?" Brand inquired, feigning puzzlement. "Emily Sinclair? How very odd. You remind me very much of someone I've recently met. Mind you my assessment is based solely on the small portion of your person that remains *exposed*." He looked pointedly at Emily, making clear his disapproval.

She managed to convey her own reaction with only the use of her eyes and lips. Apparently she was both irritated over his deduction and shocked at this audacity in speaking of it.

"What is it you mean, Davenport? Is this some sort of game you're playing at?" Colin asked curiously.

"Not at all," Brand answered calmly, "While traveling, I chanced to meet a Miss Emma Breton. Your Miss Sinclair reminds me quite strongly of her. Comparable shape and size. Similar name. The pair of them even have the identical color hair," he cited, gesturing to the glinting strands exposed where Emily's hood had fallen back slightly. Smiling with genuine amusement, he pondered, "What are the odds?"

Emily was now smiling herself, albeit rather coolly. As she tilted her head to the side in pretended interest, he could easily imagine that she was seething with frustration and anxiety.

"Come, remove your mask, and we will see if your beauty matches hers as well."

As he took her hand, he bestowed what he hoped was an encouraging smile.

"What is your intention, my lord? To flatter or to fluster."

"Neither, Miss Sinclair. But rather the harmless conversation between two people just introduced. Although I confess I don't feel a bit of the awkwardness that usually accompanies it. Strange, isn't it?"

"Most curious. Shall we discuss something else?"

He hadn't yet let go of her hand, so she tugged herself free of his grasp.

Before Brand could reply, Emily pressed on, "I assume you have not met my closest friend, Miss Sophia Penrose. She is our vicar's daughter, and I'd venture to guess, considerably more lovely than your memorable stranger."

Brand turned his attention for the first time to the quiet young lady standing slightly behind Emily and couldn't help but stare at the pair of them. Several inches taller than her friend and gowned in a sensibly demure pale blue gown, Miss Penrose was the perfect backdrop for Emily. Serene sky against turbulent seas. He guessed immediately that the comparison could accurately extend beyond their dress, and he wondered whether it had occurred to Colin when he'd begun his search for a wife. He should have thought it obvious indeed that he and Emily would not suit. Just who would suit her, he couldn't guess, but it wasn't Colin.

"Emily is prone to exaggeration, I'm afraid." Sophie decried, interrupting his thoughts. She was turning her eyebrows down at Emily but clearly wishing she could swat her friend instead.

Brand commiserated and liked her immediately.

"Clearly not in this case," he complimented smoothly.

"Thank you, my lord. Please don't think I was fishing for that compliment."

"Whether you were or not, it would have made no difference. Now, would you care to dance?"

At this point, Colin spoke up, having been momentarily silenced by the banter of the others.

"Pardon me, Davenport, but Miss Penrose has promised me this dance. Perhaps Miss Sinclair will take pity on you and allow you to partner her instead."

Turning his attention back to Emily with raised eyebrows, Brand read her answer in her eyes before she gave it.

"Forgive me, my lord. I have already granted this dance to another gentleman."

Brand wondered if his imagination had conjured the shudder that had seemed to run queasily along her body.

"How unfortunate. I was looking forward to a most interesting discussion—harmless of course. Perhaps you could be persuaded to save me a dance later in the evening?"

"Of course. I should be delighted," she lied prettily and quite transparently.

As his three companions made their excuses and turned away, Brand vowed to watch Miss Emily Sinclair closely. He was intrigued by who her next partner might be and why she would have such a reaction to him.

It was difficult to keep track of her as she moved through the crowds. Without her hair or even her gown to guide him, he found himself barely able to follow her path. And then, as a flurry off to his right sent his eyes momentarily darting that in direction, he lost her.

No matter. He would most definitely find her later.

Right now it appeared he would need to deal with a task that promised to be much less pleasant. A marriage-minded mama was bearing down upon him with the single-minded intensity of a charging bull.

He knew instantly that the woman approaching him had a daughter to pawn off, although where the daughter had got to was a confusingly interesting detail. It had been his experience that these harridans dragged their daughters with them into battle.

Not this one. It appeared she'd instead pressed Lady Willoughsby into accompanying her, and Colin's mother looked thoroughly uncomfortable with the dubious honor. He couldn't blame her. He wished he could have spared her a bit of sympathy but decided it prudent to reserve it for himself. He knew well what lay ahead of him.

It didn't matter a whit that they'd not yet been introduced, nor that he'd not been warned against her. He already knew all he needed to. When engrossed in marital possibilities, every matron was the same. He would act accordingly. He would raise his defenses, do his best to be polite, and then, should it become necessary, simply do his best to avoid her.

Pasting a bland smile on his face, he was ready. In the very next moment, they arrived.

Strangely, neither of them spoke. Lady Willoughsby no

doubt simply because she did not wish to and the marriage-minded mama because she had not yet been formally introduced. Although it was clear from the impatient tapping of her slippered foot and the wide-eyed darting glances, complete with jerky head tilts in his direction, that she would not wait overlong.

Lady Willoughsby met his eyes, silently begging his pardon, before performing the introduction.

"Good evening, Lord Davenport. I hope you are enjoying the festivities." Her eyes told him that that enjoyment would shortly come to an end. Gesturing to her companion she said, "May I introduce my neighbor, Lady Beatrice Sinclair? This is Lord Brandon Davenport, Viscount Ashwood, a family friend."

Sinclair? Good God! Is it possible that this is Emily's mother? Surely not.

Brand knew from experience that one couldn't bear responsibility for one's relations, but that didn't preclude him from being very nearly befuddled by this new development. This woman had held sway over Emily's upbringing, and still, Miss Breton had managed to slip through the cracks? Good God! He couldn't help but applaud the cleverness of the daughter in outmaneuvering her mother. Beyond that, he enjoyed the smug complaisance of knowing he had her secret identity all to himself. He could even admit that it was a great pity he wouldn't ever have any more of her than precisely that.

He had to admit the idea of marrying Emily had crept into his mind, sparking his thoughts for a single fleeting moment, before snuffing out. Ironically, he had avoided thinking of it again when he'd realized that his excuses against the marital state no longer seemed as reasonable as they once had. But here and now, he was being presented with an extremely legitimate excuse to leave Miss Emily Sinclair firmly alone. Her mother. He could never marry Emily with this woman thrown into the bargain. He would never get a moment's peace.

"Delighted, Lady Sinclair," Brand replied even though he clearly wasn't.

His feelings on the matter couldn't have mattered less. With the formalities cleared from the path, Lady Sinclair was ready to dig in her heels.

"My husband is Lord Edward Sinclair. No doubt you are aware of him?" she prodded.

"No," he returned. But feeling that so succinct an answer was perhaps a bit too rude added, "I do not believe that I am."

"If you'll excuse me," Lady Willoughsby quietly interjected, "I have to return to my other guests."

"No matter," Lady Sinclair assured him, her gaze never wavering. She apparently did not plan to acknowledge the interruption, and Lady Willoughsby didn't seem to care in the slightest. In fact, she was already moving away. Brand swiveled his eyes reluctantly back to his new companion, who, it would seem, had no plans to cease speaking anytime in the near future. Silently, he mourned his loss. *Oh to be trapped with Fitzhugh and his prey again...*

"We will see that set to rights this very evening. Mind you, I haven't the slightest clue where Edward has disappeared to—I haven't seen him since we arrived."

Smart man.

"Well, I'm certain you and I can pass the time quite enjoyably until he turns up. I would suggest we go in to supper—I am quite famished, having waited till this late hour to eat, but I've just discovered that the food is being served as a buffet. Well, 'being served' is perhaps a bit misleading. In truth we must serve ourselves."

She left that last bit hanging between them, willing him to share in her distress over such a ghastly indignity. But Brand was immune to her wide-eye appeals and encouraging nods.

"As it happens, I am not at all hungry," he lied.

"Well then, I will let you do all the talking," she trilled.

He knew there was as much chance of her keeping silent as there was of hell freezing over.

"Shall we?" she encouraged, linking her arm through his and pulling him in the direction of the supper rooms. "The instant I saw you, I knew I must be introduced, and Lady

Willoughsby was most readily accommodating. I must tell you, Lord Davenport, that your reputation has preceded you to Devon. We are delighted you decided to follow on its tails." She gave his arm a companionable squeeze. "From what I understand, you are quite the catch." He smiled blandly down at her, but her spirits remained undampened. "And I count myself lucky indeed to have caught you!" He supposed she was determined to be optimistic, but he couldn't help but wonder if she was a trifle tipsy to boot.

The twittering that ensued in response to her own witticism grated on Brand, and he heaved a deep sigh, resigned to getting the matter over with. He didn't look back to see what he was missing—it would only make things worse.

* * *

Emily was inordinately grateful that this dance happened to be a quadrille. Now at least she wouldn't have to bear the man's touch overmuch. If this had been her father's not-so-subtle way of reminding her that her engagement ball loomed close, she did not appreciate it one little bit.

Richly had simply shown up at her side and informed her that her father had promised him the dance. To his credit he did add that he hoped she would be gracious enough to honor the commitment, but the words had come out less as a request and more as a taunt. She had accepted, knowing she could not avoid him forever. And maybe not at all. The horrid truth was that she may very well have to marry him and thus be *tied* to him forever.

Desperate times…desperate measures…

Emily very nearly chanted the words aloud throughout the duration of the dance. And then suddenly, it was over. And Mr. Richly had commandeered her arm and was leading her away from the other dancers.

He led her to a private corner of the ballroom without speaking. They were now on the edge of the festivities, and everything seemed so far away, so thoroughly out of reach. Most noticeably and significantly, her good spirits.

"The dance was my pleasure, Miss Sinclair—Emily. Do you mind if I use your given name?" he asked, clearly expecting her to allow it.

"I believe that familiarity is meant to be reserved for someone with whom I have an understanding."

"I was under the impression that you and I had such an understanding," Richly answered thinly. Everything about him seemed thin, from his lean figure to his pinched face to his slitted eyes.

"Your father led me to believe…" he continued.

"My father has not made any promises to you or any other gentleman," she retorted, angry that her father had even given this man his consideration.

"Not yet," he conceded, "But my aunt has confided both your father's ultimatum as well as his indulgent allowance that you marry a man of your own choosing. Perhaps somewhat embarrassingly for you, she was also forthcoming with the none-too-surprising truth that you appear to have no other prospects. I simply thought to save you the trouble of looking further."

Now the thin lips were twisted in an ugly sneer, and Emily was incensed.

"It seems my decision to keep my own council was sensible indeed, for it is clear that Beatrice is incapable of keeping such matters private. As I am sure you are aware," she continued pointedly, "appearances can be extremely deceiving. Prospects are everywhere, sir."

At her last words, his eyes seemed to shine with venomous anger, and his jaw hardened visibly before he consciously relaxed it and allowed his smile to settle into malevolency. Her optimism surrounding the possibility that he might content himself with possession of her fortune and leave her alone was instantly dispelled. The man was utterly vile and would certainly make her life a misery if given the chance. Despite her father's intentions, she was more determined than ever not to give him one.

"But rather unnecessary," he informed her with cold confidence, "as I'm certain we will deal comfortably together…so long as we understand each other."

"We will never deal comfortably together, and neither will we understand each other. There will never be any need. For you see, as you said, prospects are rather unnecessary. They became superfluous the moment I acquired a fiancé." Plastering a superior smile on her face, Emily gloated.

She watched as a myriad of emotions flickered through his eyes: disbelief, puzzlement, anger—quickly banked— and once again, disbelief. The only outward indication that her announcement had affected him was the hardening line of his mouth and the web of lines caging his eyes.

"You'll forgive me if I don't believe you, my dear, but it hardly seems possible."

"I assure you, despite its utter improbability, it is true," she replied glacially.

The toad! Virtually implying that no one would have her. She would dearly love to see him get his comeuppance.

An idea crept into her thoughts. She tried to shoo it away, but it had gotten quite comfortable. Almost immediately, the idea transformed itself into a plan.

"May I inquire as to the identity of this mysterious gentleman?" Richly asked, very nearly chuckling in his amusement over the assumed fib.

Leveling him with her most serious gaze, she upped the ante. There would be no going back.

"Why don't I introduce you instead?" she challenged, cold and sweet.

"Delighted," he answered, finally looking and sounding a bit uncertain.

She turned away from him then, seemingly occupied with searching the ballroom for the gentleman in question. Luckily Richly didn't move from his position behind her, or he would have seen her, eyes closed, trying to summon the courage to approach Brand.

It was too late to turn back now, too late for anything but the task at hand. She would simply have to go through with it and await Brand's response. And hope she herself wasn't to be the recipient of an embarrassing comeuppance.

Glancing back to Richly to ascertain his readiness, she

ignored his proffered arm and swirled away, taking great pleasure in the cut she had delivered.

Making a steady path towards Brand who now stood alone in one of the alcoves adjacent to the supper rooms, she willed him to play along. Noticing him earlier, in close consort with her stepmother, just as her dance had begun, had nearly spurred her into abandoning her odious partner in order to bring a halt to the conversation before it could begin. She wondered whether the damage most assuredly done had been irreparable and just how the pair's little tête-à-tête would affect her imminent announcement.

She thought it best to just come right out with it, forgoing any and all pleasantries. That decided, she started the introduction while still several steps away.

"Mr. Richly, may I present my fiancé, Viscount Ashwood."

Brand had turned towards her seconds before her arrival, his concentration having been absorbed with the whereabouts of Lady Sinclair and the necessity of keeping a minimum distance between them. As such he had only heard her last five words. Whatever had come before couldn't have mattered less. He'd registered the pregnant pause between 'fiancé' and his title and been confounded over the certainty that she had not, in fact, been speaking *to* him but rather *about* him. He'd been stunned into silence.

She stepped forward, intending to rivet his attention, and wishing she could block his view of Richly. She was just barely trembling.

"Slay the dragon," she challenged under her breath.

His own words, thrown back at him, her eyes, speaking volumes. At this very moment, she was taunting him, challenging him to make good on his promise. But he could clearly see how tense and uncertain she was, waiting for his response.

Unwillingly, he looked away from her to assess the man standing some feet away. He knew Richly by reputation and wondered what he was doing in this sleepy corner of Devon. The man's tastes could certainly not be assuaged this far from London. Of even more interest was what business he could possibly have with Emily—Brand certainly intended to find out. His eyes shuttered, his own dislike mirroring Richly's, before he turned his gaze back to her. She was still turned completely away from Richly, looking up at him, and now she was batting her eyelashes quite vigorously. If he didn't already know that she was acting on his own advice, he wouldn't have known quite what to make of her. She was probably making herself dizzy, and she looked an utter ninny, but God help him, he couldn't resist her. Even with her mother in tow.

"Richly," Brand acknowledged coldly, pulling her a little closer to him and hearing her sigh of relief.

"Davenport," the blackguard answered silkily. "I must confess, I was not aware of Miss Sinclair's engagement. And had I guessed the name of her intended, I would not have been further afield. If you don't mind my asking, however did you meet?"

Richly appeared suspicious, and Brand couldn't think why.

"It was a chance meeting and a whirlwind courtship. Neither of us initially expected it to lead to marriage, did we my dear?"

Brand gazed down at her in what others might imagine to be an adoring manner, but her own smile slightly wavered as she saw the hard glint in his eyes.

"Certainly not, but now that we have come to an agreement, we couldn't be more content." Unsure what to say or do, Emily couldn't stop the words from tumbling from her mouth. It felt almost as if she was trying to write a happy ending of her own. "Could we?" she asked in a small, uncertain voice, risking a peek at Brand's face but glimpsing nothing, masked as it was with cold civility.

"Well then," Richly cut in, "I suppose congratulations are in order. I wonder that your father and stepmother didn't mention the engagement to me when I spoke to each of them earlier this evening."

"They are hoping to save the announcement for the engagement ball. Lady Sinclair especially wanted to imbue the occasion with the utmost surprise and suspense," Emily lied smoothly.

"I almost regret being privy to the secret myself—it would have been such fun to be surprised along with everyone else when the announcement is made," Brand added wryly.

"Don't be silly, my lord," Emily very nearly twittered.

Brand was staring at her, smiling in the way one might if faced with someone irritatingly meddlesome.

He couldn't have made his opinion of her inopportune proposal, such as it was, any clearer. Uncertain what else she could say, she kept silent along with her two companions.

After what seemed an eternity, Brand finally decided he had had enough of the awkward, telling silence.

Bidding Richly a good evening, Brand firmly gripped Emily's hand and pulled her towards the terrace doors at the back of the ballroom. Emily chose to pretend she was being escorted as that was most definitely more respectable and less embarrassing than being very nearly dragged.

As she sailed along in his wake, she wondered whether anyone could discern the emotions they were each attempting to conceal with brittle half smiles. Any acquainted with her would most likely be surprised that she was allowing any man to drag her along. The fact that he was a viscount and heir to the Earl of Chase would certainly cause twitters to race through the ballroom.

So as Brand continued, doggedly pressing through the crowd of people gathered to welcome Colin home, she slowed her pace a bit and slackened her grip. If she could manage to convey queasy discomfort rather than guilty uncertainty, it would go a long way towards quelling the inevitable gossip. Let the avidly curious onlookers believe that she simply needed to get some air and that Lord Davenport merely had the intentions of a chivalrous gentleman. It was true enough up to a point.

Nearing escape, they brushed perilously close to the potted palms flanking the entrance to the ballroom. While impressively exotic, the plants seemed, in Emily's opinion, a bit out of place. For while they succeeded in inspiring

thoughts of balmy breezes, those imaginary winds were no
match for the damp chilly gusts that swirled past them,
cooling the overheated room.

Why she had even spared a moment to notice them was
beyond her. She should be focusing all her time and
attention, extremely limited as it was, on deciding what she
would say to Brand. Their little excursion was bound to
come to a halt any second, and he would expect an
explanation. He deserved one, she knew, but, if anything,
that only made her less keen to provide it.

Once outside, they didn't continue across the terrace and
down into the dark of the garden where other couples were
already disappearing, apparently willing to risk the nose-
pinking weather for a few moments of privacy. Instead
Brand made a sharp right turn that had her arm nearly
jerking out of its socket. She grunted a bit in pain and
surprise, but either he didn't hear her, or he wasn't the
slightest bit concerned. Luckily he had had the foresight to
grab the hand attached to her uninjured shoulder. Or
perhaps he wouldn't have cared either way, as angry as she
appeared to have made him.

They hurried along the side of the house, past window
after window, while the frigid air streamed around them and
her slippers became more drenched with every step through
the wet grass.

She found herself thinking it a pity that they weren't
walking down the other side of the house and using the
imposing structure as a wind block. Had Brand chosen that
route, she might at least have managed to keep warm. As it
was, she had no protection whatever from the wicked north
wind that had kicked up mid-afternoon. Well, no protection
save what she was managing to get as she tripped along
behind him like a snake shimmying through water.

Her hood had blown backwards off her head almost the
moment they had stepped into the wind, and she saw no
reason to hold it in place any longer. Everything she had
intended to hide was now rather embarrassingly exposed—
quite literally. Well, she may be uncertain over how to deal
with secrets prematurely revealed, but she could very well

handle the matter of the buffeting wind. Brisk and efficient, she quickened her steps and determined to stay as close as possible to the protection offered by Brand's broad shoulders. Perhaps the cold air would serve to steam away some of his anger. As she gazed up at him from behind, she could imagine that those little puffs of air flying backwards were in fact dissipating anger rather than merely his frosted breath being carried away by the wind.

Taking a moment to reconsider, she promptly changed her mind, realizing she'd much prefer to deal with a hot temper than cold indifference.

Almost as soon as she had made that decision and subsequently hurried her steps, Brand halted abruptly, causing her to run rather awkwardly into his stiff back

Another grunt escaped her. Really, he must think her thoroughly unladylike. And why she should care whether he did or not was a question she chose not to answer.

He appeared quite convincingly single-minded and otherwise oblivious of her existence. It was obvious he didn't care a fig for her reputation, and he seemed not the slightest bit concerned that she might be in pain or even numb from the cold. She'd been *shot* just two days ago— shouldn't that merit a bit of concern? Having succumbed to Richly's promised dance, her shoulder now felt as if it was being jabbed with a red hot poker. Couldn't the man spare even the tiniest bit of pity for her? She rather thought she deserved it. Especially as she'd been dragged on indefinitely with no notion at all where he intended to take her. Somewhere he could gag and lecture her without interruption no doubt.

Bloody hell!

Just as she'd decided to yank her arm free and demand an explanation, Brand let her go. As her arm dropped limply to her side, she realized that he was occupied in viciously turning the handles of another pair of French doors that opened onto a room with which she was unfamiliar. When he ushered her unceremoniously through with a firm push to her lower back, she discovered where she was. The well-stocked shelves of books were gracefully illuminated in the shafts of moonlight that streamed through the doors' panes.

She wasn't given much of a chance to admire them.

Turning her roughly to face him once he'd heard the click that ensured their privacy (and warmth), he demanded, "What exactly was that?"

"What do you mean?" she tried, but his furious glare and angry stance were simply too much.

"Oh very well," she added petulantly, "But you can't blame me entirely."

"Can't I?" he nearly roared.

"Keep your voice down, or someone is bound to hear you and come looking," she hissed.

"Good point—if we were found here alone and unchaperoned, your reputation would be compromised, and we would be forced to…what exactly?"

"Marry," she mumbled, thoroughly contrite.

"Precisely. And God forbid that we should rush into anything or have such an important commitment foisted upon us."

"You've made your point," she conceded, somewhat irritated at him when by rights she should have been irritated only with herself.

It wouldn't matter to him that she hadn't planned the confrontation with Richly, so she wouldn't bother to tell him that it had just happened. She wasn't proud of herself, but she had to admit to being secretly pleased that the hard part was over. At least she hoped it was. All that was left was for him to decide whether or not he wished to jilt her. For although she was certain that *he* would never suggest such an alternative, her honor, or at least the fragments that remained, insisted that she allow him to back out of the neat trap she had set for him.

"If you do not wish to follow through with my unforgivable, and clearly unwelcome, overture, I will understand. I suppose Richly and I will get on well enough."

She wasn't certain whether the darkness sufficiently hid either her expression of distaste or the involuntary shiver that ran through her at the thought of wedding that man.

"I don't recall being a party to anything that could correctly be termed an overture. You very nearly taunted me into taking part in your charade, knowing chivalry offered me no permissible alternative."

Emily blanched amid the stinging truth of his words, but Brand didn't notice her reaction. It seemed his mind had just worked its way around to the rest of her words.

"Richly?" he roared, "You were going to marry Richly? Have you no sense, woman?!"

She was confident that the thundering of his voice would shortly have servants throwing open the doors to unearth the guests who had dared venture into the private library of Lord Willoughsby. But Emily realized that she no longer had the energy to care. So she stood waiting before him, allowing him to rant and bellow.

"Richly is as detestable as a vulture and just as patient. He waits, circling ever closer, hoping to prey on the unsuspecting. If you marry him, your fortune will no doubt disappear within a year, at which time he will begin his search for additional funds, and your used carcass will most certainly be banished to the country, where you will be forced to reside in shabby solitude."

Emily continued to remain silent, but her body had started to tense, and her fists were clenching and unclenching in barely suppressed anger, causing her right shoulder to throb with even greater fire.

"How could you possibly choose such a man? I can't believe your father would sanctify such a union! Does he even know the b—?"

"I have heard quite enough," Emily interrupted with carefully leashed anger, her voice ringing hollow and cold in the darkened room. She had taken a desperate chance, entrusting her future to this man, sacrificing her heart as well as her pride, and all that apparently concerned him was her highhanded method of going about it and the very idea that Richly might be the alternative. Clearly he felt no affection for her at all. And here she stood, stupidly, irrationally, irrevocably in love with him.

Well it seemed she had made a painful mistake. Faced with it now, she wished she could simply curl into herself and heal, but that would have to wait. For now she would have to put on a brave front and hide her true self from him, something she had never wanted to do. She made sure her eyes stayed steady on his as she severed all ties between them. She dearly hoped he would soon realize all that he had lost.

"Bravo! It didn't take you but a few moments, and now you have me most thoroughly convinced. You and I would most definitely not suit—on that we are in total agreement. In fact, I can't think why I ever considered you to be an improvement over Mr. Richly. I will inform Richly that we have broken off our engagement—you have no further responsibilities towards me."

With that, she swiveled on her heel, her skirts billowing out around her. She strode purposefully towards the door connecting the room with the rest of the house, not particularly caring that she might be noticed coming back into the ballroom from this direction.

Having completed no more than two strides, she was spun around again by Brand's firm grip on her upper arm. Lucky again, it was her left arm.

"Like hell," he tossed at her, dragging her close enough so that she could see the anger flickering in his eyes. Oddly enough, he appeared even angrier now than he had been before, a fact which succeeded in thoroughly bewildering her.

"You made yourself my responsibility when you fell off your horse right at my feet. Even if I had thought to avoid the task and you with it, your involvement in all manner of mischief simply wouldn't allow it. You may consider our engagement announced. It is difficult to predict who will give me more trouble, you or your mother."

Incensed by his boorish manner and demeaning words, she dug her fingernails into her palm to keep from striking him and replied as calmly as she could.

"You, sir, do not know my mother, and she is hardly in a position to give you any trouble."

"I met your mother, and I can—"

"Lady Sinclair is my stepmother, you clod."

Emily watched the surprise register on his face and then relished adding to it.

"Now, let there be no confusion. I will not be marrying you. There is absolutely nothing holding me to this engagement. I assure you, neither the embarrassment of being dragged through the ballroom, nor the scandal of calling off our engagement, matters in the slightest."

"Perhaps I can show you something that might," he tossed out before he jerked her against him and dipped his head to seal her lips with his own and stifle any further protests.

Her immediate reaction was to unclench her fists and push him away, thereby halting the hard, demanding kiss. She still wished to make her exit as dignified as possible under the ridiculously embarrassing circumstances. But her hands stopped inches from his shoulders as his kiss changed. No longer merely a way to ensure her silence, now it was something else entirely.

She marveled at his sudden gentleness given the storm of emotions that had propelled them to this point. His hands on her arms alternately smoothed, stroked, and cupped, always careful to avoid her injury. Slowly, steadily, his fingers were stimulating a considerably more compelling ache in another part of her body entirely.

The pressure of his tongue along the seam of her lips was now the barest whisper. Her mouth quivered open on a sigh, and he took her response as invitation, dipping ever so slowly in. She couldn't help but think how odd it was that such an invasion could make her feel snug and content and delightfully wicked all at once.

Deciding she was more than willing to suffer the consequences of allowing any liberties he might care to take, she verily lunged to snatch at the unplumbed depths of possibility he offered.

She moved her tongue tentatively, eager to explore. When he sucked in his breath, she pressed her advantage, licking softly into his mouth. Judging from the groan that rose up from deep in his throat, her first attempts at participation had been well received. His reaction was to take all that she offered and then relentlessly tempt her into offering more. She felt like a slip of shoreline ravaged by ocean waves, content that the wicked onslaught would never end.

The fact that he was now simultaneously plundering her mouth and reverently stroking the soft skin exposed above the neckline of her gown was making her head spin. And she was utterly content to be dizzy.

She reached for his arms, needing to brace herself against the much-anticipated unknown, but was immediately distracted by the fact that his muscles there were tense with control while hers were tense with surrender.

She squeezed a bit, testing the strength there, and the extent of control. Amazingly, the muscles tightened even further as his hands traveled to her waist, grazing the sides of her breasts on their journey. Pressing hot fingers against her back and even hotter thumbs against her front, he held her firmly in place for a thrilling kiss of possession.

When he finally tore his lips away, he tilted her slightly backward and stared. The intensity in his eyes left her breathless. He slid his finger along her cheekbone, and she realized with a shock that she was still wearing her mask. She wondered if she should remove it.

"You are so very *real*," he mused.

"Isn't that preferable in this sort of situation," she tossed back, attempting to hide the awkwardness she suddenly felt.

Clearly amused, he slid his fingers along the edges of her mask but left it thrillingly in place. "Indeed you are correct, but I assure you, that was meant as a compliment."

"You are apparently not particularly adept at flattery," she muttered. "But it hardly matters—I neither expect nor require it."

"That doesn't preclude you from enjoying it or, at the very least, accepting it when it is given honestly."

"I suppose," she acknowledged. "Thank you for recognizing my existence."

Brand's amused smile had her heart stumbling. "Your

existence was never in doubt, love. You have been taunting me with it since first we met. It is your singularity that makes you so very remarkable."

His fingers lingered on the knot holding her mask in place, but as she sucked in her breath, he slid them down to trace along her collarbone.

"You're showing signs of improvement," she said, on a breathless sigh.

"Just wait," he said and proceeded to make what she considered to be much better use of his mouth.

He trailed hot kisses from the edge of her mouth, down her throat and across the top of her bodice, scraping his teeth along her skin. She shivered, whether from the sensation or the intimacy it inspired, she wasn't certain, and truly, she no longer cared.

Thus far, everything he'd offered had been enjoyable and exciting—it had made her greedy. Now, as she savored, she sought. Waiting, wondering where it all would lead.

A mere two seconds later, he showed her.

The warmth of his hands settled comfortably around her waist had lulled her into languorous contentment; their trail of heat quickly lured her out. He was slowly pushing them upwards along her bodice, curving them around in front of her and watching her carefully with those dark, dark eyes.

Seductively, he winged an eyebrow up, then matched it with the corner of his lips just as he captured each breast in the *v's* made by his fingers and thumbs. With devilish intent, he cradled them as he dipped his head to bestow a chaste kiss upon each.

Her breath fluttered out on another sigh just as every competitive instinct slid away from her. He was taunting her, tormenting her, breaking every rule of gentlemanly play. And she never wanted him to stop.

Pulling back once again to gaze upon her as she lightly clenched and unclenched her fingers around his arms, he slowly, inexorably, pushed up her breasts until she was straining against the fabric of her gown, watching him with heady anticipation.

Smiling quite charmingly, he licked a lavish kiss into the

darkened valley between the deceptively voluptuous mounds. Digging in with her short, even nails, she struggled to keep her balance just as he determined to tip her off.

Relaxing her fingers, she spared a careless thought for the wrinkles left behind on his coat but was promptly distracted anew as he dipped his head once again to demonstrate new pleasures.

Slipping his tongue below the pearl edging framing her breasts, he flicked it over a nipple and had her pulling him closer.

"Ah, is that what you wanted?" he whispered into her ear.

"Yes...no," she managed, unable to explain that while she most certainly wanted this, she yearned for something still out of reach.

As he looked at her with raised eyebrows and seeming confusion, she quickly added, "But please don't stop."

Circling the tip of her breast with his thumb until it was thrusting against its confines, he turned his attention to its mate.

Nearly panting, Emily allowed an occasional moan to escape each time she had sufficient breath. She felt her knees weaken as she watched Brand slowly, purposefully seduce her.

Another shiver coursed through her body, and this time she recognized its cause. It was for them. What was between them already and what was still to come. She rubbed her cheek fleetingly over the softness of his hair as he bent over her and closed her eyes in pleasure. Yet tenderness was quickly forgotten as Brand lifted his head and captured her gaze. Desire flooded her senses.

She could but stare as he charmed her with a smile, gently tugging her bodice ever lower until it was about her waist. Despite the shadows shifting over her, she knew she was utterly exposed to him. She stood very still, not certain how to behave; he did the same, gazing freely. There was no disguising the two rosy nipples that seemed to be stretching, reaching, straining for his attention. She could feel them respond to his gaze and couldn't help a slightly abashed smile from escaping as she slowly, awkwardly fluttered her hands over her breasts in an attempt to conceal them.

Catching the uncooperative pair, Brand kissed the fingers of each hand before pulling them away. Once again free to look his fill, he allowed a slow satisfied smile to steal across his face.

When Brand once again managed to shift his focus upwards, he was riveted by the hint of mischief he read in her eyes and smile.

By God, but she was flirting with him.

Utterly delighted with her, Brand would have been hard-pressed to remember the argument that had spurred this heedless indiscretion. At the moment he had absolutely no complaints.

It was stunning, really, how she affected him. Thus far this evening, Emily had been responsible for his feeling baffled, surprised, irritated, and angry. As he'd watched her taste passion, he'd felt desire as never before. She was exquisite—innocently sensuous and gratifyingly eager—and he wanted her. Quite desperately in fact.

He had been rigid with desire as soon as he had claimed her lips with his own, but now, having watched her, having seen her, he was aching for her, his blood pounding out a steady, encouraging beat.

He couldn't have her. Not here, not now. And it would require total mastery of his control to uphold that decision.

But there was no convincing reason he couldn't insure that she came away thoroughly pleasured.

"You're beautiful," he said, quite in awe of the woman before him. She continued to surprise him at every turn, and he'd never found anything more seductive.

"Ahhh. Now I see how best to draw a gentleman's compliments," she smirked, glancing down at her naked torso.

"A pity you won't have an opportunity to test that theory on any other gentleman," he growled. "I, however, will most willingly oblige your attempts."

"Oblige me, please," she requested primly.

Their little chat, while unbelievably seductive, had dissipated the cloud of passion that had settled over her. He couldn't think why—his own desperation had surged dangerously close to the surface, watching this half-naked innocent flirt so skillfully with him.

He wanted to see her fall under again and felt almost reverent that he would be the man to do it.

Smiles melted simultaneously away, and eyes cloudy with untried passion met eyes sharp with skillful determination. Their bodies humming with awareness, they moved closer.

Wrapping one arm around Emily's waist and placing the other firmly on her bottom, Brand left her little choice but surrender.

Not one to give up easily, Emily wriggled about, intent on more pressure, more heat. Brand gripped her more tightly and gifted her with both.

She could no longer even feel the cold damp air that always managed to seep stealthily into every room. She was hot, so very hot, and yet she clung to the source of all the heat. Like a moth, she was drawn relentlessly forward, ever seeking; she wondered how soon it would be before she went up in flames.

Deciding she could either settle back and allow Brand to educate her in this latest partnering or share full responsibility for the evening's pleasures still to come, she chose the latter. Her fingers had been itching to touch him more intimately since their first meeting. Now was her chance. Reaching for him, she hoped her enthusiasm could compensate for her unavoidable naïveté.

Gripping the lapels of his evening coat, Emily attempted to push it over his shoulders and slide it off along his arms. She fumbled, tugged, and cursed roundly until Brand spared a moment to shrug it off himself. Dropping a quick, hard kiss on her parted lips, he shifted his attention to the delicate curve of her neck, letting his fingers move in converging circles over her breasts until they found her nipples and lingered.

Feeling decadently wanton, she didn't trouble to contain the throaty moans that seemed to be escaping her lips. She thrilled to the quivering of her legs but fought to stand, pulling, yanking at an extremely uncooperative cravat. Once it was dispatched, she turned her attention to the buttons of his shirt, but desire had made her dizzy. She fumbled, desperately impatient, before finally parting the now rumpled fabric to expose his chest.

Allowing her hands to run over him, tentatively at first and then with greedy enthusiasm, she registered his groan with satisfaction as it echoed into her mouth.

As her fingers traced a reckless path over taut muscle, she dared to pull away a bit in order to look her fill. Moonlight splayed over him, revealing an even more worthy specimen than she'd originally assumed. Sliding her teeth along her lower lip, she smiled with the secret.

Without warning, her calves were suddenly pressed firmly up against the leather sofa that fronted the fireplace. Brand had efficiently steered her from the garden door to a much more comfortable spot.

She'd thought the room had been spinning. And perhaps it had.

Relieved that she no longer need worry about toppling over, she very nearly crumpled. But not before tightening her grip and pulling him down with her.

Momentarily distracted, Emily blinked and suddenly realized how far matters had progressed. They sat together, both breathing heavily, both naked to the waist but for her mask and the seductive swathe of her domino, which remained silkily settled against her skin. Moonlight and shadow tip-toed quietly: teasing, encouraging, arousing.

This was the stuff of novels. And the climax was still to come. At least she hoped it was.

Giddy with anticipation, she squirmed onto his lap and pressed herself against him, torso to torso. He sucked in his breath and promptly tightened his hands possessively around her. As his lips once more found hers, his hand was moving on to new intimacies.

He slid his hand smoothly along her calf, and she sighed.

He touched the tender skin behind her knee, and she tensed, suddenly ticklish. He inched higher still until he was stroking the smooth warm flesh of her inner thigh, and she gasped, waiting, wanting.

His fingers stopped. Her eyes flew open in desperation.

His eyes were closed, and his jaw was tight with control. Stroking her fingers down his cheek and across his chin, she hoped to encourage him, soothe him, convince him. Anything.

Opening his eyes, he reached up with his free hand to grip hers. Holding it, and her gaze, he resumed the thrilling journey, and she breathed a quick sigh of relief before holding her breath once more.

Brand inched his fingers up until he could feel the crisp curls of hair covering her most private spot. Deepening his touch, he found the threshold they guarded. Nervous noises rose up unbidden in her throat, but she determinedly silenced them, preferring that nothing distract her as she waited frantically for the unknown.

Not wishing to keep her or himself waiting any longer than necessary, Brand shifted a bit and pushed his fingers forward to touch the slick softness ever so slightly.

By God but she was ready. And with his own mind and body nearly numb with desire, he needed no further encouragement. Easily finding the spot he knew would entice a woman almost desperately towards continued pleasure, he teased it gently, keeping his fingers busy as Emily's whole body seemed to alternately tense and relax.

Watching her was an experience all its own, he thought bemusedly. She was glorious in her newfound pleasure, and he found that all he wanted was to surprise her with further, unexpected delights.

Aware that continuing was certain to be the worst kind of torment, he slowly dipped a single finger inside her and pulled it back, steadily watching her. Emily closed her eyes and opened her mouth in awed wonder, letting her head roll back slightly. Almost immediately, she inched her hips forward, wordlessly pleading with him to continue the wicked onslaught.

He was mesmerized and this time slipped two fingers in, even deeper. Capturing her lips in a possessive kiss, he matched his fingers' movements to his tongue's, dragging her up, higher and higher.

Seconds later, he heard the catch in her throat and knew she was about to be set adrift. Keeping his mouth on hers in a desperate attempt to insure their privacy, he captured her cries of release as her body clenched around him. He was conscious of a fierce and heady satisfaction.

She dipped her head down and onto his shoulder and stayed still and quiet for several seconds—the time it took Brand to abandon his willpower in the aftermath of such glorious passion.

As he fumbled with his breeches, Emily watched with renewed, if groggy, exuberance. When his member was finally exposed, she reached to touch the hard length of him, but he stayed her hand.

"Not this time, love. I need to be inside of you," he whispered.

She nodded, obedient for once, and smiled a bit blearily.

"It will hurt a bit this first time, but I promise you, never again."

While he noticed her eyebrows dip down and her eyes narrow in confusion, he didn't pause to reassure her—he couldn't. He was much intent upon guiding himself to the threshold of all that slippery heat while he could still manage it gracefully. Finding her, he urged her up onto her knees a bit until she was poised above him, almost held up by the rigid length of him.

Then pulling her slowly but steadily down upon him, he watched her eyes grow wider until she finally bit her lip and broke her sated silence.

"I'm not certain this will work," she asserted quickly.

"It will work," he gritted out, "You will stretch to accommodate me."

He was very nearly holding his own breath, so tense he was, so determined to move slowly and carefully. He prayed he could hold on just a few seconds longer.

Emily was more than a little shocked. Certainly this was

what she had expected to happen, but then she had never expected him, or anyone for that matter, to be so very large. This would never work. She didn't want to argue with him, but it was evident that he was a bit too optimistic. It seemed strange that he would be mistaken in this aspect of the evening's proceedings, as he seemed extremely competent with everything else thus far.

Delightfully, wonderfully, unbelievably competent.

Her thoughts were interrupted by her own strangled cry. While she had been preoccupied with their unfortunate problem, Brand had snatched the opportunity to rectify it. Gripping her waist, he had pushed her down swiftly on his jutting member and buried himself deep.

"My God, Em," he groaned.

As the sharp tearing pain quickly began to recede, she struggled to shift and accommodate him. She could feel the bunched muscles of his shoulders and knew he was straining for control. Forcing herself to relax, she found she could slide a bit further down the length of him and that it felt, not wonderful, but not too bad.

"I can't wait any longer, Em." His voice carried a note of desperation, and she smiled into his eyes and nodded.

Heaving a great sigh of relief, Brand lifted her slightly and plunged her down upon himself again. And then again. Emily was shocked at the ferocity of his movements and at her own desire for them to continue. Her body reacted instinctively, further stoking the desire that had sprung up between them as she began to lever herself up and down in an attempt to match his rhythm.

She rode him unashamed and uninhibited as she once again felt herself grasping for something that was just out of reach. Willing herself to capture it and hold on tightly, she pushed herself to move even faster. Brand met and matched her, stroke for stroke.

Suddenly their movements stilled, and they stared into each other's eyes, letting wave after wave of pleasure wash over them. Until finally, overwhelmed with each other and what they'd shared, they looked away.

In a fog of contentment, Emily decided to savor the

moment and treasure the memory she'd hold forever. She supposed she should be feeling some sort of regret but couldn't think what the purpose would be. She'd had a marvelous time and would be delighted to do so again. Brand had said it wouldn't hurt the next time...but, honestly, she'd willingly risk the pain for the other rewards. She smiled to herself, thoroughly satisfied with matters exactly as they were, and she acknowledged that this was the first time since her father's ultimatum that she could make that claim. She prayed she could hold on to it.

Brand allowed the stunning impact of their actions to settle around him, relatively certain he'd never fully recover from the rash decision they had made together. She would consume him, and he'd gratefully allow it.

But not yet. He needed to be practical and prudent, at least as much as he could manage it. God help him, but it was difficult with this particular woman sitting half-naked on his lap. Hadn't his control slipped irrevocably just moments earlier?

Now he faced the disappointing task of detaching himself from her warmth and her sweet scent, covering all that glorious skin, and returning to the relative anonymity and isolation of the ballroom.

Rubbing her bare back with the palm of his hand, needing to slide her slowly into awareness, he stole one last shuddering look at her. With her hair glinting in the moonlight, her face mysteriously seductive behind her mask, and her body exposed to his sight and touch, she looked every inch a siren who had lured him from the sanity of bachelorhood. It remained to be seen where exactly she would lead him.

This very moment, however, she seemed in no hurry to go anywhere. So he would risk another moment to enjoy the fleeting calm.

After several moments resting languorously in his arms, Emily rolled her neck and stretched. Tipping her head back down, she was somewhat startled to see Brand watching her, his eyes hooded and gleaming in the trickle of moonlight. As her heartbeat hurried in reaction, Emily slowly curved her lips into a half-smile, hoping she would manage this first attempt at seduction.

"You were right," she said in a husky whisper, "It did work. But, I'll wager it will work better now that I've had a bit of practice."

The moonlight seemed to flare in Brand's eyes, but he didn't speak. His hands, which once again spanned her waist, tightened, and his thumbs rubbed intimately over the bottom edge of her rib cage.

"I wish we could," he told her.

"Why can't we?" she asked, sweetly innocent.

If he'd had any doubts as to his own ability, they were now but a memory. It seemed now they'd both go away unfulfilled. He'd make certain, however, to compensate her for the lost opportunity in the very near future.

"We need to be getting back."

She moaned a bit in complaint but slowly, awkwardly began covering all that lovely exposed skin. Seeing the difficulty she was having with her shoulder, he did his best to assist her. Then, quite unexpectedly, she leaned into him again and parted her lips for a final kiss.

Quite obviously hoping to tempt him, Emily wasn't prepared for Brand's reaction. He calmed her ardor with tenderness until she wanted simply to stay curled in his warmth.

Without speaking, they helped each other dress, meticulously straightening and smoothing to insure their clothes revealed no hints of the past hour's activities, lingering over the task that allowed them to continue touching.

Finally, knowing time had run out, they curled their fingers together and stepped out the doors and into the frigid wind.

12

"...She was acting very strangely. But that is hardly a surprise, now is it? I'm sure it is nothing."

CONVERSATION BETWEEN LADY SINCLAIR AND MR. DESMOND RICHLY
30 OCTOBER 1818

Emily had succeeded in convincing Brand to postpone the announcement of their engagement but only after agreeing to his demand for a hasty wedding.

She was to be married in a fortnight, and no one knew it but she and Brand. If she had been the least bit concerned with planning, or truly any aspect of the ceremony, this might have troubled her.

If she had been Beatrice, it would have alarmed her.

But she wasn't the least bit concerned with the ritual itself, only its result. The reality of actually being married. She truly couldn't imagine it—being tied to someone whose acquaintance she'd made only a few weeks prior to the wedding. And it was this fear, or perhaps uncertainty of the unknown, that had her insisting that they keep their secret to themselves. If no one knew of it, there was no one to speak of it, and if no one spoke of it, it was almost as if it wasn't really happening.

Part of her desperately wished to begin her new life with Brand, and the other part wanted to avoid it as long as possible. She was a ninny—she had no trouble admitting it. But that didn't help matters. He had granted her favor, and now she would be facing her fear much sooner than if she had never struck a bargain with him. She was fully aware that the entire matter made no sense, but lately nothing did.

Perhaps it was simply bridal jitters. She would, after all, be leaving the comfort and familiarity of Sinclair House (even with Beatrice in residence it was still her home). It would seem it should be more concerning if she *wasn't* nervous. Such a change was all-encompassing. While it was true she had wished for change for as long as she could remember, rather than portioning it out evenly, God had apparently decided it would be best dealt with all at once. She wasn't sure she agreed, but it hadn't been her decision, and she was left wondering whether anything ever would be again.

The knowledge that she would be marrying Brand and not someone else (most especially Devilish Desmond), *had* dispelled the weight that had pressed heavy on her chest for almost a week. But in its place there was a new, almost indescribable, feeling. It was as if her heart was tingling. She didn't know if it was with excitement or something else entirely. Something that made her wonder and worry over the possibility that this might be the end of herself. In two sure-to-be-short weeks, she would no longer be Miss Emily Sinclair. She would be Lady Davenport, wife of Viscount Ashwood, daughter-in-law to the Earl of Chase. She could already feel the loss of her identity, and it saddened her tremendously.

She shouldn't be wasting time thinking about it. Certainly things would have to change. She wasn't foolish enough to pretend otherwise. She might as well stop dwelling on the sacrifices she would have to make and consider the many benefits her new martial status would bring. Calling to mind the previous evening in Colin's library, it was easy to think of several. She could remember every single detail of the evening—at least the portion that began with her hasty and utterly unexpected proposal and ended with Brand squeezing her hand and allowing her to precede him into the ballroom following their 'understanding'.

They had decided to go in separately so as not to arouse any gossip, and as she had stepped away from him, she had vowed not to turn back or later search the ballroom for him.

The time she and Brand had spent together had been burned into her subconscious, flickering to life at the most unexpected moments for the remainder of the evening. More than once, her stepmother's far-flung voice had invaded her thoughts and sent memories of divine intimacies skittering to hide. Within a quarter of an hour, the woman had managed to leech away every bit of serenity with which Emily had returned to the ballroom, leaving her only with the desire to get away. In bed, tucked safely under the covers, Emily could cherish the last bit of solitude she had remaining, thinking of Brand and the life they would make together.

And she had, almost until dawn, at which point she had remembered with a heartfelt groan that today was to be the much-anticipated race. The opportunity to see Brand again so soon was an undeniable indulgence, but remaining abed also held extraordinary appeal this morning. The fire of excited anticipation she had been stoking for days had smoldered. She could barely bring herself to push back the down comforter on her bed, so it was bound to be a monumental undertaking to dress, ride to their meeting spot—back to the boggy forest once more—and actually muster some enthusiasm for the competition itself.

If she could forfeit the race without her pride suffering, she would, but she knew it would be impossible. She had virtually taunted Brand into accepting, and while at the time she would have considered the idea of reneging ridiculous, it wouldn't have mattered whether she did or not. She had never expected to see him again. Now she was engaged to the man, so if she didn't race him, she would never hear the end of it.

But it was most definitely the last thing she wanted to do this morning.

The glorious hour she had spent secreted with Brand had left her with a host of thrilling memories and wicked imaginings for the future...and a single uncomfortable reality. She was sore. Muscles for which she had never spared a single thought ached this morning in gentle reminder.   They had probably been every bit as uncomfortable as she had walked through the ballroom last night, but it had escaped her notice, preoccupied as she was with the long-term effects of her actions.

Now she needed to deal with them and hadn't a clue as to how to go about it.

What would the Beatrice Sinclair School of Manners and Household Management advise in this situation?

She was grinning to herself when a solution materialized. It was sufficiently ironic as to be disturbing, and she couldn't muster much enthusiasm for it. Still, she *supposed* there was the option of riding sidesaddle, for it seemed more likely to accommodate her tenderness and prevent further soreness. She would sacrifice, just this once, and hope it wasn't required of her again.   Beatrice's influence, it seemed, was even more far-reaching than she'd imagined.

Then she realized. Even if she resigned herself to riding sidesaddle to meet Brand, she would have to ride astride to win the race. Wincing at the thought, she had a second revelation.

She really didn't *need* to win this race—its outcome was irrelevant. She'd just realized the truth of the matter and was now feeling quite smug indeed. The very fact that Brand had agreed to race was enough—and precisely why she was in love with him.

It was now so wonderfully simple! She would ride sidesaddle and use a wool blanket for extra padding, and she would simply do her best. That would be enough.

As she slowly dressed, she couldn't help but wonder whether she would be uncomfortable with Brand this morning. After what they had shared, things had most certainly changed between them. But reminding herself that that had been her intention all along, she admitted it was silly to quibble and decided she would be as comfortable with him as she had been from the first.

Either that or she'd do her best to fake matters convincingly.

* * *

Brand was waiting for her, allowing his stallion to crop the reachable parts of a grassy slope he imagined would soon be frosted over. He himself was thoroughly distracted. It was difficult to believe all that had happened to him in the last twelve hours. He'd been outmaneuvered into getting himself engaged—a miracle in itself given his long-held opposition to the married state—and then he'd recklessly dragged Emily off, thinking for once to have the upper hand. Instead, she'd managed to scatter his thoughts and melt his control once again. The one thing that had gone as he intended was her agreement to a hasty wedding. Later this morning he would begin the process of obtaining a special license. He wondered if there was a necessity beyond his own urgency. Even now, a babe could be growing inside Emily. He smiled as he considered the possibility.

And as if that weren't enough to muddle a man's thoughts, he had a strong suspicion that this was only the beginning. Once he was wed to this woman, there was no telling how much his life would change. One thing was for certain—he would never be bored. But it was more than that. He had liked her from the moment he had met her, rudeness and all, but she had pushed and nudged him into acceptance, trust, and respect. Last night, he had realized that he needed her; quite simply, he didn't want to leave this quiet little corner of Devon without her.

After fleeing London to escape the marriage-minded multitude, he had succumbed to the pushiest, most presumptuous woman he'd yet had cause to meet. It was truly amazing—he couldn't help but admire her for it.

Wondering if she would always be one step ahead of him, he determined to surprise her with something before too long.

The measured gait of an approaching horse promptly drew his attention. It was sure to be Emily, and, if it was, he had a fair idea why she had adopted such an uncharacteristically slow pace.

But never would he have predicted he'd see her riding sidesaddle.

He watched her progress in stunned disbelief. She hadn't yet noticed him, and so her brow remained furrowed in concentration and her mouth set in tight lines.

He had no doubts she could skillfully manage her mount in such a position, but he knew she would never adopt it unless there was an urgent need.

Guilt snaked through him at seeing her this way, but it was rapidly overtaken by a loosening in his chest, a warm satisfaction that he had found someone like her and that they had convinced each other to hold on. He smiled in genuine affection, and it was at that moment that she decided to raise her head.

A bit flustered by the silent and unexpectedly warm greeting she was receiving from Brand, Emily dipped her eyes down, took a bracingly deep breath, gasped slightly at the biting chill that invaded her mouth and nose, and at long last, pulled her gaze back up to meet his.

"Good morning," she tried with a cautious smile.

"And to you," he answered, holding on to his own smile. "How is your shoulder?"

"In truth I've hardly noticed it this morning." Suddenly wondering if her response had hinted at other, unmentionable discomforts, she hurried on, "I suppose you are ready?" she prompted, expecting, but dreading, his acquiescence.

The ride over had been tolerable, but she could imagine that the pace she would need to adopt for the race would be considerably more jarring.

"Actually I was thinking that perhaps we could postpone." His reply came somewhat offhandedly, but he kept his eyes intently on her face.

More than a little surprised at his suggestion, Emily narrowed her eyes a bit in speculation.

"Why would we do that?" she inquired suspiciously.

"I'm...ah...a bit tired after last night and thought that perhaps, if you wanted a fair race, you might wish to delay."

She didn't believe him, not one bit. It was plain that his

suggestion was offered as a courtesy to her. No doubt he was aware of her 'condition' and thought to preserve her pride. If she hadn't already been engaged to this man, she would have proposed right this very minute.

Instead she bit her lip, and lifted the corners of her mouth in a shy smile. Offering a nod of allowance that she hoped he interpreted as appreciation, she finally spoke.

"Very well. It would be best to wait until we are assured of a fair race. Although, in your fatigued state, we may have been evenly matched—I was planning to ride sidesaddle."

"Indeed. It is unfortunate then that we will never know the outcome, but I would much prefer an even match, testing each of us at our full ability."

"There should be plenty of opportunity," she allowed, tiptoeing towards the subject of their impending nuptials.

"More than enough. In fact, I plan to use the remainder of the morning to do whatever is necessary to procure a special license. Once I have it, we can be married whenever you wish," he finished expansively. "As long as your wish falls within the fortnight we agreed upon," he added as an afterthought.

When she didn't answer, he moved his horse alongside of hers until their bodies were aligned. Using his finger, he tipped up her chin until she raised her troubled eyes to meet his steady gaze. Then dropping his hand to cover hers as it fidgeted with her horse's reins, he spoke quietly, almost intimately.

Comforted by his nearness, she turned her palm up and linked her fingers with his.

"If you would like, we can be married with only the clergy and witnesses in attendance. No planning, no elaborate ceremony, no guests. You could then announce your marriage rather than your engagement, presenting your father with a *fait accompli*. Not that I believe Lord Sinclair is likely raise any objections, but it might make matters considerably less cumbersome. I leave the decision up to you."

Realizing what he was proposing would allow her to cut

her stepmother—plans, discussions, advice, and all—soundly out of the proceedings, she grasped it with both hands.

"I would…I do…that is precisely what I would prefer," she said in a rush. But then as he smiled at her, she let her mind wander over the simplicity he'd offered and found she still had a few concerns.

She felt foolish for bothering him with such questions but thought it best that they understand one another. "Any of my gowns would require days with a seamstress before they could be transformed into a suitable wedding gown. A new gown would take even longer and require fittings." She allowed her dislike of that chore to show plainly on her face. "Is it important to you that I wear a true wedding dress, or would something else be acceptable? I have several quite lovely gowns," she offered in conciliation.

"I wouldn't mind if you came in breeches, but I daresay the others might have quite a bit to say on the matter."

"Good then. Ahh…one other thing…would it be possible for Vicar Penrose to perform the ceremony? He has been vicar here since before I was born." She looked down at their joined hands as she continued speaking. "He has been like a second father to me and I always imagined that if marriage became a necessity, he would be able to sanction it." Before he could answer, she rushed on, "And perhaps his daughter Sophie, my best friend, could act as witness?"

"If I agree to these requests, will you tell me what is really troubling you?" He looked pointedly into her eyes, not only listening, but watching for her response as well.

Her eyes widened slightly, and she flexed her fingers in his grip before he tightened on them with his own and tugged her off her horse and onto his lap.

"Come, tell me. Perhaps I can fix it for you, and you can grant me a boon. I have already decided what I shall ask for."

As he rubbed his hand along the length of her spine, she started slowly to relax and didn't realize that she had leaned into him, resting her body against the firm, unyielding muscles of his chest.

Brand pulled her closer, hoping to bridge the emotional distance between them and encourage an answer to his question. He very shortly realized that he would be content for a time just holding her in silence.

She watched her horse wander away a bit to browse amid the fallen leaves and then nestled her face close against his chest. He felt her draw in a settling breath and knew she was about to confide in him. Tightening his grip, he waited.

"I'm a little worried over the thought of getting married," she whispered.

"What exactly has you worried?"

"You," she answered quickly in a small voice.

"Ahhh, I see," he offered in response. "I can see how that might be troubling. However, you must realize that I am one of very few non-negotiable elements of this arrangement."

She stiffened slightly but held herself still when he tightened his arms on her, willing her to relax.

"I am no longer going to share any secrets with you if you persist in poking fun at me."

He chuckled but ran a finger down the tip of her nose in a placating gesture.

"Can you blame me?" he asked, clearly still amused and unaffected by her threat.

"No," she conceded, surprising them both.

"Well, then, why don't we see if we can allay your concerns. What *specifically* about me is troubling you?" Brand asked rationally.

"Oh, perhaps it is not really you at all. It is all this boundless uncertainty." At Brand's raised brow, she pressed on, offering an explanation. "This is not like an afternoon's or evening's adventure where I'm free to pick and choose—and escape whenever I wish to. This is to be my *life*."

"And perhaps we shall make it all into a grand adventure," Brand suggested.

The tightness around her heart seemed to loosen a bit at

his words, but she couldn't seem to stem the flood of questions, "Where will we live…what will be required of me…will you be a boorish, overbearing brute who wishes to dictate everything I do…will—"

"Enough! You have made your point—in not very complimentary terms. We have not discussed any of these matters, and you are justifiably concerned over their answers. Would you like to go over them now?"

"No…no…" she answered, irritated with herself. She opened her mouth to speak, seemed to reconsider what she had been planning to say, closed her mouth for a long moment and then finally did speak.

"It seems so silly really," she started, allowing her shoulders to slump slightly before finishing. "I've just…been happy here. Relatively happy anyway," she added, thinking of Beatrice and the tolerable tedium. "Marriage has me worried over what lies ahead of me, somewhere beyond these hills."

Having finally revealed her secret fear, she looked away from him, out over the rolling hills that had shielded her from the unknown. Remaining silent, he smoothed his closed fist down her cheek before capturing her chin between thumb and forefinger. He then turned her head so she was looking into his eyes.

She saw those hills, and the rosy promise of the dawn behind them, reflected in his eyes, and instantly she knew he wouldn't be taking her far. For the moment, distance was irrelevant—she knew he would only take her as far as she wanted to go away from her remembered, treasured life in Devon. She smiled, trusting him more deeply than she had ever expected. And the realization couldn't have come too soon.

"Do you trust me?" he asked innocently. She wondered if his question was a very clever deception. He seemed to know her almost as well as she knew herself, so she wouldn't have been surprised if his awareness of her sudden insight mirrored her own.

"Yes," she answered truthfully and without conditions.

His smile spoke of limitless promise, and she answered

it with one of her own. The desperation that had clung to her like a wisp of fog for almost a week now was slowly but determinedly dissipating in the face of Brand's confidence. Things would have to change—neither of them could prevent that. But right now, it seemed more than a little possible that they could very well change for the better.

"Excellent. How soon can the wedding be scheduled?" he prodded with expectant eyes.

"For someone who has clung to his bachelor existence for so long, I find it extremely suspicious that you have become so relentless in your attempts to end it so suddenly," she retorted. "Care to explain yourself?"

"You won't like it if I do, but I suppose that is too bad now isn't it?" he taunted.

Faced with Emily's puzzled and now slightly nervous expression, Brand smiled slowly and narrowed his eyes, prompting her to come immediately to two conclusions. The first was that she'd cleverly distracted him, the second that she may very soon regret it. For it appeared he planned to tease her quite incorrigibly with wicked innuendo. Flustered already, she hurried to stay his confession.

"I...really don't think it's necessary for you to..." she tried. But it appeared he wasn't about to forego this opportunity to make her squirm in embarrassment.

"A postponement, my sweet, would accomplish very little, and it would be extremely hard on me. You see, having tasted...touched...and explored as much of you as I did last evening..." With a finger's soft caress across her lips to pair with his words, Brand sent her heart aflutter once more. She was staring at him with wide-eyed intent and suddenly couldn't prevent herself from a frenzy of uncontrolled blinking.

Watching her, Brand smiled a slow, silky smile, and with a start of surprise, Emily realized he must assume she was flirting with him. She opened her mouth on denial but was hushed into willing silence by Brand's softly spoken words, "I now find I have a craving to repeat the task...over and over." As he flicked his eyes down to her parted lips, she struggled to regain her composure. She sucked in a breath and swiped her suddenly parched tongue over dry lips before pressing the pair primly together.

"And while it might be possible for us to find another opportunity before we are wed," Brand continued, "I would rather—"

"One week," Emily blurted, nearly mesmerized by his eyes. "Give me one week." Feeling almost as if she had snatched at the opportunity seconds before it was lost, she closed her eyes and breathed slowly and deeply.

Brand smiled, very obviously satisfied with his tactics.

"I am at your disposal, my lady," he quipped.

Anxious for a victory of her own, she fisted her hand in his cravat, hoping to leave at least one good wrinkle, and yanked his mouth to hers.

The kiss was fiercely demanding and considerably more desperate than either would have expected.

Emily decided that she was experiencing the effects of newfound love. As thoroughly unexpected as her recent discovery had been, it was quite logical that she'd find herself a trifle disoriented.

Brand considered his suspicions confirmed. His feelings for Emily had most definitely surpassed those of enjoyable companionship and gentle affection. He could contentedly resign himself to the idea that he was in love with her.

As the kiss melted away, both stared, quietly intent, wondering at the vagaries of fate.

Finally, they both spoke at once.

"Well then," Emily started.

"We're in agreement then," Brand offered with a roguish smile, and then, "I'm not sure how much I will see of you before the wedding. I need to get several matters in order. But you needn't worry—I will take care of everything."

Emily smiled at that. Normally she would take offense at a man's careless assumption that *he* should take charge of a situation while *she* stood idly by. Not with Brand. He made her feel comfortable with herself and spared her from proving every little thing. He trusted her, and that was just perfect.

"All right. Just wait a bit before you talk to Vicar

Penrose. I would rather tell him and Sophie myself."

In truth she had absolutely no idea what she would even begin to tell her friend. What could she say about this man, whom Sophie had just met the previous evening and she herself had met only a week before, that could possibly explain things? Even she, privy to every detail of their involvement, was still baffled by the idea that she was in love with someone she'd considered an arrogant, obnoxious stranger just days ago. Smirking to herself, she wondered if Brand felt the same. Of course, he had given her no indication that he was in love with her, but it didn't trouble her overmuch. She would work him around to the idea when she had a bit more time. In truth she already had a few ideas on the subject, ones that had her smiling in anticipation.

"If granting such small favors as postponing my talk with the vicar is all it takes to have you grinning at me, then I assure you, we will deal very comfortably together."

"A smile does not preclude irritation," Emily reminded him with a wicked gleam.

"But it can invite far more than is offered," Brand countered.

Emily pursed her lips slightly and lowered her brows but was unable to come off looking anything other than disapprovingly amused.

He sidled his stallion alongside her mare and lifted her easily, gently settling her back into the sidesaddle.

"One week," they reminded each other before riding off separately.

* * *

After stabling Gypsy, Emily entered the house and handed her hat and cloak to Pembury, who happened to be standing in the hall, seemingly with no pressing responsibility. Glancing at the hall clock, she wondered if she had chanced to spend enough time with Brand to have missed Beatrice's company at breakfast. As the hour was nearing eight, she decided her chances were fair. Her stepmother had recently been eating much earlier.

Determined to be cautious just in case luck wasn't with her this morning, she slowly moved down the hall towards the breakfast room, softly stepping along the runner carpet till its end and then tip-toeing over the bare floorboards hoping not to make a sound.

Quite unexpectedly, Beatrice made one herself. Emily started in surprise before realizing that Lady Sinclair was safely ensconced in her parlour—with a visitor.

As the new Lady Sinclair, Beatrice had wasted no time in selecting a room for herself. The one she had chosen was adjacent to the breakfast room (little surprise), which afforded a splendid view of the lawn at the rear of the house. The windows of Beatrice's parlour faced east out onto the rose garden Emily's mother had tended.

As always, the door to the parlour was open, and Beatrice unfailingly faced the door. Emily believed the tendency was based solely on her desire to trap unsuspecting passers-by into conversation. The woman was a veritable spider.

Emily was undecided, wondering whether she should risk being spotted in order to partake of a much-needed breakfast or savor her time alone, knowing Beatrice was otherwise occupied indefinitely.

Thoughts of food were momentarily pushed aside by a puzzling question. Who could Beatrice be entertaining at this hour? Clearly they did not wish privacy—the door was wide open, and their voices were not the slightest bit hushed or secretive. Well *her* voice. Thus far she had only heard Beatrice speaking. No surprise there. Now she was going to have to stand here spying if she wished to see whom it was closeted with her stepmother. Not to mention hear what they were saying…

"There is no need to be so upset, my dear. I'm sure she was mistaken," Lady Sinclair comforted.

"Mistaken? How can one be mistaken over the identity of one's fiancé?" the visitor ground out.

The voice was familiar, but lack of sleep and lack of food kept her from deducing its origin straight away.

"Easily, I assure you. You mustn't worry. Edward will handle everything. Now then, have you had your breakfast? I could accompany you. I have had mine already, but I could perhaps have some chocolate and a roll to keep you company."

How gracious, Emily thought, her sarcasm not a bit dimmed by the realization that she could be discovered at any minute.

"No, thank you, I find I am not hungry. I wish to get this matter resolved with all haste."

"Emily was up very late last night, and I think she might be a bit ill. She was acting very strangely. But that is hardly a surprise, now is it? I'm sure it is nothing."

A rude hiss that sounded as if it would rather have been a curse issued forth from the visitor. She assumed it was the visitor. Her suspicions were confirmed when her stepmother offered consolation.

"But for you, dear, I will ferret out the reason behind it."

"And when might that be, Aunt?" said the voice, and Emily could almost imagine the twisted sneer on the mouth to which it belonged.

Even without his very generous hint, Emily had already determined who stood just out of sight in consort with her stepmother. Mr. Desmond Richly. And what was worse than having that detestable toad in her home was that he was actually discussing *her* with her stepmother! He must be desperate indeed.

"As soon as Edward finishes with his business, we will discuss this matter. He will summon Emily, and confusion will be dispelled in time for luncheon."

Emily could well imagine the doting smile Beatrice had pasted on her face and knew with sudden clarity that her stepmother had no idea of 'Dear Desmond's' true qualities. That, at least, was comforting.

She needed to determine what should be done. If she admitted to Richly's accusation, neither her father nor her stepmother would agree to the plans she and Brand had just arranged. And now she was quite intent upon them. Particularly the fact that Beatrice was cut neatly out of them.

She couldn't imagine her father objecting to the match, but she supposed that was possible as well. The truth really didn't seem the most judicious option, although the thought of flaunting it once again in Richly's face was extraordinarily tempting.

If she denied it...well, she really couldn't say. If, as she hoped, her father chose to believe *her*, likely matters would continue on as they had been, with the clock ticking slowly away on a month-long ultimatum. If he believed Richly, her father was likely to threaten and cajole with the intention that she would eventually admit all. She didn't expect she'd manage to hold out very long under such pressure.

But beyond everything, she didn't *want* to tell right now—this morning—today. And certainly not as part of a confrontation with the obnoxious Richly present. She had barely gotten used to the idea herself; she wasn't up to convincing her father that she had found the perfect fiancé in the space of a week. She wanted just a little more time.

And she realized that she was willing to risk the consequences...

"I will leave you to your...self," Richly was condescending. "Please summon me as well when Lord Sinclair is available to discuss this preposterous situation."

Good grief! She was not, however, willing to risk the unpleasantness of Richly coming upon her lurking in the hallway. Where to go...?

Only one chance. Deciding to take it, she lunged across the open doorway, conscious of Beatrice's voice still speaking, and aimed for the curio cabinet standing sentry between the parlour and breakfast room doors. Feeling like a hot air balloon being launched amid a great deal of rustling and gusts of air, she held her breath, pressed up against the wall beside the tall piece of furniture. She had flattened her back against the wall and her skirts against her body to slim her profile. Had it worked?

She heard the click of Richly's boots, his steps having strayed from the parlour's Aubusson rug, and tracked his progress to the door. In a matter of seconds she would know...

His footsteps got louder…and then receded down the hall. She kept to her hiding place, giving him an opportunity to mount the stairs and close himself in the room Beatrice always kept ready for him.

Closing her eyes and letting the breath she'd been holding out in a rush, she nearly slumped with relief. Now she needed to plan, but first she needed to eat. Turning to her left, she very nearly rolled through the doorway of the breakfast room. Conscious of the need to stay relatively quiet with Beatrice tucked in next door, she moved to the sideboard and proceeded to load her plate.

* * *

Emily ate her fill from what remained on the sideboard and then somehow managed to get past the doorway to her ladyship's parlour a second time on her way to her room.

Deciding she had neither the energy, nor the inclination, for pacing, she settled into a cozy chair she often used for reading, comfortably positioned her good shoulder in one of the crooks, and brought her legs up under her.

What to do…what to do?

She'd decided at breakfast that she was simply going to deny Richly's accusations and see what came of it. So now she had time on her hands and nothing particularly diverting to do with it. She reached for a novel and thought for a moment that she might read. But staring at the cover, her mind wandered for several moments before she conceded the obvious—her concentration was too scattered for reading. She had spent enough time over the last week on inner reflection and contemplation, not to mention on her backside. What she needed was a distraction.

On that thought, and with a bit of trouble from her shoulder, she awkwardly launched herself out of the chair and began to move around the room. She knew that after she'd settled matters with her father, she would need to speak to Sophie. However, having made no progress in devising the explanation that would be required of her, she wasn't much looking forward to the conversation. She'd been so involved with her own life that she'd almost forgotten how strangely Sophie had been acting of late—her friend's behavior had made it difficult to hold even the most casual of conversations. Broaching the subject of her impending marriage and departure was certain to be an awkward and unpleasant task indeed.

Emily stopped in front of the window as the years all tumbled together in her mind. The memories formed images that flickered to life and quickly faded, only to be replaced by others. Sophie had been right beside her all along: endearing, enduring, and ever the thoughtful voice of reason. Now she would need to leave Sophie behind once more, but this time it was for good.

Tears gathered unbidden, ready to spill over, but she didn't want them. Determined to distract herself, she darted her eyes around the room. Realizing it would be hers for only a little longer, she decided to settle back into the chair and store up memories of her life as it had once been—before she had met Brand. Soon it would change irrevocably: her grand adventure was upon her at long last.

As her eyes flitted around the room, settling here and there for a moment or two, her body relaxed. Soon her eyelids pulled down with fatigue, and she fell into slumber, dreams swirling against each other, colliding, and dispersing like mist. Just as her thoughts had done in consciousness.

When she awoke, it was as a consequence of being gently shaken by Bess, who had come to inform her that luncheon was being served and that her stepmother had inquired after her, requesting her presence if she felt up to it. Now groggy, sore, and thoroughly disgruntled, Emily gradually adjusted to being prematurely awakened and rose slowly from the chair. Bess circled her like a twittering bird, smoothing her skirts and removing the pins Emily herself had randomly placed earlier that morning, having not wished to bother her maid at such an early hour.

"Her ladyship is in a bit of a tizzy. Keeps asking after his lordship. Really, Miss Emily, I thought I'd convinced you it was best if I styled your hair." Betsy tisked in disapproval. "I can't quite figure whether you tried and failed or simply didn't try at all." As she worked the matted hair quickly and efficiently into a twist, replacing the pins without conscious thought, she veered back to her original subject, "And with that Mr. Richly mad as a hornet, things just keep gettin' worse and worse. Perhaps you'd best hurry down and fix things right up."

"Thank you, Bess," Emily answered, thoroughly preoccupied. But noticing her maid standing before her, smiling at her with a touch of pride, she impulsively hugged the girl before hurrying out of the room.

As she entered the dining room, she registered that her father was still absent, and she was going to have to suffer luncheon with only Beatrice and Richly for company. As it turned out, it wasn't too painful—Richly hardly spoke, after inclining his head in curt acknowledgment, and Beatrice, as usual, delighted in speaking to a captive audience.

Emily passed the meal in mild confusion. It almost seemed as if she had imagined this morning's little drama. No one spoke of it, even the slightest hint or mention. Richly probably assumed that any discussion without her father present would prove ineffectual. And for once, he was surely correct. Beatrice, however, was another matter. This was the kind of gossip the woman determinedly sought out, so why wasn't she confronting her spinster stepdaughter with an alleged engagement and a spurned nephew?

Perhaps she agreed with Richly and wished to discuss the matter only once. Still, it wasn't like Beatrice to be efficient or the slightest bit patient. She supposed it was possible the two had come to somewhat of an understanding this morning. Emily couldn't remember overhearing anything that could be construed as such, but there could very well have been an unspoken agreement between them. Either way, she was relieved. She hadn't much cared for the idea of repeating a fib more than once. Why that should bother her she couldn't say.

Lunch, like breakfast, passed deliciously and uneventfully.

Unless one counted the escape of several rolls from their

linen covered serving dish. Lady Sinclair had been particularly up-in-arms over something, and one of those arms had clipped the footman's, positioned as he was beside her chair, causing a bobble and the resultant disappearance of a bevy of buns. Emily had found herself smiling almost indulgently as Richly rolled his eyes in disgusted disbelief.

Moments later he begged to be excused.

"Your pardon, ladies, but I have some business." Apparently not requiring a response from either of them, he tossed his napkin on the table and rose with alacrity.

"Desmond." Lady Sinclair stalled him, "What of Edward?"

"What of him, Aunt?" Desmond queried with forced patience.

"Wasn't there a matter of some importance you wished to discuss with him?" Beatrice hinted, eyes wide. Two bright spots of color had appeared high on her stepmother's cheeks, and Emily couldn't help but wonder if they'd been brought on by something more than Dear Desmond's rudeness.

"Indeed there was," he answered, his eyes flickering over to Emily before they refocused on Lady Sinclair. "Please tell his lordship that I will make myself available to him. He need only summon me." Deciding not to wait for further interrogation, Richly nodded and strode purposefully through the door.

Beatrice looked cautiously over at Emily who had pretended innocence throughout the entire exchange. Emily smiled, and Beatrice eyed her curiously but kept silent. Interesting. Deciding she would try her hand at escape she smiled gamely at Beatrice.

"I promised Sophie I would stop by the vicarage today to help her sort through the clothes she has collected for distribution to village families who are accepting of the charity."

In truth, Emily wasn't sure if Sophie had started collecting yet or not, but it was common knowledge that she did at this time every year and, as such, a relatively safe fib.

"As much as I approve of your taking an interest in such

matters, it will have to wait until later dear," Beatrice informed her. "I have a feeling your father will require your presence before too long."

"Why would you think that? He very rarely does, and I don't believe I have done anything warranting punishment." A falsehood of that magnitude had never passed her lips before.

"I should hope not dear," Beatrice agreed. "Let us just say I have a suspicion, shall we?" With raised eyebrows, she stared Emily down.

"Very well. May I be excused then to gather some clothes together in preparation for delivering them to the vicarage?"

"Of course, dear," she shooed. "Oh, and ask my maid to give you my pale lemon yellow silk—I fear it was an ill-fated choice. I have never worn it. Seeing myself reflected in the glass, I was reminded each time of a Gunter's ice."

Wishing she had had the opportunity to see such a sight, Emily nodded, "I will let Sophie know you sent it. She will be most appreciative." While it was a nice gesture, Emily didn't suppose any of the village women would ever have cause to wear such a dress. They were, however, resourceful enough to use the fabric. Perhaps it would afford them new underthings. Beatrice would expire if she ever found out.

* * *

The time had come; she had been summoned—again! The door to the study had been left open a crack, and as she spied her father behind his desk, she knocked softly, wanting only to get this matter over with. He looked up to see her peering through the doorway and promptly waved her in, rising as she stepped forward.

As expected, her stepmother was sitting in the chair by the window. Richly appeared to be blessedly absent. Excellent. Perhaps her father would relay the details of this conversation, and she would not be called upon to speak to him ever again. For even though she was to be married a week from today, she still did not wish to suffer the man's presence again if it was at all possible. It could very well mean broth and toast in her room due to meals missed belowstairs, but some sacrifices were worth it.

Smiling tentatively at her father, she waited.

"Emily, please sit down." She couldn't help but feel a bit of déjà vu. Another summons had had her sitting in the very same chair a week ago. Hopefully she'd have more success here today. As she sat, her father remained standing. Placing his hands behind him, he paced along the paper-strewn length of his desk, for the moment keeping his own council. Even Beatrice kept silent—a solemn occasion indeed.

Finally her father looked up and asked her the question she'd been anticipating.

"Emily, it has come to my attention," he spoke slowly, choosing to specify no source, "that you are engaged." He paused in his pacing and turned to look at her.

She didn't answer but stared steadily back into eyes that willed her to confide in him. She couldn't though—not yet. The effects of last evening's intimacies were still too fresh in her mind and on her body. It was her secret, and she needed to keep it a little longer. At least until Brand returned. She hadn't yet devised—let alone rehearsed—an explanation, and she most certainly did not wish to improvise. That could only lead to trouble.

"Is this true?" her father probed.

"Is it true that I promptly threw off a glorious life of spinsterhood, enthusiastically sought and—no lesser miracle—found a willing gentleman less than a week after your ultimatum was issued? What do you suppose, Father?"

Her father's lips turned up in the slightest hint of a smile.

"You needn't worry—I'll be certain to keep you informed of any and all progress," Emily assured him.

He took his time in considering, before, at long last, nodding his acceptance. Much relieved, Emily interpreted his reaction as a dismissal.

As she rose to leave and turned toward the door, the

afternoon shadows to the right of it shifted and then materialized. Richly had been in the room all along, silently eavesdropping. Apparently he was unhappy with the way the conversation, or confrontation rather, had tended. His eyes were slitted and his mouth thinned down to a mean whip.

"She is lying," he announced coldly, staring at her, into her, willing her to admit it. He must have realized she wouldn't, but he couldn't seem to draw his eyes from hers nonetheless. Speaking to her father, his voice calm with dislike for her, he began, "Last evening your daughter insisted on introducing me to Viscount Ashwood, boldly presenting him as her fiancé. I didn't believe her claim in the slightest, assuming she could hardly know the man as he is just back to England. However, when Ashwood concurred, I had little choice but to wonder, to become curious, and then suspicious."

Richly slowly panned his eyes over to her father and asked him, almost casually, "Aren't you? Curious that is? Or perhaps suspicious?"

His lips thinned with annoyance at the implication, but her father turned to face her nonetheless, " I do admit to being slightly curious about the events of last evening, Em."

"As do I," added Beatrice before retreating into silence.

"Regarding Viscount Ashwood?" Emily clarified. Her father nodded, as did Beatrice, and Richly's lips peeled back in a placidly malevolent smile.

"Well, what can I tell you?" Emily began, seeming to consider, "Um…Lord Willoughsby introduced Sophie and I to Lord Davenport, and we spent a few moments in idle conversation. Then I excused myself to grant Mr. Richly a dance that you, Father, had apparently promised him."

Lord Sinclair had the grace to flush.

"The closeness of the dance left me feeling somewhat nauseous." A pointed look at Richly was unavoidable. "Lord Davenport graciously assisted me onto the terrace for a breath of fresh air. He kept me company until I became chilly and left him to return to the ballroom. I then seated myself among the dowagers until Beatrice was ready to call for the carriage."

Apparently believing the mention of her name offered her an opening, Beatrice avidly added her own impressions.

"That is indeed the truth—she never danced again after she finished with Desmond." Emily smiled approvingly at Beatrice. "A pity she never had an opportunity to dance with Viscount Ashwood. I met him myself last evening," she enthused, "and I must say he was indeed the gentleman. He took me in to dinner and even held a second plate for me so that I could sample everything without having to make a second trip. He quite hung on my every word." She shook her head at the fond memory but then felt compelled to add, "He is the heir to the Earl of Chase you know—scads of money." Emily thought the nodding was a very convincing touch. Perhaps she *could* learn a thing or two from Beatrice.

"One would almost assume you favored his suit over my own, Aunt," Richly taunted mockingly.

Mystery solved! *That* was what had Beatrice acting so strangely. She was actually hoping to be future mother-in-law to the future Earl of Chase, Dear Desmond be damned—finally something on which they could agree.

"Don't be silly," Beatrice soothed, but her smile had faltered.

Richly turned away from her, his contempt obvious.

"Very well." Anger moved over his face, and he closed his eyes to bring it under control. When he spoke, it was with the calm of acknowledged defeat and the determination of future victory. His attention was reserved for Lord Sinclair. "By her own admission, your daughter's affections have thus far not been otherwise engaged. Perhaps I might persuade you to move our engagement forward? I am prepared to marry her as soon as I can get a license."

Emily felt a flicker of panic and wondered if it would shortly become necessary to confess all.

"I am not about to go back on my promise to my daughter. It has only been a week, and last night was the first opportunity she has had to find an alternative. It is unfortunate that she was not feeling well enough to dance after she danced with you. But time has not run out." He smiled at his daughter encouragingly, affectionately.

Turning back to Richly he said, "Emily may have the rest of the month." He then inclined his head, waiting to have his decision acknowledged. Richly's lips compressed further, but he nodded curtly.

Satisfied, her father added, "At which time, there will be an engagement ball." Words were left unspoken, but no one confused his meaning. She and Richly would be engaged at that ball if no one else materialized.

But someone had. Someone perfect—or as close as Emily had ever imagined finding.

She breathed a deep, confident, relieved breath and didn't bother to spare Richly another glance. He was now in earnest discussion with her father, and she resolved not to eavesdrop on the drivel of a tattling toad. Quite suddenly, amid his muffled fury, several words were quite easily discernible.

"...all rather inconvenient and—you must admit—melodramatic...a month to find a willing gentleman after years of rejections and indifference...?"

Emily froze, her entire body tensed, but she forced herself to keep walking, keep moving until she was out the door and had closed it behind her.

Inconvenient and melodramatic.

She had heard those exact words uttered with the same icy hostility once before. At midnight in the cemetery one week ago. A faceless coward had kept to the shadows then and ever since. He had shot and wounded her without remorse or even purpose. He was the gentleman highwayman. And the gentleman highwayman was Richly.

Not even for a moment did Emily fall victim to the misguided denial most cling to when faced with troubling knowledge regarding acquaintances. She knew in an instant, with no proof and no confession, that Mr. Desmond Richly was indeed the elusive highwayman that she and Brand had hoped to ambush. It was so believable she couldn't fathom how she hadn't thought of it until now. Richly had recently been spending quite a bit of time in the area, and it was even possible that Beatrice had been innocently feeding him information via her gossipy monologues.

Good heavens! She needed to talk to Brand, but she wasn't sure how to contact him without giving everything away. The only thing she knew with relative certainty was that he was not whiling away the hours at Clifton House.

He had said he had some matters to take care of, and that probably meant a trip somewhere. London? Cornwall?

She could send a missive to Danenbury Hall but should she? How would she get it there without arousing suspicion?

Deciding she couldn't risk it, she realized she was on her own. She most certainly did not wish to arouse Richly's suspicions.

Two days ago she'd been ready to relinquish all such adventuring indefinitely. Now with the knowledge that Richly was the target for apprehension, her spirit was filled with renewed—almost gleeful—determination. Her visit to the vicarage would need to be postponed. Otherwise it was almost a foregone conclusion that she would slip and come dangerously close to revealing too much. Especially after this afternoon's revelation.

What she needed to do was keep a close eye on Richly. Any mysterious outings and she would have no choice but to follow him. He could already have plans for another attack and, with Brand unaccounted for, she would have to be prepared to handle matters herself, using whatever means were necessary. Preferably violent ones, she admitted, smiling to herself.

First things first, she needed to get away from this door. Having paused to absorb the proof of Richly's perfidy (an assumption that had been long-standing), she was still positioned right outside her father's study door. Richly would be exiting at any moment. Where to hide? She couldn't go up to her room and expect to accomplish anything; she needed to be lurking about down here, waiting to see which direction her quarry took.

Her eyes scanned the hall until they stopped directly in front of her. Perfect. She would curl up in the library, conveniently located right across the hall, and be perfectly positioned for the requisite spying. Within moments, she was ostensibly selecting a book for an innocent afternoon of reading when her father's study door opened with a click. Hearing the string of curses that clearly identified Richly, Emily moved deeper into shadowed concealment behind the open library door.

She was able to visually track him through the crack between the hinges until he reached the stairs. Then she listened for his footsteps as his boots clicked on the stairs and along the corridor above her until finally she heard what she'd been waiting for. The slam of his bedroom door and the resounding thud that, she assumed, could only be something hitting the wall.

So Richly was in his room. Excellent bit of detective work. Now what? She could either stay down here or go up to her room and wait. But her room was several doors down from his (thankfully)—she'd have to keep her ear to the door. Her current hiding place was ideally located but put her at risk for a visit from Beatrice. Although this was, after all, the library. She should be safe here for quite awhile. She'd even indulge in the comfort of a chair.

Arbitrarily pulling a book down from the nearest shelf, she selected the cracked and faded leather armchair in the corner and curled up to wait. And wait and wait.

Hours had passed when she finally stood, stretching her unused muscles. Oddly enough, she had become engrossed with the book she had chosen—a work on Ancient Roman civilizations—and she'd only just realized it was time she dress for dinner. Laying her book aside, she swept through the door, and chanced to see Richly descending the stairs. Not wishing to be discovered, she whipped back into the room and huddled behind the door, hoping she would have the opportunity for another bit of eavesdropping.

As Richly reached the bottom step, Pembury approached him, no doubt with the announcement that dinner would shortly be served. Her quarry, however, brushed past the servant with a dismissive shake of his head and quickly walked to the door and out into the darkness of early evening, his great coat whipping out behind him.

Bloody hell! She was going to have to follow him. And she'd best hurry if she had any hope of catching him and thwarting any nefarious plots he had planned for the evening.

The inconsiderate weasel! She had lost count of how many meals she had already had to skip because of this man. Tonight would quite obviously be one more.

She wasn't at all looking forward to donning those filthy breeches again, and while she didn't know where exactly she'd lost the cap, she couldn't pretend any regret. Except that now she would need to find something else to confine her hair. For that matter, she'd need something to confine her torso as well—Brand had ripped the entire top of the shirtsleeve clean away when he'd tended her wound.

It was obvious that she was going to have to improvise a bit. *Why* hadn't she been considering all this while lolling away the afternoon in the library? Apparently ancient civilizations were as riveting as Vicar Penrose would have her believe—who knew?

Now rather than settle into a quiet dinner, she would need to don her disguise, risk retrieving his father's pistols—not forgetting the bullets, escape unnoticed, fetch Gypsy and make chase. Rolling her eyes, she resigned herself to a most unpleasant evening.

Without any leads, clues, or otherwise useful information, she had no choice but to assume his intent was thievery and his destination, that same shadowy stand of trees. And as she slid from behind the library door, she had to admit she was looking forward to the outing just a little bit. She would sacrifice. And her reward would be the sweet satisfaction of revenge.

With a bit of devilment in her eyes, she hurried to the stairs.

13

"I confess Mr. Richly and I are hardly related. I had no idea he was so utterly unsuitable!"

CONVERSATIONS BETWEEN *LADY BEATRICE SINCLAIR*
AND ANYONE WHO WOULD LISTEN
5 NOVEMBER 1818

Emily considered it impressive indeed that she had somehow managed to accomplish everything and leave the house within fifteen minutes of Richly. Comfortable once again astride Gypsy, she urged her horse in pursuit and allowed herself a moment's appreciation of her daring ingenuity. As expected, her own shirt had been irreparable. So she had snuck into Richly's room—cringing with every step—and pilfered one of his. Each time she thought of its fabric rubbing against her skin, she shuddered, forced herself to breathe deeply, and pushed the reality to the back of her mind.

Finding a cap had been an entirely different matter. Richly had had nothing of the sort—nor had she expected him to—and while she hadn't expected her father would, she certainly hadn't been willing to risk a search of his things. She hadn't supposed she would have received prompt assistance from the servants or stablehands either. Such an odd request would have been commented upon and wondered over, and she hadn't the time for that. It had taken her two weeks of prodding and persuasion to obtain her first disguise—she rather doubted she could get anything in the space of two minutes. But she couldn't spare any longer.

So with no suitable way to cover her hair, and desperate to be on her way, she had cut it. All of it. Clean off. Her hair was now as short as a boy's.

Her determination had held long enough for her to finish the task, but as she had gazed at herself in the glass, shorn locks in hand, her heart had stuttered, and her breath had come short. Slowly, carefully, she had raised a hand to touch the gentle curls that framed her face and attempted to convince herself that it was actually quite flattering. She knew it would take some getting used to but felt certain she would become quite fond of it. She hoped Brand would also. If not, it would grow back. Eventually.

Turning from the mirror, she'd shrugged on her vest and found that, with the cap absent, the seemingly unoffending garment had an odor all its own. In truth she much preferred the grubby garments of the stablehands with their stink of stale sweat over the pristine lawn shirt that had come from Richly. Shaking her head over the level of deception one could achieve simply by one's manner of dress, she'd crossed her fingers that her luck would run stronger than Richly's this evening.

Then she'd slipped out and away.

It would be necessary, she knew, to tread carefully. She would need to be silent, vigilant, and quick. If she wasn't, it could very well mean a missed opportunity or worse. 'Worse' being a tragic and painful death. She didn't want to think about consequences, didn't want to consider what could very well happen to her tonight. But she couldn't seem to stop herself as Gypsy moved relentlessly towards an unavoidable conclusion.

If she died here tonight at the hands of two contemptible, cowardly villains, she would never know what she'd missed in a life spent with Brand. Ever since she'd proposed to him—for that was how she preferred to remember things— she had eagerly anticipated each and every aspect: the adventures (whatever they may be), the arguments, the quiet conversation and, martyr that she was, even the wifely duties. A week seemed a lifetime away, but she had only two choices. Ignore Richly, or deal with him. The latter option, while more dangerous, had otherwise presented itself quite attractively. So she'd chosen it, and now she hoped she'd not regret it.

As the consequences of carelessness were now even more precarious than before, Emily was determined to think and act as prudently as possible. So noting their location—still quite a distance from the trees—she slowed Gypsy to a walk, and the pair began their painstaking plodding through the darkening evening, stealthily moving from shadow to shadow. Willing herself not to become distracted, Emily focused on anticipating each and every landmark they would pass. She had ridden this countryside since she was a young girl, and there were memories everywhere. But tonight she couldn't risk them clouding her thoughts. She would just acknowledge the scenery that triggered them and move on.

It was in this tedious manner that she and Gypsy reached their destination. She knew the next part could very well be extremely tricky, for as she moved into the shelter and shadows of the trees, she could easily find herself face to face with either highwayman with barely a moment's notice. Pulling her father's pistol from the waistband of her breeches, she placed her index finger on the trigger and laid it across Gypsy's back. It was fully loaded, primed, and ready. With a deep breath and a quick prayer, she nudged Gypsy silently into the shelter of trees.

Having not the slightest clue as to where Richly had gone, Emily felt a bit foolish prowling around in the dark, steadily creeping closer to the road. She kept her eyes alert, scanning her surroundings, and her ears pricked for any noise at all. She knew there was every possibility that nothing would happen here tonight. And just as good a chance that something already had and she'd missed the entire proceedings.

What could she do but wait? So she did, quite patiently—for a time. Then she began to fidget, wonder, and consider. She checked her gun, her position, her surroundings. She smoothed Gypsy's mane and then her own—what was left of it anyway. Finding it very difficult not to get distracted with life while out alone in the chill darkness of approaching winter, she truly hoped this evening would finish matters. She would wait for Richly to arrive.

What she saw next had her desperately hoping that he was somewhere else entirely.

Being a little distance from the clearing, her view was overlaid by criss-crossing branches and a stubborn leaf or two, hanging on despite the rapid approach of winter. But there could be no mistaking it.

Bloody hell! What is he doing here?

It appeared that once again she and her notorious stranger would rendezvous amid these same trees.

She wondered if it could possibly be a coincidence that in the next few moments he would be riding right past her hiding place. For it appeared he had no weapon drawn, and he was hardly troubling to keep his presence a secret. Just as he came even with her, he began to whistle horridly off-key.

Hoping to prevent the nicker of greeting Gypsy was sure to offer his stallion, Emily shoved a handful of sugar wafers in front of the horse's nose, tempting her to distraction.

Gritting her teeth and tracking his slow progress along the road, Emily willed him to hurry. When he didn't, she impatiently edged herself forward, needing to be certain that no one else watched him as she did.

Twigs snapping loudly off to her left had her leaning even further forward for a better look. Another visitor had joined their cozy little gathering, and it appeared this was no chance encounter. They might as well have been serving tea—any more and they'd bloody well have a foursome for cards!

Had Brand actually planned to meet the weasel Sneeves and told her nothing of his intentions? Was it possible that the two of them knew there was to be another attack this evening?

How dare he presume to keep her in the dark about it!

The indignity she felt over his arrogant high-handedness

promptly dispelled her earlier wish to be left out of it. Narrowing her eyes and contenting herself with thoughts of the lecture she would deal him, she risked stepping Gypsy a bit further forward to make certain she could see and hear the entire exchange.

As soon as the newcomer began to step his horse out of the trees, Brand pulled in the reins of his stallion and tensely waited. Sneeves moved tentatively, nervously forward, looking ready to bolt at the slightest hint of a threat.

"Got yer message and come like ye asked, milord. I've kept to our agreement, pokin' round for news of 'im, but none 'er talkin'."

"You've heard nothing of him?" Brand demanded.

"Not a thing, milord."

"And he never sought you out after the last attack?" Brand prodded.

"'E may 'av tried, but I kept to meself for a bit after that, hopin' he wouldn't come lookin'."

"I see," Brand allowed, seeming to consider, "And while I respect your motives, you must realize that self-preservation is at odds with our intention here. You are our only connection with him, and I'd appreciate your continued assistance."

In the light remaining, she could no longer make out anything more definitive than their shadows. Brand's was particularly unobliging in that he now had his back to her. But even at this distance she could easily judge that his companion was resigned and more than a little fearful of what his new employer would require of him.

"Aye, milord," he murmured, fiddling with his horse's lead.

"Good man," Brand nodded, probably hoping to inspire confidence. "You will be well compensated. Perhaps it would be best if you simply make it known that you have returned and are hoping to resume your previous employ. We'll have to hope rumor will circulate far enough to reach the ears of your elusive cohort. Wherever he may be." Brand shook his head in discouragement, apparently as unsatisfied with his plan as everyone else who had heard it.

"Aye, milord," the lackey repeated.

Emily could only assume the man didn't trust his composure to say anything further. Either that or he didn't trust Brand's reaction to anything other than outright obedience.

"Fine," Brand spoke approvingly, "I will meet you back here in three days. If you need to get a message to me, leave it with the tavern keeper—anything at all could help us."

So *this* was what Brand needed to see settled before they were wed. Interesting he hadn't mentioned it. There wasn't the slightest possibility that she wouldn't.

She'd had quite enough of secrets, not to mention the behavior necessary to keep them. Everywhere she looked, she saw her own behavior mirrored back at her. Cagey omissions and sly fibs now seemed the expected behavior. It was a guess, but she assumed she'd been the only one willing to delve into the tricky business of outright and unscrupulous lies, except perhaps Richly. She wasn't proud of herself, just desperate. As soon as this business was taken care of she would set everything to rights.

"Why wait?" came a disembodied, silkily smug voice.

Having been caught up in her own thoughts, Emily wondered for a fleeting second who had had the nerve to intrude. As the voice hung on the air, she realized exactly to whom it belonged and just what was happening.

Startled over the interruption, both men turned their eyes in unison, no doubt recognizing the fact that their quarry had found them.

A midnight black horse materialized in the clearing (or perhaps it was another color—she really couldn't tell for sure), its rider cloaked and hooded. There was no mistaking the two pistols he carried. Both glinted in the moonlight, and each, no doubt, had a target of its own.

"Ah…Richly. Of course," Brand allowed, and Emily imagined his lip was curled in contempt.

The unspoken subtleties of the exchange, it would seem, were to be left open to speculation or disregarded entirely. For with an utter lack of cooperation, the darkness had now obscured her view quite thoroughly indeed. The conversation was clearly audible, and she could still make out each man's silhouette, but their faces were concealed in shadow, and expressions had to be assumed rather than observed.

"Ashwood," Richly replied with an equal amount of distaste as Brand slowly turned his horse. "I am of the opinion that we get this matter nicely settled here and now. You have insinuated yourself into what I had planned would be a rather profitable scheme. As such, I fear I must now include you as one of a number of things that must be dispatched with all haste."

From the moment of his appearance, Richly had kept his attentions focused solely on Brand, not even bothering to give his misguided partner a cursory glance. But visibly trembling, Sneeves foolishly reminded both of his presence.

"How did ye know we was here, milord?" he puzzled.

"Surely you did not believe that you had managed through such feeble efforts to elude me?" Gauging the expression on the man's face, he continued. "Or perhaps you did. Pity. I have employed someone to keep an eye on you almost from the first. Ever since the full measure of your ignorant stupidity became clear. The only reason you have continued on thus far is that your disappearance was temporarily inconvenient. That is no longer so. Now that I no longer intend to mastermind this nighttime thievery, you are merely unnecessary baggage."

Despite his callous assessment, Richly apparently felt words were not sufficient to make his point and so fired the weapon in his left hand. As the remorseless sound tore through the clearing, Emily watched, wide-eyed and helpless, as the bullet struck the unsuspecting fellow full in the chest. Amid her stunned horror, she tried to draw a bit of comfort from the familiar task of soothing Gypsy, but it wasn't nearly enough for what she had just witnessed and what she feared may lie ahead. She couldn't think, couldn't decide what should be done. Should she reveal herself? Should she use the element of surprise to her advantage and fire while still in shadow? She couldn't decide—truly she'd never expected this business would end in death. Worse still was the reality that she had witnessed a murder.

For there was no doubt in her mind that Sneeves was dead. He lay crumpled, motionless, and silent, and neither of the other two men even spared him a glance.

She felt—no, desperately wished—that she was watching a play being staged, but of course she wasn't. Still, it seemed Act I had come to a chilling end, and Act II was about to begin.

As the roar of the gun died, Brand remained motionless, compelled by the pistol Richly now aimed at his chest. Emily expected his own pistol was tucked conveniently away in either his waistband or the pocket of his greatcoat. She turned nervously away from him to stare at the dark shadow he faced.

"Just like your brother, Ashwood. You have become a noose hanging from my neck, slowly tightening, threatening to choke off my livelihood."

He was calm even in hate, disturbingly so. Suddenly fear clutched Emily's heart as she realized that Richly intended a second killing this evening, was perhaps anticipating it with even greater pleasure.

"I was not aware that you knew my brother, Richly. The company he tended to keep did not often tend to your sort."

Brand was clearly taunting, but Emily sensed he had grown wary at the mention of his brother's name. Richly was content to toy with him as well.

"Certainly I was not his choice of companion, but our paths crossed one evening, and let us just say we both regretted it. Although he much more so than I."

Emily was thoroughly confused but hanging on every word, curious as to what Richly knew and would say of Brand's murdered brother.

Brand was apparently not so interested as she, for he turned the conversation around to the present.

"Matters must be desperate indeed for you to be rusticating in the country, not only seeking a dowry from an unsuspecting young heiress, but playing at highwayman as well. Although perhaps 'playing' is not the appropriate word. Highwaymen are by nature nasty cowards. One would assume you'd fit right in with such a breed, but it seems you don't even rise to meet those lowly standards. They, at least, are a fearless lot, willing to stand and face the consequences of their reckless thievery. You have not even that—you are but a shadow, faceless and slippery."

Richly was probably seething by now. His horse was stepping side to side, no doubt sensing its rider's tension...or fear.

"So very like your brother, Ashwood," Richly answered, "How fitting that you should meet the same end. You should be pleased. Your brother's murder was contracted for a bottle of gin. Yours will be at my own hand—you have become a project in which I am personally interested."

Licking his lips at the sight of his prey (or so Emily could imagine), Richly kept still and silent, waiting for the gratifying rage that was sure to flow over him when Brand absorbed the harsh reality of his brother's death paired with the bitter irony of his own.

Now wishing desperately that she had never involved him in her selfish desire for adventure, Emily waited helplessly for his reaction to this truly unbelievable turn of events.

"*You* were responsible for my brother's death?" Brand asked quietly. So quietly that Emily could barely make out the words. Apparently he was still puzzling over connections and possibilities in his mind and hadn't yet allowed the need for revenge to make him careless. She willed him to hold tightly to his control.

"I was," Richly acceded coolly, with a measure of smug satisfaction.

"What possible reason could you have had? My brother was without fault, a true gentleman, friend to everyone, unquestionably honorable—ah...I am beginning to see. Should I hazard a guess, or would you care to enlighten me yourself? I have heard that criminals, murderers in particular, quite enjoy the boast of their villainy. Some even prefer it to the deed itself."

"Ah, yes, well it will be difficult to come to any

conclusions strictly on the instance of your brother's murder as I did not actually carry out the deed. However, I do believe I'd rather enjoy the telling of it."

Here Richly paused, but Brand chose not to be bated.

"I can't even remember how long ago it was—although I'm sure it has not escaped your memory—but I was facing an extremely unpleasant future. I was in desperate need of funds but prepared to sacrifice. I was, in fact, planning to marry. The wedding was set for the following week, but the bitch jilted me, leaving me with no dowry and no reasonable options. There was no choice left but the unreasonable. I spent the fashionable hours mingling with society, hoping to lure another heiress, and the wee hours I spent in the most sordid gaming hells in London, blindly hoping to win myself a fortune. Neither was working. And coincidentally, it was the evening your squeamish brother put in an appearance that I resigned myself to an extremely risky alternative."

Here Richly paused for a long moment. While it was possible he was absorbed in sordid memories of the past, Emily rather suspected he was hoping to make Brand squirm with impatience.

"Suffice it to say that your *esteemed* brother caught me cheating at cards and informed me with the self-righteous confidence of privilege that he had no choice but to expose me."

The beginning of the confession (except the part about the clever girl who had narrowly escaped the same fate as Emily herself) had been spoken with cold amusement and had probably slipped through quirked lips, but there was no denying that Richly was angry now, his hand likely tensing on his weapon. Emily's tensed on her own, but she waited with nervous, jittery uncertainty, wondering what to do and when to do it.

"It seems, Ashwood, that you are no better schooled than your brother. It would have been a wise lesson to learn not to intrude in matters that are quite obviously not your concern. A pity your brother was not around to teach you. And now, alas, it is much too late to reform. But still, I find

I want you to know the ugly truth of this unfortunate incident. Being labeled a cheat in a gaming hell is not nearly the same as having such a label attached to you in a gentlemen's club. It is, quite simply, a death sentence. Every blighter who has chanced to share a game with you suddenly materializes, threatening to take the winnings he believes are owed him out of your hide as well as your pocket. I couldn't allow that to happen. Surely even you must realize that."

Brand gave no answer, so Richly continued, now sounding rather nonchalant.

"And so I convinced him, the heir to the Earl of Chase, to listen to my explanation, insisting it was all a misunderstanding. We agreed to meet at a back table after I had played out my hand, but I sent someone in my place. And handed over enough for a bottle of blue ruin when the nasty fellow returned. It was money I would have rather not spared, but what choice did I have? I rather expect you know the rest."

"Yes, I know the rest. Tis a pity your confession did not reach the ears of a cleric. For you see I have neither the spiritual authority nor the inclination to ease your conscience prior to death."

Richly chuckled, apparently mistaking Brand's meaning. "Rather ironic, wouldn't you agree? You finally know the truth, and it is too late for you to act upon it. If you'd only known earlier. At the Willoughsby ball, perhaps, when we were introduced by your fiancée. You may as well add the tiresome wench to the list of things I have, quite effortlessly, stolen from you. But I hardly think you'll be needing her where you're going. And I most assuredly do."

Emily's now overactive imagination had Richly leering arrogantly. When she heard an evil cackle echoing in her thoughts she quickly tamped down on her imagination and raised her pistol. Ashamed of herself for watching the two men with a detached eye instead of remembering her own involvement, she vowed to clear her mind and focus on opportunity. Relieved she had chosen to wait, she now fervently hoped the distance in the darkness would not spoil her aim.

Nothing had ever mattered more.

Lining up the barrel of her pistol to strike a bullet against the visible glint of Richly's gun, she regretted she would forfeit the opportunity to exact a more fitting revenge. She would dearly love to make the cad yelp in pain, but she wasn't certain she could gauge the shadows well enough to avoid killing him.

"How unfortunate that you're to die disappointed," Brand promised.

Neither of them had spoken in so long, Emily couldn't even remember which words Richly had uttered last to provoke Brand's resolute response. Further, she was determined not to try—she needed to keep her concentration on her target.

The final taunt had apparently proven too much for Richly, and he extended his arm to fire. As if expecting such a reaction, Brand whipped his arm back to palm his own pistol and sent his stallion plunging to the side.

Faster than either of them, Emily shifted her own barrel a whisper up and over and squeezed the trigger.

* * *

The bullet had gone in exactly as she intended—ripping into his chest and perhaps his heart as well. A fitting end for a man who had so casually torn apart the hearts of so many others.

Relieved her aim had been true, Emily felt the tension ease out of her, only to be replaced by searing pain. Having not allowed herself even the tiniest bit of laudanum, she was now feeling the consequences of that decision. Still, she'd had little choice.

But now it was finally over, and she could partake—a liberal draught with a cup of chocolate and then blessed oblivion. It sounded wonderful but was likely hours away. She knew very well she was going to have to discuss this entire matter with Brand, and she wasn't looking at all forward to it. There would be no avoiding a lecture—for either of them. She just wished it could wait.

Simply holding the pistol steadily for so long had strained her throbbing shoulder, and the shot had jarred the wound into numbing pain. Knowing she surrendered matters into Brand's capable hands, she doubled over, hunching in on herself, willing the pain to stop.

It was thus that Brand found her, faint and weak. He wasted no time in contenting himself that no new wounds had befallen her before tenderly scooping her up and settling her in front of him on his horse. Moments later her eyelids fluttered open, and at the question in her gaze, he confirmed what she had expected—Sneeves was dead and Richly not far behind.

Determined not to lose consciousness a second time, Emily focused her attention away from the pain, instead concentrating on distracting observations... the shadows roaming over Brand's face, moving on the breeze, and the stationary one that hinted at his need for a shave... Gypsy's glassy eye as she stood beside them, warily watching her equine companion of late or perhaps just being coy... the transparent clouds trailing across the moon... Brand's comfortable smell of leather and horse with just enough spice to distinguish him from his stallion...

She could imagine herself smelling of lavender water, but it was difficult to ignore the foul odor of stale sweat she knew came from her. She was determined to be optimistic and so assumed it was the vest.

Enough was enough. If Brand didn't plan to lecture her tonight, she'd just as soon get home and into bed. As nice as it was being held in his arms, conditions were detracting from her enjoyment.

"Would you take me home?" she asked, her voice softly sleepy and pleading.

"Of course, love," he soothed. "Is your shoulder all right? I was hoping to give it time to settle a bit before you have to endure the trip back."

"I'm extremely motivated. Laudanum, chocolate, and a soft, warm bed are waiting for me." She smiled up at him blearily and then added as an afterthought, "You're nice too."

"I'm flattered you'd even think of me with so many other indulgences available to you," he teased. Leaning over a bit, he took up Gypsy's reins and clicked both horses into motion.

Suddenly registering what they were leaving behind, she awkwardly asked, "Should we...er...just leave them?"

"Once I get you home, I will return with the magistrate. You needn't concern yourself any longer."

She knew he hadn't meant to sound patronizing, but she couldn't help but challenge him, even despite the pain.

"If that is a hint of the lecture you intend to deliver when you believe me fully recovered from this evening's misadventure, please do not keep me in suspense."

The tender concern that had suffused his face was instantly dispelled by an amused grin that told her exactly what he thought of her haughty sarcasm.

"Why do you always seem to find my comments amusing?" she queried.

"Perhaps I was wrong when I told you that you could not slay every dragon on your own. I'm beginning to think you yourself are the dragon, always breathing fire." Seeing his words were irritating her further, he sighed. "I am not used to women like you. You are utterly unexpected, opinionated, fiery—" He drew out the word and lifted his brow, willing her to make the connection to his previous comment, "—and brave. And I do not plan to lecture you."

At Emily's smirk of disbelief, he elaborated, "I have no cause. You warned me of this eventuality, so I can hardly quibble now, can I?"

Utterly lost and reasonably certain it wasn't because her thoughts were mired in a fog of pain, she blinked several times and shook her head silently in obvious confusion.

"What?" she finally managed.

"Did you, or did you not, tell me that you would ride with me, mine to command, or ride alone, answering only to yourself?"

"I did," she answered decisively. She had a vague memory of saying something to that effect but didn't wish to appear uncertain.

"Well then, I haven't any cause to lecture or even to complain, have I?" he finished.

"You hadn't before either, but it never stopped you," she muttered.

"Leave it alone, Emily," he warned. "Shall we agree not to speak of the matter again?"

"Fine," she conceded, relieved.

"Good. But allow me to say just one final thing."

Emily gazed at him with a mixture of irritation and exhaustion and waited.

"Bravo, my clever girl."

At her start of surprise, he silenced the inevitable questions with a quick kiss. "You will, of course, have to explain everything to me. But later. Much later."

More relieved and contented now than she ever would have expected, given the circumstances, Emily closed her eyes and enjoyed the feel of him next to her. She was relaxed enough to sleep but didn't wish to waste this time with Brand, choosing instead to close her mind to everything but his warmth as the chilly breeze skimmed over and around her. Brand must have assumed she'd fallen asleep, having settled so quickly into silence. And in truth she was lingering not far off.

Until he whispered.

"Perhaps you could even explain just how you succeeded, despite my most well-intentioned, determined efforts, in capturing my extraordinarily well-guarded heart."

Emily stilled, perhaps even tensed, but just the slightest bit. Then she waited, hoping.

Brand's arms tightened around her gently, ever careful of her injury, before he placed a soft, tender kiss on the top of her head. Suddenly she remembered her hair—all of it gone, and he hadn't even mentioned it. Perhaps he hadn't noticed.

The thought came a mite too soon—he was noticing now.

As he tentatively touched his fingers to the gentle curls and then buried as much of them as was possible in the hair at her temple, she heard a quiet chuckle. He then covered her exposed ear with his hand, pillowing the curve with warmth.

"Good God, I love this woman beyond measure," he announced quietly to the empty darkness that surrounded them.

Emily fought the inclination to disentangle herself from his embrace and sit up, confronting him with this latest revelation. Instead she stayed silent, trying to keep the reaction his words had inspired to herself.

At long last... She had been beginning to despair that she was going to have to initiate every step of their relationship. She had already been bold enough to challenge him to a race, involve him in a dangerous ambush (although not by choice), and propose twice (once to him and once by proxy to his father's coachman). If neither of them had admitted to it by their wedding day, Emily had planned to tell Brand that she did indeed love him. Now she needn't feel so nervous. Even if he wasn't ready to tell her directly, she knew. And that was enough.

She cuddled closer, utterly delighted with her good fortune. She had gone looking for adventure, thought to find it by ambushing a pair of highwayman, and instead been ambushed herself. The life she would soon start with her perfect stranger was sure to be a greater adventure than either of them had ever dreamed. The excitement would of course be mingled with much lecturing, bullying, pleading, and eye-rolling, but it was a small price to pay—if Brand felt such pretense was necessary, so be it. She would bring him around in the end.

Smiling contentedly, relaxed at last, she settled into the comfort of dreams.

* * *

Brand knew the exact moment she fell asleep. He'd known when she'd been warding off sleep and when she'd been faking it, and he couldn't help but smile. She would lead him a merry dance, figuratively and no doubt literally as well, but he couldn't wait.

He'd felt the breath rush out of him when he'd come upon her, huddled over her horse. Seeing Richly shot through the heart, knowing the bullet had stayed Richly's own intentions, Brand's thoughts had flickered to Emily, and he'd wondered, for a single second, if she'd ridden to his rescue. But he'd shoved the thought from his mind, done what was necessary, and then gone looking, hoping it had been anyone else.

He couldn't argue she wasn't competent, brave, and clever—a perfect companion for such an evening's work. But none of those qualities could counteract the reality that his mind swirled with apprehension whenever she was within harm's reach. When had she become the center of his thoughts, his emotions...his life?

The minute he'd seen her.

He could admit it to himself now—some small part of him had known all along and helped her to convince the rest of him. Quite suddenly the possibility that he might fall in love, marry, and fill a nursery had no longer seemed the slightest bit unpleasant. Emily had somehow managed to overturn his foolish convictions and reverse his way of thinking. He now realized what a tragedy it would have been if he had ignored his heart and allowed her to marry someone else. It was as Colin had predicted: he'd fallen in love where he'd least expected it and had spent the ensuing days bumbling around without even realizing it.

Having wanted not only to make the declaration of love first but also to make it as unorthodox and unexpected as Emily's proposal had been, he decided it couldn't have been better planned. He had said it first, as was his intent, but she had pretended not to hear. As such, she could hardly tease him about it later. Further, she couldn't very well complain he hadn't made any overtures—her conscience wouldn't allow it. Ingenious—a neat solution befitting their unique relationship. Perhaps she had had the chance to realize the same before she'd finally dropped off to sleep.

Looking down at her again, he remembered the fantasy he had conjured: she had been gloriously naked but for the fall of her hair. Obviously that would have to wait. But the advantage of this pixie cut sprang immediately to mind. With all those shining locks of hair gone, she would be thoroughly and thrillingly exposed. His original fantasy now impossible, he spent the remainder of the ride back to Sinclair House envisioning a very vivid new one.

* * *

She hadn't slept so peacefully in what seemed an eternity, but she awoke to uncertainty and the troublesome task still ahead of her. Today was the day—she could avoid it no longer. She'd already idled away the morning, and time was running out on the day. It would be dark before long. Hoping to distract herself with thoughts of a pleasant afternoon tea, she painstakingly saddled Gypsy and was off to the vicarage at long last. Her wedding was in five days, and she still hadn't explained things to Sophie. She didn't like to think she'd been avoiding her friend, but rather, that she'd been preoccupied with other matters.

She certainly felt entitled to such an excuse even if it wasn't precisely accurate.

For she wasn't nearly so comfortable with the truth… the sad fact that she had become uncomfortable with her friend's mercurial moods and subtle impatience… the fidgety awareness that she'd have to say goodbye, have to confess that once again she was to be the one having the adventure… the disturbing possibility that the awkwardness between them might continue on indefinitely, long after they'd parted ways.

On occasion, knowing the truth simply made everything worse.

The past week very likely qualified as one of those slippery 'occasions'. If she confided in Sophie, things between them would only be more uncomfortable. Emily knew she'd need to contend with a lecture, and the scope of misbehavior Sophie would need to address was sure to drag it on indefinitely. In truth she didn't wish to be subjected to any of it. Just as she didn't wish to subject Sophie to the worry such confidences would inspire.

So she would be careful in what she revealed. She would tell Sophie just enough to quell suspicion. The rest would remain a secret she would share with only Brand. For she felt certain he would not tell their tale either, no doubt out of concern for her reputation. Which, oddly enough, she now found herself a trifle concerned over as well.

Sophie would be proud.

With that thought bolstering her confidence, she decided it was time. She'd prolonged the ride as much as possible and then lingered over Gypsy's tether, but she simply couldn't delay any longer—she was literally standing at the backdoor to the vicarage, willing herself to knock.

Clenching her hands into fists and holding them almost rigidly by her sides, she took a deep breath. She needn't have bothered, for she was caught distressingly off guard when Sophie opened the door on her quite unexpectedly.

Emily supposed the welcoming smile that promptly replaced Sophie's startled surprise was at the very least encouraging. Unexpected, given her friend's recent behavior, but encouraging nonetheless. She wondered what it was that had returned Sophie to good spirits but was determined not to press. Sophie would confide whatever it was as soon as she was ready. Or perhaps she wouldn't. Emily knew she would need to accept that possibility as well.

"Emily! Hello. What are you doing standing out here? Why didn't you just come in straight away?" Sophie continued chattering as Emily stepped inside and removed her hat. Then she simply stared, apparently speechless.

As impossible as it seemed, Emily had forgotten. It was quite astounding, really, when one considered all she'd had to contend with that very morning at breakfast, but there it was. With everything else on her mind, her hair had quite simply slipped from her thoughts. Now she was to be caught off guard, for without the distraction of full confession, her shorn locks would most definitely warrant a lecture. Perhaps she could forestall it with the explanation that she had given her father and stepmother. For she was of the opinion that if a lie was to be required, it may as well be consistent—she'd found that made for considerably less work.

At least Sophie wasn't likely to require any sniffing salts. Lady Sinclair had needed most of the morning and afternoon to recover from Emily's 'ghastly surprise'. Although the shock had receded sufficiently so as to allow her ladyship to descend the stairs for a hearty, restorative luncheon, at which time she'd informed Emily that she simply couldn't bring herself to speak to such an ungrateful stepdaughter who persisted in behaving so shockingly. The announcement was repeated no fewer than ten times, leaving little question as to her stepmother's true feelings on the matter. Her father hadn't said a word.

Even the news of 'Dear Desmond's' demise had not warranted as much discussion. Nor had the news of his stint as the area's elusive highwayman. Her stepmother had, of course, been justifiably embarrassed and upset and had refrained from speaking his name ever since. No other mention of a rapidly approaching engagement ball had yet to be made, by her or anyone else.

Perhaps they had decided they couldn't possibly marry her off in such a state and had no choice but to wait until her hair grew out again. If that had been all that had been necessary for a postponement, she would have loped it off within seconds of hearing her father's ultimatum.

Now it no longer mattered. The man her father had intended she marry was dead, and her hair would not grow back for some time. But if her suspicions were correct, Brand didn't appear to mind her shortened curls in the slightest. If she was lucky, he may even come to find he preferred them as she now did.

As she'd explained to her father and stepmother, she'd simply been tired of all that hair. So it had seemed sensible to cut it. While truthful, it was, of course, not exactly the truth. Still her new style definitely had its advantages. There would be no more time wasted, waiting while it was washed, brushed, pinned, curled, twisted and braided. No resigned irritation as it snarled, snagged, loosened, and defiantly fell. Now she could refrain from worrying about any of it.

As she finished telling Sophie the very same, it was obvious her friend didn't believe her—not a bit. Emily could almost hear the thoughts moving through her friend's mind, *"That's it? That's the best you can do? Surely you don't think I believe such an unimaginative lie coming from you?"* Sophie's response, however, was quite proper indeed.

"Well, I never would have expected such a drastic step, but knowing you as I do, I really shouldn't be at all surprised. It looks lovely on you. Truly. I wish I were as brave. But I daresay I'm not, and never will be, so I'll just have to go on as I am."

Where was the scolding, Emily wondered? This was a changed Sophie indeed.

Sophie reached a gentle, tentative hand up to pat her own perfect coiffure. Emily didn't know why she bothered. Never was there a hair out of place.

"You, my dear, do not even have benefit of a ladies maid, but still you manage to look perfectly presentable for every occasion," Emily graciously returned the compliment. "I confess I've always been envious."

"Oh Em, stop teasing!" Sophie batted the compliments away as a rosy pink glow infused her cheeks.

Emily was delighted that the easiness between them had been restored.

"Very well, then let's talk of something else," she agreed, linking arms with Sophie as they moved down the hall to the comfortable parlour. When Sophie remained silent, she prompted, "You first—tell me the exciting news of the vicarage this week."

Sophie seemed to be considering very carefully.

Perhaps a few nudges were in order, Emily decided.

"How is your father?"

"Very well. He is closeted in his library working on this Sunday's sermon. He has been so busy lately, it seems he has left it to the very last minute."

The last minute indeed! It was only Thursday. But to Sophie, no doubt, this did signify considerable procrastination. In her defense, she would need to transcribe everything, surely no easy task. Interestingly enough, another blush had risen to Sophie's cheeks when she had mentioned her father's busy schedule, but it could very easily have been attributed to mild disapproval over her father's lapse in responsibility.

"Any new artifacts uncovered?" Emily queried, not because she was the slightest bit interested, but merely to draw Sophie out. It was clear her friend was holding back something that she desperately wanted to reveal. So what was it?

"Father did just receive a bit of correspondence in the post this week chronicling some of the recent discoveries in Egypt. I could interrupt him if you—" Sophie made to rise.

"Not necessary," Emily hurried to answer, "Any visitors of interest?"

Sophie had now turned so red she looked positively flushed, and her eyes were settling on everything but Emily who was now seated directly in front of her.

"Sophie?"

"Visitors are always interesting in their own way, don't you think?"

"No," Emily succinctly, and rather rudely, replied.

"Oh…well…tea?" Sophie offered, rising from her chair.

"Perhaps later," Emily deferred.

Sophie lowered herself back down and looked thoroughly uncomfortable. Then, visibly struck with inspiration, she leaned towards Emily.

"*You* must have some news. Come, tell me what has been happening during the past week. Where have you been? Father and I have puzzled over your absence."

Sophie was chattering again, most suspiciously.

"I do have news. Considerable, life-altering news, but I want to hear yours first," Emily admitted.

"Mine?" Nervously Sophie gestured towards herself, fisting one hand against her chest while the other fidgeted in her lap.

"Yes, Sophie. Clearly you have news of considerable magnitude to impart."

"You don't wish to go first?" Sophie wasn't troubling to hide her surprise or her reluctance.

"No, Sophie, I do not," Emily assured her firmly, "You've very graciously offered me plenty of opportunities to do just that over the course of our friendship. It's long past time I returned the favor." Then Emily had a sobering thought—maybe Sophie really didn't want to tell her. So she quietly added, "Unless you don't wish to tell me."

They stared at each other, both nervous with anticipation, both wondering how this afternoon's confidences would change things between them, until finally Sophie spoke.

"I haven't yet told anyone else—I was waiting to tell you first. But I confess, I'm not certain just how you will react." Sophie had glanced down to pluck at her skirts during this confession, but now she glanced up to meet Emily's puzzled and slightly troubled gaze.

"If it's made you as happy as you appear to be, how else could I react but with matching delight?"

With the whisper of a sigh, Sophie answered, "Very well. I am...engaged to be married."

Whatever Emily had been expecting, it hadn't been this. For a moment she was too stunned to even respond. Luckily, she recovered quickly.

"Oh, but Sophie, that's wonderful! For it appears to be exactly what you want! And he must be a paragon among men to have you glowing with such happiness. Who is he?"

Please not Sir Fitzhugh, Emily prayed. Sophie's tidy decorum wouldn't last through a single meal with the slovenly squire. And it was difficult to imagine which Sophie would find more objectionable—suffering her wifely duties in the marriage bed or periodically finding bits of food among the linens.

Emily shuddered, wondering who else it could possibly be.

"Lord Willoughsby—Colin," Sophie answered quietly, now almost cringing before her.

Emily's heart beat once, twice in heavy staccato, a dramatic accompaniment to the news.

Colin?

Rather than dispelling her confusion with the skittish confession, Sophie had succeeded in thoroughly bewildering her. This was…well…certainly unexpected. And yet, Emily promptly decided, ridiculously logical—the two were a perfect match—and most definitely suspicious. It was clear Sophie hadn't revealed everything, and it was this very obvious omission that grasped Emily's attention, not the newfound knowledge that two friends she had known since childhood planned to marry. One look at Sophie confirmed that the entire situation was making her friend nervous. Curiously, it didn't appear to be the engagement that she worried over but rather Emily's reaction to it.

But why? Why would Sophie believe that she would be anything but congratulatory?

After all, Sophie and Colin had been friends since childhood, and he was a wonderful man—hadn't she considered marrying him herself not two weeks ago?

Realization dawned.

Was Sophie so nervously preoccupied because she believed she was trampling both her best friend's feelings and future at once? It wouldn't be the least bit out of character for her selfless friend, but Emily suspected there was something more. Sophie, who had vigilantly reminded Emily of the inevitability of marriage, and done her best to ensure that Emily's reputation remained intact until the occasion of it, had curiously never spoken of marriage for herself.

Yet here she sat, engaged. And within a fortnight of Colin's return to his estate.

So much had happened in the last week. And Sophie's curious behavior could be traced right back to the beginning—back to that fateful stormy day in which Emily had barged into the vicarage, trailing mud and expecting a miracle.

She'd been too self-absorbed that day to notice, but it was clear to her now that Sophie had been hesitant to include Colin in the list of potential candidates for her best friend's future husband. Hindsight really was rather useless, and troubling to boot—it didn't solve a thing and only made one feel inadequate. Sophie had, in fact, made no objection, and Emily had heard only the silence of acceptance and approval. Apparently the relief she'd felt over finding the ideal husband so very quickly had diminished her powers of observation. So she'd been oblivious as well as foolishly optimistic…

She'd truly believed Colin was the one for her—the one she would marry. Now Emily knew just how big a mistake she would have made in marrying Colin—she would have deprived him of Sophie. And Sophie of him.

She suspected that Sophie was in love with him, but the notion seemed as far-fetched as she herself falling so quickly in love with Brand. Having so recently returned, Colin could only have managed one, or perhaps two, visits to the vicarage over the past fortnight. One or two visits in ten odd years! Could Sophie's feelings have reached such depths to have spurred such a reaction after only a few hours of visiting? It seemed improbable, even impossible. Unless…

"Emily?" Sophie's voice broke on the interruption.

Emily realized she had been staring blindly out the parlour window, which overlooked an extremely well-tended herb and vegetable garden that was even now showing signs of its winter bounty. She slowly turned her gaze back to Sophie.

"Hmmm?"

"Aren't you going to say anything at all?"

"Are you in love with him?" Emily asked pointedly.

"Yes," Sophie mumbled, looking down into her lap once more. She appeared embarrassed and, what was worse, dejected. How curious.

"You managed to fall in love with him over a single afternoon's tea?" came Emily's disbelieving reply.

Sophie's eyes jerked up, and she answered immediately, "No! I…" She fell silent again, having reconsidered her intended response.

"So you've been shooing me away, avoiding me, all in an attempt to court Colin yourself with the intent of garnering a proposal from him before I could manage it?" Emily winged her eyebrow up as if expecting a reply but then added, "How fortunate you are able to converse knowledgeably about ancient civilizations." Emily wondered if Sophie would even register the wry humor lacing her words.

Sophie sat wide-eyed and attentive, waiting for the opportunity to speak, too polite to interrupt. When Emily stopped, Sophie launched into an apologetic explanation.

"I know it looks awful of me, and it was, but not to the degree you've assumed. I will admit that your decision to pursue him was the impetus for my own actions, and that is quite horrid of me. But you must believe that I didn't want Colin merely so you couldn't have him. I have..." she halted, gathered her courage, and rushed on, "...well...I've loved him my whole life. And I saw my last chance with the perfect husband slipping away from me, or rather, being wrenched away by your very determined fingers. It was undoubtedly presumptuous of me, but I was certain you didn't love him, and then once he and I became reacquainted, I knew for certain that you and he wouldn't suit. At least not like he and I would. So I decided to pursue him myself despite your intentions. I'm truly sorry, Emily, but this one little thing—this one terrifyingly huge thing—I had to do for myself. I truly hope my actions will not cause you pain—I never intended that." Finishing, Sophie took a deep breath, and Emily heard the quaver in it.

Before she could respond, Sophie added, "As to avoiding you, I can't imagine what you're thinking of—we always visit here at the vicarage, and, in case you've forgotten, I live here. I *will* admit to shooing though."

Sophie wasn't as downtrodden as she appeared, and Emily smiled at the rarity of her friend speaking in her own defense. It was well past time. She grinned at her friend, hoping to convey how very proud she was. Yet it seemed, in doing so, she had made Sophie even more nervous—best to practice smiling into a mirror as soon as possible.

Anxious to put her friend's heart and mind at ease, she finally spoke.

"Sophie, you have absolutely nothing of which to be ashamed. You couldn't be more justified in your behavior—each and every aspect. In fact my only regret is that you didn't wish to confide in me sooner. Fifteen years sooner would have been ideal, but any time between then and now would have been preferable to enduring the uncertainty and confusion I have been living with for the past week."

"You're not hurt...angry...disappointed?" Sophie inquired in disbelief.

"Of course not! You were right—Colin and I wouldn't have suited—I found that out for myself after spending no more than two minutes alone with him." Emily smiled at the memory.

"You were teasing me?" Sophie demanded. "I suppose I deserve it for keeping such a secret from you but really, Emily—how childish!"

"Come now, Sophie. Don't act the role of prudish vicar's daughter." Emily giggled and had Sophie searching for something to throw at her. Emily quickly held up her hands with intent to call a truce. "Let us celebrate an end to secrets, at long last. Perhaps over a companionable cup of tea."

Sophie rather thought Emily was spreading it on a little thick.

"The difficulty," Sophie admitted, "in offering tea to ill-mannered visitors is that it only encourages their return and requires that I suffer through an extended visit. You are perilously close to being counted among their number," Sophie warned, attempting to look stern and succeeding admirably.

"I'll forgive you your lapse in judgment if you'll keep my name on the list of visitors worthy of a delectable tea party."

Sophie smiled absently, realizing that soon everything in her life would change, just as Emily's would. But for now, the pair of them could enjoy the comfortable familiarity of afternoon tea as best friends.

Rather suspecting that Emily was thinking the very same thing, she answered with fond forgiveness, "Fair enough."

Sophie was relieved to have a moment alone and an excuse to go with it. She needed to inform Cook that tea should be served with as many pastries as could fit on the tray. It was a special occasion after all. With the task completed, she let herself—for a moment only—glory in the relief she felt in knowing that her secret was one no longer. And that Emily was neither hurt, nor angry.

Returning to the parlour to see her friend seated, rather nonchalantly, on the sunny window seat, Sophie realized that Emily hadn't yet revealed anything about her own dramatic husband hunt, not to mention her whereabouts over the past week. Emily had stalled, and Sophie had forgotten, caught up with nerves over her own secret. But now she'd remembered. So seating herself beside her friend, Sophie promptly set about the task of unearthing a few secrets.

"If we are to celebrate the end of secrets, you must tell me, what is to come of your impending engagement?"

The broad nature of Sophie's question and the gentle tone of her voice, implied that she had heard the gossip surrounding Richly. And as Emily didn't care to discuss it even the slightest little bit, she decided to answer simply.

"Marriage I suppose."

"You're quite the wit, Em. Just *who* do you propose to marry."

"The deed is already done."

"What deed exactly is done?" Sophie asked suspiciously.

"I've proposed to marry someone."

"You've…?" Seeing Emily's slow smile, Sophie promptly forgot her irritation. "Who is he?" she demanded excitedly.

"Viscount Ashwood."

"The title sounds familiar. Have I met him?" Sophie was clearly straining her memory.

"At the Willoughsby ball."

"Oh!" And then, "He isn't that gentleman who likened

you to another of his acquaintances, is he? The one to whom you were quite abominably rude?" she asked pointedly.

"That hardly narrows the field," Emily pointed out, hoping to distract Sophie from that incriminating line of conversation.

"True," Sophie admitted. "But I'm referring to the gentleman to whom Colin introduced us."

"Yes, he's the one." Emily knew she was grinning like a fool and couldn't have cared less.

"Had the two of you met previously? I can't imagine that he would have otherwise sought out your company after that ill-mannered display? Certainly you are an heiress, but that doesn't excuse everything," Sophie puzzled.

"Please don't concern yourself with my sensibilities," Emily retorted.

"Oh, Em," Sophie protested, thoroughly exasperated, "Even you must admit that it is a rare occasion indeed for which you decide that a bit of good behavior is warranted."

Realizing that the words she had just uttered had been quite rude indeed, Sophie decided it would be best if she stopped speaking and waited for Emily to continue.

At the distant sound of hoof beats, her friend had turned away and leaned towards the window. Sophie was fully aware that with one's face nearly pressing against the glass, it was possible to glimpse the narrow lane that led to the vicarage. But patience was necessary for success—visitors could be heard long before they came into view. And patience was a quality that Emily possessed in extremely limited measures.

And yet, her friend sat calmly gazing out the window, silent for only a few seconds. Then, without turning from the window, she began speaking.

"As it happens, he is the boorish, abominably rude, arrogant beast of a man I met in the thunderstorm little more than a week ago."

Sophie could hear her friend's amusement and couldn't have been more baffled. She didn't speak, couldn't think what to say. Emily, it seemed, didn't expect her to say anything and confessed more.

"We have had occasion to meet several times since then and have decided that a marriage between us would be mutually beneficial."

Now Sophie was downright suspicious and very nearly glaring at her friend's back. She didn't even want to hazard a guess as to what secrets Emily was carefully stepping around, for even a vivid imagination was no match for Emily's ingenuity. Emily was probably hoping that her best friend either wouldn't realize the omissions or wouldn't press for an explanation. But Sophie had decided she wasn't of a mind to be accommodating.

"When have you had occasion to meet?" she asked, hoping she sounded merely innocently curious.

"What a delightful coincidence," Emily announced, ignoring Sophie's question entirely, "It appears that Colin has decided to pay you a visit. And who should accompany him but the conveniently tolerant Viscount Ashwood."

Not the slightest bit surprised over the possibility of visitors, and these visitors in particular, Sophie huffed in exasperation before exclaiming, "Oh for heaven's sake, Emily! Are you wishing for a formal apology for my earlier teasing or are you content now that you've gotten in a few pokes of your own?"

"I suppose I'm through now," Emily offered, turning back.

"Thank heaven for small favors," Sophie muttered, shaking her head.

Suddenly she realized she hadn't yet offered Emily her good wishes for her impending marriage.

"In that case, I shall offer you my most heartfelt congratulations! How lovely for you to have found someone with whom you share an…understanding."

Sophie's final words came out haltingly as she realized their clumsiness. Not knowing what else to do, she elected to begin bobbing her head in the nod that so often accompanies awkward situations.

Emily stared at her for the space of a moment and then laughed with genuine amusement.

"Dear Sophie." Still grinning, Emily reached for her friend's hands, now clasped tightly in her lap. "It is difficult to believe I've found someone at all, particularly in the space of a week, but more difficult still when you consider that he and I share considerably more than the requisite 'understanding'."

"Are you...in love with him?" Sophie asked in bewildered awe.

"It seems so. In fact rather madly I fear. But I don't feel as foolish knowing that he feels the same. Well, perhaps not the same," she allowed, "but at least he loves me." She finished the admission with a satisfied nod.

"That's wonderful, Em!" Sophie enthused. "More wonderful still as it is not Colin who has earned your apparent devotion," she added teasingly.

"On that we can amicably agree," Emily nodded, clearly relieved over her narrow escape from a life with Sophie's intended.

"When can we expect the grand wedding, planned and orchestrated by your doting stepmother?" Sophie inquired, tongue in cheek.

"Actually, we are to be married by special license in five days, just witnesses present. I had hoped you would stand beside me—Brand is no doubt asking Colin—and I wondered if, perhaps, your father could conduct the ceremony on such short notice."

"Gracious, Emily! You certainly are a one for secrets. Beatrice will be apoplectic when she learns of this."

Sophie attempted to look mildly disapproving but then abandoned the pretense and pronounced enthusiastically, "What fun! I will make certain Father's schedule will accommodate such a momentous occasion," she promised.

Grateful for Sophie's blessing, Emily breathed a sigh of contented relief.

"Beatrice will simply have to content herself with a wedding ball two weeks following the ceremony, that is if she can bear my many indiscretions. My hair, or rather the lack of it, came as quite a shock—so much so that I'm not certain she is up to the personal affront she will, no doubt, consider our elopement to be. Still, she should be somewhat mollified with her newfound connection to the Earl of Chase."

Sophie gasped. "He's an earl? Odd. It was always my understanding that the higher the gentleman's rank, the more discriminating his search for a suitable wife...." Absorbed with the implications, it was a moment before she slowly turned to Emily and noticed her friend's single raised eyebrow.

"I'm only surprised you didn't manage to snare a duke!"

Her attempt at recovery was weak, and Sophie well knew it, but she didn't wish to start in on apologies again.

Emily rolled her eyes dramatically and was prevented from saying another word by a knock on the outer door.

Sophie hopped up, delighted with the reprieve her errand would provide. Emily remained, sitting in the slanting sunlight, considering her changed circumstances. She heard the booted step at the door to the parlour and slid her eyes away from the chilly bleakness of winter to the cozy warmth of the room.

And there he was, stealing her breath, crowding her thoughts. He was staring at her with an intensity that almost made her uncomfortable. It didn't, only because she knew she stared back just the same. Suddenly, unexpectedly, he smiled, and her heart hammered, and her breath hitched. He was hers. She had found him, claimed him, won him. And her happiness was now boundless. This was what she had hoped for but despaired of never finding.

As Brand moved towards her, her eyes never strayed from him, and in a matter of seconds, he was close enough to shield her view of Sophie and Colin who had followed him into the room in quiet consort.

He greeted her simply, but his choice of address spoke fluently of everything between them. "Emma," he prompted, extending his hand for hers.

The word was certain to be muffled enough to remain for her ears alone, but still she sent him a quelling glare as she offered her hand. It wouldn't do at all for Sophie to hear him calling her by that name—she would wonder over it, and that was the last thing Emily needed. Her attention was drawn back to Brand when, with deliberate defiance, he twisted her wrist around and placed a heated kiss on her palm, bestowing a wicked grin as well.

Startled and inexplicably skittish, she attempted to snatch her hand back, but he was faster, capturing her fingers before they slipped through his grasp.

"Odd indeed that you should object to such a chaste kiss after we've—"

"Will you hush?!" she whispered through gritted teeth.

He nodded solemnly but then brought her fingers to his lips once more, this time for a nipping kiss on her fingertips.

She gasped, hoping she hadn't been loud enough to draw attention to herself, and thereby revealed the intimacy between them that Brand was determined she remember.

"Desist, Davenport," she fairly snarled. His only reaction was a chuckle before he nudged her aside on the window seat and positioned himself beside her, his thigh pressed scandalously up against her own. And as if that weren't enough (they were in the vicarage for heaven's sake!), he boldly reached his hand into her lap to snatch back one of the hands she'd just managed to demurely settle there. She thought it best to relinquish it and avoid a struggle.

Now she could do nothing but hope that Sophie would fail to notice what she was sure to term their improper behavior. For it was apparent that further glaring would produce no useful result—Brand didn't appear the slightest bit affected or contrite. So, cozily resigned, she turned her attention to Sophie and Colin.

Only to witness her best friend leaning into Colin, her graceful hand pressed lightly to his chest! Colin's own hand was covering hers as he smiled down at her.

It was possible nothing would ever surprise her again.

Deciding she had nothing to lose and everything to gain, she squeezed her fingers around Brand's and smiled adoringly up at him, batting her eyelashes like mad.

14

"Twas quite a coup and my intention all along…"

PRECURSOR TO EACH AND EVERY CONVERSATION
IN WHICH LADY BEATRICE SINCLAIR TOOK PART
5 NOVEMBER 1818
(AND FOR WEEKS AFTERWARDS)

"You, my dear, are extremely fortunate that I have chosen to forgive you so promptly…*and* so graciously."

Emily desperately wished to roll her eyes but feared Beatrice might retract her oh-so-generous offer of forgiveness.

"I assure you, it is your choice of a *husband*…" Brand, standing close beside Emily, received an approving nod, "that has managed to redeem you after your flurry of *faux-pas*."

A new pronunciation of her ladyship's favorite French word now joined the ranks of many others while, quite oblivious, Lady Sinclair kept on, "And it is as a favor to *him* that I have decided to resume speaking to you."

With the wedding ball proving itself a huge success—even Emily had to admit that her stepmother had done wonders, despite the monumental grudge she'd been holding—and Emily's hair, while not exactly in fashion, at least styled quite fashionably, Beatrice was apparently in a charitable mood. And very obviously expecting a humbly appreciative reply.

"Perhaps I should be thanking *him*," Emily muttered dryly. But gently prodded by Brand's warm palm squeezing her elbow, she added, "I appreciate your gallantry in the matter, Beatrice, not to mention your tireless efforts in planning this celebration. Everything has turned out beautifully—I can never hope to be so cleverly capable."

You, my dear lady, are fortunate indeed that I have quelled sarcasm so promptly and chosen instead to respond graciously.

"My dear, you mustn't worry. I will *teach* you," Lady Sinclair consoled fervently. Now that you are married, it is more important than ever that you understand how to fulfill the duties demanded of you, not only by your husband, but by his title as well."

At this point Brand interjected, "You need have no worries, Lady Sinclair. I will personally see to it that my wife is schooled sufficiently as to enable her to perform any wifely duties I should demand of her."

Beatrice nodded approvingly, and Emily bit her lip to hold back a fit of giggling.

Brand continued, "I will also arrange for her to be in prompt attendance for afternoon tea whenever we can manage it."

Emily stiffened beside him and turned to protest, but he tugged on her arm, willing her to keep silent.

"But right now, we must beg your pardon. My wife has promised me this dance, and I do believe my father wishes a word with you."

As soon as word of his son's nuptials had reached him, the earl had diagnosed himself fully recovered. Upon receiving an invitation to the celebratory ball, he had set off promptly for Sinclair House with the intention of getting better acquainted with his new daughter-in-law. The two were becoming extremely fond of each other and getting along quite famously. By all appearances, the relationship between father and son had softened slightly but not enough to eliminate the good-intentioned jabs and teasing pokes that had been all that had connected them for so many years. Still, as Emily told Brand, it was progress that would be helped along by the influence of grandchildren.

Emily was equally delighted with the knowledge that her

relationship with her own father had, after too many years, flickered warmly to life once again. When she and Brand had informed Lord Sinclair that they were, in fact, already married, his reaction had been one of proud approval.

"I couldn't have chosen better for you myself, Emily. As for you, Ashwood, well, I bid you good luck."

After they had all toasted the occasion, Beatrice had caught Brand's eye and patted the seat beside her, eager for a cozy conversation. Emily had looked on, fondly sympathetic, until her father had taken her hand and turned her around to face him.

Holding both of her hands in his, he'd gazed silently at her for several moments. Then he'd smiled and pulled her close to embrace her as he'd not done since she was a little girl.

With her eyes closed on a sigh, she heard him whisper, "Don't go too easy on him, my dear. Give him a bit of a challenge. We'll see if he fares as well as I did."

When she pulled away to peek up at him, he added, "Managed to get you married, didn't I? And with only a bluff."

A tingle of awed disbelief ran down Emily's spine as she pulled away staring. "A bluff? The ultimatum? Richly? The engagement ball? It was all a bluff?! Emily opened her mouth on a tirade of words but shut it without speaking them. Staring at her father, she slowly eased her face into a smile. "Bravo."

She knew she could afford to be forgiving—it had all turned out all right. Rather perfectly in fact.

Miraculously, she had even managed, with Brand's unsolicited assistance, to make amends with Beatrice. And it hadn't been too painful, all things considered.

Now, looking around the ballroom, her hand in her husband's, she was thoroughly content. Sophie and Colin were moving slowly towards the doors that would lead them scandalously (for Sophie anyway) to the darkened gardens—they would be married themselves before too long. Brand's father and hers were laughing heartily over something one or the other of them had said, unaware that

Beatrice was even now bearing down upon them. And in the corner, Sophie's father was expounding on some topic or other to a riveted Sir Fitzhugh. It hardly mattered to either of them that the squire's interest lay, not in the conversation, but in his plate of food.

She smiled, a bit sentimental over being back in her childhood home, wishing to snatch a few more memories to take with her. It had been a marvelous evening, and she was truly grateful to Beatrice. She'd graciously accepted congratulations and behaved with an almost unprecedented amount of decorum. Now she was to be rewarded—she would dance with her husband.

It suddenly registered that Brand appeared to be heading in the opposite direction from the dancers. She tugged on his arm in question.

"Are you going to dance with me or not?" she challenged.

"I decided I'd prefer to save my energy," he answered cryptically, never stopping.

Considering a moment, Emily offered an alternate suggestion.

"Seeing as we are leaving for your estate tomorrow, perhaps we could use the morning to prove who is the better rider?"

"I'd prefer you try your abilities with another sort of riding." As he glanced back over his shoulder at her, his gaze had her dreaming of surrender even as her lips curled in challenge.

Suddenly flushed with heat and thrilled with the implications of his daring suggestion, she lowered her voice in an attempt at seduction.

"I should tell you that I am a very demanding rider. I expect to be well pleased with my mount."

"I am at your service, milady," he growled, swinging her up in his arms as they reached the staircase that would lead them to an evening's pleasure.

Epilogue

She would never have imagined her own daughter behaving in such a fashion. It mystified her anew each time she witnessed it. But as she sat resting yet again, stroking her rounded belly and attempting to ignore the poking kicks her future son, or daughter, saw fit to bestow, she was, at the very least, amply entertained. Beatrice was jointly presiding over the tea tray with her oldest granddaughter Annabelle, and it was unclear who was the more fussily demanding of the two. Annabelle was enjoying the proceedings immensely, dressed in a pale blue dress so encrusted with lace that it nearly made Emily cringe just to look at it. The dress had been a gift from Grandmama and, as such, was 'perfectly proper' for tea. Or so she'd been told.

Beatrice was utterly devoted to the child and had begun requesting her presence at afternoon tea before she had even reached her third year. Seeing great potential in her, Beatrice had ordered a miniature tea set from London and had promptly taken Annabelle on as a most willing pupil in the Beatrice Sinclair School of Manners and Household Management.

Soon afterwards Emily had begun receiving very pointed advice on the management of Rathern Hall, their home for most of the year, from a very prim little miss who seemed most oddly informed. Brand thought his daughter's antics delightful and thoroughly amusing. Emily rather suspected Beatrice was using her granddaughter as a spy through whom she could collect information and then plant unwelcome advice and instruction. Beatrice denied any and all accusations.

A flurry of activity at the entrance to the room drew her attention. It would seem her son would need to deal yet again with the consequences of arriving a few minutes late for tea despite a valiant, if misguided, effort. In his haste it appeared he hadn't even paused to wash his hands or face. She needn't worry over scolding him—it would be well taken care of.

As her eyes shifted from four-year-old Henry to the matched set of disapproving frowns marring the brows of Annabelle and Beatrice both, Emily could but sympathize. He was almost a mirror image of her in appearance and behavior, while his sister, now in her sixth year, was clearly Brand's child.

"Henry," Beatrice scolded.

"Woof," admonished Prissy gently.

"You are late, and, what is more, you are quite filthy," Annabelle added mercilessly.

"Still, your intentions were good," Beatrice allowed, "You are *here* after all." The last was spoken a bit more loudly and directed, Emily knew, more at herself and her past transgressions than at her son.

"Strive to do better next time," Annabelle encouraged. "Come, let us get you washed up. You cannot hope to sit down to tea looking as you do."

Grasping a bit of his shirt at each shoulder blade between two prissy fingers, she nudged him ahead of her out of the room.

"Cook has made gooseberry tarts," she whispered quite loudly in the vicinity of his right ear as she hustled him away, easily transforming herself back into a little girl as she stepped through the doorway and out of her ladyship's parlour.

Emily watched them until they were out of sight and then tilted her head down closer to her abdomen and murmured, "If you should happen to be a girl, you might try to be a bit more like your mother in certain respects."

"I heard that, Emily," Beatrice informed her archly.

"Grrr..." added Prissy, exposing two rows of sharp white teeth.

"I only meant in appearance," Emily lied, smoothly and easily, referring to the difference in her daughter's dark coloring and her own.

"Surely you don't imagine I believe that?" Beatrice shrewdly skewered her with one eyebrow raised. "But it hardly matters," she relented. "Children have a sense of what is important."

Gooseberry tarts.

Beatrice continued, "They thrive on learning."

How to acquire more gooseberry tarts.

At least in that respect both children took after their mother.

Lady Sinclair's eyes softened, and a smile tugged at her lips as she glanced down to Emily's rounded form.

Forever awkward in the face of her stepmother's seldom conferred approval, Emily was relieved to hear the approach of voices. It seemed her father and husband would be joining them for tea today. No doubt they had heard the whispers from Annabelle and Henry.

If word of Cook's gooseberry tarts ever reached Town, all of London society would be eating out of Beatrice's hand or, at the very least, her parlour. Emily's lips were sealed.

As her children hurried into the room just ahead of their father and grandfather, Emily's heart swelled with pride and contentment at the happiness she had found and made with Brand. Catching her husband's eye as he strode into the room, she smiled and rose with awkward determination, her thoughts having already strayed to the temptation of the tarts.

Alyssa Goodnight

left a stable, sensible career as an engineer (testing microcontrollers) for the wild existence of being a mom. Apparently lacking in things to do, she decided to spend her spare time writing a romance novel—it only took her four years—and then resolved to get it published. She is now at work on her second novel and is desperately hoping to improve upon her completion time.

Send Alyssa some feedback by visiting her website at

www.AlyssaGoodnight.com